# KABBALAH

Other books by David Scott Milton

THE QUARTERBACK
PARADISE ROAD

# KABBALAH

## DAVID SCOTT MILTON

HARCOURT BRACE JOVANOVICH
NEW YORK AND LONDON

Copyright © 1980 by David Scott Milton

All rights reserved. No part of this publication may be reproduced or transmitted in any form or by any means, electronic or mechanical, including photocopy, recording, or any information storage and retrieval system, without permission in writing from the publisher.

Requests for permission to make copies of any part of the work should be mailed to: Permissions, Harcourt Brace Jovanovich, Inc., 757 Third Avenue, New York, N.Y. 10017.

Quotations from the following songs are used by permission of their publishers: "I Love You Because," by Leon Payne, © 1949, renewed 1976 by Fred Rose Music, Inc.; "Out of Time," by M. Jagger and K. Richard, © 1966 Abkco Music, Inc., all rights reserved; "If You Need Me," by Wilson Pickett, Robert Bateman, and Sonny Sanders, copyright © 1963 Cotillion Music, Inc. and LuPine Publishing Co., all rights reserved; "When My Blue Moon Turns to Gold Again," by Wiley Walker and Gene Sullivan, copyright © 1941 by Peer International Corporation, copyright renewed by Peer International Corporation, all rights reserved.

Library of Congress Cataloging in Publication Data

Milton, David Scott, 1934–
Kabbalah.

I. Title.
PZ4.M6617Kab  [PS3563.I448]    813'.54    79-3360
ISBN 0-15-146608-4

Printed in the United States of America

First edition

B C D E

There is in God a principle that is called "Evil," and it lies in the north of God. And what principle is this? It is the form of the hand, and it has many messengers, and all are named "Evil," "Evil." And it is they that fling the world into guilt, for the *tohu* is in the north, and *tohu* means precisely the evil that confuses men until they sin, and it is the source of all man's evil impulses.

*The Bahir Kabbalah*

*This day is poised in time.*

Two boys not yet twelve years old sit on the grassy hillside of a park. Below is a river and beyond that, seen through a scrim of hazy smoke, a row of black steel mills.

It is a warm afternoon in late summer. The boys, one blond, one dark, sit lost in thought. Summer's end is unimaginable.

"Tell me about Kabbalah," the blond boy says.

The dark boy gazes up at the clouds, magical forms, scudding by: swans, elephants, giraffes.

Time yawns with drone of summer flies, grasshoppers flitting through the fireweed, sweet odor of goldenrod and rose mallow, churn of brown river, hum of far-off mill.

It is an hour for telling stories.

"There is a great distance between us and God," the dark boy begins. "He wants us to reach him. He has given us something like a map. Sometimes it takes the form of a tree and we call it the Sephirot. Sometimes it's in the shape of a man, and this we call Adam Kadmon—the first Adam, even before Adam of the Bible "

"But Adam was the first man—"

The dark boy knits his brow, ponders. "Before him was a perfect Adam, but God felt that was too easy so He made an Adam with a flaw. He gave this Adam a choice: good or evil. If Adam had made the right choice, we would all be perfect."

"I want to be perfect," the blond boy says.

"Then you must follow Kabbalah. This map." The dark boy takes up a twig and draws a figure in the ground. "It's made up of ten lines, forming thirty-two paths. And each leads to an attribute of God. And you must come close to these attributes. And then you will come close to God."

"I want to come close to God," the blond boy says. "I want to be perfect."

"The map, though, the Tree of Kabbalah, has another side. If you were to look at it in a mirror, you would see the other side."

"That is the bad side?"

The dark boy nods. "God has given us this choice, good Kabbalah or bad. And they are both here at the same time. One is a reflection of the other." The dark boy's voice is soft, serious. "If a man follows bad Kabbalah, he will be lost. He will spend his days in loneliness and pain. He will wander from town to town, shunned by everyone but the most miserable, the evil ones like him. He will be stupid like a golem. His life will not be his own. He will suffer and he will cause suffering."

A shiver passes through the blond boy. "I don't want to be stupid like a golem."

"You must follow good Kabbalah."

"I wish I was smarter," the blond boy says plaintively. "I'm strong, but I'm not as smart as I'd like to be."

"And I want to be strong like you," the dark boy says.

"You don't need to be strong. You have me to take care of you," the blond boy says. He is silent for a while. "Promise me you will show me the right Kabbalah."

"I promise."

"Forever?"

"Forever."

The great, sharp disk of the sun slices behind the mill tops. Dusk gathers like smoke in the woods below the park. The day grows cool. The sky beyond the river is fiery with flame from the mills.

The blond boy puts his arm around the dark boy's shoulder as they stroll from the park.

At a corner opposite a granite school building they enter a candy store.

This day is poised in time.

# PART
## 1

# 1

Mirror Street. He had been haunted for some time now by the conviction that his life was a fun house mirror. Or a show seen on television, the reception not always clear. Curved, distorted, fragmented, a war of reflections, it often filled him with horror and a terrifying sense of impotence.

He strolled past Mirror Street, where he had spent a part of his youth, walked along Murray Avenue, and turned up the hill, moving in the cold dusk. Harsh lines of neon cut the buildings, slashes of blood palpitating in his gaze: JIFFY LUNCH where the Hot Puppy Shoppe had been; THRIFT DRUGS in place of the Murray Avenue Pharmacy. FORWARD AVENUE BOWLING remained from the past, its sputtering sign sad and remote, its dark exterior a lie to him: he could not shake an apprehension that the insides were gutted, that nothing existed beyond the facade.

The world of his youth was real, the time of his present a fun house. Fun house mirror. Mirror Street.

In his mind now he saw a dying bird. He was eight years old, pressing against the leg of his mother, weeping. And there was a fragrance of flowers. After that he had run from the house . . .

The street was empty. The Squirrel Hill movie house lights were on, but the marquee had not yet been set with the week's attraction. A jumble of meaningless letters created something like panic in him. He tried to make out a message, but if it was there, it was much too arcane, dense consonants, brutal configurations. He moved on.

The street was cold. He pressed his hands deep into the pockets of his pea jacket. His right hand gripped something that felt colder than the cold outside and he squeezed it to bring warmth to it. Squeezed. It should be warm, he thought.

He was possessed of an idea of himself as The Destroyer. He had visions of an ancient man with long, flowing beard and prayerful hands peaked together at the fingertips, eyes of no color, expression menacing in its emptiness. He dreamed about this man and he thought about him often. The old man had sent The Destroyer out into the cold autumn night.

His right hand was warm now. What it held burned now in his grip.

He turned and moved on past the high school, Taylor Allderdice. Pale, cold, dirty yellow brick. Beyond the high school, where Shady Avenue angled left, was the old synagogue, the Ohave Zedek, built from what appeared to be the same dirty yellow brick as the high school.

An old Jewish woman, the first person he had seen since leaving the streetcar at the bottom of Mirror Street, moved down the steps from the synagogue.

The woman caused him to shudder. It was a Jewish neighborhood and Jews upset him. Old Jews upset him most of all. He didn't like stooped, dark people. He was tall and blond, his eyes a washed blue, eyes the color of clouds.

He glared at the woman in her dark, formless coat, mud-gray stockings sagging about her calves, her face the texture of aging newspaper. Frightened, she looked away and hurried on past him up Tilbury Street. Had she recognized him? He weighed the possibility: he had spent more than half his life in this neighborhood. At one time everyone had known him.

He walked past the fence surrounding Colfax, the elementary school. In the school yard a gang of teen-age boys was tossing around a football. One of the boys stared at him. He did not acknowledge the look. The boy grew embarrassed, dropped a pass, jogged about awkwardly, shaking his head.

The blond man with gray-blue eyes watched the boys playing football for a while. They were not very good. Had he been in the mood, he could have shown them a few things.

A sudden feeling of enormous, impenetrable, chilling loneliness came over him, a feeling that no one on earth mattered less than he. The boys were stealing glances at him, and he realized how awful he must look, thin, pale, needing a shave, his clothes—ragged pea jacket, khaki trousers, workboots—old and torn. His long hair was dirty blond, scraggly, knotted. There was a time when it was golden blond. The boys were looking at him with pity and the disgust he felt for himself was almost overwhelming.

He moved off toward the candy store.

It was directly opposite the school, run by an old Italian, Cervino. What would Cervino look like now? In the days when he attended Colfax, Cervino had seemed elderly. How must he look now? Ancient, ancient. Bearded man with eyes of no color? No, Cervino had been clean-shaven. His skin had been pink.

He remembered a time when Cervino had held him. He had been surprisingly strong with muscles like stone.

Would he recognize him? Thousands of kids had spent their after-school days in Cervino's, browsing among the comic books, buying penny licorice, orange soda, banana mallows. Years and years of kids. Why would he recognize *him*?

Would Cervino recall that once, a long while back, they had had a few moments together? It was a knot in time and it would be undone.

On one corner had been a pharmacy. It was gone. There

was now an empty lot. An old Italian man crossed the street. He wore a heavy black sweater and baggy trousers with no belt. It was not Cervino; the candy store owner had been tall and elegant.

No, Cervino, if he was still alive, would be tending his counter.

He saw in his mind now a dying bird, an Easter chick. Its mouth gaped open, fighting for breath. And then he was burying his face against his mother's thigh. There was a fragrance of flowers, her fragrance. And he was weeping. Later, he had watched the rain. Then he had gone to Cervino. Oh, that was long, long ago.

He entered the candy store. It was empty.

He advanced on the counter, studying the store. It had changed since he had last been there. He had been a kid, then: of course it had changed—but in small ways. Fun house mirror. The counter had been moved from the side to the rear wall. The flower seeds, which used to be in a metal rack near the door, were gone. There were still racks of comic books. The floor was still the same: small, dingy white tile squares. The phone booth was still in the back.

At the counter he looked down at the case. Dark wood, wavy, thick glass. Inside, a sorry selection: Hershey and Clark bars. Hershey kisses. Licorice twists in plastic wrapping. Where were the wax lips and the small wax milk bottles? The jawbreakers, licorice dots, bubble gum baseball cards?

The old man moved out of a back room, buttoning up his sweater. Perhaps he had been napping, although he looked fresh. Perhaps he had been in the toilet or watching television. It was after five. School had been out a couple of hours. He would be closing in an hour or so.

He had not changed at all and the blond man with gray-blue eyes wondered at this. A tall handsome man of indeterminate age: Cervino might have been sixty-five, he might have been eighty. Old, but not infirm, curiously stately, curiously gentle.

Were the muscles beneath the sweater still like stone?

If, after all these years, Cervino had not changed to him, had he changed to Cervino? The old man was smiling, as though, indeed, he had recognized him. The blond man's heart began to race. "Yes?" the old man asked in his softly accented voice.

The blond man drew a revolver out of his jacket pocket. The sorrow within him was immense. *A little bird was dying, rain was falling, he was weeping.*

He did not talk, but motioned toward the register. Cervino, whose whole life had been spent among small children, who was only dimly aware of evil in the world, did not understand. He continued to smile. "Is this a joke?" he asked.

The Destroyer shot him twice, once in the head and once just below the heart. He had thought he wanted the money, but after shooting the old man he realized that was not it at all.

The old man lay on the tiled floor, dying. The Destroyer, exulting, watched him die. And yet—

An abberant pale dwarf of his self curled in his skull and wept.

The blond man hurried from the store.

It was almost dark now. He did not walk past the elementary school. He hurried along Frick Park and turned off at Nicholson Street. He gazed for a moment down at the high school field. The football team was practicing in the heavy gloom. The figures colliding on the dark field appeared as waves of chaos smashing on a black shore.

He dropped the revolver in the bushes and went at a run back toward the park.

He was heading in the direction of Saint Philomena's, the churchyard, the deserted coal mine there.

The Destroyer ran with easy, beautiful, swift, elegant strides. When he turned it on, no one could catch him.

Running with him stride for stride, whispering to him, weeping, persisted the pale dwarf of his innocence.

"Hey, John, listen to this one. If two black guys in a black Cadillac is black power, and two white guys in a white Cadillac is white power, what are two Polacks in a green Cadillac?"

"What?"

"Grand theft auto." Jackie Palmer, detective third grade, was talking to his partner on the homicide squad of the Pittsburgh police. They were standing between a small freezer and the telephone booth, behind the counter. "Want a cho-cho bar?" Palmer said, indicating the ice cream freezer.

"Food makes me sick. Like razor blades in my stomach."

"Sure. Only a ghoul could eat in circumstances like these." He smiled, revealing uneven teeth. He finished his ice cream bar and threw the stick to the floor. Then he lit a cigarette.

The old man's body lay just in front of the telephone booth. There was a small wound in his forehead and a patch of blood on his blue sweater just below his heart. The face of the old man was pale, though peaceful. He might have been asleep.

"Put out the cigarette, Jack." Strahan had turned his back on the room and spoke in an even, quiet voice. Jackie Palmer looked over the room. It was filled with uniformed police, police brass, and men from the medical examiner's office. "Fuck 'em," Palmer said out of the side of his mouth. "What have they done for me lately?" His eyes shifted behind dark glasses.

John Strahan and Jackie Palmer, the initial detectives, had lucked onto the case. They had been going through the motions, putting in hours on a cold lead involving another case, ancient business. Strahan, who had grown up near the neighborhood, suggested a drive into Squirrel Hill. They were on Beechwood Boulevard just up from the candy store when the first call came in over the radio. Now

8

the murder of the old man belonged to them. A pain in the ass, Jackie Palmer thought.

"That your school over there?" Palmer said, indicating Colfax.

"Saint Philomena's. I was from Greenfield."

"Not Kike's Peak, huh?" The largely Jewish Squirrel Hill was often called Kike's Peak by people outside the area.

Jackie Palmer laughed. He had a dry, tense laugh. His eyes combed the room. In his wing-tipped, light brown shoes, canary yellow sport jacket, and sunglasses, he looked more like a small-time hood than a detective.

Strahan, who was in his early thirties, ten years younger than Palmer, resembled a lawyer or an accountant. He was tall and solidly built, on the lean side, with a serious, intelligent look. He wore steel-rimmed glasses. He spoke so softly you had to strain to hear what he was saying.

He moved away from Palmer, who was still smoking a cigarette, and approached a group of men gathered near the body. The ambulance attendants were waiting to remove the body.

A uniformed cop led a man in his early forties to the body. The man stared down at the body and shook his head and made a quiet clicking sound with his tongue.

Outside on the street a crowd had gathered. Police cars, sirens at full scream, were approaching from all directions. "They're late, but they're coming on strong," Palmer called over to no one in particular.

"I'm his nephew," the man who had just been led to the body said. "I'm his nephew," he repeated, though no one seemed to care. He continued to shake his head.

A tall man in a gray topcoat approached. "Frank Rikert," he said, offering his hand to the man, "Superintendent of Police of the City of Pittsburgh."

The nephew appeared impressed. "Oh, yes. I recognize you." Rikert looked surprised. "Television."

"This is Bob Harris of the District Attorney's office,

Lieutenant Busik, head of the homicide squad, and—"
The superintendent looked at Strahan and drew a blank.

"Detective Strahan," John Strahan said softly, disappointed that the superintendent had forgotten his name His stomach tightened.

"Is there anyone you want notified?" Busik said to the nephew.

"He has no one. He had a sister who used to run the store with him. She died five years ago. My father, his brother, is back in Italy." The nephew shook his head. "Forty years this store's been here. Would you believe that?" He stood there shaking his head.

Busik motioned Strahan and the man from the D.A.'s office away from the body. Rikert conferred with a uniformed captain. Jackie Palmer joined Busik and Strahan "What do you think?" Busik asked.

"Junky," Jackie Palmer said. He dropped his cigarette butt to the floor and ground it in with the sole of his shoe The pain in Strahan's stomach increased. Palmer had a habit of making grand leaps of logic to a single conclusion: if it was murder, it involved narcotics. Another belief: no crime scene was too sacred not to be muddied up—cigarette butts, coffee containers, used Kleenex, his own fingerprints. Still, he was a good detective, relentless and tough.

"A junky, huh?" Busik said.

"You got my marker on it."

"The register's untouched. What do you figure?"

"That's a rough one to figure."

"What do you think, John?"

"Could be a junky. I don't know."

Superintendent Rikert motioned Busik over. "There's a kid out there who thinks he knows the guy who did it."

They brought the kid in, a redhead with a fleshy nose. "This guy come by—" the kid said, scared.

"Wait a minute. What do you mean, 'this guy come by'?" Palmer said.

very angry closed down inside him. "If it's Gray Eyes, I went to school with him. His name is Buddy Hall."

"Why would he do something like this?" Busik asked.

Strahan didn't answer. "It's all yours, you two," Busik said. He moved off with the superintendent.

"This is prime stuff," Jackie Palmer said to Strahan. "Fifteen seconds on the Action News. You could make gold shield off this." He flipped his cho-cho bar into a far corner and lit up another cigarette.

The cold had a metallic sting to it. Strahan wondered if it would snow. He had meant to get the chains out of the garage and carry them in the trunk. He had forgotten. If it snowed, making it up Polish Hill, where he lived, would be anything but fun.

He wouldn't mind getting in some snowmobile hunting, though. Should he and Palmer be able to swing four or five days off, they'd head upstate and go buzzing around looking to bag bobcat and rabbit.

He parked his car in the back of Bluestone's Restaurant and he and Palmer got out. They walked down Beacon Street to Murray Avenue. Murray Avenue, the main thoroughfare in Squirrel Hill, was quiet tonight. The number 60 streetcar, one of the last in the city not to be mothballed in the car barn, glided by, heading for Homestead across the river. Its wheels ground out harsh sparks as it slowed on the hill.

The avenue had a run-down, used look to it. There were several Jewish bakeries, kosher butcher shops, two movie houses, a supermarket. Everything was quiet now in the chill evening of a late fall Monday.

In the spring and summer Murray Avenue at Beacon, both walks of the street, would be thronged with sidling hustlers and petty gamblers. On a night like tonight they would be in Bluestone's or in the Malta Social Club, just above the Beacon Art Cinema.

"We were tossing around a football and this guy come by."

"You were tossing around a football?" Palmer said.

The kid looked as though he might break into tears. He was pale and very nervous. "A group of us were over in the school yard—"

"Roll up your sleeves!" The kid just blinked.

"Hey," Palmer said louder. The kid rolled up his sleeves. Palmer pulled his arms toward him and examined the veins, then pushed his arm down. The kid's lower lip was trembling.

"Go on, go on," Busik said.

"This guy come by and watched us awhile. Then he left. Then a little later we said let's get a soda at Cervino's."

"We?" Palmer said.

"C'mon, Jack," Busik said. "Let the kid talk."

Palmer retreated to the ice cream freezer and took out another cho-cho bar. He dropped the wrapper on the floor.

"We were coming down the street, the street back there."

"Beechwood," Busik said.

"We were crossing Beechwood when I saw this guy coming out of the store. He was walking up Beechwood. I said to this other kid, Paulie Sablowsky, 'He got a gun in his hand.' Paulie Sablowsky said, 'Holy shit,' just like that."

"Did he see you?" Strahan asked.

"Naw, naw. He was on Beechwood, but toward the park. We were behind him."

"Do you know this guy, the guy with the gun?" Busik asked.

"They call him Gray Eyes. When I was just a small kid, everyone used to point him out. He played quarterback for Allderdice the year they beat Westinghouse for the City."

"You were there when they beat Westinghouse, weren't you?" Jackie Palmer said to Strahan.

"I know him," Strahan said. Something very cold and

"C'mon, I'll buy you a bowl of matzo ball soup," Palmer said, smiling a thin, humorless smile.

The two detectives entered Bluestone's.

It was a large restaurant, decorated with much red leatherette, its walls and pillars mirrored. In one section there was a long delicatessen counter with a case displaying slabs of sturgeon and lox, corned beef and pastrami, cheeses, salami, herring in sour cream.

Palmer and Strahan slid into a booth. Though the street outside was deserted, Bluestone's was thriving. The whole neighborhood seemed to be in the restaurant.

"Hey, Reagen," Palmer called over to a hefty, red-faced man sitting at a nearby table with three other men. "What's good?"

"Can't go wrong with the beef flanken," Reagen said in a ragged voice.

"Who do you like at the Market House on Friday, Chappy?" Palmer asked.

An older, bald man was eating a corned beef sandwich. He did not look up. "Bet your money on the black," he said with a vague Yiddish accent.

Palmer feigned great surprise. "I thought you were managing the hunky."

"That's why he says to bet on the nigger," commented Reagen without a smile.

"Pat, you been hanging with them sheenies too long," Palmer said to Reagen. "Your nose is growing a hook. You even been making mocky moves with your hands."

"He's playing with himself," another of the men at the table said, fishing a matzo ball out of his soup.

"But is he making any fucking money?"

"What money? He got a *goyish kop*, Reagen," the man fishing out the matzo ball answered. He was small and thin and had bulging eyes.

"Talk English, Jo-Jo. I don't understand them Jew words."

"You understand *gelt*, though, don't you, cop?" the fourth man at the table said without humor. He was a hulk of a man with soft, feminine hands and hooded eyelids. They called him Turtle.

Palmer smiled his thin, joyless smile again. "That I understand," he said.

"Know why Jack talks out of the side of his mouth? So when they're settling the payoff no one can read his lips," Jo-Jo said.

"Every wrongo cop I ever saw talked out of the side of his mouth," Reagen said.

"Hey, my mother taught me crime don't pay," Jack Palmer said. "But then again police work ain't so prosperous neither." He laughed.

"How's it going, Johnny?" Jo-Jo asked Strahan. Strahan made a small motion, not quite a shrug.

"Strahan's a winner," Reagen said. He pronounced the name "Strawn." "He got ice in his heart."

"Hey, Chappy," Palmer said. "Is it true Strahan here could have been another Billy Conn?"

Chappy continued to chew on his corned beef. "Johnny was good, don't you worry," Chappy said. "He could have done all right."

"He told me you stole him blind," Palmer said.

Chappy stared at Palmer. "I never took a cent. If he said that, he's a liar. He was a kid. What did he know?"

"He knew enough to get out of the game and get on the police force where the real money is," the man called Turtle said.

"How's Sid Hall?" Strahan asked.

"Why?" asked Reagen.

"I heard he was set to hit the jackpot."

"Nickel stretch. He beat it," Reagen said.

"Don't tell me about Sidney," Chappy said with a wave of his hand. "Sidney will always beat the jackpot. Know why?" No one appeared interested. He tapped his skull with his forefinger. "*Tsechel.*" He smiled a gap-toothed smile.

"I know a lot of people who worship the ground Sidney got coming to him," Jo-Jo said.

"Anybody seen Buddy?" Strahan asked the question offhandedly, as though bored.

"Buddy Gray Eyes?" Jo-Jo said.

There was quiet for a moment.

"Why bring up that disaster?" Turtle said at last. "No one's seen him in years."

"Gray Eyes is a good kid," Chappy said.

"I love Gray Eyes. I'd love to French kiss him," Jo-Jo said.

"Ask Mother Shadman," Turtle said. "They were A-hole buddies." Palmer cocked his head, mimed sticking a needle in his arm. Turtle winked. "He claims diabetes," he said.

"Diabetes, my dick," Palmer said.

"Where's Mother been?" Strahan said.

"They got him bronzed, hanging in the men's room at the Old Jew's Home out on Brown's Hill," Reagen said.

No one laughed.

Strahan got up and looked around for a waitress. "Order me a corned beef," he said to Palmer. He started for the phone booth in back.

"You want that on white bread with mayonnaise, don't you, Johnny?" Turtle called after him.

Strahan phoned his wife. "I don't know when I'll be home. The old man who ran the candy store across from Colfax has been killed."

His wife's voice was weary. "Yes. Yes. I heard it on the six o'clock news."

"You remember Buddy Hall, don't you?"

"What about him?"

"He did it."

He waited for her to say something. There was a long pause.

"Buddy? Dear God, *why?*" she said.
"When I see him I'll ask him."

Upstairs at the Malta Social Club things were quiet. A group of men were playing a Yiddish card game, kupkis. They cut the deck into small stacks and bet on the stacks. Then the top card of each stack was turned up and the high card won. It was a simple game, but they played for respectable stakes. There was perhaps five hundred dollars on the table when Palmer and Strahan entered.

"Homicide's not on this pad here," one of the men standing behind the players said. He was joking, but he did not smile. He was a short, blond Irishman, about the same age as Strahan.

"A buck for you, a buck for me. Halvesies," Palmer said.

Sidney Hall, a man of fifty-five who looked ten years younger, sat at the table banking bets. "Halvesies you got to earn," he said, without looking up. He was a well-muscled man with dirty blond hair and pale blue eyes. Manicured nails; bright, though not flashy, clothes. His face showed no fat and few wrinkles. He had a broken, ex-boxer's nose and scars above each eye.

"I earned it," Palmer said with his tight smile.

"Not by me," Sidney Hall said. In repose there was something cold and unpleasant in his look. When he smiled, however, he was a dazzler. He smiled now at Strahan. "What's the good word, Johnny?"

Strahan motioned with his head. "Let's talk."

"Call your lawyer, Sidney," one of the men at the table said.

"Not with Johnny," Sidney Hall said. He gave his chair to the Irish kid and moved with Strahan to the far end of the room. The room was large and drab with a number of plastic-top tables. There was a small kitchen area and a service bar at one end of the room. The wall was lined with framed photographs of old-time Pittsburgh prize fighters, Harry Greb, Fritzie Zivic, Billy Conn.

16

Sidney Hall offered Strahan a cigarette and when the detective declined, he lit up. They stood by the service bar. "Three packs a day," Sidney Hall said. "And I can still take the kids in handball. My natural constitution. Stop by the Y, we'll play some time."

"Downtown they play mostly doubles now. I only play racquetball now."

Sidney Hall made a sour face. "You're only using one arm. You got that racquet so you don't have to get down for those low shots."

"I get a good workout."

"Oh, sure." He shifted his weight from one foot to the other and looked over at the card table, eager to get back, uncomfortable with Strahan. He knew Strahan disliked him. "Still over in Greenfield?"

"We moved to Polish Hill."

"You got the blacks coming in there, don't you?"

"It's close to work."

"Oh, yeah. You guys in homicide work out of the Public Safety Building."

Strahan didn't say anything, but watched Sidney Hall coolly, without overt hostility, as though studying an object. Hall, who knew the game, did not allow himself to become intimidated. He would wait Strahan out, heap him with trivialities. "Still following the fights?" he said.

Strahan shook his head, no. "Ever think you should have maybe stayed in that game? You were good," Sidney Hall said. "In my prime I could have given you a lesson, though."

"I remember seeing you fight Charlie Affif when I was a kid."

"Did you see that fight? I could have beaten him."

"Not that night."

"You're right about that. Not that night. I pissed blood for a week after that fight."

They did not talk for a long time. Strahan continued to stare at Sidney Hall, who did not look away.

17

After a while Strahan said, "We're looking for your son."

"Buddy? What for?"

"Where is he?"

Sidney Hall threw his cigarette to one side. "Buddy's gone. Years now."

"He's back."

"That's not so, John."

"Oh, yes."

"You know something I don't know then." He walked over to where the cigarette was still burning on the faded linoleum floor, picked it up, and ground the butt out in the ashtray. He lit up another cigarette.

From the card table sounds of an argument erupted: "Jake was managing him, then!"

"No, sir!"

"I'm telling you Jake was managing him!"

Sidney Hall turned back to Strahan. "What did Buddy do?"

"Killed a man," Strahan said.

"Hey, Sidney," one of the men at the card table called over. "At the end there who was managing Ezzard Charles?"

Sidney Hall had grown very pale. He held his cigarette cupped in his palm. His hand trembled. "Hey, Sidney," the card player called out again.

"Jake Mintz," Sidney said.

"You sure about that?"

"Yes." His voice was constricted, as though his breath had been cut off. "Kill? Who did he kill?" Sidney Hall said to Strahan.

"A man. Two shots, head and heart." Sidney Hall shook his head in disgust and disbelief. He hitched up his belt. His face was contorted, terrible. "How long ago did you see him?" Strahan said.

"Years ago. He was living out in California. My wife was dying and I took her out there to see him. She wanted to see him so badly. To her Buddy was—" He paused. He hadn't the breath to get the words out. "She died out there," he said at last. He stood leaning on the service bar, staring at the end of his cigarette.

It was strange what happened to the voice, Strahan was thinking. Sidney Hall's voice had become very small, as though he were strangling. "He was some athlete, that kid. I thought he'd have a career with football, you know?" Sidney Hall said.

"Yes."

"Well, you know what happened with his leg. You know that, John. Then out in California junky niggers got him." He leaned back against the counter and took in a deep breath, gazing up at the ceiling. "When his mother died, we had a fight in the hospital. I beat him up. He was thin like my little finger. Who did he kill?"

"The candy store owner."

"Cervino?" Sidney Hall stared at the detective. "I don't believe that. Why would he kill an old man like that?"

"I don't know."

"No. Not the old man. I don't believe that." His gaze had hardened; his eyes looked as though they would cut right into the detective's skull. Strahan, his look cold, opaque, stared back from behind his wire-rimmed glasses. "What are you doing to me, Johnny?"

"It's true."

"Why? Why?" His voice rose. "Don't shit me like this."

"Give him up, Sidney, before he gets hurt."

"I don't have him to give up!" Sidney Hall shouted. "Get out of here, you fucking weasel. You have no right hassling me like this!"

Strahan looked over at Palmer. The room had grown very quiet. The card players were looking at Strahan and Sidney Hall.

"He's trying to crucify my son! Buddy's a good kid, everybody knows that. You did him in one time, Johnny. You're not going to do him in again. You fucked him over,

Johnny. You know that, fucked up his leg. He's trying to crucify Buddy—" Tears of anger were streaming down Sidney Hall's face.

Strahan moved to Palmer at the door. "Let's go," he said.

Sidney Hall was yelling at the top of his voice: "Tell them all he was a good kid. You knew him, Johnny. Don't let them hurt him. Tell them all what a good kid he was!"

One of the card players, a large, balding man in a T-shirt, got up. He kicked a chair over. "Get out of here, fucking scumbags!" he shouted at the detectives.

Palmer's expression hardened. "Hey, Maish, you want something?" he said. The other card players held the man in the T-shirt. Strahan patted Jack Palmer on the shoulder, edged him toward the stairs.

Sidney Hall continued to yell: "Don't let them hurt my kid, John! I hold you responsible! If they hurt him, I'll come after you. I swear it to you, don't let them hurt him!"

His face was red now, saliva foamed at his lips, tears stained his cheeks.

Strahan felt embarrassment and a powerful loathing for the man. Cockroach! He loathed all these people, hustlers, con men, cheats, schemers, liars, wheeler-dealers.

They had polluted the blood of the world, these cockroaches. If he had his way, he'd wipe them from the earth.

Bartolomeo Cervino, the nephew of the dead man, was not home when Palmer and Strahan came to visit. The house, a neat frame affair, was in the Hazelwood section, on a hill overlooking the Baltimore and Ohio Railroad yard. Across the Monongahela River you could see the McKeesport and Youghiogeny Railroad Company yard.

His wife, a very thin, though not unattractive, woman with black hair and eyes, told them he would be working until midnight. He was a dispatcher for B & O.

They drove down the hill to the railroad yard. They found the nephew in a small office. Palmer did most of the questioning while Strahan looked out over the yard through a window gray with soot and ash. Large maroon freight cars moved slowly past the office area every few minutes. From where he stood Strahan could see long bands of glistening rail curve along the dark river toward the Carnegie Illinois Steel Mill upstream, skeins of silver unwinding in the night.

Strahan's soul seemed to be unraveling with the cold, silver metal of the rails toward something—what? He was filled with a great yearning for truth and rightness, an end to evil and murder. He had become a detective for many reasons, but at bottom, he told himself, it was to see an end to evil. And yet he somehow knew—and it gnawed at him—that evil was not only outside him, but inside also, and he felt terror at that knowledge.

"We think there might be a dope angle to this thing, if you see what I mean," Palmer said.

Bartolomeo Cervino did not commit himself. He stared pleasantly, dully at Palmer. "The murder of your uncle could be a junky's work. Is it possible your uncle in some way knew this fellow, this guy they call Gray Eyes? Is it possible they had some dealings?"

"Oh, I don't think so," Cervino said. "My uncle was a very moral, gentle person. He lived a quiet life, was a regular churchgoer."

"Which church was that?" Palmer asked, as though he cared.

"Saint Philomena's on Beechwood."

"You went to school there, didn't you, John?"

"Grade school. They used to have a coal mine right on the church grounds," Strahan said, still staring out the window. "The kids would play down in the mine."

Palmer was growing impatient. "What we're trying to get at here—your uncle, did he make trips overseas?"

"He traveled to Italy once, oh, many years ago, when his sister was alive. They visited my father."

"Your father lives—where?"

"Just outside Naples. He used to work on the railroad. He retired back to Italy."

"What's his house like?"

Bartolomeo Cervino appeared confused by Palmer's question "What?"

"Does he own a big house over there?"

Strahan turned from the window, annoyed. Palmer was off spinning dope theories again. Strahan could see where it was heading: international narcotics ring leading from Naples to a small Squirrel Hill candy store, with Buddy Gray Eyes somehow involved. Perhaps the dope was entering Pittsburgh by freight train. Ridiculous.

"He owns a farmhouse. That's all."

"When I was a kid I used to spend time in your uncle's store," Strahan said. "He was a good, kind man." He would come down from Saint Philomena's after school and buy penny licorice. His mother would give him one penny a day for candy. The old man would lean down and place the licorice in his hand and close his fingers over it. Sometimes he would hug Strahan gently. He had a clean smell, like fresh laundry. "I promise you: we'll get the man who killed your uncle."

"Pray God. He didn't deserve to die like that."

"No, he didn't."

Strahan and Jack Palmer began to cross the railroad yard to where their car was parked. A freight train glided slowly by. Strahan had an image: he held Buddy Gray Eyes. He had his head on the silver rail. The freight train sliced the head neatly off the body.

The image caused a wave of nausea in the pit of his stomach. He hated Buddy Gray Eyes with a maddened, unreasoned hate, a hate that had nothing to do with the murder of the old man, a hate more intense than anything he had ever felt in his life.

# 2

KABBALAH, Kabbalah, Gnosis, Kabbalah.
Rabbi Akiba Moldavan had a savage headache. He had taken three aspirins earlier, then three more. The pain continued to throb behind his brow.

He closed his eyes and tried to will it away. It seemed to grow stronger, pounding now. He felt as though his head would fly apart.

For days he had had the headache. He should visit a doctor, he told himself. No, no, it was his nerves. It was his world crushing in on him.

The air in the study was oppressive with the smell of old books and dust. His father sat in the corner of the study, watching him. Words jumped around in Akiba's head: Kabbalah, Kabbalah, Gnosis, Kabbalah.

It had been a difficult evening, though not very different from most of his evenings. The early part had been occupied by his sister—she had been acting up again—then some trivial, nagging business with the synagogue. Now he would try to work. His father would sit there and stare at him with watery, pain-filled eyes.

His father, who had suffered a stroke some months earlier, was a manageable burden. His sister, Hannah, was another matter.

She had been hopelessly insane for a number of years.

When his father had been healthy and his mother alive,

they had taken care of her. Now that responsibility had fallen on Akiba and his wife.

For an hour this evening Hannah had been wandering the house, raving. The Nazis were coming after her. They had infiltrated the state. They were coming into the house. They were preparing to cut her up with long, sharp knives.

She refused her medication. She roamed the house, wailing, a sad, mad woman of forty. She had been quite pretty when she was young, before the breakdown. She was no longer pretty, an old lady at forty.

The children had become upset at her behavior and this was painful to Akiba. While Ruth, his wife, tried to comfort them, Akiba had at last persuaded Hannah to take her medication.

Just before she drifted off to sleep she said, "God doesn't like us." Akiba explained to her that that was not true, that they were blessed. "No, no," she insisted.

When the medication had taken effect, Akiba sat with Ruth and the kids for a while. Ruth read to them from a book of Hasidic tales.

Afterward Ruth said, "You're tired, Akiba."

She was right. He was exhausted. A pleasant-looking man, lean, with dark hair and eyes and pale skin, he could not conceal fatigue. It would show in his face. Dark smudges would underline his eyes; his skin would take on a chalky appearance. Constant tension produced in him a driven, harried quality.

"I'm fine," he said.

On his way to the study he took a phone call. It was Izzie, a half-wit who did odd jobs at the synagogue.

The synagogue was in the Hill District, an area once heavily Jewish, now almost entirely black, a crumbling, dying neighborhood; the congregation had been his father's and he had refused to leave; with his illness, responsibility had fallen to Akiba.

Izzie was one of a few dozen Jews who had neither the wit nor the will to escape the slum. He had called now to say that the toilets were stuffed. "The old *kockers* been using newspaper again."

"We have a plunger. In the closet next to the basement sink."

"They shouldn't use newspaper."

"I'll talk to them."

Izzie began to sing, "It's Only a Shanty in Old Shanty Town," the only song he knew. He sang it for no reason, as he always did, in an empty, off-key voice.

Akiba listened for a moment, then hung up in despair. His headache had come on with a fury.

Downstairs in his father's study he tried to work on his manuscript.

His father, in a corner of the room, sat pale and trembling, and it angered and pained Akiba that a man of such towering strength and learning had been blasted like this. What was God's reason, his plan? What? God's ways are not man's ways, he told himself, believing that as much as he believed anything.

In medieval Jewish lore it was said that each person had his *memuneh*, or heavenly deputy, which could be conjured up in a waxwork representation. And that is how his father appeared to him now, a waxwork doll, a *memuneh*: certainly not the great Rabbi Isaac Moldavan, renowned scholar in *halakah*, Jewish law, whose *Responsa*, formulated when he was a teen-ager in his native Galicia, were still referred to in Orthodox Jewish courts, a rabbi who was quoted in the margins of the latest edition of the *Talmud*, a monument of intellectual and moral force.

Akiba stared down at his manuscript, a translation of the *Derekh Etz Hayyim*, "Way of the Living Tree," of Moses Luzzatto, an eighteenth-century Kabbalist. He could make no sense of it today; the fragile and complex threads of its thought had become hopelessly tangled in his aching head.

He separated the pages, tried to concentrate. The clock in front of him jumped each minute. Time jumped. His father sighed and muttered in his chair.

He struggled to deal with Luzzatto's words, yet it all seemed to be slipping away. Footnotes, some of them going on for pages, seemed incomprehensible to him now: references to Heraclitus, Saint Thomas, Maimonides, Philo, Vital—a whole spectrum of Jewish, Greek, and Christian thought—eluded him, danced mockingly out of the grasp of his mind.

He had been working on the manuscript for years. He had a dream of someday publishing it. Perhaps when he finished it, he would see a wholeness to his life.

"*It's only a shanty in old shanty town—*" The words of Izzie, the moron, sang in his head.

Akiba Moldavan's head pounded. He felt it would burst. He felt like crying out to God—Show yourself to me! In one small way show yourself to me!

God's ways are not man's ways.

"*It's only a shanty in old shanty town—*"

The clock in front of him jumped time. His father sighed and trembled in the corner.

He got up and went into the kitchen. He poured himself a cup of cold coffee from a pot on the stove.

He sipped at the cold coffee. The taste was bitter on his tongue. He emptied the cup into the sink.

Kabbalah, Kabbalah, Gnosis, Kabbalah. It taunted him, tortured him. When he had been younger, there had been a war within him, a war in that gray area where Kabbalah approached Gnosticism, the ground of *aggadat shel dofi*, "offensive narrative," Sabbateanism.

He often questioned: had he been alive in the seventeenth century, would he have been taken in by the false Messiah, Sabbatai Zvi? Gifted Talmudist, brilliant Kabbalist, Sabbatai Zvi had become convinced the *Zohar*, the "Book of Splendor," presaged his arrival as the Messiah.

Thousands had followed him. When the Sultan of Turkey offered him apostasy or death, he had chosen to become a Moslem. The whole affair had been cataclysmic for Judaism, a spiritual disaster. Yet the ideas—they held powerful, seductive promise.

Kabbalah, Kabbalah, Gnosis, Kabbalah . . .

He was aware his wife was watching him from the door to the kitchen.

"Do you want some tea?"

"All right."

He sat at the table while Ruth busied herself at the stove.

"I'm thinking of Sabbatai Zvi. The First Cause," Akiba said. "Sabbatai Zvi and his followers believed that the God of Israel and his *Torah* are entirely divorced from the First Cause, that Christianity, rabbinic Judaism, and Maimonides distort the nature of God, mistakenly confuse God with the First Cause. The First Cause is an absent God, unknown and unknowable, yet it is the root of all things."

"Drink your tea."

"It's inverted Gnosticism, that kind of Kabbalistic thinking, that the Good God and the Absent God are not the same. That's what Sabbatai Zvi says, however—"

"Does he say what to do with a sore throat? Debbie is coming down with a sore throat."

Akiba massaged his brow. "I felt like screaming earlier." He stared at his tea for a long time. "What about Debbie's throat?"

"It's a little irritated."

"Maybe you ought to keep her home from school."

"We'll see."

He sipped at his tea. His wife, a small, redheaded woman with a freckled, almost pretty face, sat at the table opposite him, her chin resting on her hand, watching him, a playful smile at the corner of her mouth.

Akiba's mind was racing. As a young man returning to theology—he had abandoned religion during his teen-age years—he had found the Sabbatean formulation seductive. The more he pondered it, the more powerful it became.

He would lie in bed at night worrying it. His sleep became filled with wild and terrible dreams, dreams of an insane and ravaging Messiah. Of what power was the revealed God, the God of the *Torah*, if the First Cause held no moral force?

There had been a breakdown. On the day of his *smicha*, his ordination as a rabbi, he began to spit blood. His brother, Yakov, who had long since abandoned all religion and had become a successful fashion photographer in New York, took him to an Orthodox tuberculosis sanitarium in Brown's Mill, New Jersey. He remained there three months. He relinquished Sabbateanism, saw the ideas for what they were: manifestations of the *yetzer ha-ra*, the Evil Inclination. He returned to Luzzatto and Maimonides.

Over the years, though, the problem of the First Cause and God continued to plague him.

Finishing his tea now, he rose from the table. "I better get my father to bed," he said.

He entered the study. His father was staring at the wall. He motioned for Akiba to sit. It was a great effort for him to speak. Bubbles of saliva gathered at the top of his beard.

"Charlie Waldenblatt called earlier," he said at last. "Your letter to Rabbi Rose. It upset—upset Charlie."

Emmanuel Rose, an Orthodox rabbi of flashy but superficial learning and unbounded ambition, for years had been attempting to undermine Isaac Moldavan's influence in the Jewish community.

Since the old rabbi's illness Rose had led a concerted effort to wrest control of the Institute of Jewish Studies from the Moldavans. Despite its lofty name, the institute was a one-man operation that published pamphlets and books on matters of Orthodox Jewish law. Charlie Waldenblatt, a wealthy Jew of the city, was one of the backers of the institute.

Akiba had dashed off a stinging letter to Rabbi Rose. Rose was now using that letter as ammunition in the fight for the institute.

"Charlie—Charlie told me your letter was very hostile."

"Just because I told Rose he was more of a *mohel* than a rabbi? I don't think that's *hostile*." A *mohel* was one who performed ritual circumcision.

"Akiba—" The old rabbi knitted his brow, fought to remember something. The thought would not come. He had once known volumes of *Talmud* by heart. Since his stroke there were only great black holes where the knowledge had once been.

He motioned impatiently toward the bookcase and indicated a shelf. Akiba ran his hand over the volumes until his father nodded, then removed a book.

It was the *Pirke Avot*, "The Ethics of the Fathers," a tractate of the *Mishnah*, the first part of the *Talmud*. Rabbi Isaac mentioned a section, a paragraph. He could see the page in his mind; he could not find the words.

Akiba read: "The Holy One, blessed be He, judges the world with his attribute of mercy; and when a person is neither thoroughly righteous nor thoroughly wicked, the Holy One, blessed be He, judges him with His attribute of mercy as a righteous man."

His father, of course, was forgiving Emmanuel Rose everything.

And now Akiba became aware that his father was weeping. Tears poured from his eyes. He spoke softly in Yiddish, spoke to God. "Give back my learning. My *Talmud*." And now he cried out, louder: "Give it back to me! Please, please. Give it back to me!"

His whole body was wracked with sobs. Akiba, who had never seen his father weep—not at his wife's death, his daughter's breakdown, his eldest son's defection from the faith—was stunned. His father's voice was almost a moan now: "Give it back to me. Give it back to me."

Akiba moved to the old man and attempted to hug him, but he did not know how. In their whole life they had never embraced. He touched him and drew back, then turned to the bookshelf. He replaced the *Pirke Avot* and waited for his father to control himself, pretending none of it had happened.

Later, after putting his father to bed, he came back down to the study. He watched television with the sound off, "Monday Night Football."

Plagued by shame, he stared at the set. He had let his father down—not only in the Rose matter, but in the conduct of his whole life, his unconventional theology, his inability to carry out properly his duties at the synagogue.

He was aware he was only one disappointment, a minor one, in a long line for Rabbi Isaac. There was his sister's madness, his brother's turning away from the faith. Yakov, the paragon of the family, a man who knew whole tractates of the *Talmud* by heart, had become *am haarez*, the most despicable kind of ignoramus, one who, though versed in *Torah*, still rejected it. His father had gone into mourning for him, sat *shibah* as though he were dead. He never spoke to him after that, never mentioned his name.

Hannah's breakdown followed Yakov's desertion and Akiba became a rabbi. What else could he do? What else? He had tried, and still he was a disappointment.

The football game ended. The news came on. Akiba turned up the sound.

Ruth entered the study and sat on the couch next to him. The television commentator was talking about the murder of Cervino, the candy store owner.

"What did he say?" Ruth said, craning forward to hear. Akiba made the sound louder. "Shot?" Ruth said. "How?"

Akiba listened, profoundly shaken. "Terrible," he said. "Terrible, terrible."

"Oh, Akiba—"

He sat there riven, touched by an awareness of the chaotic power of evil. He thought of his childhood days, days of innocence, baseball cards, bubble gum, wax lips, Mr. Cervino in his gray sweater. Akiba knew nothing then of the world; he felt as though he knew even less now. He knew nothing. Nothing. Nothing.

He told himself now, desperate in his sense of impotence: if a man through Kabbalah could somehow unify the chaos, bring light out of dark, the world would be saved.

Kabbalah, Kabbalah, Gnosis, Kabbalah.

# 3

It was past midnight when John Strahan entered the White Tower on Baum Boulevard in the East Liberty section of town. Jackie Palmer had gone home. Strahan, on his way home also, had decided to stop for coffee.

He was sweaty and in need of a shave and he hated the feeling. That was the worst thing about detective work: a person went about it in such grubby condition most of the time. The soul became involved with filth, and to be physically filthy also was a last, unbearable affront.

Inside the White Tower the air was dense, the windows fogged with steam. Strahan ordered coffee and waited while the girl made up a new batch. The place reeked of grease. A black junky woman at the end of the counter was nodding into her food.

"Patsy," the waitress said to the woman, while the coffee dripped into the pot, "get your eye out of your mashed potatoes." The woman lifted her head; half her face was covered with potatoes and gravy.

Strahan took out his notebook, a small yellow spiral. It was divided into two sections: current notes and things to be done. He looked at things to be done. There were a dozen mundane chores neatly lettered there.

He took a red marking pencil out of his jacket pocket

and with delicate strokes ran a line through those things he had accomplished.

He studied a chess problem he had copied from a magazine: white to mate in three. He could not solve it.

He turned back to current notes and printed out GRAY EYES. He repeated it, pressing harder on the marking pencil: GRAY EYES. He underlined it: <u>GRAY EYES</u>.

He thought about him as a youth. He had been enormously popular, a natural athlete, cool, intelligent, with a kind of spectacular charm that had always galled Strahan.

They had been rivals in many areas, played football on opposing sandlot teams—Strahan for the Greenfield Hilltop Aces, Gray Eyes for the Mirror Street Ramblers—later boxed against each other. Though they played football on the same high school team, the rivalry continued. And there were other things . . .

"Dot the *i*'s and cross the *t*'s, John."

Strahan looked up from his notebook. Jo-Jo was smiling over at him. He and Turtle were seated at a small table off to his right.

Jo-Jo, with his thin, pockmarked face and wide bug eyes; Turtle, huge, flabby, with a pasty womanish complexion and lugubrious air, were watching Strahan with the cool indifference of nighttime hustlers. Constantly seeking to impose their own terms, though ultimately forced to play the cops' game, they related to the police with heavy-handed banter.

There were only a few all-night places in Pittsburgh. Wherever you went you would see the same faces.

The Pittsburgh underbelly: con and scam artists, pimps, pushers, dealers, small-time gamblers, siding men, strong-arm hoods—they were cockroaches to Strahan. That's what he called them and he often had the feeling that he would like to get them underfoot and crush the life out of them. The world would be better off without them—if only for sanitary reasons.

There were cockroaches and cockroaches, stupid cockroaches, vicious cockroaches, cunning cockroaches. Jo-Jo and Turtle were of the cunning variety. They kept their hustles just inside the confines of the law, or so deviously performed them that the law could never grab them. To Strahan they were, nevertheless, cockroaches and he would have loved to be able to rid the earth of them.

"Is my name in there?" Jo-Jo said, indicating Strahan's notebook.

"Only if you put out," Turtle said.

"I'd put out for John. I always went for guys who wore white socks and Thom McAn shoes."

With a paper napkin Strahan wiped the moisture from his steel-rimmed glasses.

The blind, unreasoned hate Strahan felt for these people, creatures who were nevertheless human, disturbed him. It hadn't always been like that, the hate. Years on the job had eaten into him. What had once been merely disgust and annoyance had evolved into something lethal.

"You hear about Herbie Malik?" Jo-Jo asked. "They found him in Ambridge, half his head in his lap. I'd say it was a thirty-thirty. Might have been a forty-four Mag."

"I didn't know that," Strahan said.

"Got in with bad people, John."

"That's what happens."

Turtle, who had been reading a newspaper, shrugged and went back to it.

"Someone twisted his arm to light a few matches. He burned down a bakery in New Kensington. They grabbed him, he talked and walked."

Turtle, without looking up, said: "He went bing, bing, bing and someone went bing, bang, boom!" Jo-Jo signaled for a refill of his coffee.

"I'll have to charge you," the waitress said.

"Forget it," Jo-Jo said. "You know my philosophy on life? When they give, take. When they take, holler."

A hamburger patty sizzled on the griddle. The tattooed short-order cook chopped onions. The place filled with greasy smoke. The waitress shook the junky woman who had nodded back into her mashed potatoes. "Patsy, you're making a spectacle of yourself," she said.

"I heard on the television somebody offed the old guinea from the candy store," Jo-Jo said. "Who would want to off an old guinea, John?"

Turtle looked up from his newspaper. "What's black and blue and floats down the Allegheny River?"

"Tell me," Jo-Jo said.

"People who call Italians guineas."

The black woman at the end of the counter was nodding slowly back into her mashed potatoes, her head dipping down in precise increments.

"Patsy, goddamn it, you're making a spectacle of yourself again," the waitress said. Patsy continued to make a spectacle of herself, down into her plate.

"Give me some news about Gray Eyes," Strahan said.

Jo-Jo said, "I always liked Gray Eyes."

Turtle studied the newspaper. "There's a jock strap sale at Yankowitz's," he said. "I need a new jock strap. My balls are suing me for non-support."

"With that gut when was the last time you seen your balls?" Jo-Jo said.

"Tell me about Gray Eyes and Mother Shadman," Strahan said. In his head he had been shifting around a lineup of hustlers, a Pittsburgh all-star team. One player hadn't been on the field for a while: Mother Shadman, an old-time Squirrel Hill junky. Gray Eyes and Shadman had hustled siding together many years ago. If Gray Eyes was into heroin—a rumor Strahan had heard a long time back—it was conceivable he would look up his old hustling buddy, Mother Shadman.

There was a problem, though. Shadman, whose nickname came from his inordinate devotion to his mother, had disappeared from his usual haunts. His mother had died in the Jewish Home for the Aged, and he had taken her death very hard. Strahan hadn't seen him in months.

"Last I heard he set out for the boneyard," Jo-Jo said. "You know, a Mother Shadman is like an elephant: they set out to die in their secret boneyard."

"Where's that?"

"Miami Beach. *Emus*, John. I heard he's in Miami Beach."

"There's an outfit called Duquesne Glass. They manufacture steel tubing," Turtle said. He was reading from the stock market page.

"Duquesne Glass and they manufacture *steel* tubing?" Jo-Jo said incredulously.

"They developed a new process. The stock is going like a motherfucker."

"Where is he?" Strahan said to Turtle. He was losing patience.

"Who's that, John?"

"Shadman."

"You're asking me to drop a dime on somebody? Hey, I go bing, bing, bing, you go bing, bang, bong, and maybe we hit off a bargain."

"I'm not going bing, bang, bong for a fat asshole like you," Strahan said.

"What do you know about my asshole? While I'm bending over for the soap you been sticking your nose up there?"

"That's funny," Jo-Jo said. Strahan did not laugh.

"Why don't you ask the *shvartzer?*" Jo-Jo said.

He nodded toward the open kitchen. An elderly black man was washing up some pots. "Crawford, talk to the man here," Jo-Jo said.

The black man looked over. "What's he want to talk about?"

"Remember Gray Eyes?" Jo-Jo said.

"Gray Eyes? I don't remember no Gray Eyes."

"Buddy Gray Eyes," Strahan said.

"Oh, that Gray Eyes. I haven't seen him in a long time," the dishwasher said. "How's he doing?"

Strahan motioned the dishwasher over to him. "What do you want?" the black man said, approaching.

Strahan pulled him gently by the wrist and pushed up the sleeve of his white jacket. His forearm was scarred with old needle tracks and craters. "So?" the black man said. "I'm clean now."

"John, the man got his arms in hot soap and water ten hours a day. He's clean," Jo-Jo said.

"Where can I find Mother Shadman?"

The dishwasher looked over at Turtle and Jo-Jo. They did not look back. Turtle had returned his attention to the newspaper.

Jo-Jo lit a cigarette and held it limply next to his face; he was watching the black woman at the other end of the counter. "Patsy, you're making a spectacle again," he said, waving the cigarette in a vaguely effeminate manner.

"Patsy," the waitress said, "get your damn face out of them potatoes." The black woman made a humming sound and buried her face deeper into the mess.

"He be up at Manny's in Squirrel Hill," the dishwasher said.

Strahan looked long at Jo-Jo. "Miami Beach, huh?"

"The *shvartzer* knows something I don't know."

"*Shvartzers* always know something you don't know," Turtle said.

"I don't know anything," the dishwasher muttered, returning to his sink.

Patsy, at the end of the counter, looked up from her plate. She glowered down the counter. "Who you calling a *shvartzie*?" she said belligerently.

"No one's talking to you," Jo-Jo said.

"Don't fuck with me, chump," Patsy said, brandishing a dull butter knife. "I'll cut your white dick off."

"Watch that language in here," the waitress said as

Strahan rose to leave. "You come around here, Patsy, make a spectacle of yourself—"

"Kiss my black ass," Patsy said. "If it were as white as your face, I wouldn't be in the condition I'm in now."

Strahan paid for his coffee. "Give them a refill," he said. He made an entry in his book.

"Putting it on the expense account, John?" Jo-Jo said.

"Right beside your name."

"Keep my name out of it."

Strahan winked. It was an uncomfortable gesture. John Strahan never had been one of the boys.


"Where's Mother Shadman?"

Ijack, the late-shift baker at Berman's on Murray Avenue, looked up. Someone was standing in the alley, just outside the open back door, behind the screen.

"Who's there?" he said, sucking on a Marsh Wheeling cigar as he pounded at the dough. He was in a sour mood: his helper, Willie the Greenhorn, had been giving him a rough time. Ijack wanted pans scraped, the big refrigerator washed down. Willie refused. He was supposed to get the bagels out, he said.

Buddy Gray Eyes moved into the baking area. "Hey," said Ijack. "How you doing?" He hadn't seen Gray Eyes for years. In the old days he had liked him, tough kid, good athlete. "Where you been?"

"On the Coast."

"Nice out there," Ijack said. He remembered Gray Eyes as a handsome, slick character. He looked thin now, wasted. "You been sick?" he said.

"I'm all right," Gray Eyes said.

"How about a roll? Willie, give him a roll. What do you want, onion?"

"Fine."

"Don't sweat on it," Ijack admonished the Greenhorn. Willie lobbed an onion roll over at Gray Eyes. Gray

Eyes tore the roll apart, but did not eat it. "I have to get to California," Gray Eyes said.

"Yeah," Ijack said, cutting the dough into loaves. Willie stood beside him at the worktable and dusted the loaves with corn flour.

"Mother Shadman still around?" Gray Eyes said.

"Try upstairs at Manny's." Manny's poolhall was around the corner, above the bakery.

"Could you get him for me?"

"Hey, Willie, run upstairs and get Mother Shadman." Willie busied himself with the doughnut vat. "Did you hear me?" Willie slammed pans around in front of the oven. "Whenever I want something from him he suddenly can't speak English. Hey, you fucking hunky, did you hear me?"

Willie glared at Ijack, then moved out the back door.

"Sure, California's good," Ijack said. "I never been there, but I hear. I been to Florida. Same thing, right? Sun, right?"

Gray eyes did not answer and Ijack continued pounding the dough on the worktable.

Willie returned with a short, pudgy man with soft, white skin and a hardly perceptible beard. The man wore lightly tinted prescription glasses over large, baleful, liquid eyes; he moved with small, almost delicate steps.

"Someone here for you, Mother," Ijack said. He spotted a shadow moving in the corridor leading to the store. "In the hallway."

Shadman walked to the back of the baking area. "Who is it?" he called into the darkness.

"Gray Eyes," Buddy said softly from the corridor.

Shadman moved into the corridor. "Buddy, Buddy," he said. They embraced. Mother Shadman held Gray Eyes to him for a long time. He fought tears.

"How have you been?" Mother Shadman said. He patted Gray Eyes on the face lightly. "I get emotional. I'm sorry. So many memories."

Gray Eyes retreated down the corridor into shadow.
"What's the matter?" Mother Shadman said.

"I came to town with a friend. Now I have to leave. I don't have any money."

"You're carrying a habit?"

"No, no, I beat all that. I need money to get to California. I have this friend out there. He'll take care of me."

"I could maybe get you a few bucks, but you know I have a jones—"

"Get me what you can. If I can get to New York first—"

"If it's dope, I could score enough for both of us—"

"No. I have friends in California, New York," he said.

"It'll be tomorrow before I can get you anything," Mother Shadman said. He tore off a corner of a paper bag and jotted down his phone number. He handed it to Gray Eyes. "Where can I get a hold of you?" he asked. "Here—" He offered him the pencil and a piece of paper bag.

Gray eyes wrote down a phone number and address. "This girl is staying out by Kennywood. She'll know how to reach me," Gray Eyes said.

He moved up very close to Mother Shadman. His blue-gray eyes gleamed with a brilliant feverishness. "I was by Allderdice field earlier," he said. "The high school team was practicing. Remember the game I played against Westinghouse? You were there, weren't you?"

Mother Shadman could see a lean young man flashing across the field, dodging, leaping, twirling in the bright day. The ball soared into sunlight and it was golden and the young man was golden also. "I remember it," he said.

"That was some game, wasn't it?"

"The best I ever saw."

"Right." Gray Eyes stood there, staring at nothing.

"You're all right?" Mother Shadman said. "You're sure?"

Gray Eyes shrugged, smiled. His smile was dazzling and suddenly Mother Shadman felt better. "I'm fine," Gray Eyes said.

Later, Gray Eyes stood on the cobblestone street overlooking Kennywood amusement park. He could see the skeleton of the Jack Rabbit Roller Coaster outlined against the night sky. Beyond the amusement park was the Monongahela River and beyond that a carpet of pinpoint white lights: Braddock. To his left the steel mills of Homestead; to his right, the steel mills of Duquesne.

A great flower of molten orange light spilled out from a mill in Homestead, a snaky flower of fire whose tendrils coiled through the black sky whipping red spark filaments all about.

He thought about Cervino. He saw in his mind's eye the blue-gray fabric of the old man's sweater. The threads of the sweater had been unusually thick, a broad, thick weave, probably foreign made. A relative in the old country must have sent it. He wouldn't have had money to buy handmade Italian imports.

Had he been wearing the same sweater many, many years ago, that time they had been together? Gray Eyes decided it had been a similar sweater, but not the same one. No, too many years had passed.

And once again he saw the dying Easter chick, felt the warmth of his mother's leg, smelled the flower of her perfume, saw rain falling over the park.

Suddenly he was seized with a sense of desolation so complete that he moaned with it. What had he done? And why? He was The Destroyer . . .

That day many years ago—he had been to Cervino's, yes, and afterward, the fight, yes, and then he had run off.

He had come to Saint Philomena's, past the lily pond and the ball field, to the coal mine. He had come to the coal mine and crouched in the shaft. And then his mother had come to him . . .

"Oh, dear God, get me out to California," he whispered. "Get me to California, to Alex and Stanley, to the ocean and the sun. Get me to California."

He stared behind him, up the hill. The light in the room

he shared with Julie was off. She wouldn't be back from work yet.

He would wait till she returned, then call her. He wouldn't go to the house. That would be too dangerous.

He had intended saying good-bye to her earlier, but he felt they should talk. He felt he should try to explain certain things to her.

He would explain to her about the Easter chick and his mother and Cervino and—and—

He would not excuse what he had done to the old man. That was something for which he would offer no apology. No, he wanted to talk to her about what he had done to her, what he had caused in *her* life.

He wanted to tell her about The Destroyer and The Protector and what the old man had done to him.

He moved down the cobblestone street and hurried into the darkened amusement park. Mother Shadman would come through. He would get—to New York, to Earl. Earl would see to it that he made it out to California!

He had a tattoo on his chest of a stick figure man. He rubbed the tattoo under his shirt. The world was a network of lines, the drawing over his heart, a map. It was all interconnected. Pittsburgh, New York, California . . .

How blessed he was to have such sweet friends!

Mother Shadman arrived back at the pool room to find John Strahan waiting for him.

He pretended he did not see the detective and seated himself in a corner of the room beneath a green-shaded wall lamp. He studied a paperback he carried in his coat pocket, while eating red pistachios from a paper bag.

Randall, an old gimp who managed the poolhall, limped around the room like a wounded jackrabbit, racking balls, adjusting cues, cleaning ashtrays. It was nearly two o'clock and he was preparing to close up shop. Two men in their early twenties were the only other people in the place.

Strahan lifted the book out of Mother Shadman's hands

and studied the worn cover. It was *The Philosophy of Edmund Husserl.*

"Phenomenology," Shadman said.

Strahan turned the book over in his hands, leafed through it. "What is it?" he said.

"Consciousness in relation to objects," Shadman said.

Strahan returned the book to him. "You hear a man was murdered this afternoon?"

"Doesn't surprise me."

"The man from the candy store."

"Cervino?"

"Buddy Gray Eyes did it."

Shadman gazed around the room, licking his lips nervously. He passed his hand over his forehead as though wiping away perspiration.

The two men at the pool table were having a heated argument. Randall limped over to them, brandishing a broom. "They'll be none of that in here," he said.

The men quieted down and went back to their game.

"The older you get," Mother Shadman said, "it's like one ax chop on top of another. First my mother, then this. Do you have a cigarette, John?"

"I gave it up," Strahan said.

"Randall," Shadman called out. "Give me a cigarette."

Randall limped over. "All I got is menthol." He gave Shadman a cigarette. He leaned between Shadman and Strahan, winking. "Those punks fuck with me I'll be on 'em like ugly on an ape; no one fucks with me."

"Good, Randall, good," Mother Shadman said.

"So," said Strahan. "He came to you, didn't he?"

Shadman stared at the end of his cigarette. "What can you do me?"

"What do you need?"

"There's one or two things need cleaning up." Shadman shook his head, sighed. The weight of the world pressed down on his junky's soul. "What is this life, John? What is it?"

"I don't know."

"With all the great books I'm privy to I still look at life in amazement. People are vicious, unreliable." Strahan shifted his weight uncomfortably. When you paid for the show, you had to take it all, the bullshit, the self-pity, the philosophic con. "People will murder and lie and betray. I'm not telling you anything you don't know." Shadman puffed on his cigarette, pondered. "In the old days it was different. There were *menshes*, then. No more. Cervino is dead, murdered by my one-time good friend; my mother died. But let's look at it from another angle—Let's say they didn't die, that no one really dies, because there is no death."

"Some people'll be happy to hear that."

"I knew Cervino forty years—"

"I knew him, too."

"Everyone knew him. A refined man. Quality."

Randall opened up a window wide to air out the place. A cold draft blew through the room.

"My mother, may she rest in peace, for years was up in the Jewish Home for the Aged, the Moshav Zakainim, up there on Brown's Hill Road. I wanted better for her. She deserved better. But she ended up in a little four-by-ten cubicle there. A narrow iron bed to sleep on. She used to complain to me about that bed. 'Everett,' she'd say, 'that bed is a pain in the ass.' Everett's my name. Not many people know that."

Mother Shadman sighed. "At home my father would say to me, 'Everett, remember three things in this life: Don't be ridiculous. Make a living. And there's an angle to everything.' So all my life I've been ridiculous, never made a dime, missed all the angles."

"You done all right with the angles," Randall said, pushing the broom along the wall.

"Close the window," Shadman said.

"We got an odor in here. When the odor's gone, I'll close the window."

"Fifty years the odor'll still be in here."

"Don't listen to him," Randall called over to Strahan. "We run a disinfected place here."

Shadman waved him off, disgusted. "I wanted better for my mother," he said to Strahan. "But at an early age I came down with an incurable disease—heroin addiction. Still, in the jackpot and out, I did what I could for my mother. I would visit up at the Home for the Aged and I'd bring her some fruit and candy. She had a sweet tooth all her life—"

"Can we cut the horseshit now?" Strahan suddenly said. "Do we slice a deal or what? You know, a guy your age should be thinking about retirement."

"I think about it all the time."

"Miami Beach."

"Sure."

"Certain people are upset about this thing, killing an old man for no reason. Certain officers of the law wouldn't bring him in, they'd shoot him like a dog. They don't know Buddy the way you and I know him. So I'm looking out for Buddy, too."

"I know you are."

"I'd make sure he got to the station house."

"Slice," Shadman said, subdued. "I'm too old to do hard time anymore."

"Okay."

"I got one count of possession pending up in Fayette City."

"No problem."

"If anybody asks—you know, the boys—tell 'em I did it for him."

"I will."

"Be sure to tell them, John." Shadman removed a piece of paper from his pocket.

"This is out near Duquesne," Strahan said, studying the paper.

"It's his girl friend. It's right by Kennywood."

Strahan copied the address and phone number in his little yellow book. He also wrote: Edmund Husserl, Phenomenology. Consciousness in relationship to objects—telling himself that some day he must read up on it.

He closed the notebook quickly, as though embarrassed by the notation on Husserl.

He started for the door. Mother Shadman was staring at the wall. He shivered in the cold. The bag of pistachios on his lap fell to the floor, spilling all over. "Now look what you've done," Randall, the gimp, yelled. Cursing, he moved to sweep them up.

# 4

THE address Mother Shadman had provided him with was a large gabled house on a cobblestone street above Kennywood Park. It was off season and the amusement park was dark.

Strahan eased his car in against the curb on the hill opposite the house and shut off the motor.

He huddled in the front seat, cursed the weather. Snow threatened. A few wet flakes pasted the windshield.

He longed to go in after Gray Eyes. He might be able to claim the doctrine of hot pursuit. He demurred. While technically it might be valid, the courts had been coming down hard on the doctrine's abuse.

He would wait till the sun came up, then wake Jackie Palmer, have him visit the magistrate and get a valid warrant. In the meantime perhaps Gray Eyes would show.

He fought sleep. There was a pack of cigarettes on the car seat—Jackie Palmer's—and although he had given them up more than a year ago, he tried one. He drew on it without enjoyment, angry with himself for backsliding. He crushed out the cigarette after several drags.

He removed his service revolver and checked the cylinder. He carried a backup gun, a snub-nosed .32, in a small holster on his hip, and he checked that, too.

He thought about the old man and Gray Eyes. He

thought about the past, how it was penetrating into the present now, upsetting the fragile equilibrium he had established in his life.

He thought about his wife, not the way she was today, but in the past, in those high school days when Buddy Gray Eyes had been king of the school.

He weighed his service revolver in his hand. And he knew that if he were to confront Gray Eyes now, he would use it on him.

There were old scores that had not been settled entirely.

The inside of the car was like a refrigerator. So much of a cop's work was in the cold, Strahan was thinking. So much of it was done when you were tired and hungry and angry. So much of it was done when your stomach burned with fury. "Put out the fire," Strahan told himself, hunching low behind the wheel of the car. He hugged himself, attempting to get warm.

He lit another cigarette.

In his mind's eye he saw Gray Eyes and his wife together, when they had all been younger. Gray Eyes and his wife were naked. Strahan's stomach turned with nausea at the image.

And then he saw something else: Cervino's store, Gray Eyes as a child coming toward him.

They had had a confrontation. What had it been about? The memory died. Strahan's breath fogged up in the cold. Strahan suffered: a purgatory of deep night surveillance, cold, lonely, tired—vicious imps of the past dancing in his brain.

His eyelids began to flutter shut. He forced them open. White spots swirled down out of the dark sky. Strahan continued to fight to stay awake.

It had begun to snow. The snow fell in large, feathery flakes across the white light of the corner streetlamp.

Julie Tripp, idly brushing her hair, stood by the window watching the snow. She liked the snow. She had been raised in the mountains and it reminded her of home.

Nothing else in the scene reminded her of home, though; not the ribs of the amusement park roller coaster, not the mills across the way spewing flames, not the thick soot and grit of this town.

Where she had grown up everything had been white and clean. Her life had been clean. No more.

What to do?

She continued to comb her hair, trying to apprehend some direction in her life, some core. She had been combing her hair for more than an hour; before that it had taken her nearly as long to remove her makeup. She could not bring herself to attempt sleep.

She sensed that something was wrong.

She had fought with Buddy the night before and he had rushed out into the night. She had not heard from him since.

She feared that something had happened to him.

It was almost daylight. She had been back from work for nearly two hours. She should sleep. She couldn't. She was desperate with worry.

She prayed that Buddy hadn't gone to the cooker again, returned to dope.

"Everything is all right, Julie. Everything is *all right*." She spoke aloud, trying to reassure herself. "Go to bed now. Everything is all right."

She stayed by the window, continued to comb her hair.

For the past hour or so a car with a man inside had been parked outside the house. The engine was off. The man sat in the cold. She was certain he was a cop. Over the years she had had some experience with cops.

Watching the snow like delicate lace falling now, the bleak landscape shrouded in a mantle of white, power lines heavy with white, the dark river moving through white, she thought back on the past, of home, and of the first time she had met Buddy Gray Eyes.

She had just turned eighteen, a silly kid just out of high

school, an ex-cheerleader, counter girl at the Big Bopper Burger—a local hamburger joint. With her long, reddish blond hair and Kewpie-doll face, she had been the prettiest girl in town. Everyone in her senior class had expected great things from her.

The town she had grown up in was on Lake Chandler in California's eastern Sierra Mountains. Eight thousand feet above sea level, the area was a minor resort—fishing and boating and hiking in the summer, skiing in the winter. The year-round population had been fewer than three hundred people.

She lived with her father and two younger brothers in a mobile home overlooking the lake. Years before, her mother had abandoned the family—just ran off with a man from Reno.

Buddy had a job that summer with the Forest Service in the bristlecone pine area—the oldest living trees on earth, he had told her. In the winter he lived in a cabin up at Lake Chandler. He stayed pretty much to himself.

During the summer she had seen him only a few times. He was living, then, in a tent in the bristlecone pines. He walked around in western getup, blue jean outfit, Tony Lama cowboy boots, Stetson hat.

In the winter he moved to Lake Chandler.

She would see him in the Big Bopper Burger day and night. He rarely spoke to anyone. He would sit smoking cigarettes and staring out over the snow-packed mountains. He drove a battered old dump truck that constantly was on the fritz. He was always out in the lot tinkering with it, trying to get it started.

She couldn't take her eyes off him. There was something so pathetic and lost about him, yet enormously attractive. He was perhaps the most handsome man she had ever seen. He had long blond hair and light blue-gray eyes, peculiar eyes, startling eyes. He had a dazzling, though sad, smile. It wasn't often he smiled, however.

"Why are you always alone?" she asked him one winter

afternoon as the dark mountain shadows swept over the white expanse of snow.

He talked in a vague way of hassles, problems living in Los Angeles. He needed to get the smog out of his lungs, to clear chemicals from his brain cells.

Later she learned that he had been involved in dope—moving, trading, selling. And that certain people had labeled him a police informer.

He told her he had been misunderstood. "They play everyone like a yo-yo," he had said, referring to the narcs. "The game's nothing but talk and walk. One of these days I'm going to straighten everybody out as to what I did and did not do."

She went off with him one evening after work and they drove back to his cabin. It was a plain, pine-board structure set far back from the lake. They had made love and it was the easiest and most natural thing she had ever done in her life.

"He taught me things I would have never imagined," she said aloud now, still gazing out the window, still combing her hair. "Good things and bad." Some very bad. He had turned her on to heroin.

The man in the car below had lit a cigarette. She could see the ash glowing in the dark.

She took her nightgown from the closet and laid it out on the bed. She sat down on the bed.

The evening was so quiet! Everything was so quiet! A white blanket of snow muffled the world . . .

She prayed for Buddy to appear, smiling, sliding along in his easy, cool, relaxed way—his old way—to tell her that everything was all right.

She prayed that he arrive now with—a pizza! In the old days he would do that sometimes, stay out half the night, then suddenly appear, loaded down with bags and boxes of Italian food.

When he was in a fine mood, there was no one who could put away food the way he could.

In the good days they would go to ball games and rock concerts, drive-in movies, restaurants of all sorts.

Buddy was always bouncing, laughing, whistling. He whistled between his teeth and could create a whole combo of sound. In a short time, wherever they were, he would have everybody perking with his rhythm, bubbling with cheer.

In the beginning she had imagined that was how their life together would be: one long party where even strangers suddenly became friends.

It never was. Instead it had been dope deals and hustles, embarrassments, recriminations, rip-offs and narc entrapments . . .

He had been doing dope heavily when she first met him, trying to throw it off. He always seemed to be trying to throw it off.

He told her he wasn't addicted—just habituated. He would smile shyly and explain it was his sense of adventure that drove him to it. And in a way she found it to be true: he took dope the way some people climbed mountains, testing his strength and endurance, aiming for some impossible height, rappeling off obdurate acclivities, flirting with black chasms.

Occasionally the results would be disastrous.

She would look at him and he would be wasted on windowpane acid or PCP and his eyes would take on a sad, dead look and he would talk about The Angel of Death, The Protector, The Destroyer.

He would bare his chest to her and run his fingers over the tattoo he had there, a stick figure man spread-eagled above his heart.

Seated on the bed now, watching the snow fall in long, slow, ever increasing waves, soft white curtains of snow billowing down, obscuring the amusement park, obscuring the mills beyond, she realized how far she had come since those innocent days in the mountains. She had traveled not only across time and distance, but more: she had done the road to the end area of her being, some desolate, rusting, garbage dump of the soul.

She moved back to the window. The snow was falling faster. The ground beneath the streetlamp was coated with snow.

The man in the car was still there.

She started to undress when the telephone rang.

At the other end of the line no one spoke for a long time. She could hear quiet breathing and a hollow whooshing sound: an outdoor pay phone. "Hello? Hello?"

At last: "Little Julie," said softly, flatly, not in the old Buddy way.

"Bud? Where are you?"

"The fun house."

"In Kennywood Park?" Silence, except for the breathing. "Buddy, please—"

"I'll be leaving town," he said after a short while.

"Why? What's the matter?" He didn't answer. "Where are you now?"

"I told you. The fun house."

"Shall I come there?" Silence. "Bud?"

"Is anybody watching you?" he said.

"Yes. There's a man in a car. Buddy, do you want me to come to you?" He did not answer. She could hear him breathing. They did not speak for a long time. "What have you done?" she said at last.

"I'll tell you about it sometime," he said, sounding very much like a small boy.

"Buddy, right this minute are you in the fun house? The Kennywood Park fun house? Is that where you're calling from?"

But he had hung up.

She stood in the center of the room for a very long time, staring at the phone. "I don't know what to do, I don't know what to do," she said over and over again.

One night, when they had first arrived in town, they had gone walking in the amusement park. They had investigated the fun house, surprised there had been no guard.

Was Buddy there now, waiting for her? Was that what the call meant?

Or had he been talking about the fun house of his mind, his perpetual, walk-around horror show?

His voice over the phone had been so cold, so empty. What had happened to him?

Was it dope? Had he scored? Was the chill in his voice dope modulated, heroin chill?

What should she do? What?

She wanted to go to him, yet couldn't move. She was paralyzed by *possibilities*. She had seen so much: dope encounters, ugly schemes, death flirtations, heroin scares. They were all waiting for her in the black heart of the night.

Chemical goblins skulked in the night, filled her with terror. Rush to him now, she told herself; yet she did not move. Drugs had done it, had poisoned their life, and now, though she wanted to save him, the past and its pain rose up in her mind, immobilized her.

He had been off drugs when she first met him. Their time together had been bliss. Over that winter he had started back.

She hadn't known. Suddenly one day, after weeks of silence and lethargy, he had come to her exploding with exuberance, filled with grandiose ideas.

They went off skiing by themselves, not on the regular slopes, but on the back of the mountain. He wasn't a very good skier, but he seemed absolutely fearless.

Later, she discovered his lack of fear came out of dope: methedrine, cocaine, acid.

He had formulated a theory, he told her: skiing was like life. If you got the speed up fast enough, you couldn't fall and you couldn't get hurt. He *would* take falls, but he never seemed to injure himself. In football it was the same way, he would explain to her. It was only when you held back that you got hurt.

She didn't want to hold back. She would go to the end of her being with him.

He started doing heroin. Her reaction when she first learned it was one of anger and indignation. It was a sham emotion: she really envied him, envied that realm of experience outside her ken. "How does it feel?" she would ask him, feigning only mild interest.

"It's all right," he would say.

"Why do you do it?"

He would sigh: "Hey, it's something to kill time with." Then he would laugh, a slow, nodding laugh.

"Let me try it," she asked one day.

"Ah, no. It's not for you."

A charade between them began. He would lecture her on the pitfalls of junk, preach and use, and while using not believe a word he preached. They both played at a game the outcome of which had already been determined. The question now was who would shoulder the blame. Who forced whom? Who was guilty?

He would brood; she would sulk. Days would go by and they wouldn't talk to each other. All the while they were doing a slow dance around the eye dropper spike and bottle cap cooker, both knowing all the time that, of course, he would eventually usher her into his world.

The first time she used it, she threw up. After that it became easy, a routine flirtation with death and the abyss.

They would monitor each other's habits, look out for one another, make sure they were just dipping and dabbing —weekending. During the week they might indulge in a whole range of chemicals; heroin they saved for Saturdays and Sundays.

They would hang around his cabin making slow, dreamy love, nodding out, immersing themselves in death without dying.

They would spin off on long, rambling talk journeys. He would unfold for her his life, his experience, the lessons he had learned.

He told her of his ambitions. He had been a hustler, the son of a hustler, yet he loathed hustlers. He wanted something grand, majestic, some powerful, governing idea for his life.

He tried politics. Through a girl friend—the girl who had introduced him to heroin—he became involved with a group of metaphysical revolutionaries.

Alex Zayas, an ex-con, was the leader. He was very bright and very persuasive. He had read all the books, could mouth all the rhetoric. Revolution would redeem not only Alex and Bud and the rest of the group, but the whole world.

It was a race between revolution and dope, and dope won out. The chemical explosions in their brains became surrogates for cataclysms in the world.

Buddy came to realize it was all sham and self-con, blood-and-brain-barrier technology. They were nothing more than prisoners of chemicals. He tried to escape.

From time to time he would. Then he would return.

At rock bottom he was left with himself and that was not enough. Alex Zayas, politics, dope—he embraced them again and he was no longer alone.

What was it he wanted, Julie would ask him? He would try to articulate it, but it never came together. "I want to protect the weak," he would say. Or: "I want to remove pain." Or, in desperate moments: "I want to destroy—"

What? What? Julie would demand. What do you want to protect? What do you want to destroy?

He couldn't answer it. He would grow quiet. He would go back to dope.

Sometimes he would say, with a touching, small-boy simplicity: "I was a hero as a kid. Everybody looked up to me. I want to be a hero again."

Pacing the room now, Julie thought about the day she had left the mountains with Buddy.

Hurtling down the narrow road from Lake Chandler,

a sudden panic had seized her. They were on a road she had traveled a thousand times and yet nothing seemed real or recognizable. Where am I? Where am I driving? What lies ahead?

As they drove south, the day grew somber. On switchback roads above the salt-thick and dead Mono Lake Julie stared out over barren undulations of gray rock vastness. Glacier snow gathered at the crests, rocky, desolate volcanic escarpments. Julie was glad to be leaving this land.

They were heading toward the sun-blessed lands of southern California. She was sure they would both find a bright, clean, dazzling dream.

She was wrong. The time after leaving the mountains was composed of nightmare years, dope hustles, throwing herself away. She shuddered at what she had done in those years, looked back on herself as though at a stranger.

And now this: cop traps set, fun house sanctuary, dead madness in his voice.

She roamed the room now like a locked-in animal. "I don't know what to do."

In an agony of despair she dressed, threw on her cotton coat, and hurried from the room.

She moved down the stairs to the first floor of the house.

She stood in an alcove between the heavy front door and a glass outer door and watched the street. Through the falling snow she could see the dark form of the man waiting in the car.

She felt cold all over, not only from the frigid air trapped between the doors, but more: Buddy's voice whispering in her head, *the fun house*.

Was he there? Desperate, insane, waiting for her to somehow save him? Were there shards of sanity in him crying out to her?

What had he done? Something terrible, too terrible for him to tell her, but what?

The wind rattled the glass front door. Snow danced

across the cobblestones. The man in the car did not move.

If Buddy was waiting for her in the fun house, then it was essential that she get there without the man seeing her.

But how?

She waited. She tried to think of a way of getting past the man in the car. She would have to go down the hill. There was no other way.

She stood shivering in the alcove, unable to get herself to move, hoping that the man in the car would go away.

The man in the car had lit a cigarette; the ash glowed, cooled, burned hot again, slow, hypnotic, lambent winks of color.

Should she wait? Attempt to go for it now? Run? Or stroll with forced casualness? From where she stood she could see the entrance to the amusement park, just down the hill across the streetcar tracks. The fun house was at the far end of the park.

The cigarette ash flared, cooled, then flared again.

She moved briskly out the doorway and started down the hill, whistling as she went, frightened, yet amused at her assumed insouciance. Whistling!

The car started up, its headlights snapped on; it began to follow slowly after her down the hill.

She did not look back, forced herself to keep a steady, casual pace. She could hear the crunch of the car's tires over the snow-covered cobblestone street.

She crossed the streetcar tracks and stood waiting. The entrance to the park was directly behind her.

How to get into the park? How? Was Buddy just beyond the entrance, waiting for her? Was he cold, desperate, insane, dope high? Was he watching her?

The detective car suddenly speeded up, swerved ahead of her, and came to a stop at the next corner. She was staring directly ahead into the car now. Although she could not make out the face of the man, she was sure he was watching her, waiting for her next move.

She glanced back at the park entrance. Run for it, run! Come on, Julie. Do *something*. She could not move.

She stood there for a long time. The man in the car waited.

At last she heard a rumble in the distance, then a grinding of steel wheels as the streetcar to the South Side eased around a bend toward her.

The streetcar glided to a stop. The door opened. Julie just stood there. "Well," the conductor said.

"I don't know what to do," she heard herself say.

She looked beyond the tracks. The cop's car waited there, its motor running.

She boarded the streetcar. "Is something the matter?" the conductor said.

"No," she said. The streetcar pulled away. The cop car did not move.

Around a curve at the bottom of the hill she said, "I'll get out here."

She rushed from the streetcar along the steel fence that bounded the amusement park.

She found the open side gate, the gate she and Buddy had used.

She walked through the darkened amusement park, hurrying along, trying to keep warm. She moved across a maze of concrete paths that looped through the park. She passed the Jack Rabbit Roller Coaster, Noah's Ark, The Whip. The artificial lake in the park was drained, the refreshment stands boarded up.

The park, with its closed-down rides, bizarre cutout signs, surreal forms, appeared in the snow as some extraordinary alien world, a landscape in a white nightmare.

She moved along the walk toward the fun house. A huge, yawning clown's face formed the entrance. A train of open cars would move on a track through a water-filled channel into the mouth of the clown. The cars were gone now, the water drained.

The wind had started up. A metal sign on a wooden cubicle creaked and banged against the shuttered front.

She stepped onto a plank walkway and followed the empty channel into the maw of the concrete clown's face. She entered a tunnel and groped her way along the damp tunnel wall. The air was stifling, with a rank smell of mildew and rotting wood. The dark pressed in on her. Julie's voice echoed down the tunnel: "Buddy!"

She felt along the wall where she and Bud had discovered a switchbox. She found it now and threw the lever. Light burst on her in shattered chunks: a room of mirrors, fun house mirrors, distorted, dizzying.

Her reflection grew fat and waned, weaved at her.

"Bud?" she said. "Buddy!"

Her reflection in spectacular multiplicity bobbed in the white light.

"Buddy, please!"

There was a soft rustling sound behind one of the mirrors. It opened outward and he appeared.

He looked thin and pale to her. His eyes were empty; they gazed past her.

She felt as though she would weep. "What's wrong?" she said.

He did not speak for a very long time. He stared past her. Their reflections in the fun house mirrors surrounded them, a grotesque and silent array.

"I'm in trouble," he said at last.

He spoke rapidly now, still not looking at her. "Something happened—the old man—I went with my mother to the old man and—"

His eyes were brilliant, fevered. He was looking beyond her, beyond the mirrors.

"What old man?"

"He's been holding something over me."

"Who are you talking about, Buddy? What old man?"

"It's all on the tattoo," he said. He smiled, slowly. "I'm going out to California, Julie. Alex will take care of me.

First I'll go to New York and see Earl and maybe Adele and they'll all take care of me. They all love me."

Julie fought tears. "What have you done?"

"I have a lot to make up to people. It hurts me that—"

"What have you done? What? Tell me, Buddy? What have you done?" She was screaming now, hysterical. His face was so drawn, his eyes so empty, sadness without end in his gaze. "Please tell me—"

"Sweet, sweet Julie," he said. He held her to him. She was trembling. He stroked her hair. "I'm sorry, Julie. Little Julie. I'm sorry."

They stood like that for a long time. Then they walked outside. The sky was streaked with gray light. It was almost dawn.

"Give me some money," he said.

"I'll go with you."

He shook his head. "It's serious," he said. "You can't go with me."

"Did you hurt someone?" He didn't answer. "Did you kill?"

He opened his shirt, baring the tattoo. "The Destroyer did it," he said, stroking the tattoo. "He did it." His voice was cold again. "Now give me the money."

She fought to control her sobs; still they came. She rummaged through her coat pocket, found her wallet. She had less than fifty dollars. She gave it to him.

"A man will see you with some more money for me. His name is Shadman. I'll call you later."

"Will I see you again?" she said.

"Oh, sure." He shrugged. "It was just something I had to do. Alex will make it right."

He started to walk away, then, as an afterthought, turned back to her. "You might run across this person— I've told you about him. His name is Akiba. He'll know what to do—"

Akiba. A Jewish man, a rabbi. He had spoken of him before. "About what?" she asked.

He stood there, his shirt open, stroking the stick figure man tattooed on his chest. "Kabbalah," he whispered, then he was off, moving quickly through skeleton struts of amusement park rides, a shadow racing before the light. It was morning now and he was gone.

# 5

THE wheels of procedure turned slowly. John Strahan sat in Lieutenant Busik's office at the Public Safety Building and waited.

Busik, at his desk, nibbled at an egg salad sandwich. Bits of egg dribbled from the corner of the bread onto the wax paper wrapping. Busik ignored it, continued eating. He studied a report in front of him. He did not look at Strahan. He was peeved with him.

On the wall just above Busik's head, Scotch-taped to the wall, was a yellow rabbit's foot; next to that, a framed plaque with an American flag and the exhortation: "Keep America *Strong*."

Jack Palmer stood by the window, flipping a coin. Strahan marveled at his simple-minded doggedness. He would flip the coin, catch it on his wrist, study it, flip it again. Over and over he performed the ritual.

From time to time he would gaze out over the street below. A work crew was repairing the sidewalk; the sound of a jackhammer continued in a low, incessant, ratcheting drone.

Steam heat hissed from an ancient radiator beneath the window. The walls were a sickly bureaucratic green. Busik and Palmer were perspiring. No one thought to open the window.

Strahan felt a terrible distance between him and his co-workers. He was of a different breed. Watching Palmer's involvement with a *coin*, Busik's concentration on his report, he realized how limited their imaginations were: they were like horses—you pointed them in a direction and they plodded their way there. And it was just this plodding quality that was responsible for their effectiveness as cops. They never worried, never panicked, never pursued with passion, never quit. They just continued on, straight ahead.

And they accomplished the job.

Palmer, with his crooked smile and garish attire, might be taken for a racetrack hustler. Busik, solidly built, pleasant-looking, could have been a life insurance salesman.

Strahan realized with a pang of envy that both of them, in their easy affability, were what you would call regular guys. Most of the men in the department were. Strahan wasn't, never had been.

He was painfully aware of how different from them he was. He was tight. He looked cold. He did not smile easily. He played chess, read philosophy. Beneath his vaguely removed, grayish exterior, a terrifying anger raged. He covered it up. It took great effort.

His stomach burned. "Put out the fire," he told himself. He walked to the cooler and drew a cup of water. The pain eased in his stomach.

"So what do you think, John?" Busik said, still without looking at Strahan. "Will he go back to this Shadman guy?"

"I have no idea."

Strahan and Busik had had words earlier, and the resentment still smoldered.

At dawn, after the young girl had boarded the streetcar, Strahan had returned to the rooming house. He had roused the landlady and questioned her about Gray Eyes. She had not seen him for several days. The girl worked in the checkroom of a restaurant on Mount Washington.

He had the woman take him to the room, then sent her

downstairs. He removed his service revolver and pushed the door open. The room was empty.

He searched it without a warrant.

When he arrived at the Public Safety Building, Strahan told Busik what he had done. The lieutenant, normally easygoing, had chewed him out in front of everybody. "We been having a helluva time with the D.A.'s office over that hot pursuit thing. You know that, John!" He had slammed drawers, banged his desk, hollered.

How could Strahan communicate the passion he had felt, what Gray Eyes meant to him?

All the ferocious evil in the world had consolidated for him in the idea of Gray Eyes. All doubt in his soul melted away. Cervino represented everything that was decent in this world; Gray Eyes, that which mocks, desecrates, slaughters decency.

How to explain that to Busik? How to impress on him the awesome rage he felt? He would have to explain so many things; he would have to lay bare his soul, peel away layers of the past, display the pain buried there.

In the outer office things were speeding up. Detectives moved in and out; doors slammed; phones rang. There is a rhythm to any case. What appears desultory and stagnant is often just the prelude, the necessary warm-up—the department testing the water. When they finally did enter, it was with an energy and sense of purpose that often surprised Strahan. They may have been plodders, these detectives in homicide, but the accumulated force of their activity created something powerful, inexorable.

That morning a search had been completed of the area surrounding Cervino's store. The murder gun had been found several blocks away. A palm print had been taken off the gun, a Smith & Wesson, single-action, bottom break model. It was an unusual weapon for a murder, a pre-1865 service model—an antique really—employing .32 rimfire shells.

A man from ballistics studied the gun. He recognized

immediately its special character: only one company in the Pittsburgh area carried .32 long rimfire shells. The owner of the company had been called in with instructions to bring along his records.

He was brought to Busik's office, a tall, elderly man in a dark suit; he looked like an undertaker. He was nervous. He chain-smoked and had a hacking cough.

Busik wiped some residue of egg salad from his hands and offered the gun seller a chair. He displayed the revolver for him. By law a gun seller must take application for purchase of any firearm and submit a copy to the sheriff's office and the state police. The gun seller leafed through his records and came up with the information: he had sold the revolver to a man by the name of Jim Smith.

"He gave you identification to the fact that he was Jim Smith?" Busik said.

The man in the dark suit nodded. Busik stared at the man. The man grew nervous. "It was more or less an antique gun. He said he collected them."

"And you sold him ammunition?"

"Yes."

"For an antique gun?"

"He asked me if it would be hard to get ammunition for it and I said it would. I told him I had a box of thirty-two long rimfire and he bought the box. You know, that's a single-action revolver, you have to cock the hammer back to fire it, and I just never thought—"

"What did this man look like?"

"Early thirties. Good-looking fellow, though scroungy. Dirty blond hair."

"What color were his eyes?"

"Light, you know, nice eyes. Nice-looking boy. Maybe a little undernourished."

"Maybe a junky?" Jackie Palmer said.

"Oh, I wouldn't know about that."

After he left, a man from the coroner's office arrived with a preliminary report.

Strahan, who had not slept in more than a day, felt himself drifting off as the man read from the report. He had seated himself in a chair out of the line of sight of the coroner's man; he leaned his head back against the wall. The radiator hissed softly; the jackhammer growled on the street below.

The man read in a monotone: "A bullet wound of the skin of the forehead located at the level sixty-nine inches above the undersurface of the heel and two and three-quarter inches above the supraorbital ridge and one and three-quarter inches to the right of the midline. The wound was round and gaping, measuring five-sixteenths of an inch in diameter, and was surrounded with an areola of deep brownish red excoriation to the right and slightly below the wound. The penetrating wound passed to the left and slightly toward the back and upward through the skull—"

That morning Strahan had arrived home, intending to catch a few hours of sleep. Kitty Lou, his wife, was already up, curled on the living room couch watching television, some inane game show. They had argued.

The fight had had a special ugliness to it. It had been about Gray Eyes.

He had not wanted to discuss the case. Kitty Lou had persisted, following him into the bedroom. There was concern on her face and he knew it was for Gray Eyes.

For years he had sensed it, denied it, felt it rising in him again—a devastating realization: she had ceased to love him before they had been married. She had been carrying on with someone behind his back. In high school, when they had been going together, he suspected she had been sleeping with Buddy Gray Eyes.

He had never had evidence of it, but he had felt it with as much certainty as anything in his life.

And on this morning she had shown concern and he had refused to tell her anything. She had grown agitated, almost hysterical, and Strahan lashed out at her. He said some ugly things. He had not voiced the thing that truly rankled him; he never did. He attacked her in other areas.

She drank too much. She let herself become sloppy. She did nothing all day but stare at television. She neglected the kids.

They had shouted at each other and Strahan had walked out of the house. And the rage toward Gray Eyes was monstrous within him.

The coroner's man's voice continued on, a soothing purr: "—by a roughly circular hole measuring three-eighths of an inch in diameter and through the dura by a ragged wound and through the right frontal and left parietal lobes of the cerebrum by a ragged tract measuring as much as three-quarters of an inch in diameter to end against the inner surface of the left parietal bone of the skull, over which the dura was lacerated at a point two inches above the level of and one inch behind the superior point of attachment of the left external ear where the bullet was found—"

Had he hated Gray Eyes before he had suspected his involvement with Kitty Lou? Yes. Yes—the hate had gone way back, from the time, the time . . . He had been ten years old, a student at Saint Philomena's. After class he had gone along Beechwood Boulevard toward Colfax. On the corner had been another kid and they had fought and—

Strahan bolted straight upright in his chair. "That's what he'll do," he said aloud.

The coroner's man halted his presentation. Busik looked over. "John?" he said.

"I just realized something," Strahan was suddenly wide awake, brimming with energy. "Buddy Hall kills a man. Who does he turn to? He's been gone from this town a number of years—"

"Yes?" Busik said.

"He had a friend in school. They were like brothers. He'll go to him."

"Who?"

"His name's Moldavan. He's a rabbi."

"This guy Gray Eyes is a Jewboy?" Busik said. "I would have never made him for a Jewboy."

"Oh, yes."

"Go to this rabbi, huh?"

"It's a possibility."

"Yes," Busik said, considering it. He moved to the hot plate at the far end of the room. "A Jewboy? I would have never made him on that one. Anybody want any coffee?" He poured out a cup for himself. "Where do we find this rabbi?" he said without much enthusiasm.

The news of the murder had filled Akiba Moldavan's night with bad dreams. He was in Colfax School, a kid. Someone was chasing him. He rushed to Cervino's store. Cervino was smiling at him, offering him candy.

He overslept and once again missed the early *minyan* at his synagogue.

On the way downtown on the bus he rationalized his dereliction. It's an obligation, *hovah*, technically in the law, to come to the *minyan*. On the other hand, there is no legal prohibition against missing it. He told himself, the Zohar says prayers go up to the throne of God on various levels. On each level the prayer is inspected by a group of angels; they can send the prayer back down, reject it. In a *minyan*, however, when a person *davens*, the prayer goes straight up. The prayer itself does not have greater quality, but since it is made by a group who have gathered for that purpose, it is sent directly to the throne of God.

Akiba Moldavan's hope was that his prayers had genuine quality and would pass muster.

The bus was moving along Fifth Avenue through the black area, the Hill District. Off to his left were the Monongahela River and the mills; to his right, clapboard shanties rising in bleak array up the side of the gray cobblestone hill.

The city was washed with gray, a heavy smog-haze that softened all harsh lines. Buildings, mills, bridges seemed suspended in gray.

Akiba got off the bus just before it reached downtown. His first stop that morning was a breakfast meeting with Leon Frankenthal, one of the backers of the Institute for Jewish Studies. Charlie Waldenblatt had set up the meeting. He reminded himself that he must be diplomatic.

Akiba was nearly a half hour late for the meeting. Waldenblatt and Frankenthal were already having breakfast in the dining room of the Fifth Avenue Plaza, an apartment building–office–shopping center complex on the edge of the downtown area. Frankenthal owned the whole thing.

Charlie Waldenblatt, a large, expansive, florid-faced man with narrow, smiling eyes, was attacking a stack of pancakes; Frankenthal, lean and dyspeptic looking, was studying a dish of prunes and a bowl of bran flakes.

"Sorry I'm late," Akiba said.

"We didn't wait," Frankenthal said. He had a tight mouth and an intermittent twitch that caused his lips and nose to pucker like a rabbit's. His father had been A. J. Frankenthal, steel and banking, the first Jew in Pittsburgh ever to have been admitted to the exclusive Duquesne Club.

Akiba was always uneasy with these people. They had no religion, really. Both men were married to non-Jewish women and Waldenblatt's children attended a private Catholic school. Still, they were the largest supporters of Jewish charities and institutions in the city. Out of guilt, Akiba supposed.

"Rabbi, I'll get right to the point," Frankenthal said tartly. "I'm disturbed, as you know, about certain directions the institute is taking, and since you think of me as a four forty man—"

"Four forty man? What's that, *gematria*?" Waldenblatt said.

The Kabbalah propounded that the name of a thing was

its essence since the world was created through speech: in Genesis as God spoke, the thing was created. *Gematria* was a form of interpreting *Torah* on the basis of numerical equivalents for words and phrases.

"I'll tell you something, Rabbi. In high school I ran the *hundred-yard dash*. I did not run the four forty." Frankenthal settled back and glowered at Akiba.

With *gematria* the use of numerical equivalents—*proprehos le hachma*—could have mundane as well as sacred employment. Akiba had taken to referring to Frankenthal behind his back as a fast guy, a "440 man." In his angry letter to Emmanuel Rose he had characterized Frankenthal as "running the 440 quite well." Combining the numerical values of the Hebrew letters *shin*, *mem*, and *qoph*, one arrived at 440: *shmuck*. Rabbi Rose had obviously made the connection and relayed it to Leon Frankenthal.

Akiba stared down into his coffee, fighting to keep control. Frankenthal cleared his throat, waiting for a reply.

What was he doing here, trying to play this game, a game he was totally unsuited for? He had told himself on the way over: be diplomatic with Frankenthal. Butter him up just the slightest bit and he'd give you anything. The institute would be saved. Just butter him up . . .

He couldn't do it. He was not cut out for this, not cut out for this at all. He looked up at Frankenthal, stared him in the eye. "Hundred-yard dash? To me you'll always be a four forty man."

"What is this, a breakfast meeting or a track meet?" Charlie Waldenblatt said with a forced laugh.

Frankenthal reddened. His nose and lips threatened to pucker out of control. "All right. All right. And another thing—my plant manager out at Mag-Lee Beverages told me you refused to give him a *hekhsher* on our new line of root beers—"

"He wouldn't tell me what was in the beverages. He expected an automatic stamp."

"Now wait just a minute here—"

"Your manager told me you had said that because of the support of the Frankenthal family for my father's institute—"

"Now wait just a minute. You know." Frankenthal was twitching wildly now. "If you think that was a *bribe*, you know, if that's what you're accusing me of, then—then—"

"Akiba isn't accusing you of anything, Leon," Charlie Waldenblatt said. "Tell him, Akiba. You don't mean to say—"

"If I'm going to be bribed, Leon, you'd have to come up with maybe a half million. Then *maybe* I'd *think* about it. But this kind of small-time stuff—you've got the wrong boy, baby."

Charlie Waldenblatt, smiling tensely, tried to defuse the situation. "Nothing is meant by this, Leon. He's just joking."

"I'm not joking. The man *was* trying to bribe me."

Frankenthal's twitch snapped his head in short tics; he grabbed the back of his neck with his hand.

"Something else," Akiba said, warming to the attack. "Last month I applied to the Jewish Center for three hundred dollars for a lawyer to help out one of my convicts at Western Pen. The Jewish Center, which the eminent Rabbi Emmanuel Rose runs, and on whose board of directors you are the most prominent member, turned me down. They informed me that the president and the board felt they did not have a 'channel' for such a request. A channel to piss on people—that's what you have."

"We don't have channels for renegade rabbis who want to throw away money on two-bit thieves, you know? We don't have channels for rude, hostile rabbis, you know?" Frankenthal was twitching so convulsively his head appeared about to fly from his neck. "We don't have money for that sort of thing." Charlie Waldenblatt looked unhappy. He was still smiling, but the smile was frozen on his face.

Akiba got up from the table. "I know," he said quietly.

"Times are hard." He withdrew some money from his pocket, selected a ten-dollar bill, and let it fall to the table in front of Frankenthal. "Lunch and carfare—till times get better for you."

"Akiba," Charlie Waldenblatt said, shaking his head. "Sorry, Charlie. I just can't stomach this fool."

Akiba hurried from the table. He felt stupid, awkward, and worse: impotent. Frankenthal was a man one couldn't insult. He was sure they had all been tried and had slid like oil off his thick, slick skin.

As he pushed his way through the revolving door, he caught his coat. Of course, of course. Make a grand, stupid gesture, attempt a sweeping exit, and catch your damn coat! He yanked hard, heard a tear, and continued out through the door.

On the street he examined the coat, a stained gabardine half a dozen years old. The rip was in the rear at the seam. A portion of ragged lining fluttered in the wind. No problem. Ruth could sew it. The coat would be good as—well, as good as it had always been.

He paid a quick visit to the Jewish slaughterhouse, then dropped in on a downtown hotel. An ex-prisoner whom he had known in Western Penitentiary had been working as a cook in the hotel restaurant. The ex-con had been a fink in prison and was still a fink: he had run into Akiba several days before and told him the hotel restaurant had been mixing the kosher dishes with the nonkosher dishes.

After a short period of negotiation—the hotel catered to a number of Jewish organizations and was eager to keep the business—the kitchen manager agreed to replace the offending dishes. Akiba felt he had been hampered only slightly in impressing his position by the ragged state of his topcoat.

Next he walked over to the county jail, a huge, gloomy, stone fortress just off Fifth Avenue downtown. One of the Jewish prisoners, Klaris, had requested an interview.

Klaris, a gaunt, ratty-looking man in his early forties,

was depressed. "The colored are out to get me," he said, nervously twisting the ends of his hair.

"Why do you say that?"

"They're Muslims. They don't like Jews in here."

"There are only two Jews in the whole jail. You and Cavanaugh."

"Cavanaugh's not a yiddle, Rabbi. How naive can you get? *Cavanaugh.*"

Cavanaugh, an obvious demento, claimed his mother was Jewish, which in rabbinic law indeed would have made him Jewish. Akiba, however, accepted his claim on a more complicated basis: in Hebrew the word *kavvanah* meant "intention": in Kabbalah it was the mystical intention accompanying the formal ritual—the rite was the body, the *kavvanah*, the soul. If Cavanaugh's *kavvanah*—intention—was Jewish, and he was in jail facing a long stretch, Akiba would accept it.

"What can I do? He has an Irish name, but a Jewish nose."

"Look at his pecker," Klaris said. "I seen it. That's not a Jewish pecker."

Klaris was fighting tears. "Get me a good lawyer, Rabbi. Get me out. I can't take hard time anymore. Help me."

"If you stop stealing, Jerry—"

"*I can't* stop stealing."

It was true. Klaris was a pathetic case, a man to whom stealing seemed as essential as breathing. No matter how many times he made it out of prison, he always managed to steal his way back in. "I'll do my best, Jerry."

Klaris held onto Akiba's hand and squeezed it tightly. "Please!"

Please. Please. Liars, cons, thieves. Please. He would do his best. He would beg, cajole, wheedle, to try to get a proper lawyer for Klaris, who would then get out, pull another job, and end up right back in the jackpot. Yes, he would do his best, torn topcoat and all.

Klaris was taken from the room and Yousif Abdul brought in. Abdul, a black dope dealer awaiting sentencing, had claimed a vision: Moses had come to him in his cell and told him to renounce his Muhammadan faith and embrace Judaism. Akiba suspected a scam of some sort but agreed to talk to him.

Abdul, totally bald and incredibly muscular, looked at Akiba with dark, impassive eyes. "Call me Jacob," he told the rabbi after being addressed as Yousif. "That Arab stuff is nothing but a lame shuck as far as I'm concerned. Moses told me my name is Jacob."

"Okay, Jake. What do you want to know?"

"Point one: 'cause I'm a Jew, do they have to cut a piece off my privates?"

"Jake, let me say *technically* you're not yet a Jew—"

"Moses give me the office. How much more technical can you get than that? Point two: a guy told me any Jew can get out of this place and go to Israel—"

"Who told you that?"

"Cavanaugh."

"I see."

"Point three: if you're a rabbi, how come you don't look like no drawf?"

"Drawf?"

"You know. The little old man with a long beard in the third-grade reader."

"Dwarf."

"Drawf. Right. With a beard. How come you don't have no beard?"

"It's like this. There's a mystical element as far as the *tozurrik*, the visage, is concerned. In the Kabbalah you have these channels where the energy comes through the hairs on the face. However, technically, there's nothing in the everyday laws about it."

"Ra-ight," Yousif Abdul said slowly. "I can understand that. I didn't mean no criticism by it, you understand?"

"Now as far as the other thing goes—your becoming a Jew. I want you to think it over. Being a Jew is not all roses. Being a black Jew is even tougher."

"It weren't so tough for Sammy Davis."

"I get your point there, Jake."

"Moses told me I was a Jew, baby. That comes straight from the mountain, like the Ten Commandments, and the rest of you kikes got no right to fuck me around."

"Right, Jake."

"'Cause the next time I'm coming back with a hand-carved *original* of the Ten Commandments."

"That should help your case considerably, Jake."

"All right."

As Akiba was moving down the hall toward the front gate, a guard waved him over to the reception desk. "There was a call for you, Rabbi. Your wife. She said to call a detective Strahan at the Public Safety Building. Also she said a woman had called about an old friend of yours, a man named Buddy Hall."

# 6

Akiba Moldavan moved through the dingy marble lobby of the Public Safety Building. He did not wait for the elevator. He took the stairs two at a time. He had a strong, inexplicable sense of foreboding.

It had to do with Strahan and the call from the girl. Akiba had spoken with Ruthie: she said the girl had sounded agitated. She wanted to talk about Buddy Hall. She would call back in the evening.

Buddy Hall and Strahan! Strange, strange how these things moved, he was thinking. An old man is killed, a figure from his childhood. And now two people with whom he had had much to do in days going back to grade school, days of hanging out in front of the murdered man's candy store, suddenly reenter his life.

Buddy Hall, who in some ways had been a brother to Akiba, he had not seen in years. Strahan he ran into from time to time. He did not like, or trust, John Strahan.

A detective ushered Akiba into an office, Lieutenant Busik's. There were three men there. One was Strahan, who greeted Akiba coolly, almost formally. "It's been awhile," Akiba said to Strahan.

"When was the last time?"

Akiba remembered. There had been a problem with kids painting swastikas on the sidewalk in front of his father's house. Strahan had been a uniformed cop then. "That trouble out at our house—"

"The house on Hobart?"

"Yes." Akiba had never felt comfortable with John Strahan. He sensed hostility, envy from him. And he knew that Strahan did not like Jews.

"Why don't you have a seat, Rabbi," Jack Palmer said.

Akiba took a chair by the window.

"We also played some chess at the YMCA," Strahan said.

"Yes, yes." Akiba played in a league at the YMCA, where some of the better players in the city gathered. "John is very good at the game," Akiba said.

"Is that a fact?" Busik said with forced interest.

"We want to ask you about Gray Eyes," Strahan said. "Buddy Hall."

"When was the last time you saw him?" Busik said.

"Oh, long ago. Long, long time ago. Is there some problem?"

"Yes, yes," Busik said. "There's some evidence he murdered a man."

"Murdered?" Akiba wasn't sure he had heard right.

"The old man. Cervino," Strahan said.

Akiba leaned forward, suddenly faint. "Murdered Cervino?"

The men in the room did not speak.

Akiba could feel the floor sinking beneath him. A wave of nausea spread over him. I'm going to black out, he realized, and he fought it. He gripped the arms of the chair tightly. Please, not in front of these people. Too embarrassing. Hold on.

Jack Palmer moved to the water cooler and brought him a cup of water.

At last the feeling subsided. "Why? Why Cervino?" Akiba said.

"We don't know," Busik said.

The air in the room was thick, stifling. Buddy Hall a

killer! How was it possible? There was a mistake. There must be. Cervino? Buddy Hall? "We used to steal from him," Akiba said at last, so softly he could have been talking to himself.

"Steal?"

"When we were kids, Buddy and I would steal from Cervino's store. Dumb stuff."

A rush of memory came to Akiba Moldavan now, terrible days in Colfax School before Buddy Hall had been his friend, days of torment and ostracism. Akiba would go to school wearing his yarmulke and carrying banana sandwiches in a brown paper bag. The kids would taunt him and beat him up—the Jewish kids as well as the gentiles. He was the only kid in the school who wore a yarmulke.

In certain respects the Jewish kids were the worst: he represented something to them that they and their parents were ashamed of—the Orthodox, European ghetto Jew. They were modern, American. They went to synagogue twice a year, on Rosh Hashanah and Yom Kippur. Their religiosity was timed to the social season, a chance to parade their fall outfits at the Conservative and Reformed temples of the city. Judaism was Bar Mitzvas and weddings, the Hadassah and B'nai B'rith. What did they know of Talmud and Kabbalah, of Law and Mysticism, of the *Hester Punim*, God's Hidden Face, the Sephirot—the Ten Spheres through which God manifests himself in the world? They knew *kosher* and *kichel* and perhaps a hundred Yiddish words that they carried into English, a comedian's storehouse of bad jokes. *Shmuck* they knew best of all.

Buddy Hall, who looked more like a *goy* than the most *goyish goy* in the school, who didn't even have a Jewish-sounding name, was a Jew and had become Akiba's protector. Why, Akiba never quite understood. He was the most ignorant of Jews in Jewish matters and yet he had a passion for justice and he took Akiba under his protection. He became Akiba's idol, his hero. He was an athlete, he was tough, all the kids looked up to him; and he had chosen Akiba, the freak, for a friend.

There had been an incident with Strahan. Akiba couldn't remember the details. Grade school. There had been a fight; Buddy had come to his rescue.

Afterward—had it been that day or another?—they had sat on the grass in Frick Park and pitched buckeyes down the hill. Akiba remembered telling Buddy stories of Kabbalah and the Thirty-two Paths of Wisdom, of the Sephirot, and the golem—a being fashioned from clay, a Frankenstein monster who could perform either good or evil. He had told these stories to impress his new friend, to demonstrate the wondrous knowledge he possessed.

Later, in high school, after Akiba had broken away from religion, he and Buddy Hall would drive out to Homestead, out to the black whorehouses on Seventh Avenue opposite the mills. The whores would be gathered around potbellied wood stoves in the front parlor, voodoo ghosts in red panties and bras, their dark, smoky skin sunk deep in shadow, flickers of orange flame reflecting from the stove, shimmers of red silk coiling in the dark. Voodoo ghosts.

Buddy would go off with the whores while Akiba would sit there, tense and fearful. The whores would kid him. "What's the matter with you? You not a fairy, are you?" Eventually he went with one of them. The experience had been painful, ugly.

For weeks after, Akiba had had nightmares about the girl, her bored, dead eyes, the stench of her—perfume and perspiration.

It was then that he had spoken to Buddy of *yetzer ha-ra*, The Evil Inclination, The Destroyer. He told him that, according to the *Talmud*, The Destroyer seduces in this world and accuses in the next.

And now this man, his friend of days gone by, was himself *yetzer ha-ra*, a murderer.

Lieutenant Busik had taken a pipe out of his desk and

was attempting to light it. "Even though you haven't seen this man in years"—the pipe would not light; he tamped it down with his thumb and jammed his lighter deeper into the bowl—"it's just possible he might contact you." At last a puff of grayish smoke rose from the pipe; Busik looked infinitely satisfied. "We just thought, Rabbi, you should be cognizant of the situation, if you get my meaning." He looked over at Strahan. "Anything else?"

Strahan moved to Palmer and Busik and they conferred in quiet tones at the far end of the room. Palmer looked bored, jiggled several coins in his hand, and stared out the window; Busik puffed contentedly on his pipe.

After a moment Palmer and Busik excused themselves and Akiba was alone in the room with Strahan.

"When was the last time you saw Buddy?" Strahan asked.

"I haven't seen him since high school."

"He didn't turn out well. He became a hustler like his father," Strahan said. He stood above Akiba, his eyes serious behind his spectacles. "I've been trying to recall—in high school Buddy took out Kitty Lou, didn't he?"

"Your wife? Not that I know of."

"Before we were married?"

Yes, Akiba remembered now. There had been a time when Buddy Hall had been seeing Kitty Lou Ozimek, the woman who later became Strahan's wife.

Buddy Hall's leg had been severely injured. Strahan had done it. While Strahan was at football practice, Buddy would take Kitty Lou Ozimek to Frick Park. He told Akiba he was doing it out of revenge for what Strahan had done to his leg.

"Yes, I remember something—"

"What?" Strahan's face was very close to Akiba's now. There was a frightening desperation in his eyes.

"I remember Buddy hurt his knee playing football—"

"Yes. At that time. He began to see Kitty behind my back. What went on?"

"That was years ago—"

"Yes, yes," Strahan said. "But something went on. I'm sure of it."

"I think he saw her once or twice—"

Strahan moved away from him. "Yes. He saw her behind my back. I seem to recall that. I've been wondering what went on. I've been thinking about that. Yes."

"I don't know."

"Yes. Something." Strahan was at the window now. He stood staring out at the street below. He did not talk for a long time. "You can go now," he said at last, as though talking to a stranger.

# 7

JOHN STRAHAN was as tired as he had ever been. Still, he could not get himself to go home. After Akiba left, he met again with Busik and Jack Palmer. "Well?" Busik said.

"If he stays in town, he's going to come back to Shadman or contact the rabbi," Strahan said.

"The rabbi? What's he going to do, pray?" Jack Palmer said. "My bet is Shadman. He'll look to get high."

Bob Harris, the man from the D.A.'s office, arrived with a search warrant for Gray Eyes's room. "Get some sleep," Jack Palmer said to Strahan. "I'll go out there with the search team."

"I can't sleep," Strahan said.

At the clapboard house on the hill across from the amusement park, the landlady explained that his girl friend had been back to the room, then left again, probably to work.

While the search team went over the room for fingerprints, Strahan phoned the restaurant, the Silver Princess. The girl was not due in until late in the evening.

"Look at this," one of the search team said. In a drawer he had found a cigar box filled with photographs. Strahan took the box and emptied it on the bed.

It was a collection of high school graduation pictures,

two-by-three inch prints that the kids used to autograph and exchange.

Strahan went through the pictures. They were from his graduating class. Akiba Moldavan's picture was there; he wore a small cap on his head and looked gaunt and serious. He had written: "From that day at Cervino's to this day, to all the days of the future, I will never forget you. Akiba."

Cervino's? Cervino's? What day at Cervino's? What did it mean?

He put the picture in his pocket and went through the rest of the pile. A gallery of forgotten faces passed through his hands, callow, pimply-faced kids trying to look grown-up in front of the camera.

How strange that Gray Eyes had kept them all these years. He read the autographs. They spoke of Gray Eyes's success with women, his great charm, his athletic prowess. They all predicted great things for him in the future.

Could they have imagined murder?

He searched for his own photograph in the stack. It was not there.

He found his wife's. A pang stirred in his heart: she looked unbearably beautiful, soft, young.

He turned the picture over and read: "Gray Eyes, sexiest eyes in the world. Remember me forever. Kitty Lou Ozimek."

Strahan tore the picture into small pieces.

"What's that you have over there?" Jack Palmer said.

John Strahan shrugged. "Nothing."

At the pathetically small, woefully neglected Adath Jeshuron Synagogue on Webster Avenue in the Hill District, they had trouble getting a *minyan*, the ten men necessary for the evening service, the *maarib*. Akiba had finally to walk over to Logan Street and escort one of the shut-ins, blind Heschel Glick, to the synagogue.

The area was inhabited almost entirely by blacks. To be

old, infirm, white, and Jewish was not a good thing in the Hill District. To be blind was even worse.

It was a problem for the old people to come to the synagogue as night approached. They came and they were robbed on the way. Every member of the synagogue had been robbed at some time. Several had been killed over the years.

Not that it was a blessing to be black in the area. They, too, were robbed and killed. They lived with failed plumbing, inadequate heat, rats, in rotting frame houses whose soot-covered exteriors dated back to the terrible Smoky City Pittsburgh days.

The rats had increased in recent years. Great portions of the blighted area had been leveled to make room for urban renewal. On the edge of downtown, imposing apartment and office buildings had gone up; housing projects had been built. From the steps of the Adath Jeshuron Synagogue the great retractable dome of the new Civic Auditorium could be seen. The rat population shifted, consolidated, crowded more and more into the shrinking older section.

A no-man's-land of rubble-strewn lots where construction had not yet begun separated the rebuilt area from that portion of the Hill District that had not yet been touched. The old area—cursed, bleak, decaying—stretched, shunned and forsaken, beyond the sleek and shining high-rises.

Akiba Moldavan had not shunned or forsaken the district. The twenty or so old Jews who still lived there, trapped by poverty, age, and habit, had been his father's congregation and were now his. Services attended by hundreds were once held in the main hall; it had been jammed to capacity. Now the faithful met in the *Bes Midrash*, the study room in the basement.

This night, after the *maarib*, Akiba had walked the old people to their homes. The blacks for the most part lived in ramshackle wooden buildings, two- and three-story shanties. The old Jews were a cut above that. They all lived in red brick tenements.

He returned to the synagogue and sat in the main hall. It was dark, musty, and cold. He sat there shivering in the damp and cold and realized it was not only from the cold that he trembled. He trembled from an awareness of evil.

A simple, defenseless old man had been killed, slaughtered by someone who at one time had been the most important person in the world to Akiba. It was a nightmare, incomprehensible. It was *tohu*, emptiness, a void. Why old man Cervino? Why?

His friend was an animal, devoid of moral sense, a murderer. This knowledge shook him to the very foundation of his being.

He sat thinking in the unheated synagogue and he moved his lips and no sound came out as he formed words, trying to sort out his thoughts. God's ways are not man's ways. The Master of the Universe is unknowable. Though I may not apprehend Him, He apprehends me, reaching me in a terrible, ferocious way. He thought of his father's illness, the insanity of his sister, his brother's estrangement. And now this!

What did God want of him? He was being tested, of that he was certain. Yet to what purpose? It was of monumental importance that he discover why this was happening in his life, this confrontation with evil. A pattern had appeared—Cervino, Strahan, Buddy—embers of his youth exploding into flame now with sudden, stunning fury.

The *tohu* was presenting itself to him with rage, with murder. To what purpose? And why?

Or was it without meaning, aleatory, haphazard, splinters of quantum light, riving an uncaring universe? Was *Hester Punim*, the Hidden Face of God, no more than a mask to delude mankind? Were His ways so imponderable as to be a nothingness, one's whole existence forfeit to a mask concealing—what? Shadows . . .

Was what had occurred a celebration of that nothingness? The word *holocaust* at its core meant "burnt whole," a burnt offering: was Buddy Gray Eyes's action a holocaust, a ritualistic affirmation of emptiness?

Was the flame of gunfire a torch that said: there is no God, there is no providence, there is no *Olam ha-Ba*, World to Come?

The murder of one—was it the murder of many? The burnt offering of a man, the holocaust of a people? Flames of emptiness? *Tohu? Tohu?*

He thought of his father's father, how he had died. The Chief Rabbi of Przemsyl in Galicia, he had remained in Europe, had been trapped there when the Nazis moved in.

While his horrified congregation looked on, soldiers had slashed the *Torah* into a thousand pieces, set fire to his synagogue. A tributary of the San River ran behind the synagogue and the soldiers threw the charred and torn *Torah* into its waters. When the old rabbi saw the desecrated Scroll of the Law he waded out into the creek and, weeping, clasped the strips of parchment to his heart.

He wore his *tallith*, the prayer shawl, and *tefillin*, the phylacteries containing portions of the law, when the SS took him down to the edge of the same creek and shot him through the head.

His bloated body became trapped in debris at the creek's edge and it bobbed and floated for three days, the *tallith* streaming over it, whipping around it, shrouding it, at last submerging it.

The faithful of his congregation, held prisoner, witnessed this. They could do nothing. Later they were shipped to Belzec near Lublin. Most of them died in the Zyklon B gas chambers.

Was this God's plan, even as the murder of the old was God's plan?

Or was it the flames of *tohu*, the burnt offering to emptiness?

It is impossible to calculate providence, he told himself. Sometimes a person suffers for himself, sometimes for his generation. Luzzatto had said, even with the sword of your oppressor lying poised at your neck you must believe in God. Luzzatto had said—Luzzatto had said—his words were black wings beating inside his skull. Luzzatto. Maimonides. They said—they said—

The pressure of their belief rose and strained with such power that he felt it would split his head. Millions slaughtered, innocent children, pious old folk, the most *frum*, devout, of people killed with unspeakable brutality—and still you must believe. Luzzatto, Maimonides. They demanded so much! The Hidden Face of God demanded so much!

Akiba told himself this now: there's nothing outside of God's Oneness. When a person is being tortured, when his children are being murdered in front of his eyes, he is contributing to the eventual revelation of God's Oneness. Evil is not God's conqueror, but part of His Oneness. The good will be revealed one day and shine forth and evil will be displayed as its adumbration only, a dark aspect of God's Goodness, the shadow that sets forth the light.

And he thought of a parable his father used to tell: a *zaddik*—a holy man—and a sinner lived in the same house, the holy man in the attic, the sinner on the level below. A wood ladder separated them. The holy man, after a lifetime of deprivation, prayer, and righteousness, grew weary and began to envy the sinner. "To suffer. What's the *mitzvah* to suffer?" he asked of himself. And the sinner, whose wasted life had brought him only emptiness and unhappiness, envied the holy man. "I have done everything and I feel nothing. What is the reward, then, in sin?" Each decided to transform himself, to visit the other and learn his ways. Both stepped at the same moment on the ladder linking the two levels. Their combined weight was too much. The ladder snapped. Both plunged to their death in the basement below. And what became of their souls? The soul of the holy man, moving downward, was consigned to hell. The sinner, on his way up, went to heaven.

One may not reach God, but one must strive toward Him. At some time before the end one must strive toward God.

Even Buddy Gray Eyes, Akiba told himself. Even he must strive toward God.

The door opening behind Akiba startled him. He turned. A man in nylon windbreaker was standing just inside the entranceway—John Strahan.

Hands in his jacket pockets, he stood in shadow, silhouetted against the open doorway. "Your wife told me you'd be here. I was in the neighborhood."

He moved partway down the aisle and gazed around at the interior of the synagogue. Akiba felt embarrassment at the shabbiness of the place. He sensed Strahan's disapproval.

"We don't use this hall much," Akiba said. "We meet downstairs."

"I didn't even know there were Jewish people still living up on the Hill."

"Not many."

Strahan nodded. "Everyone's trying to get off the Hill," he said. "Even the blacks." He was staring at the Ark now. Above the Ark, which contained the *Torah*, was a slab on which the Ten Commandments were carved in Hebrew. "I only live a few minutes from here, over on Brereton. That whole area over there, it's white, but the blacks are moving down."

He sat across the aisle from Akiba; he shivered. "Cold," he said. "The churches are the same way. I guess heating is pretty expensive."

"Pretty steep."

"First time I've been in one of these places. What do you call it in your language?"

"Shul."

"Like a church, I guess. I'm not much of a churchgoer.

Kitty is the churchgoer. She has the spirit." He remained quiet for a while. "She was an attractive woman, Kitty."

"Yes, she was."

"She's still lovely—" Strahan's fingers formed a tent at his mouth. "I have few complaints. She's a fine wife and mother." He sat there for a long time staring straight ahead.

Akiba grew uneasy. Even when they were younger, in school together, Strahan's presence was unsettling to Akiba. He always seemed a person who felt nothing, a person, who, because of that, could not be trusted. Even as a child he seemed to have loyalties to no one or nothing.

"Who can understand it? Gray Eyes a murderer?" Strahan said. Behind his wire-rimmed spectacles his eyes were chilling in their marble opacity. "If he contacts you, or someone contacts you for him, you'd tell me, wouldn't you? As an old friend?"

Akiba did not answer. The discomfort he felt was physical: his skin was cold; the cold seemed to penetrate to the core of his being. He thought of the *Talmud*, the *Pirke Avot: Beware of the ruling powers! For they do not befriend a person except for their own needs.*

John Strahan removed his spectacles and began to clean them with a tissue from his jacket pocket. "He's living with a girl out near Kennywood. They have his room staked out. He won't go back there. The girl might contact you—"

John Strahan smiled. It was not an attractive smile. He was not a man used to smiling. "As kids we did some crazy things, didn't we? Fights, one neighborhood against another, Squirrel Hill against Greenfield."

What is Strahan doing here? Akiba asked himself. It's not just about Buddy. . . .

Strahan continued to smile.

*Do not think the lion is smiling when he bares his teeth; it is only to devour. When you have dealings with the ruling powers, beware their smiling faces and honeyed* words. *Let them not seduce you into revealing to them the secret in your heart.* . . .

"You know, I can't stop thinking, I don't know why I can't get it out of my mind—Cervino's when we were kids. You and Buddy—what went on at Cervino's?"

"What do you mean?"

"Was there something special, some special occurrence?"

"I first met Buddy at Cervino's."

"Ah, yes. I see."

"That's when I first met you. At that same time."

"Really? The three of us? We first met there?"

"I believe so."

"Yes, I do remember something about it. What was I doing there?"

"Oh, it's so long ago. Kid stuff." They had been ten years old. John Strahan had come along and for no reason that Akiba could understand had begun to beat him. A boy came running out of Cervino's. He had pulled Strahan off Akiba, then fought him. He had given Strahan a bloody nose. It was Buddy Hall, Gray Eyes.

"Ever since the murder I've been thinking back on those days," Strahan said. "That poor man, poor kind old man. You see, Akiba, that's why I'd like to reach him before the police. I want to protect him. The police don't like it when a defenseless old man is murdered like that." Strahan spoke with quiet sincerity, and yet Akiba did not believe him.

Strahan's eyes shifted behind his spectacles, as though Akiba had read the thoughts there. "Nothing really went on," Strahan said quietly.

"What?"

"Between Kitty Lou and Gray Eyes. In high school. They just saw each other a couple of times."

"Oh, yes. I'm sure nothing went on."

The eyes shifted, roamed, were tortured. "I have to find him," he said. "I have to find him."

"What will you do when you find him?"

"Save him," Strahan said, and his voice was hoarse, unnatural. "Help me," he said. "We were good friends, Buddy and I. I want to save him. I swear to you. Believe me." Akiba did not answer. "Please, believe me."

Still, Akiba said nothing.

A fear started in Akiba, a recognition: *he wants to kill.*

Strahan wrote out his home phone number on a slip of paper and gave it to Akiba. "Kitty Lou will be happy to hear from you. Maybe you can come to dinner. We could play some chess." He walked to the door. "Strange, isn't it, how you and I have gone along a certain path, conventional path? Got married, became upstanding citizens. And Buddy Gray Eyes—who can understand it?"

"It's a terrible, mysterious thing."

"Yes." Strahan's eyes remained opaque behind the spectacles, marble cold. Akiba did not trust him at all. "If anything comes up, call me at home. Don't call at Public Safety. Okay?" He stood for a moment at the door, thinking. "That day when we were kids—Buddy stole something from Cervino's."

"He was always stealing from Cervino's. Sometimes I was his accomplice."

Strahan smiled again. "I should put you under arrest," he said. The smile was tight, forced, chilling.

After he left, Akiba sat in the cold synagogue and tried to figure out what to do.

No, he did not trust Strahan at all. He had seen hate, murder in his eyes.

Kabbalah is here, Akiba said, a working out of old destinies, a complex and tangled knot of the past.

Strahan had always functioned in his life as some malignant force of viciousness and duplicity. There had been the incident when they first met, the fight in front of Cervino's candy store. Some years later, when they were both sixteen, another incident took place.

Akiba had played baseball with a Squirrel Hill team, the Tartars. They had been challenged by a team from

Greenfield to play on their field. After the game the Greenfield kids provoked a fight. Older men from the neighborhood joined in, beating the Squirrel Hill kids, calling them dirty Jews, kike bastards, Christ killers.

Akiba had gone to Strahan, who was captain of the team, and tried to get him to stop the beatings. Strahan smiled. He spoke quietly, apologetically: he was sorry, but this was the way things were.

And then he began to punch Akiba; he kicked him. He stood above him kicking at him, still smiling, his voice soft, filled with regret. Akiba Moldavan had been hospitalized with a concussion and three broken ribs.

Gray Eyes, who had not been there for the game, learned what had happened and went searching for Strahan. He caught up with him behind the high school and they fought out at the large concrete smokestack there.

Gray Eyes had beaten him badly, pushed Strahan's face into the ground, twisted it hard into the dirt until his blood mixed with the dirt and his face was nothing but blood and dirt.

Strahan did not smile very much after that. He had become very quiet. He waited. At the beginning of football season, during practice, he wrecked Gray Eyes's knee, blind-sided him as Buddy was standing relaxed at the end of a play.

Buddy Hall had had a chance to become all-state. The injury ended his football-playing days.

And so, behind Strahan's back, Gray Eyes had taken up with his girl friend, Kitty Lou Ozimek.

That had been the tangle of their relationship, extending even to this day.

There is a knot here, Akiba was thinking, and bound up in it are Strahan, Buddy Hall, and myself. It had begun many years ago in a fight in front of the store of a very decent man. The man was dead now. One man was a murderer, another his pursuer. It all carried forward to this day.

And now he realized his life would be forever without meaning unless he untied this knot, laid bare each tangled skein, understood the pattern they formed.

He dug the knuckles of his hands into his temples. There is something here, there is something of Kabbalah, there is a revelation at the heart of this. He thought of the Thirty-two Paths of Wisdom, of the Sephirot, of white Kabbalah and black.

My friend is no longer Buddy Hall, he is Gray Eyes and he is outside the realm of the human: he has shed innocent blood. God's providence pertains to him no more. He must await *din*, God's swift judgment.

In his *Massilat Yesharim*, "The Path of the Just," Luzzatto had written: "On the basis of justice alone it would be dictated that the sinner be punished immediately upon sinning, the punishment be a wrathful one; and that there can be no correction for the sin. How can a man straighten out what has been made crooked? If a man killed his neighbor, how can he correct this?" But then he had asked: "What function does the attribute of mercy perform?" And answered: "The attribute of mercy is the mainstay of the world."

The attribute of mercy is the mainstay of the world. . . . The Tree of *Sephirot*, the Thirty-two Paths of Wisdom, glowed before his eyes now, a palpable presence, numinous, magical, a knot of divine power, tying him to the destinies of Strahan and Buddy Gray Eyes.

An idea came to Akiba, possessed him with a rush, an outcry rising from his soul, an outcry, desperate, beautiful, promising to break the bonds of mundanity strangling him. He would insinuate himself into this action, would attempt to reach out and pull Buddy Gray Eyes from a swamp of sure destruction; he would search for him, save him. He would operate not only on a level of divine justice, but with an idea of divine mercy.

Nothing is due this man, he thought. He doesn't deserve to live. But even as we do not deserve to be created, we are created. Akiba, therefore, would involve himself in an act of true creation. He would bring something out of nothing, would lift a man who had descended to the level of an animal back into the realm of the human.

He thought: I will act like Maimonides' good governor, without passion, act only for what should be done. I will perform a deed of mercy, of loving kindness, not because of my passions, but in order to come near God. The Talmud holds: *He who sustains one life is regarded as if he created the world.* . . .

Coldly now, objectively, he examined what needed to be done. There's a nothingness, *tohu*, where this man, this once friend, once known as Buddy Hall, had been; there's no reason why this animal should exist, why I should associate myself with him. Nevertheless, I will enter into this action and see if I can fulfill God's plan with an act of loving kindness, of mercy, to see whether, indeed, there might be some reason for his existence. I'll give him the time necessary for repentance, for return, for *teshubah*. "The gates of *tefillah*, prayer, may be shut, but the gates of *teshubah*, repentence, are ever open."

First nothingness was created. Nothingness was Buddy Gray Eyes. And then the world. When you get into the world, you cannot see God because of the enormous ocean of nothingness. Buddy Gray Eyes. You must get out of the world, get through the nothingness and come near God . . .

He would go through *tohu* to approach God.

And there was Strahan. What of him? He, too, was there at the edge of *tohu*.

Strahan would try to kill Gray Eyes! Why was Akiba so certain of it? It was the pain in his look, the restless shift behind his glasses, the passion in his voice: *I have to find him.*

Akiba roamed the darkened synagogue now, moved down the aisle to the *bimah*, the platform from which the Scroll of the Law is read, pounded its base with his hand, moved back up the aisle, talking aloud to himself. His thoughts were on fire, with Kabbalah, with the mystical tree, the Sephirot. Its burning tendrils coiled and uncoiled in his skull. He felt as though he were hurtling along a twisting, dizzying roller coaster track: Kennywood Park, diving through vertiginous colored lights . . .

Strahan will try to kill him, and—and—

Akiba will go through *tohu*, he will save Gray Eyes and—

He will stop Strahan.

In ancient Jewish law a person pursuing another with the intention of taking his life is *rodeph*. You are obligated to prevent this killing, even it means taking the life of the pursuer.

Akiba felt as though he could not breathe. He stood trembling in the center of the synagogue.

He must not only find and save Gray Eyes, he must prevent Strahan from killing him.

He knew now why he was here, what he must do with his life.

Softly, from the rear of the synagogue, he heard a voice, a soft crooning: "It's only a shanty in old shanty town . . ."

He turned. Izzie, the moron, stood smiling and singing in the open doorway.

# 8

*The chosen people.*

John Strahan couldn't sleep. Returning home, he had collapsed on the bed without discussing the case with his wife. He hadn't slept in two days. He was desperately tired, sick, disgusted. And he couldn't sleep.

*The chosen people.* The phrase kept ringing in his head, a mocking litany. Children's voices singing in his head. *The chosen people, the chosen people* . . .

He saw himself standing on the ballfield of Saint Philomena's, just above the entrance to the old mine shaft. He was with a group of boys from Greenfield. They had a Squirrel Hill kid surrounded and they were chanting, *the chosen people, the chosen people,* laughing and chanting, while they pelted the other boy with small chunks of coal. The kid wore glasses. The glasses had been broken. His face, a mole's face, was streaked with coal dust and blood.

Why did that scene come back to him now?

The muffled sound of the television blasting from another part of the house thudded into the room. Kitty Lou, his wife, was watching a cop show, the sound turned way up.

He rolled over and buried his head in the pillow.

The pain had started in his stomach again. His wife's selfishness and vulgarity was a dagger cutting into his stomach. It would have been ludicrous were it not so angering and demeaning: the wife of a detective compulsively watching television police shows, volume full up. She was mocking him, throwing it up to him: the television cops were the real heroes; he was a fraud.

And yet to call her on it was futile. She would love to do battle over it. She knew how to drive the dagger in and twist it.

Since the first year of their marriage it hadn't been right with them. Contempt had bred contempt, smothering whatever affection might ever have existed. Why, then, had they continued on with it?

For some people a quiet misery is preferable to admitting a mistake. Strahan had always been dimly aware of this. He and his wife had settled for the barely tolerable against going it alone. Without ever discussing it they had made the choice to build a life out of the meanest ingredients. It was a dry life, a life of narrow purpose with few satisfactions; yet, nevertheless, a life.

Strahan buried himself in work and the gym. Kitty Lou watched television, visited the beauty parlor, played canasta with her girl friends. He had his wife. She had her husband. They had their children. They had their life.

She hated his job and expressed only contempt for it. She ridiculed him. She went her own way.

He suspected her of cheating on him, but had never been able to catch her at it. Long ago he stopped trying.

Buddy Gray Eyes had been the earliest deception, had had her when they were still in high school. Strahan always suspected it, but said nothing. That had been the first knife blade twisting in his gut.

Over the years there had been others, slashes of fire in his stomach.

He thought about his police work. Even there he had not been his own man: he had gone into it to please Kitty Lou. She had always admired a certain toughness in men, and Strahan, with his quiet intelligence, had not been sure he had it. He had boxed and played football, but he had also liked chess and mathematics and, at one time had thought of becoming an engineer. It was through his father-in-law, Thaddeus "Polish Ted" Ozimek, a retired cop and Greenfield ward chairman, that he had been brought into the force.

Because of Polish Ted's influence Strahan had made detective at a relatively young age. He'd had a promising future on the force, until his father-in-law, an ebullient, charming, brutal man, suffered a massive coronary at a Polish Falcon Society fund raiser: they said he was dead before he hit the floor. Thousands attended the funeral and Strahan couldn't help but feel that the brightest part of his police career was being lowered into the grave with Polish Ted.

Still, Strahan slogged on, did his job, suffered slights— Superintendent Rikert's not knowing his name, Busik's humiliating him before the other detectives—and looked to get ahead as best he could. He was ambitious. He coveted promotion. He had grown to love police work— not the razzle-dazzle television stuff—but the day-to-day grind and grit of it. He loved pushing on ahead, nibbling on a case, moving on relentlessly, grinding the cockroaches down. He had a highly developed, if personal, sense of right and wrong, and he pursued it with ruthless single-mindedness. There might be things off the mark in his life. In his work he was always on the side of the just.

*The Chosen People.* He tossed on the bed from side to side, his nerves electric, singing. He thought about Akiba Moldavan and Buddy Gray Eyes. What, after so many years, had suddenly drawn them into his life? Childhood was past, best forgotten: it had been a bitter, barren time. Strangely, only the old man, Cervino, glowed in his memory, a singular element of purity.

Now he had been destroyed and only the past's ugly waste remained, threatening to overwhelm him.

*The chosen people.* As he lay on the sweat-dampened bed, churning into blanket and pillow, the loathing inside him was immense, terrible. *The chosen people . . .*

Bam, bam, bam! The scream of sirens, the screech of tires. Muffled sound pounding from the living room television. He got up. His pajamas were soaked with perspiration. He had a chill.

It was eating at him that Buddy Gray Eyes had slept with his wife. Were he to bring it up, though, he knew she would deny it. Over the years he had delicately probed the edges of its possibility.

It was like probing steel. She yielded nothing.

The more he brooded about it the more certain he became. Of course, Gray Eyes had slept with her.

*The chosen people . . .*

He dressed and entered the living room. Kitty Lou sat in a housecoat in front of the set. She was smoking a cigarette, lipping it in an affected tough-broad style that Strahan found particularly offensive. On the cocktail table in front of her was a half-empty highball glass.

Her attention was on the television screen, where a young cop flashed a forced, grotesque, cap-toothed smile. Strahan had an urge to kick in the picture tube, to shatter not only the falseness and complacency of the actor, but that of his own wife, her whole world.

In the kitchen he put on water for a cup of instant coffee. He wiped his eyeglasses with a paper napkin while waiting for the water to boil.

When he was very young, he had been taunted by kids with the name Four Eyes. His eyes had always been bad. They were getting worse. Perhaps the eyes were one of the reasons he so hated Buddy Hall.

It was in high school that the girls started calling Buddy Hall Gray Eyes. Everybody picked it up. His eyes were *stunning,* the girls would say, and John Strahan would study them and suffer a terrible ache of envy at their loveliness.

John Strahan always believed that had his eyes been better, he would have been something above mediocre in athletics. As a boxer he was all right, but he never had a take-out punch: he just couldn't make that solid connection. Bad eyes. In football, too, he would just miss an essential shade of accuracy. Bad, bad eyes.

Buddy Hall as an athlete never missed. Strahan had come to believe it was all in the eyes.

He returned to the living room with his coffee. The credits on the show were rolling. Kitty Lou barely glanced at him. "Thanks," she said.

"You want some?"

"What do you think?" She sloshed the ice around in her glass.

"I didn't know you wanted it."

"Okay," she said. "O-fucking-kay."

"Did the kids eat?"

"Yes, the kids ate."

"Frozen pizza with Cokes?"

She did not answer.

"Can you turn that thing off? Please," he said.

She made no move to accommodate him and he kicked the side of the set hard. She shrugged and clicked off the television with the remote control.

"I came in this morning and the set was on. I wanted to sleep and you started with me," Strahan said, fighting to keep his emotions in rein. "I need to sleep. That's too much to ask, isn't it?" He tried to control himself; it was always like this, their time together, prelude to quarrel, quarrel, or sullen aftermath. "I just want to know one thing: do I deserve to sleep? Huh? Do I *deserve* to sleep? That's all I want to know."

She didn't answer. He sat on the couch. The cover of the couch was rose-patterned and he began to count the flowers to calm himself.

Kitty Lou lipped her cigarette, toyed with the ice in her glass. He looked at her without talking for a long time, thinking that, yes, he supposed she was an exceptionally attractive woman: tall, athletic body; fine, blond hair; delicate features. She never failed to turn heads when she entered the room. She was stunningly beautiful and perhaps that was part of their problem: her appearance had created in her a self-absorption than canceled it all out for Strahan. He could only concentrate on her flaws. Why, when she had been so breathtaking in her teens, did she now seem so unappealing, lips too thin, eyes too narrow, voice harsh, grating, nasal? Even the smell of her, a vaguely sour odor unaffected by baths or perfumes, annoyed him. Her cool unapproachability, which had so excited him in their youth, was now only irritating.

In high school she used to torment him with her penchant for wealthy, weasely Squirrel Hill types, the rich Jewboys who used to arrive at school in their Cadillacs and sports cars, the Buddy Gray Eyes crowd.

In those days he considered himself unaccountably lucky to have won her. He regretted it now. She had never let him forget what she had sacrificed to marry him. "I could have had a home north of Forbes," she would throw up to him. North of Forbes was where the wealthiest of the Jews lived.

At times like that he would feel the cutting pain in his stomach, the knife being driven in.

"You came home this morning and I asked you a simple, human question," she said. The long ash on her cigarette was about to fall. Her chair and the carpeting around it were scarred with black-slash cigarette burns. "I asked you about Buddy and you abused me."

"I was tired. I just wanted some rest."

"But you said he killed somebody. Isn't that what you said?"

"He killed the man from the candy store."

"How do you know he did it? How do you know it?"

"Knock off your ash," he said.

She looked over at him and did nothing. The ash fell to the carpet. "How do you know he did it?"

"Why do you care?"

"What do you mean, 'Why do I care?' "

"Just what I said."

"I liked Buddy. Everybody liked him. He was the best."

"Not in my book."

She remained quiet for a moment, lipped her cigarette, inhaled deeply. "So why do you say he killed this man?"

"I didn't say it, witnesses said it."

"I don't believe it."

"Why the fuck do you care?" Strahan's voice was tense, rising in anger.

"I care because I care. I care about certain people. You don't care about anybody."

"I care about the old man who was killed. And I'm going to get the man who killed him. All right?"

She didn't answer. She stared at the end of her cigarette. "And another thing," she said. "What about the back door? That's another thing."

"Oh, please—"

"And the goddamn kitchen floor's rotting."

She had walked to the yellow plastic bar-stand and was pouring herself another drink. He tried to take the bottle from her hand, but she pulled it away from him. "Watch it, mister," she said.

"I just want to have a coherent conversation. I don't want to jump from Buddy Gray Eyes to the back door to the rotting floor—"

"This fucking house," she said. "This fucking house."

"What about it?"

"This fucking house." She nodded her head, waved her drink around the room. "And the back door. And the kitchen floor."

They occupied the ground floor of a red brick duplex bought from an uncle of hers at the suggestion of Polish

Ted. The house had turned out to be a disaster. It was old and drafty and there was something constantly wrong with it—if it wasn't the furnace, it was the plumbing. The idea behind buying the house had been twofold. First, because it was on Polish Hill, it was only ten minutes away from the Public Safety Building where Strahan worked. Second, the rent from the upper apartment would cover the payments on the house. It hadn't worked out that way. In order to come out financially on the deal Strahan would have to do most of the maintenance work himself. He just didn't have the time. When they hired someone, the work was sloppy and took months to complete; it was expensive; for every repair made, two problems seemed to develop. It was all a rip-off.

And the blacks were moving in. When they tore down a section of the Hill District, blacks moved across Bigelow Boulevard to Polish Hill. If Strahan wanted to, he couldn't sell the place now. They'd never get their investment back.

"Well?" she demanded.

"Put down that fucking drink."

"Well? The back door. And the floor. And—and—"

"I can't fix it now!" He squeezed his hands into tight fists, digging his fingernails into his palms. She knew he couldn't possibly repair the door at this time. She had brought the whole thing up only to aggravate him further, to suggest whole areas of his dereliction as a husband.

"Let the goddamn floor rot then," she said.

"What do you want from me?"

"That's a laugh."

"I'd really like to know. What do you want from me? What? What?" He was yelling and he felt ugly and foolish as he did it. His voice was constricted with emotion, and that made him loath himself.

"And then there's Buddy," she said.

"Yes. Yes, I know."

"There's the back door, and the floor, and—and—"

"Buddy."

"Gray Eyes."

She turned and looked at him suddenly in a very direct way, not drunk, not hostile. She looked surprisingly young and beautiful, as she had looked in the high school graduation picture. "Oh, John," she said. "He really killed that old man? He really did that?"

She came to him, leaned against him. He could feel her body trembling under his hands. He didn't know how to hold her; it had been too long.

He wanted to ask her: Did you sleep with him? When we were young and I was so much in love with you, did you sleep with him?

He was aware now of music coming from the apartment upstairs, a radio or phonograph. He strained to make out the song.

She relaxed under his hands and moved away. She sat on the footstool in front of the couch. "Poor Buddy," she said to no one in particular.

He walked into the kitchen and poured himself a glass of milk. He had a sharp, raw pain in his stomach. It was almost eleven. He had figured on sleeping until midnight. He knew he must go out again, but he didn't relish it now. He was just too goddamn tight. How had his life become so strained and ugly?

When he finished with Buddy Gray Eyes, it would be right again.

He returned to the living room. Kitty Lou reached forward and snapped on the television set. She kept the sound off. "I'm sorry," she said. "I'll be very, very quiet. I'll just look at the pictures."

"I'm going to get him," he said.

"Yes," she said. "I suppose you will."

"What went on?" he heard himself say.

"What do you mean?"

"What went on with Buddy?"

She looked at him and smiled as though at some private joke.

"What did you used to do with him?"

She stared at him very directly and spoke with the voice of a young girl. "He liked to stroke my hair. He would tell me how good and beautiful I was. And that's all you need to know, you motherfucker."

He could clearly hear the song from upstairs now: Elvis Presley singing "I Love You Because," and Strahan considered, it must be an old recording. He forced his attention to the song. He would show her nothing, not a quiver, not a blink of an eye.

Strahan removed his windbreaker from the closet. He took his holster and service revolver from the shelf and checked out the cylinder.

"I could have married him," Kitty Lou said. "I could have had a large house north of Forbes. And he wouldn't have killed anybody because I would have taken care of him."

From upstairs Elvis sang in a youthful, plaintive voice: *"I love you because you understand, dear / Every single thing I try to do / You're always there to lend a helping hand, dear. / I love you most of all because you're you. . . ."*

Though he tried, Strahan could not quite recall when or where he had first heard that song. Years ago. Junior high. Sometime.

"How was he?" Strahan asked quietly.

"He was fine," Kitty Lou said, forcing a tight smile.

"Good," said Strahan, donning his windbreaker over the holster. He replaced the revolver in the holster.

"Are you going to kill him?"

Strahan did not answer. He was at the door now. "He used to make me cry, John. He was very gentle and I used to cry because he was so sweet."

"I'm going to give you something to cry about," Strahan said, and he left.

It was bitterly cold and snowing and Strahan immediately regretted not taking his overcoat instead of the windbreaker. He was trembling from the cold and from anger.

He walked down the hill, entered his car, and started it. He sat in the car for a while, waiting for the motor to warm up.

His hands were tight on the wheel; he squeezed it and felt like crying out, screaming. He hated this neighborhood, the cobblestone street, the rickety slat-board houses that climbed in topsy-turvy fashion up the hill. Across the Allegheny River, on the North Side, an orange CLARK BAR sign burned through the falling snow. Down below, on this side of the river, he could see the signs for Iron City Beer and Duquesne Beer—"Have a Duke"—and he felt trapped, deeply, hopelessly trapped, trapped by the blacks, trapped by the Jews, trapped by his wife's disdain for him and the hostility he felt in return, trapped by this house, this neighborhood, trapped by all the hustlers and con men and murderers in this world. He felt like taking his gun and blowing his brains out.

He drove along Paulowna Street to Herron Avenue and down to Brereton. He drove past the Polish Falcon Society and the Roman Catholic Church, Ecclesia Polonia Immaculati Cordis Mariae. This was the church Kitty Lou attended with the children. Strahan had long ago given up on church.

In front of the church was a large plaque erected by Our Lady of Victory Club in honor of the men from the church who had served in World War II. "Faith, Valor, Loyalty," the plaque said, then listed the names; the Janickis, Olzaks, Kruszewskis, Pulkowskis, all the Poles of Polish Hill who had served the United States of America so well.

Strahan had walked by the church often and he would stop to study the plaque. Although he had not grown up in this neighborhood, the names were so familiar to him now that he felt as though he had known the men. Whenever he would meet someone whose name he recognized from the plaque, he would think, Here a son, husband, or brother gave his life in war; and he would treat the person with a certain deference.

He felt a kinship to those ghosts of another time. To Strahan they represented something pure and brave, something lost irrevocably. He felt in a strange way that they would have liked and accepted him, those fallen soldiers of the Second World War. He imagined between them and him an easy comradeship. They would have called him Johnny or John-O, given him encouragement, included him in their private jokes. He had entered the police force expecting this comradeship; he had not found it. There had been a hint of it with Jack Palmer, but even there he sensed a gulf: his youth and seriousness had made Palmer uncomfortable.

Continuing now along Brereton, he drove by the recreation center where he played racquetball and boxed several nights a week, as many as his work would allow.

At Thirteenth Street he crossed the Pennsylvania Railroad yard to Smallman, heading downtown. He was in the middle of a warehouse district now. Black, wooden-backed produce trucks, dark, bleak storage buildings, remnants of rotting fruit and vegetables, crushed cartons and crates, rubble-strewn lots, streetcar tracks rusted from disuse, railroad sidings clotted with grease stretched through the area. Signs for Gullo Produce, Pittsburgh Banana, Otto Milk, faded and ghostlike palimpsests, covered whole sides of warehouse buildings.

Strahan felt as bleak and desperate inside as the area around him, and though he was heading downtown for the Public Safety Building, he turned off at Twenty-first Street.

Buried in the heavy blackness of the warehouse buildings, amid the detritus of the day's market, was a small red brick building surrounded by a wrought-iron fence. A scattering of watermelon rinds rotted at the front door. Above the door, a large, yellow wood affair, carved in stone, were the words *Ad Majorem Dei Gloriam*. A plaque to one side said: PLEBANIA PARAFIT SW. STANISLAW KOSTKI—Saint Stan's Church, as the people on Polish Hill called it.

Strahan parked his car and walked along a narrow path

to the parish house in the rear. The light in the house was on and Strahan pressed the buzzer.

A man opened the door. "Johnny," he said, "I was thinking about you. I run into Jack Palmer downtown." Father Walter Nagorski, pastor of Saint Stan's, admitted Strahan to his apartment.

The television news was just ending. The priest turned off the sound. Strahan seated himself in an armchair and stared at the set. Small, colored figures played out a foolish, silent charade. "Bad business with this old man," Father Nagorski said.

"Yes."

"I was down there by the Art Cinema, looking to get a sausage by Podalak's. An' I see this character in a green striped sport jacket made him look like a walking peppermint stick, rocking back on his heels studying rear ends up on the movie poster, getting ready to go in, X-rated thing. 'Hey, fella,' I yelled. 'I'm goin' to have you up on report!' I tell you he jumped three feet!"

"Who was it?"

The priest looked disappointed that Strahan hadn't figured it out. "Jackie. Three feet he jumped. So we get to talking an' I ask about you an' he tells me you're up to your ears on this case, this ol' man gets himself killed and so forth. Tough business."

"It never gets easier."

"That's the pity of it." The priest poured out a couple of scotches, added a splash of soda water, and placed the drinks on a table next to Strahan. "How about a little diversion?" Father Nagorski said, indicating a chess set on the table.

"Not tonight, Walt."

The priest relit the stump of a cigar. He had thick fingers and the cigar appeared ridiculously small in them. A large, muscular man in his late fifties, he had been a wrestler in his youth, had fought pro, and had given it up for the priesthood.

Strahan had known Nagorski since he had been very young, when the priest would stop by Saint Philomena's to play ball with the kids. Strahan was in grade school then. Walter Nagorski was a legend: he had once hit a softball from the Beechwood Boulevard side of the field, past the coal mine shaft, beyond the driveway, and out onto Forward Avenue. It was a shot some old-timers compared to Babe Ruth's towering home run, during the last game of his career when he was with the Boston Braves, over the right field stands in Forbes Field.

Years later they met again in a chess tournament at the downtown YMCA. From time to time they would get together and have at it over the board. Strahan played a cautious, methodical game, a game whose power arose through accretion rather than illuminating strokes, while Father Nagorski played in a slashing style, full of inventive combinations. Strahan usually won.

"Was the old man a friend of yours?"

"Not really. I knew him. I liked him a lot."

"I know what you mean. It's tough."

"Yes."

Strahan didn't speak for a very long time and the priest grew uncomfortable. He cracked his knuckles loudly. At last Strahan said, "Was I interrupting you, Walt?"

"Not at all. Not at all. I was watching the television with one eye and working on my model. Let me show you something." The priest lumbered to a card table in a corner of the room. He lifted the whole table and brought it to Strahan. On it were a number of small plastic pieces. "Rolls-Royce."

"Hmm."

"This here is the motor." The plastic motor was half-assembled. Nothing else was. "Trickier'n hell. See these gee-gaws here? Each one of 'em got to be separately glued together."

"Some job."

"I'll say." Father Nagorski puffed for a while on his cigar. "Jackie told me the guy killed the old man is a local boy."

"I went to high school with him."

"Is that so? I didn't know that."

"Yes."

Father Nagorski shook his head, puffed on his cigar, took a sip of his whiskey.

"Did you know this man, Cervino?" Strahan said.

"It seems to me I've been in his store. A gentleman of the old school, as I recall."

"Yes, he was. You know the crazy thing, Walt?"

"What's that?"

"When I was going to Saint Philomena's, I would often be in the candy store. And the fellow that did the killing, he would be there, too."

"Is that so?"

"I fought him once in front of the store. The old man broke it up. Oh, we were maybe ten years old. As a kid I didn't take to people, older people, you know. But I liked this man. He had a kind way about him. That's what gets to me about this whole thing."

"Why do you think this other chap killed him?"

"It made no sense. He was a good athlete, clean-cut guy. A Jewboy."

"Jewish? Is that right?"

"Something's eating away at me, Walt," Strahan said. "I have a terrific hate for this guy, a hate that goes way back for him. It has to do with a lot of things that I could never explain."

How could he tell the priest that Gray Eyes had had the woman he loved when they were young? That Gray Eyes had had money, looks, an easy way with people? "You see, Walt, I've never killed a man. I've come close, but thank God I never have. With this guy, if I find him, I'm going to kill him."

Father Nagorski said nothing. He cracked his knuckles, one by one, slowly. "He's a Jew," Strahan said. "I hate him for a lot of reasons, but I hate him also because he's a Jew."

He had never discussed these things with Father Nagorski and he knew now that what he had just said had not set well with him.

The priest's face grew serious. He puffed on his cigar. "You're wrong for that, John," he said.

"I don't want to hate. It's just in me." Strahan suddenly felt a deep shame. He was sorry he had come here. The disappointment he had caused the priest was apparent and profound.

"I grew up on Locust Street, on the Bluff," Father Nagorski said. "Went to Duquesne University up there. I was raised with Jewish people. Some fine people, I loved them like my own. There was an old Jewish man used to come down the street with a broken-down horse and cart and the boys in the neighborhood would pelt him with garbage. It turned my stomach, John. I don't like that sort of thing. I never did."

"The hate isn't just that, Walt. It's a lot of other things. I've known this guy since we were kids—" In his mind's eye Strahan saw Buddy Gray Eyes and Akiba Moldavan; they were ten years old; he had been fighting Akiba; now Buddy was coming toward him . . .

"They're the chosen people, Walt."

"Yes."

"Why? Chosen for what? If you knew this guy, this Gray Eyes, Walt. If you knew what he had done to me . . ."

"What?"

Strahan could not answer. He wanted to say: He was beautiful and I wasn't. He was accomplished and I wasn't. He had the woman I loved . . .

"This will sound crazy, Walt, but from the time I first met him, as a little kid, I had a hate for him. Does that sound crazy? And he did this, killed this sweet, defenseless old man. What am I supposed to do?"

"Do your job. But don't do it out of hate. Because this man is a murderer, don't you become one, too. Purge your heart of hate, John."

"I can't," Strahan said, and he was in deep pain as he said it. He suddenly knew he must leave this place: he should never have come. He questioned why he had come and felt somewhere that he must have been looking for absolution for his hate. And he knew now that the priest would not give it to him. "There are other things, Walt. I can't explain them."

"What other things?"

"I can't say."

Father Nagorski was puzzled, saddened. What did John Strahan want from him? And what would he do? "Sit down. Let's talk some more, John," he said.

Strahan shook his head. His face was pale, frightening. His eyes behind his spectacles burned with a terrible cold anger, and Father Nagorski was deeply troubled.

There were things the priest would have liked to say. He would have talked of his days as a young theology student, sitting in a small luncheonette owned by a Jewish woman, opposite the university. She would feed him when he was hungry and had no money. She would tell him stories of her childhood in Lithuania. She would teach him words in Yiddish. There were four daughters in the family and he harbored a secret love for one of them.

When the woman died, he wept as though it had been his own mother. Years after, the daughter, the girl he had loved from afar, also died and the sadness he felt had been monumental.

He would have liked to convey to John Strahan how important people were in this life, how worthy of respect and love. He would have attempted to get him to abjure hate, envy, small-mindedness.

He would have talked to John Strahan as to a son.

But it was too late. John Strahan had gone without even a good-bye.

Back at the Public Safety Building Strahan put through a call to Mother Shadman. Gray Eyes hadn't contacted him. "Did you set that deal for me up in Fayette City?" Mother asked.

"I'm working on it."

"Yeah, that's like the check's in the mail or I won't come in your mouth."

"I'll be by to see you later."

"Don't come here with an army of bozos in Robert Hall suits, crew cuts, and toothpicks in their mouths. You'll ruin my reputation."

"What's your address?"

"Mills Avenue in Braddock. Four oh five."

At the elevator he met Busik on his way out. The lieutenant, who had been working late, looked tired. "I promised this guy Shadman we'd do him some good up in Fayette City," Strahan said.

"What's he have?"

"One count, possession."

"Fuck him. Unless he brings the joker into us slung over his shoulder."

"That's what I figured."

"Where's Jack?"

"Porno film."

"Nice. What'd he get, a report this Gray Eyes was seen sniffing the seats? My ambition in life is to die and come back to earth as Jack Palmer."

He banged the down button and he and Strahan rode to the street level in silence.

It was nearly one o'clock when Strahan arrived at the Silver Princess, and the place was nearly deserted. He was taken to a small, round Formica table with a view, through the rear glass wall, of the Golden Triangle, the city's business district where the Allegheny, Monongahela, and Ohio rivers converged. The Silver Princess was perched on the edge of Mount Washington. From his table Strahan could see Three Rivers Stadium across the way on the North Side. He could see the tall, sleek buildings of downtown Pittsburgh's Gateway Center, and the Fort Pitt and Point bridges spanning the rivers.

Three girls were at work in the Silver Princess, two Amazonian blacks in tinfoil costumes that revealed large expanses of rich, chocolate flesh, and a young white girl who sat in the check room. She was the same girl Strahan had followed to the streetcar stop.

A dark, swarthy man worked behind the bar. He looked to be Lebanese or Syrian.

One of the black girls, extraordinary breasts threatening to overflow her costume, smelling of a tropical-sweet perfume, took his order. She spoke with a clipped, elocution-school, phony English accent. "Tonight, for entrée, the Silver Princess is proud to present a special treat: the New York Strip Steak—a cut of prime meat done on our charcoal broiler to the proper perfection of your taste desire. We also have the Surf and Turf Special, Lobster Bits en Brochette, and Duck à la Maison. Prime Ribs of Beef au Jus, with our Silver Princess Baked Idaho Potato. And a Filet of Sole with Amandine Sauce." He ordered the Surf and Turf Special.

An incline car glided gracefully up the steep side of Mount Washington. Through the gently falling snow it appeared unconnected to any track, appeared to be floating. A huge flower of molten orange fire blossomed from the blast furnace of a steel mill upriver on the Monongahela.

The waitress returned with an hors d'oeuvres platter and pointed out the various items: "There are hearts of artichoke in a vinaigrette dressing, cauliflower and crabmeat dip, honeydew melon wrapped in prosciutto ham. The rest I believe are self-explanatory." He looked at the platter:

the rest consisted of tomatoes, cucumbers, and salami slices.

As he was being served his Surf and Turf, Strahan said: "I think I know the checkroom girl. What's her name?"

"She's a cute one, isn't she? We all call her Paper Doll."

"She have a boyfriend?"

"I believe she does."

"Blond, dirty hair? Very light eyes?"

The waitress studied Strahan for a long moment. Her look bled off its affected dazzle, replacing it with a street toughness. "You're the heat?" she said.

He showed her his detective's badge. She smiled. "And you're such a clean-cut-looking fellow."

"Bring her over."

Julie Tripp joined Strahan at his table. She appeared drawn and tense. She was on the verge of tears. "What did he do?" she said as soon as she sat down.

"He didn't tell you?" She shook her head, no. "He killed a man," Strahan said.

The girl stared at the table for a very long time. She put her right hand up to her forehead, but she did not cry. She sat like that for quite a while. Strahan did not speak.

"Who?"

"A defenseless old man. He owned a candy store. Your boyfriend just went in there and put two bullets in him."

A shudder went through the girl. She stared directly at Strahan. Tears welled up in her eyes, but she continued to look directly at Strahan. "Why?" she said.

Strahan shook his head. "You tell me."

"He's sick. He's just sick."

"Where is he?"

"I don't know."

"Did he contact you?"

"I can't do this," she said. "I can't tell you anything."

"Where is he? He killed an old man. Killed. Understand? Now where is he?"

"What will you do with him?" Strahan did not answer.

"You'll do away with him. I know it. I'm never going to see him alive again."

"He killed a defenseless old man."

"Why did he do that? Why?"

"Give him up."

She just shook her head. Tears streamed down her face. "I can't do this. Please." She broke down. She turned to the window and tried to compose herself. The tall waitress stood a few feet back, glaring at Strahan.

"Why do you people do this?" Julie said. "Why do you try to force people to turn on people they love?"

Strahan looked genuinely surprised. He pushed the remainder of his meal away: the Surf and Turf Special tasted like cardboard. "That's not the way I operate. You don't understand—I go way back with Buddy. He's not a murderer. Whatever he did, he did out of sickness." He leaned forward and took Julie's hand in his. It was cold and thin, fragile, like the wing of a bird. She pulled it away immediately. "I want to save Buddy," Strahan said.

Julie Tripp did not answer. Strahan felt an alien pang inside: the girl appeared soft, vulnerable, and he was suddenly reminded of Kitty Lou when she was in high school. Paper Doll, the waitress had called her. Yes, she did have the delicacy of a paper doll. She would tear, she would crumple.

Strahan felt a loathing for himself, knowing that he would use her, lie to her, play on her vulnerability. He wished he could do otherwise, but he could not. "Please. Believe me. The boys downtown want to destroy Buddy. I don't want that. I beg you, for Buddy's sake, if you know anything, *anything*, please tell me."

She stared at him for a very long time. Strahan fought to maintain a look of concern, but he could feel it draining under her gaze. He could feel his face grow hard and he could do nothing about it.

He saw something shut down in her gaze and he knew

he had lost her. "There's nothing I can tell you," she said.

Strahan leaned back and stared out the window. The lights of the city glistened like slivers of ice. A shadow clouded his reflection in the glass, the waitress at his side now, cooing in her fruity voice: "For dessert we have the Silver Princess Parfait, which is vanilla ice cream in a cassis and Kahlúa sauce; Brandied Pears; German Black Forest Cake, which is a creamy chocolate, whipped cream, and maraschino cherry."

Julie was wiping her eyes with a napkin. Strahan declined dessert, asked for the check. When it came, he paid with his Master Charge.

He gave the girl his home number and the number of the Public Safety Building. He jotted them down on a match cover from the Silver Princess. "What's going to happen to him will not be very nice. They'll put so many bullets in him, he'll be lucky if his pretty eyes are still in his head."

If he thought he would make her cry again, he was wrong. She did not pick up the match cover. She stared at him with an empty toughness that caused him to regret he had ever felt pity toward her. "Please," he said, and it was without feeling, flat, harsh.

"Please what?" she asked, as though nothing else had passed between them.

"Okay," he said, and walked to the door. He looked back at Julie Tripp. She was watching the snow fall.

The house where Mother Shadman lived was a scag center, two-story shack in the black section of Braddock; rotting, sooty slat-board, it was peopled by pimps on the slide, hookers hooked, former mill workers, truck drivers, day laborers, shop girls, all scraping bottom now, all brought low by junk draculas; vampire geeks whose sign was not fang marks on the neck, but blue-black craters in the crook of the arm, the back of the knee, between the toes.

John Strahan climbed the weary steps with a feeling of fatigue that had nothing to do with the hour. He had made the climb so often in so many other places. He knew what to expect: the wheedles and imprecations, the lies, the deadness. There would be flecks of dried blood, scabs, pits, scars.

It was nearly two A.M. and the living room, wood-burning stove glowing quietly at its center, was filled with men and women on the nod. It was a waiting room in the strictest sense: one waited for nothing, and did nothing but wait.

"Hey, my *man*," a black Mills Avenue pimp said languidly as Strahan entered. The room smelled of joss sticks and garbage.

"You got the wrong man," Strahan said. With no guarantee that Gray Eyes was not lurking there, Strahan was fastidious: he kept his back to the wall.

"I got the wrong man? You mean you're not my *main* man? Well, shit." The pimp laughed and laughed.

There were scratches and yawns from the others, a few smiles.

A toothless old black next to the pimp laughed softly and massaged his bald head with the knuckles of his hand. It was the dishwasher from the White Tower. "Hey, champ," Strahan said. "How's it going?"

"If I'm the *champ*," the dishwasher said, "I sure hate to see the *losers*."

"I'll tell you something," the pimp said to no one in particular, adjusting the stained white fedora on his head. "The man once promised to fly me to the moon. I said, 'God bless you, but go it alone. Just bring me back some cheese.'"

"I hear this," said the dishwasher, grinning. "I hear this."

"Some people, you know, will promise you the sun, moon, and the stars and work down from there," a junky whore said without opening her eyes.

"Uh-huh. I hear this."

"What you want, my man?" the pimp said, tilting his fedora back on his head.

"I'm looking for Mother," Strahan said.

"What you want with my mother?" the pimp said.

"I don't want anything with your mother," Strahan said.

"Don't come 'round here then asking 'bout her, then. Lest you want your asshole where your mouth be."

"He's upstairs in his room," the dishwasher said.

"Pale-ass motherfucker," the pimp said.

As Strahan started up the stairway the pimp called after him: "I'll put a hurtin' on your ass, you come here throwing your gold badge weight around. I'll *dust* your ass."

Shadman had the bureau pushed against the door. He called out to Strahan to wait, and there was a sound of movement within. It took him awhile to push the bureau out of the way.

The room, filled with books and magazines, was nevertheless painfully neat. Shadman, clad in a terry-cloth robe, moved to a small, stained enamel sink in one corner of the crowded room. He sucked air from exertion. "No locks on the doors. They steal the fillings out of your teeth, junkies," he said. His rheumy eyes looked infinitely sad. "Coffee, John?"

"All right." Strahan noticed Shadman's hands were trembling as he drew water for the coffee.

Strahan seated himself on an iron chair next to the bed. There was a small, hand-carved chess set on the nightstand. Next to the board were several books—Ouspensky's *In Search of the Miraculous*, *Chess Praxis* by Aron Nimzovich—and a stack of nudie magazines. It occurred to Strahan that Mother Shadman had created for himself a replica of a long-termer's prison cell, a home away from home.

He leafed through one of the magazines, gazing without interest on the color shots of female genitalia, thinking that human flesh, no matter the region, was not meant to be seen close up.

Shadman, preparing the coffee, couldn't stop his hands from shaking. Spoons rattled against cups, cups against saucers.

"Shit," Shadman said. "I can't stop these fucking nerves. Shit."

"You got yourself a jones."

"No," Shadman said. "I'm scared. Someone rang the phone before, John. They didn't speak. I could hear them breathing."

"If it was Gray Eyes, why didn't he speak?"

"How do I know?" Shadman was on the verge of hysteria. "Maybe he knows I snitched him off. He could be on his way over right now to cancel my mail. You didn't put the word out that I snitched him off, did you?"

"Oh, come on," Strahan said. An excitement had started in the pit of his stomach that was almost sexual. Gray Eyes was on his way over! He would face him. They would talk.

He removed his revolver, checked the chambers, rested it on his lap. Then he checked out his back-up gun.

"That thing up in Fayette City?" Shadman said.

"We'll take care of it."

"I just can't do hard time anymore."

"Sure. Hard time is a bitch. Nothing but boy-ass for diversion."

Shadman's chalky-pale face, wide watery eyes, plump womanish body, filled Strahan with revulsion. He was a cockroach, a plague, a fungus. Strahan was thinking: I'd love to eradicate this creeping evil; burn the whole house down.

There was a sound in the hallway outside the door. Shadman stopped moving. Strahan's hand went to the revolver on his lap. A woman's voice sounded on the other side of the door so clearly it seemed she was in the room. "Don't you fuck with me like that, flat-nosed motherfucker.

Don't you ever fuck with me like that. I'll break your motherfucking jaw." There was a noise of weak scuffling. "Grab hold on my shit, I'll kick your black ass all over this place."

A man's voice now: "What you hit me for, bitch? What you hit me for? Broke my damn bridge, bitch."

"I'll break your ass."

"Crazy bitch."

The junky-mumble argument receded down the hallway. A door slammed.

Mother Shadman, still trembling, poured out hot water into two cups, stirred the instant coffee, and placed the cups on the nightstand.

Strahan took a sip of coffee. "Good," he said.

Shadman selected a cigarette butt from a neat row on the nightstand. He had trouble inserting it in a metal holder; his hands wouldn't stop shaking.

"What are you afraid of?" Strahan said. "Gray Eyes might blow you away?"

"Oh, no. There is no death," Shadman said. "Turning in an old friend bothers me. It upsets my nervous system to turn in a friend."

"Who's your friend? Gray Eyes?"

"Well. I *fantasize* we were friends. If I think it, it's real. If it's in my mind it exists."

Strahan just smiled.

"The world is not real unless it's in my mind. Nothing is real unless it's in my mind. If a tree falls in the forest—you know that concept? Well, if I didn't see it, it didn't fall. And no one dies. Ever."

"What kind of concept is that?"

"That's a very Oriental concept."

Strahan studied his coffee cup. "You see this? That's a coffee cup. It exists. And when a man *dies*, he's *dead*. Whether you see it or not."

"Oh, no. There is no death."

"No pulse. No breath. Death."

"Are you kidding *me*? How many times did dope fiends go out in my arms? We dumped their bodies, all right? And you know what I believed? This man is not *dead*. I can't feel his pulse—that doesn't mean shit. How do I know he's dead? What if you get him in the ground and he opens his eyes? That's what I'm afraid of."

There were footsteps down the hall. Strahan moved behind the door. He listened as someone entered the bathroom at the end of the hall. There was the sound of urination, the flush of the toilet, footsteps back up the hall. "They piss like horses," Shadman said with disgust. "Waterfalls. All night."

Strahan paced, went to the window. The street outside was dark; someone had knocked out the streetlamp.

He returned, seated himself facing the door. Shadman toyed with a chess piece. After a while he said: "I hated like hell giving up that kid, John. All right, philosophically, it doesn't really happen. Still, it's a rotten thing, giving up people."

"Killing an old man's not so nice, either." Strahan could feel the excitement coursing through him. Gray Eyes was on his way! He fought to rein his emotions in. Cool, cool, like Jack Palmer, cool.

"You know my problem," Shadman said. "I don't like myself."

"I can understand that," Strahan said.

"And how about you, John?" Shadman said. "You think you're Mister Nice Guy? You could use a personality course, learn to relate."

"You think I want to relate to the class of people I come into contact with?"

"I'm sensitive to your situation, John. You should have been a shoe salesman. Then you'd enjoy relating." He sighed. "Nothing exists," he said.

"Oh, there are some things," Strahan said.

"You know what exists, John? A spike in my arm. That exists." He stared off toward the wall, puffing his cigarette butt right down to the metal holder. "An accident of chemistry did me in. As a young man hanging out with musicians, the stuff was there, I was adventurous. I tried it." He smiled wanly. "Genius IQ, hundred eighty-something. The hope, pride, and joy of my mother. All into the cooker."

Strahan was tingling with anticipation now: Gray Eyes would arrive soon. Yes, he would arrive. When he faced him, when he removed him from his life, how would it be? "What's heroin feel like?" he said.

"It's good," Shadman said. "You never tried it?"

"No."

"If you're going to throw away your whole existence it's the best thing I can think of. Better than suicide. You got a personality problem, John. It'd do you good." Strahan smiled, a thin, tight smile. "You know the biggest drawback with smack?" Shadman said. "Constipation. That stuff'll block you up like you got cement up there. Got to blast it out with dynamite." He continued to toy with the chess piece, made a desultory move. "What will you do when Gray Eyes shows?"

"I'll tell him he doesn't exist. I'll tell him you don't exist. I'll tell him no one exists."

"You do that, Johnny."

They remained quiet for a long time. Shadman began to move the pieces on the chess board, sliding them back and forth, testing the possibilities, rearranging them. "What I mean is," he said, "it could be no other way. There was no choice. What happened was the only thing that could have happened."

"Yes, yes. How did Gray Eyes get into doojee?"

"I don't know. Ran into the wrong person at the wrong time, I suppose. Sad, you know? Sad. Sad he got into it. Sad I'm turning him in. It's like Schopenhauer's bulldog ant. You know about the bulldog ant?" Strahan didn't answer. "You cut the bulldog ant in two, his head and tail will bite and sting the shit out of each other. How about a game of chess?"

"If you can stop your hands from shaking." Shadman held his hands out. They were not trembling now.

In the recesses of the house someone was playing an old Dinah Washington record, "Time Out for Tears."

# 9

AKIBA MOLDAVAN, sitting in front of the television set, stared at the screen. Johnny Carson was on. The earplug lay loose on the table next to him. The show played out in silence.

His mind was chaos, raging with Kabbalah. From time to time he would get up and pace the study, twisting the hair on his head, pressing his knuckles against his skull, muttering aloud to himself.

He was exhausted and he was frightened. Earlier something had occurred which had profoundly shaken him.

He had discovered a link between his past and the terrible events of the present. Kabbalah, which until this day had existed in a realm of speculation, seemed suddenly to have thrust itself on him with a force bizarre and magical.

What was real? What was symbol? It was all converging, coming together.

The early evening had been difficult: problems with Hannah. He had arrived home to find his sister raving. Ruth was a Nazi agent, she screamed. She would not take her Thorazine. The pills were cyanide, she cried.

She whimpered and screamed and moaned and the kids had become upset, infected by Hannah's terror. He had had to take care of her, then deal with the kids. Fortunately Rabbi Isaac, who had gone to bed after dinner, was asleep.

He managed to get Hannah to take her pills, then quieted the kids with a story.

Afterward, he went downstairs to the study. He took his high school journal from a shelf. He had not looked at it in years, since his graduation.

He came across John Strahan's entry: "Football team captain, homeroom president, track, basketball, chess. Golden Gloves boxing, Science Club; high honor student. Ambition: Engineering." Strahan stared, stern and serious, out at the world.

Leafing through the book he came across Strahan's wife's picture: "Kitty Lou Ozimek, the minx of our crew, will add her potion to a heavenly brew." With her beehive hairdo and quizzical expression, she gazed from the picture as though questioning, seducing the world.

She had signed the book for Akiba: "To a good friend of Gray Eyes, all the best, Kitty." The handwriting was a childish scrawl.

"A good friend of Gray Eyes—" Gray Eyes. How had Buddy received the name? It seemed to have had something to do with Kitty Lou Ozimek. He tried to remember its origin, but could not.

He turned to Buddy Hall's entry, studied the picture there. Buddy had short hair then, a semi-crew cut, and he was smiling at the camera. His accomplishments listed under the picture were mostly athletic. There was mention of his charm and popularity, followed by a poem: "A gridiron great, Buddy Gray Eyes's fame is unbounded / a swell fellow to know, by his feats we're astounded." He had autographed the book: "Your true friend forever, Gray Eyes."

As he stared at the autograph, Akiba Moldavan felt a rush of disquietude, a cold spread of panic.

There was a sketch drawn next to his name, a sketch that Akiba had no memory of: a crude stick figure of a man. Above the head Buddy Gray Eyes had printed EMETH.

The figure was constructed of ten lines: the Tree of

Kabbalah, the figure of Adam Kadmon, Primordial Man.

A whole world of days came back to Akiba now, days of his youth when he and Buddy would laze around Frick Park, stretched out on the grass, and stare up into the buckeye trees above them.

It was during these times that Akiba would talk about Kabbalah, the Tree of Life and the Tree of Death. He would tell tales of the golem. On the forehead of the golem the ancient rabbis would carve the Hebrew word for truth, EMETH. Should the golem threaten to rage out of control, the first letter would be erased and EMETH would become METH—"He is dead"—and the golem would crumble back into clay.

Akiba had told Buddy a story of a *Baalshem*, Master of the Name, a great mystic, Rabbi Elias, who had constructed a golem that had grown so large the rabbi was unable to reach his forehead to erase the magical letter.

The golem grew in strength and ferocity, became *yetzer ha-ra*, The Destroyer. He had gone over to *sitra ahra*, the other side, and was now in the service of the Prince of Demons, Samael.

Soon the golem would loose himself from the rabbi's house and roam the world, a rampaging, indestructible monster of evil intent. Rabbi Elias, who had created him, could not control him, could not bring him down.

Out of desperation he resorted to a trick. He asked the golem for a last favor before he went out into the world. Would the golem help him off with his boots?

As the golem bent down to perform this last service, Rabbi Elias was able to erase the odylic letter, EMETH became METH, and the golem was destroyed. His weight, though, came crashing down on the rabbi, crushing him to death.

Akiba had told Buddy this story when they were children and he had echoed it in his autograph. He had drawn a stick figure in the form of the Sephirot and crowned it with the Hebrew word for Truth. He had drawn himself as a golem.

Why? Why? What was its significance?

Did it mean that all these years he had moved through life thinking of himself as The Destroyer, as a golem?

Was it coincidence or was it magic, that even as Akiba planned to save his once friend through Kabbalah, the friend had accepted a vision of himself as a thing made of clay?

Akiba roamed the study, his life suddenly chaos, a whirlwind. What did it all mean, stick figure Kabbalistic man, golem?

I am becoming insane, he thought. I am becoming like Hannah or Izzie, the moron . . .

He thought of Gray Eyes, the *name*. The name of a thing is its essence, the *Talmud* held, determined its future; the alteration of a name could avert even the Angel of Death.

Buddy Hall, by changing his name to Gray Eyes, had performed an inversion of this principle: he had shifted himself from good to evil, from this world to the *sitra ahra*.

Was it possible? Was it reality, symbol, madness?

There is a reality beyond reality, veils separating the two. The veil shifts and we see—

I am becoming insane. How is this different from Hannah's delusions? Izzie's moronic chanting?

*The name of a thing is its essence.* Gray Eyes? How had he received the name? When? In grade school? Junior high school? Akiba couldn't remember. He fought to bring it back. It escaped him.

Kabbalah, the Thirty-two Paths of Hidden Wisdom, golem, Buddy Gray Eyes. He was perspiring now, cold with fear, haunted.

There is a rock of reality beyond all this, he told himself. There is God here, somewhere. There is God!

Buddy Hall, Gray Eyes, wandering the *sitra ahra*, lost in

*tohu*, possessed by his golem twin, his human self usurped by The Destroyer . . .

The *Talmud* held that whoever pondered four things—what is above, what is below, what was before time, what was hereafter—it were better he had never been brought into the world. Four rabbis, it was said, had gazed on the innermost secret of Kabbalah: one died, one went mad, one became an apostate. Only one entered in peace and left in peace.

Yes, and—a man in a dungeon sees through the bars of his cell a splendorous light. With all of his strength he attacks the walls of his prison and breaks out. The light, however, is no longer visible. He is confronted by the wall of a precipice and he despairs. Yet, though he is unaware of it, the light is there, shining from a magnificent palace, and what is more, it is the dimmest and most concealed emanation of the true light and still it is beautiful beyond imagining. If he persists, if only he persists, he will see the light in all its glory!

The light is there, Akiba told himself. The light is there.

The name Gray Eyes. Gray Eyes. How had he received it?

And now Akiba Moldavan remembered: Kitty Lou Ozimek had conferred the name on him. It had been in their junior year in high school. It had occurred after lunch, at the smokestack behind the school.

Akiba could see the scene as though it had happened just that day, could feel the cold snap in the early fall air, smell the vague burned odor that always seemed to hover over the smokestack area, could hear the sound of an electric saw screeching from the open window of the carpentry shop.

A discussion had been going on over what constituted sex appeal. Kitty Lou Ozimek had said that bedroom eyes were the essence of sex appeal, and gray eyes were the sexiest eyes of all. Who has gray eyes? someone had asked.

Buddy Hall was seated on a brick wall just beyond the group, smoking a cigarette. Kitty Lou looked over at him and said, Buddy Hall has gray eyes, Buddy Hall is Gray Eyes, and Buddy smiled and bent his head low in a mock bow as though accepting the name. Yes, she had offered it to him and he had taken it. From that day forward Buddy Hall had been known as Gray Eyes.

Yes, the name. Gray Eyes, the inversion of Primordial Man, the dark Sephirot, the golem.

It all clashed in Akiba Moldavan's mind, name and essence, sign and significance, black Kabbalah, white Kabbalah.

"I am going insane," he cried out aloud.

No, I must do this. I must, he told himself. I must go after Buddy Gray Eyes, I must skirt the *sitra ahra*, walk the edge of the *tohu*.

On the television figures shifted, laughed, danced. Colors flashed in front of his eyes.

There is *Ein Soph*, the Infinite, the Endless, a glowing coal whose presence is known only by the fire which rages about it.

Plunge into the fire, he told himself.

The *Ein Soph* is Hidden Wisdom and there are thirty-two paths to it, the paths and limbs of the Sephirot, and by following them he would approach God. And he would redeem Buddy Gray Eyes.

Gray Eyes was in black Kabbalah, the obverse of the divine Kabbalah, in the *sitra ahra*, where The Destroyer roams. And it is there that Buddy Gray Eyes is trapped; lost, lost, desperate, mad.

And more. More. "No, I am babbling," he cried. "I am mad."

The Tree of the Sephirot is the Tree of Life, the dark Sephirot is the Tree of Death. And it is there that Buddy Gray Eyes now exists. The tree is also in the form of a man, Primordial Man, Adam Kadmon, and from his eyes, ears, nose, and mouth the attributes of God explode as light. There is the dark side, the evil side of Adam Kadmon, the *sitra ahra*, known as Adam Belial. Gray Eyes is there. The light from Gray Eyes is black light . . .

The tree of Kabbalah was on fire in Akiba Moldavan's head.

I must follow the paths of the Sephirot, the thirty-two ways, God's sublime attributes; and I must confront the *tohu*, gaze on the thirty-two paths of the *sitra ahra* . . .

Yes, yes. I must follow the paths, follow the Sephirot, find Buddy Gray Eyes, redeem him. Only I can do this. Only I understand sign and significance, name and essence. I must turn him from golem to man.

I am insane, he told himself. He pressed his knuckles to his temples and tried to squeeze the terror out of his head.

He sat in front of the television set, his head in his hands, his mind swirling with images of the past, his whole self immersed in the past. He could feel it, smell it, the coldness of autumn past, the burned odor of the past.

And binding past to present, days of innocence to days of murder were the Tree of Sephirot, limbs of Primordial Man, knot of Kabbalah.

He did not notice Ruth when she entered the study. She carried a tray with tea and cookies, set it down on the round mosaic cocktail table next to Akiba's chair.

She looked at Akiba with alarm. "What is it?" she said. She held him to her, stroked his head. His hair was damp with perspiration. "What is it? What?"

"I'm going to hunt for him," he said.

She did not speak for a long while. She poured out their tea. "Drink it, Akiba. It'll get cold."

He sipped at the tea. "It's going to be very difficult," he said. "For me and for you. But I must do it."

"Akiba," she said gently.

"I must."

Suddenly he embraced her. There was a terrible desperation in the embrace. He had never in their whole marriage held her like that. He hugged her to him and hung on, an embrace of extraordinary love; or a drowning man holding on.

At that moment the phone began to ring.

# 10

THE night was cold, the avenue dark save for a few pale neon signs in the store windows along the street: Gerber's Kosher Meats, Hebrew National Delicatessen, Rosenbloom's Bakery. A bare white bulb shone outside the door leading to Manny's, the local poolhall.

It was snowing.

Akiba Moldavan stood on Murray Avenue waiting for the streetcar. At this hour, past one A.M., he knew it would be a long wait. There were only two streetcar lines still operating in the city and the late-night service on neither line was predictable.

The phone call earlier had been from Gray Eyes's girl friend, Julie Tripp. She was distraught. Police were watching the place where they lived; she had no idea where Buddy was, but sensed he might be near. He might be hiding in the amusement park. She begged Akiba to meet her there.

He hung up the phone, possessed, filled with Kabbalah.

To start a journey through the paths of the Sephirot, one had to start at the root. It was there that God reached out to man through the Shekinah, his feminine aspect. The blind Shekinah who had lost her sight from weeping for Israel in exile.

His reaction was idiocy: Akiba knew it, but he couldn't help but feel the woman on the phone had come to him from the root of Kabbalah. She was the Shekinah reaching out to him.

The girl on the phone had been weeping.

The solitary light burning outside Manny's Poolhall radiated loneliness, a faint, cold beacon to an infinitesimal world. Up at Manny's, Randall, the gimp manager, at this hour would be sweeping up. A few last, lost players would be running cool balls along the felt-covered slate. The tables, rafts of the night, were the haven and consolation of these men, their women, their friends, their homes.

Akiba thought back on his youth, on all the lonely nights he had spent at Manny's, on that special pang he would feel when closing time came around, on the lost looks on the faces of the regulars as Randall would limp from table to table, yanking at the soiled, waxed overhead lamp strings, cutting the lights off one by one. They knew little of the day, the regulars. They desired to know less of the night. They coveted for their existence only the glide and carom of clean, cool ivory balls whispering over perfect, smooth felt-covered slate. They asked only for that special confinement to their lives, that hushed and banked-down control of all their fires.

From the time he had entered the sixth grade until his graduation from high school, Manny's had been the center of his life. Akiba had taken up the game of pool with the same obsessiveness and determination with which he had attacked chess. There were chess players, too, up at Manny's. They would play off to one side. But pool was the bread-and-butter game.

In those days Akiba and Gray Eyes were inseparable. He was called Shadow: Gray Eyes was the blond dazzler, Akiba the dark umbra that swept after him.

In the sharp, metallic cold of the night Akiba watched as a streetcar approached. Sparks showering from an overhead guide wire, steel wheels grinding along the avenue, it passed in the opposite direction. The trolley bell clanged, echoing in the night. Akiba, forlorn, gazed after the streetcar, a patch of glossy red swaying away, sparks diminishing, everything receding, seeming to implode into the night and the snow.

And Akiba thought of the old days, of the adventures he and Buddy Gray Eyes used to have.

One afternoon two mill workers from Hazelwood had come up to Manny's. Buddy had beat them for nearly a hundred dollars and when it came time to pay up, the men did not have the money. They held a conference with Buddy. He came over to Akiba glowing with excitement. "They have a girl, a gang bang. They're going to bring us in on it."

Akiba had not wanted to go along. Since his experience with the whore in Homestead he had not been with another woman.

He tried to beg off, but Buddy Gray Eyes shamed him into participating.

They had driven with the two men across the Murray Avenue bridge to a small frame house on the edge of Greenfield. Akiba saw it now in his mind's eye: early May, late afternoon, the air sweet with spring, the sky a clear, dazzling blue. The girl, in a thin cotton dress, came out of house and shyly entered the car.

She was short and quite pretty, perhaps twenty years old. She had light reddish brown hair done up in a bun in the back. She smiled a lot. She did not talk. She had friendly, pleasant eyes and she kept turning around and smiling at Akiba and Buddy in the backseat, while the two mill workers made vague, lewd remarks. She just smiled and smiled and Akiba was touched by her and wanted to protect her in some way, yet doubted that she needed or wanted his protection.

They drove over to Mount Royal Road in Squirrel Hill. There was a wooded area sloping down to a hollow just off Mount Royal. They could see the mills of Homestead across the river. A faint blue haze hung over the mills and gathered at the river's edge.

The two men led the girl from the car down a path that curved into the trees of the wooded area. One of the men told Buddy they would signal when it was their turn with the girl.

The men did not return to the car for a very long time. Buddy decided they should investigate. They left the car and started down the path into the trees, Akiba's heart thudding heavily, his hands wet with perspiration. He felt his father was watching him. He felt God was hovering above him.

Gray Eyes was the *yetzer ha-ra*, the Evil Inclination, leading him on. He must escape, he must! Yet he moved on with his friend, on through the trees.

Late afternoon shadows had begun to close down over the woods, and the path ahead of them was dark. Thick boughs weighted with leaves pressed in on them, smothering what was left of the afternoon. Occasionally blades of the sun would slice through the foliage, blinding Akiba with stabs of light, then flash behind the trees and leave the path in gloom.

All around them were Seckel pear trees and the air was heavy with the smell of the ripening fruit.

Above the wooded area, in the not very far distance, a group of men were at work nailing struts for the frame of a new house. The sound of the hammers echoed through the stillness of the woods.

Ahead was a clearing in the trees, bathed in bright sunlight. There was a clump of bushes beyond the clearing. Akiba saw something shimmer behind the bushes—bare skin, a figure.

Buddy crossed the clearing and approached the bushes, then turned to Akiba and waved him forward. Akiba could not move; he felt rooted to the ground. Buddy laughed and jerked his arm in an insistent wave. Akiba walked slowly toward him, dreading each step.

At the bushes he looked down. Through the leaves he could see the two men and the girl. She was lying nude on one of the men's shirts at the foot of a Seckel pear tree. One of the men was on top of her, pumping furiously into her with clumsy, ludicrous energy. The second man, his shirt off, was seated on the ground, smoking a cigarette. He had seen Bud and Akiba and was smiling.

Beyond the men and the girl was a stand of white birches, straight, thin, delicate, arrayed like ghosts in the cool gloom of the deeper woods.

Akiba stared down at the man slamming awkwardly into the girl; the man snorted sharply with each thrust, his pale buttocks and hips shaking like rubber, doughy, sickening, obscene.

The girl's eyes were closed, her body limp. After a while the man on top came. He rolled off, damp with perspiration. He motioned Akiba and Buddy forward.

The girl's eyes were closed. She was not smiling now. Her face was pale and devoid of expression. Akiba studied her, amazed at his sudden objectivity, vaguely aware that his objectivity was a defense against terror. She had very short legs and surprisingly large, firm breasts. The area around her sex had been shaved. Scattered over the ground were fallen Seckel pears and the girl's shaven sex appeared as a ripe, delicate fruit to Akiba. Her breasts had large, reddish brown nipples and they, too, resembled some rich, ripe fruit.

Buddy knelt down and began to knead her breast. He squeezed and smoothed and stroked it as though it were a lump of wet clay.

Wood fleas had begun to flit around the damp, reddened wedge of her sex and Buddy brushed them away with his hands.

The second of the hammers on the house above continued to echo through the dying day.

The man who had just finished looked over at Bud. "She's yours," he said.

Buddy said to Akiba, "You go first."

"I can't," Akiba said softly. "Not with them around."

Buddy moved over to the two men and talked with them in a low voice. They laughed and moved off through the bushes into the sunlit area. Buddy knelt beside the girl. "Feel that," he said. He gently ran his hand over the girl's breast. "It's lovely, Akiba," Buddy said.

Akiba sat on the ground next to the girl and placed his hand on her breast. It felt marvelously firm, rich, velvety. "Don't be afraid," Buddy said.

Akiba stroked the girl's breast, but did nothing more. "Is it that fringe thing? Are you embarrassed about that?" Buddy said.

When he was younger, Akiba had worn under his clothes the *zizith*, ritual fringes required of Orthodox Jews on any four-cornered garment.

The wearing of the *zizith* followed the biblical injunction: "That ye may look upon them and remember all the commandments of the Lord, and do them."

In school he had suffered greatly over them. When Akiba would have to undress for gym class, the other kids would ridicule him. Since deserting his religion he had given up the *zizith*. "I don't wear them anymore," Akiba said.

"You don't have to do this if you don't want to," Buddy said.

"I want to do it."

Buddy Gray Eyes moved off through the bushes to the sunlit area. Akiba was alone with the girl.

He had begun to tremble. He couldn't stop. The white birches stood in the gloom, tall, pale, thin sentinels, imprisoning him, guarding him, accusing him, visitors from the *sitra ahra*, this world and the next, here together, gathered in this dying afternoon, this cave of dark woods. "The *yetzer ha-ra* seduces in this world and accuses in the next," the sages of old held, and Akiba felt it now and he believed it.

He looked down at the girl. She was breathing with deep, irregular gasps. Her eyes remained closed.

The sound of the workmen hammering beyond the woods resounded through the trees.

He moved his hands over the girl's breasts and he felt a deep embarrassment at the tremor in his fingers; he stroked her breasts and the trembling eased off.

He moved one hand down across her belly; her velvet skin felt marvelously rich, soft, imparting to him a sense of the miraculous, as though her desire was entering him, some inductive gravitational field suffusing him with need of her. Terror and guilt subsided. He moved his hand down to her bare pink cleft and slid his finger into her. She moaned quietly, a soft exhalation of breath, and she opened her eyes and looked at him with an expression that was questioning and sad and he, too, felt sad.

With his trousers down, feeling brutally exposed and awkward, he moved on top of her. He sensed eyes watching him, eyes of Buddy and the two mill workers, eyes of the men building the house on Mount Royal, eyes of his father, eyes of God.

He had trouble entering and he felt her hand guiding him and then he was moving into the center of her, swept along in a corrivation miraculous, ineffable, tender beyond imagining. And he felt, even in that moment, that he had caught some glint of God's excruciating beauty. And with it came terror again, and beauty flooded over the terror and yet the terror remained, ugly, drowning, still there, still accusing him.

She moaned over and over, "oh, oh, oh," little, sharp animal cries and he did not want to leave her . . .

Afterward he was dizzy with anxiety and guilt. For years he would be assaulted by a vision of the scene—the girl limp and naked as the two mill workers tried to dress her.

She had been dragged to her feet by the men and one of them was attempting to get her breasts into her brassiere.

They kept flopping out and the second man began to slap her, saying, "Let's go. Time to go."

One of the mill workers, the man doing the slapping, was grinning back at Bud and Akiba as they moved off.

The sound of the men at work in the house above contined to hammer through the still air.

The next day Akiba had returned to the spot, terror-filled, half expecting to find the girl's dead body concealed in the bushes. He found nothing.

Akiba never saw the two men, or the girl, again.

Greeeeeeeeeeeeeeeeeeeeech! A streetcar was screaming its way down Murray Avenue toward him, gliding to a halt. He suddenly realized how cold he was. His feet and face were numb from the cold. It was two A.M. He had waited almost an hour.

There was a scattering of riders in the car, workmen in thick twill clothes, heavy workboots, carrying lunch pails. They dozed or read newspapers or stared ahead, lost in thought.

He considered the past, how it stayed with him, how more vivid than the present it was. What, then, of the future?

The streetcar rocked along through the night and snow and Akiba Moldavan played with the idea of time, where life was not a continuum, but an entity, a mirror with quirky warps, smiling and winking back on itself, reflecting itself—a mirror looking forward and back, reflecting to any point where one stood.

And God would be the face behind the mirror. A one-way mirror. And He is staring out through the glass.

The streetcar started down Brown's Hill Road and Akiba thought of his friend, Gray Eyes, a murderer, and the streetcar wheels cried out and old man Cervino was crying out and the world seemed to be shrieking about him and Akiba Moldavan's thought shrieked: Why? Why had he done it? Why?

The girl would give him some ideas, some answers.

And what if Buddy was with her? What would Akiba do then?

He fought to control the anxiety within him. He told himself all this is frozen in God's mirror; I am on the path of Sephirot.

Speeding down the hill, approaching the High Level Bridge from Squirrel Hill to Homestead, the streetcar passed a large, gray concrete building, Buy-Wise Discount House Plumbing and Electrical Supplies, and Akiba realized the building had not been there the last time he had been through the area: for many years there had been an empty lot on that spot.

The Ringling Brothers and Barnum & Bailey Circus would arrive in town for one week every year and pitch its tent where Buy-Wise Discount now stood. As kids, he and Buddy would visit the circus, con their way into the big top, filch peanuts and Cracker Jacks.

Most of their time, though, they spent at the freak show.

They derived no pleasure from observing the freaks; yet study them they did, as though seeking out some key to life's mystery. And though the more elaborate lessons were still in the future, life did admonish them: Look, I have twisted surprises, grotesque disappointments.

Buddy had always been profoundly moved by the freaks. He would walk away from them with tears in his eyes. He would grow silent for hours. Why are they here? he would ask Akiba. Why are they on this earth?

And Akiba would tell him: God's ways are not man's ways.

And now time had passed and Buddy Hall was a murderer.

The streetcar continued down Brown's Hill Road, moved past the Sealtest ice cream plant and behind it the Jewish Home for the Aged, the *Moshav Zakainim*, a large red brick building overlooking the High Level Bridge and Homestead.

Akiba thought now of the old-timers living out their days in the *Moshav Zakainim*, awaiting *Malaka ha-Mavet*, The Angel of Death, who, with his terrible venom-tipped sword poised to fall, sits at the bedside of the sick, the infirm. Many of these people had been powerful, accomplished. Now they lived out their days gazing down at the oily waters of the Monongahela River and the rust-colored corrugated roofs of the steel mill on the other side, U.S. STEEL HOMESTEAD WORKS painted on the mill roofs in blue and white, brown smoke rising from the huge mill stacks, muddying the black sky.

Now the streetcar was moving across the High Level Bridge. Ahead was the steep West Street hill, climbing to the borough of Munhall; a ramp off to the left led to the steel mills, Seventh Avenue where the whorehouses once had been. Did the whores still lounge in doorways and peer out of windows and stroll the streets just opposite the gate to the mills, waiting for the workers to change shifts?

Now they were moving along Main Street in Homestead, past pawn shops and dreary mill-town bars, jewelry stores, credit dentists, drab clothing emporiums featuring Sweet-Orr work apparel, Red Wing and Georgia Giant steel-toed boots.

An acrid odor like burned rubber pervaded the air. Tacky, siding-covered frame houses spread up from the river and the mills, carpeting the hillside; a plague of siding salesmen had descended on this land, leaving in its wake a desolation of phony brick, imitation wood, and false stone.

The streetcar ground to a stop at Harrison Street, just beyond the entrance to the Carnegie steel mill. The workers got off and hurried across the narrow bridge to the mill gate.

As the car started up again, Akiba realized he was alone. He began to think about the day he had first met Buddy Hall. He had been in Cervino's store and had bought candy; another boy was there, a blond boy with very light eyes. And now, even as the streetcar rocketed forward, Akiba was moving back in time. He could see the boy clearly. He had been crying. His face was streaked with tears. After Akiba had left the store, another boy, a Greenfield kid, had approached him: John Strahan! Extraordinary. The three of them had come together for the first time on the sidewalk in front of old man Cervino's store so many years before.

Strahan had taunted him, called him dirty Jew, snatched the cap from his head. Akiba had tried to get away, but Strahan blocked his path.

And then the blond boy had come rushing from the store; he had thrown himself against Strahan and knocked him to the ground. They fought; Strahan had been beaten. It was Buddy Hall and he had just entered Akiba Moldavan's life.

Yet there was something else about that day. Something else had happened. Akiba fought to remember it. He could not. In his mind's eye he could see Strahan retreating toward Colfax School, and—and—

What? He could not remember. It's important, it's at the root, he now told himself. He could not remember.

The streetcar shot past the mill sections of Whitaker and Homeville; the banks of the Monongahela were glutted with black mills: Carnegie Illinois, Bethlehem Steel, U.S. Steel, Mesta Machine; ingot, bar steel, and pig-iron mills. Kennywood Park and the skeleton ribs of its roller coasters came into view.

Akiba moved to the front doors of the car. Outside it was snowing lightly. Approaching a curve, the streetcar slowed and now plaster clown faces, giraffe and elephant heads rotated out of the night. The streetcar came to a stop at the darkened entrance to Kennywood Amusement Park.

The doors opened and he moved out into the night. The streetcar glided away, trailing sparks along its guide wire.

Akiba looked around. The area was deserted. Across from the entrance to the amusement park, the Blue Mill Café, a wooden building with a series of gabled roofs, was dark and shuttered. Beyond it, up the hill, was a cluster of old houses.

Was it here that Buddy Hall had been living, Akiba thought, this strange, lonely area, opposite a closed-down amusement park? And where was he now? Above him on the hill? Insane, murderous, watching Akiba from the dark? What would he say? What would he do?

There was a sound behind Akiba. He turned, startled. Someone stepped from the shadowed entrance to the park.

It was Julie Tripp.

They walked through the darkened amusement park and did not talk for a long time. Akiba could feel the tension and despair in the girl beside him. He wanted to say something comforting, but no words would come.

She was extraordinarily lovely, delicate, with skin so white it seemed almost translucent. Her eyes were a very pale blue and it occurred to Akiba what a spectacular couple she and Buddy Hall must have made. It was the eyes, a particularly lustrous quality, a shade of blue he had never before seen.

She was wearing a thin cotton coat and the wind, gusting through the deserted park, caused her to shiver. She hurried along, trying to keep warm.

She led him through the park and Akiba had no idea where he was going.

Metal signs creaked, banged against shuttered fronts; canvas flaps snapped in the wind like gunshots.

The concrete path curved its tortuous way through the park, and it seemed to Akiba he was moving into Kabbalah.

"He called me, you see, and he said he was in the fun house, and—" They were near a small man-made lake. The water had been drained. From where they stood they could see the boarded-up merry-go-round building. "I just didn't know what to do, so I called you."

"Did you see him?"

"Yes. I came to the fun house yesterday. He was just—

he was crazy—and he mentioned your name and I had no one to turn to—"

"Mentioned my name? In what way?"

"It was just a crazy jumble of things. He said he was leaving town. A man was supposed to contact me with money for him."

They moved around the empty lake toward the fun house. Akiba felt that each shadow held the possibility of Buddy Gray Eyes and he was afraid. Signs groaned in the wind, Dipsy Doodle, Cat-A-Piller, Bump-A-Ride ghosts.

They entered the fun house along the plank walkway. "Buddy!" Julie called out, her voice echoing in the darkness of the fun house.

"Bud!" Akiba shouted.

Julie threw the light switch; the mirrored room was suddenly bright with light.

Something moved from behind one of the mirrors: a rat, its sleek coat the color of slate, pinpoint eyes burning in the white light, scurried forward. It turned and its reflection turned, a room of rats reflected in the surrounding mirrors. Akiba stomped his foot and the rat scooted off into the dark tunnel behind them.

"Bud," Julie called out again. He did not appear.

They left the fun house and moved through the park. "I don't know what to do," Julie said. "I don't know where he'll go. I don't know where I'll go."

Akiba wanted to reassure her in some way but he could say nothing. She was so fragile, so vulnerable. He had an impulse to take her in his arms, to comfort and protect her; he grew embarrassed at the thought. He felt awkward, inept, foolish.

The tracks of a roller coaster, the Thunderbolt, dived into a deep hollow in front of them. Akiba peered down, watched the snow drifting between the tracks; he felt as though he was moving with the sweep of the tracks, swooping, sinking. He pulled back, dizzy. "I used to ride this with Buddy," he said. "I don't know how I did it. He'd get in the backseat and stand up and wave his arms. I liked that about him. He was never afraid of anything."

"I liked that, too," Julie said. She drew her coat about her, trying to keep warm.

"When you saw him yesterday, did he talk about the old man?"

"Yes. He said the old man held something over him—"

"Held something over him? What?"

"He didn't say. It was just craziness, rambling—"

"Why did he kill a harmless, kind old man? Why?" Akiba said.

She shook her head. "I don't know. I just—he had become empty, like a shell. I saw it coming, but—he had been on drugs and then he got off them and I thought everything was going to be fine—"

"But why kill this particular man?"

"I don't know."

"Did he ever talk about him before yesterday?"

"Once, a long time ago. After his mother died, he was in very bad shape and he would ramble on about her and he told me a story, I don't know, it made no sense. He had had a pet that died, then something about his mother and the old man who owned the candy store across from the school. He told it as though it had been a bad dream. He would go off like that and you never knew what was real and what was a nightmare."

"You said he mentioned me. What did he say?"

"He talked about—he called it The Destroyer. Akiba and The Destroyer. He talked about you all the time. He had told me you were a rabbi."

"Yes."

She smiled. "I've never met a rabbi before. Buddy was the first Jew I had ever met."

They stood staring down into the hollow for a while, watching the snow. Akiba's mind was racing with possibilities. "He mentioned The Destroyer?" Akiba said. "This was yesterday?"

"Yes. He said The Destroyer made him do it."

"What else?"

"He said something about Kabbalah—"

"Kabbalah? What about Kabbalah?"

"He would always talk about it. You, Kabbalah, The Destroyer—this whole crazy jumble of things. He and this friend, Alex, would have these charts and drawings. It was just all drug madness. He had a tattoo done on him just after his mother died, a figure of a bearded man with arms and legs outstretched—"

The stick figure Buddy had drawn in his journal, the golem! "Was there anything, a word, in the tattoo?"

" 'Meth.' "

"You're sure it's 'meth'?"

"Yes. Yes. I'm sure."

"Not 'emeth'?"

"It was 'meth' because I thought it had something to do with a drug, methedrine, which they call 'meth' on the street."

Akiba suddenly broke away from her and moved to the end of the walk. When he turned back to Julie, his face was flushed and he was trembling. His look was wild, agonized. " 'He is dead,' " Akiba said. "The name of a thing is its essence."

Julie stared at him with alarm. "I don't understand—"

" 'Meth'! It's the Hebrew word meaning 'He is dead,' 'Death.' He's tattooed himself with 'Death'!"

He moved back to Julie Tripp, fighting to control himself. "There is much in the world that is incomprehensible. There is the body of the world, and its soul. We only see the body. I'm not talking about voodoo spirits, cult metaphysics—"

He stood there trembling, fighting to make sense to her, to himself. "God is Knowledge, that which Knows, and that which is Known. They are all One. And there are paths to this Knowledge—"

He realized his voice had shrilled out of control. He was

trembling violently now and he could not stop. Julie Tripp stared at him, stunned, bewildered. How to convey a vision of the inexplicable? he thought. How do you explain He who encompasses Everything and therefore is No-Thing? God's Hidden Face? How to convey to her Kabbalah? "I must get to him," he said, and he meant Buddy Gray Eyes, but also something deeper, more mysterious.

"He said you'd know what to do—"

"He told you that?"

"Yes."

He took her hand, squeezed it hard. "I'm going to find him. I promise you. I'm going to discover why he did this thing." Her eyes were wide and frightened and he knew he must do this, as much for her as for himself.

"Where did he say he was going?"

"New York, then California. He said this man, Alex, would take care of him."

"Where will he go in New York?"

"He had an old girl friend there. And a man by the name of Earl. They had been in California: Alex, Earl, Adele. Earl and Adele went back to New York. They were all very close at one time."

"All right," Akiba said. "All right." He was breathing hard now, as though he had run a great distance. It was freezing cold out yet he was drenched with perspiration.

"Can you save him?" Julie said.

"It's not so simple. It depends on what you mean by 'save.'"

He continued to hold her hand. He led her toward the exit.

They hurried along the dark and twisting paths of the park, moved through swirling snow.

Could he save himself, Akiba Moldavan was thinking. For all about him, *tohu*, emptiness, raged.

# 11

GRAY EYES prowled the whorehouse bars of Seventh Avenue in Homestead, paranoia trailing him wherever he went. He knew he must get to Shadman's, then leave town. He could get to New York, to Earl, and Earl would take care of him and then he would make it back to California and Alex.

Alex Zayas was radiant in his mind, a merciful angel. Alex would gather him in his arms and take care of him. Alex would understand. All energy flowed from Alex and to Alex.

The Coast, with its perpetual springtime, easy breezes, opalescent waters, salt-tart air, smooth, white, warm sand, would cleanse everything, make it all right. He would turn his life around. Again.

He must get to California.

Why, then, did he hesitate going to Mother Shadman's? There had been something in his old friend's tone when he had answered the phone that disturbed Gray Eyes, a certain tension. He must have found out about the old man. And if he did, what then would he do?

Everywhere Gray Eyes felt people watching him. He'd warm himself for a few minutes in a bar, feel eyes on him, and move on.

After meeting with Julie in the amusement park, the realization of where his life now was had come down hard on him. He had been seized by a loneliness immense and chilling, a loneliness that turned the world to ice.

Everything had been destroyed, his coming back to Pittsburgh, his plans for change.

His whole being seemed composed of regret. Not over the killing of the old man: no, that was necessary and right. It had to be done, an ancient debt owed by him to the old man.

No, the regret he felt was for his whole life, regret that he had ever been born. The killing was a footnote to regret, not regret itself. My life is nothing—and at the bottom of the page: an old man dead.

He walked along a cobblestone street opposite black mills. Snowflakes delicate as feathers brushed his face. Several mill workers huddled on the corner under the rusting wrought-iron balcony of the Homestead Hotel. A young prostitute in a mini-skirt, gold platform shoes, ratty fake-fur coat, stood in the cold bargaining with the men; ringlets of blond hair framed her tiny, painted-doll's face. She reminded Gray Eyes of Julie, that same used, lost quality.

Suddenly he saw his mother's face in his mind's eye. She was dying. Her mouth gaped as she fought for air, and then he saw a dying chick and it, too, gasped for air, and then Julie, her mouth open, struggling for breath, trying not to cry.

Why hadn't he been able to explain things to her when he had seen her? He had meant to, had meant to tell her all about his mother, about the old man, but it seemed to him, there in the fun house, that the *world was the fun house*, all of it warped, fun house mirrors, everything distorted—not just the room they stood in, but *everything*.

He had intended to explain to her about the old man, then cut away from her clean. But he had not realized how fierce the bond was to her. To sever it was like cutting flesh.

What to do? Risk going back to her now, take her with

him to California, or visit Mother Shadman as he had planned? He must cut her loose, he told himself. Otherwise he would destroy her. Yes, he must cut her loose, reach Shadman, make it to New York, then California.

He must finally get to California.

In the railroad yard beyond the mills the long, low bellow of a diesel train sounded.

He hurried along the cobblestone street, moving past slat-board buildings, nailed-up houses with walls of peeling paint.

He thought of Akiba Moldavan. He had wanted to visit him. What would he look like? How would they get along together? Would they play chess and pool? Would Akiba regale him with stories?

And what would he say about the death of Cervino? Gray Eyes would explain to him about the dreams he had been having, about the stained-glass windows in the Beth Shalom Synagogue, ancient hands forming a bridge. In one dream an old man was standing in front of him. He had a long beard; his hands were tented at his lips, the hands in the stained-glass window. The man was looking at him with blank eyes. The man had appointed him, without articulating it, The Destroyer.

And so he had gone to Cervino. He would not tell Akiba why. That mystery would remain buried in the bloody coffer of his soul.

In front of him now another prostitute moved out of the doorway of a boarded-up building, a black girl with bleached platinum hair. She wore sunglasses and thick white pancake makeup on her face. She turned to Gray Eyes and his heart jumped.

She is my future staring at me, he thought. A bleached future, grotesque. He pushed on by her. She licked her tongue over her lips and made a soft, hissing sound.

He continued on. Where can I hide, he thought, where in the world? I should reach Mother Shadman. A brutal disquietude stirred within him. Still, if not to Shadman, to whom? Where?

At the corner a taxi, the motor running, was parked in front of a run-down tavern. The outside wall of the place, the Rustic Bar and Grill, was covered with false brick siding, cracked, the asphalt composition within exposed. The driver of the taxi dozed behind the wheel.

Gray Eyes got into the backseat. The driver started awake. "Take me to Mills Avenue in Braddock," Gray Eyes said.

On the bridge across the Monongahela the driver talked about his son: "He's seventeen years old and he can't keep his hands off his own mother. He doesn't have a girl friend so he uses my wife, kisses her arm, says, 'Mom, what a nice body you got.' My wife, she got so upset she stabbed him with a fork. And then she feels bad and she kisses him all over."

"A mother shouldn't act that way," Gray Eyes said.

"Ah," said the cab driver, "don't you see? You and I are from the old school."

The front room at Mother Shadman's house was empty except for a solitary black man sleeping in a chair. He had a fedora pulled down over his forehead. Gray Eyes started up the stairs to the second floor.

He felt eyes on the back of his head and he stopped halfway up the stairs. The black man was awake, staring up at him. The black man said softly, "It weren't me that done it, man."

"Done what?"

"You know the game, baby, you want to pitch, you got to catch," the black man said languidly.

Gray Eyes heard the sound of footsteps moving along the hallway above and he started back down the stairs. "Cut and run, champ!" the black yelled and Gray Eyes leaped the stairs and bolted for the front door.

He hit the door and almost took it off its hinges, then

vaulted the porch railing. Coming off the curb onto the cobblestones, he heard footsteps slamming down the porch stairs. "Buddy, it's me! John Strahan! I want to talk to you!"

He looked over his shoulder. A man was moving at a run down the walk, his nylon windbreaker flapping open, revolvers in both hands. Gray Eyes was seized by an incredible feeling of distortion, fun house mirror feeling, the sense that a man in his dreams had burst into his reality.

It was Strahan, his schoolmate Strahan, older now, his hair thinning, a bit heavier—but Strahan nevertheless. What was Strahan doing here, chasing him, hands flashing blue of revolver steel? Fun house mirror.

It was as though he had just seen Strahan, had been jogging across Allderdice High football field, and Strahan had moved up behind him and cut him down; it was as though it had only been yesterday—yet it had been more than ten years. He had changed, but in ways so subtle that Buddy Gray Eyes would have been at a loss to explain them. A thickening, that was all—a vague spreading out, a warped perspective. Fun house mirror.

Akiba, Strahan, and old man Cervino—a knot of his past, twining back thick and tight to some distant point where it all began.

This all came to him in a flash and with it came a panic that sent Gray Eyes racing down the street, toward the mill.

"Buddy!"

A gunshot sound cracked the icy air, then two more. Gray Eyes hunched low to the ground, junked from side to side. There were 150 feet between him and Strahan; he'd outrun him any day, any field, he told himself. No way Strahan could catch him.

In his mind's eye Gray Eyes was streaking down the Allderdice High School practice field, late afternoon of an autumn day, the field hard and oily beneath his feet, and

John Strahan out to do him in, pounding after him, out to wreck his leg!

There was a low concrete wall and a wire fence and Gray Eyes was up over both of them in a motion so easy and fluid that it surprised even him.

He's a cop, John Strahan's a cop, and he's trying to kill me. Ah, knot of the past, knot to the beginning.

Another gunshot ripped the night. Another miss.

A narrow labyrinth cut at wild and ridiculous angles through the heavy black mill buildings: a slag pile, a heap of pig iron, steel shavings, coal. The sulfur smell of the place burned in his lungs. He saw an opening at the end of the labyrinth.

Strahan's footsteps had softened now, a distant pitter-patter behind him.

And then his knee went, the injured knee, Strahan's ancient damage, and he went down on the concrete. As he got to his feet, another shot cracked at him and he felt as though someone had sliced his upper arm with a knife.

He stumbled and limped up a short concrete ramp and threw himself over a low wall. Catching his leg on some chicken wire, he went sprawling on cobblestone, but was immediately up and, hunching low, headed for a storage yard filled with sheds, girders, machinery.

Gray Eyes hit the wire gate and scampered over it. Across the goal line. Touchdown.

He lay low in a large drainage pipe for a while. He could hear Strahan's voice calling to him in the distance; it moved off in the other direction, grew faint, then stopped.

He picked at the palm of his hand. Small hairlike splinters of slag were embedded there from his fall. Next he examined his arm. There was almost no blood. The bullet had carved a gash into it, exposing pink and white flesh.

He made his way down the drainage pipe to a concrete walk at the river's edge. He hurried along the walk to a metal footbridge that linked the Braddock mill with another mill across the river.

He followed the bridge to the other side. At the entrance to the mill he could make out a figure in the gatehouse, one of the mill guards.

He turned from the mill and moved at a half run up a steep cobblestone street. The snow had started again and was coming down fast, stinging his face with hard, ricelike granules.

The mill town—it must have been Duquesne—was silent, sleeping.

He saw at the end of the block the red neon sign of a tavern, STAN KUSCO BAR, and he fled toward it. He entered breathless, damp with snow.

Inside everything appeared limp and tattered. A Polish dance was just winding down. Crepe paper streamers littered the floor. A large silver ball spun from the ceiling, sending out slivers of reflected light. A trio—accordion, guitar, drums—plodded through a weary polka.

Gray Eyes stood by the door watching the dancers revolve slowly around the room, spinning in counter-motion to the silver ball rotating from the ceiling. It all seemed a dream, smoky and unreal, bizarre contrasts, absurd combinations: women in long gowns, men in workshirts; tall men with dumpy women, straight-backed, aristocratic-looking women with shrimpy men. An elderly woman in a mini-skirt and high cowboy boots, a man in maroon jacket and white shoes; another woman in a yellow pants suit; a man, extraordinarily tall, with a ferocious lantern jaw, elegant in a white ice cream suit; a dark-haired, lovely girl in a black ballet dress dancing with a ratty-looking man in striped wash-and-wear suit.

Everyone seemed to know everyone else. Some of the men looked like off-duty cops—or perhaps firemen. A husky man standing beneath an exit sign was staring at him.

He turned to leave and a fat lady in a bright red dress blocked his way.

Perspiring heavily, her eyes barely focused, she caught at Gray Eyes and pulled him to her and then he was on the dance floor, clopping around in a clumsy polka. They spun about the room. The pace of the dance increased. The woman smelled of perfume and sweat. She rolled her eyes and laughed loudly, stomped her feet while emitting yelps in Polish. "*Dobri, dobri,*" she cried over and over.

Then the music stopped. The fat woman leaned on Gray Eyes. A smear of blood from his wound came off on her dress, but she was soaked with perspiration and the blood on the red dress appeared as sweat.

He tried to get out of her grasp. A short man, his face flushed with alcohol, came to them.

"My husband," the woman said. She hugged herself closer to Gray Eyes.

"What's your name?" the husband asked.

"Jim Smith."

"Hey, long time!" the husband said, hitching up his trousers.

The woman called over to another man, a fat man in a T-shirt. "Andy, you know Jim here, don't you?"

"Hey, Jim," Andy said warmly.

The three of them whooped over this unexpected meeting, tugged and pulled at Gray Eyes. They were under the impression he was a Jim Smith they had known from McKeesport. They had supposed he was dead. "We heard it was lung cancer," the fat man said.

The fat man in the T-shirt insisted they all celebrate Jim Smith's resurrection at another tavern. They tripped toward the door, pulling Gray Eyes along. "*Julayda, Julayda, you are my honey, Julayda, Julayda, I've got lots of money . . .*" the fat man in the T-shirt sang, performing a quick polka turn and hop.

Then they were out in the cold night air, skipping and hopping along the cobblestone street, dragging Gray Eyes with them.

His arm did not hurt and Gray Eyes was thankful for

that. He had stained all three of them with his blood, but no one seemed to notice it.

They went several blocks and then they were at another tavern, Uncle Bela's Gypsy Club.

The tavern was one wide, drab room, empty of people except for two tattooed men in sleeveless undershirts sitting at the bar, a large bleached blond, and a short, bearded man with sharp, dark features at a table.

The place smelled of beer and disinfectant.

The blond got up and escorted them to a booth against the wall. She and the fat woman's husband joked in Hungarian. "Keep out of trouble, you hear?" the fat woman's husband called to the men at the bar. They grinned. Neither man had front teeth. "I've locked them both up more times than I can count," the fat woman's husband said.

"Rudy's a cop," the fat woman said. "You knew that, didn't you, Jim?"

"Oh, sure," Gray Eyes said.

Rudy reached under his sports jacket and brought out a .38 police special. He pointed it at Gray Eyes. "Bang-bang, Jim," he said. Everyone laughed.

Rudy ordered boilermakers for all, and when they arrived made a rambling, mostly incoherent toast to Jim Smith's miraculous recovery from lung cancer.

Then he began yelling for Bela to get the show on the road. He waved his revolver in the air to demonstrate he meant business.

The fat woman said Bela was a genius. She pointed to an accordion on a chair where a small bandstand had been erected at one end of the room. "He'll make that fucker sound like an eighty-piece orchestra," the fat woman said.

"I like Bela's music better than Montovani," her husband said. He continued to wave his revolver in the air. "Hey, Bela, get the show on the road. Where's the dancer?"

"In the crapper," one of the men at the bar yelled back.

"Wait till you see this one," the blond said, arriving at the table with another round of drinks. "A hippy."

"What are you doing with a hippy?" the fat woman said.

"Does she have big tits?" the fat man in the T-shirt said.

"Hey, Bela, get this show on the road!" Rudy yelled.

Bela, the dark, bearded man, rose from his table and started toward the bandstand. He wore a blue plush suit, tan platform shoes, and very thick eyeglasses. The bleached blond moved behind a set of drums.

Bela launched into an elaborate introduction as though the room was filled to capacity. Then he and the blond played a rickety version of "Lady of Spain." "Eighty-piece orchestra. Didn't I tell you?" the fat woman said.

"Play something by Montovani," her husband yelled.

Bela grinned and perspired and continued on with "Lady of Spain."

When he had finished, he gazed around the room through eyeglasses thick as Coke bottle bottoms and launched into another flowery introduction, this time for Milena, the gypsy dancer.

Gray Eyes probed at his arm. The bleeding had stopped.

The dancer, dressed in a diaphanous turquoise costume, had black hair and a fleshy body. She had a round, pretty face. She danced barefoot, throwing her body about the stage in a swirling approximation of a gypsy dance. No one seemed very interested.

Zombielike, the girl undulated, gazing into the lights with a flat, dead look. She completed a spin and then she saw Gray Eyes. She began to perform her act to him, staring at him with an eerie emptiness. She shook and gyrated toward him, her movements slow, viscous, without feeling. She completed three numbers and did not take her eyes from him.

The show ended. Rudy asked for the check, then began to argue with the blond. The check included a cover charge because they had sat at a table.

After he had paid he leveled his revolver at Gray Eyes. "You're under arrest," he said.

"What for?"

"Beating the rap. The Big C." He laughed and hugged Gray Eyes, kissed him wetly on the side of the face.

When the three had left, the gypsy dancer joined him at the table. She had changed into two-tone jeans and a jersey. Stenciled on the front of the jersey was the word GREED.

"Like the act?" the dancer said.

"Oh, yeah."

"Shake and bake." She lit a cigarette and stared at him with empty eyes. "There's a lot of wild shit around, heavy-duty stuff," she said.

"For sure."

"For sure. There's stuff the government won't even tell us. A lot of stuff is killing us. Lasers."

"Uh-huh."

"They want to encourage a consumer society. They want you and me buying aspirins and deodorants and Kotex, those fucks." Her voice was as dead as her eyes. "They feed it to us on television. Lasers. Lasers of fear. It's fantastic the way they control the world. You know, babe, the shit's on the doorstep and we're stepping in it all the time."

Gray Eyes was exhausted. His body felt drained, and deep within him a cold, cold feeling gnawed at him, seemed to be burrowing into his bones.

He would need to rest before he ran some more.

"What are you floating on?" the dancer said, staring emptily at him.

"I'm just a little worn out."

"I know what you mean. You've been spinning your record too fast."

"Uh-huh."

"I spin my record at its proper speed. My gynecologist told me I got the organs of someone ten years younger. And I'm only twenty-two."

"Can we go someplace?" Gray Eyes said. "I need to lie down."

"Who can resist Oliver Twist?" she said. She took a long, slow drag on her cigarette, kept her dead eyes focused on him. "What's a heavy dude like you doing in this sleazoid scene, babe?"

"Just come in out of the cold."

"Definitely. What's your name?"

"Jim."

"I'm Tracy. They call me Milena here. That was the girl used to work here. I adopted it as a nom-de-fucking-plume. Jim what?"

"Smith."

She laughed. It was an empty laugh and not attractive. "You may even be Jack-the-fucking-Ripper, but I'm your match." She got up and disappeared into the kitchen. Gray Eyes waited. She did not return for a long time. He had decided she had left by a rear exit when she came back into the room wearing a full-length hooded coat. "Come on, babe. Shake and bake," she said, and he followed her out of the place.

They climbed the cobblestone hill in silence. It was very cold out now. The snow had abated. Their breath fogged up in the crystal air.

Gray Eyes began to shiver violently, attacked by a ferocious chill. He couldn't stop quaking. Tracy, the gypsy dancer, eyed him without concern out of the corner of her gaze, coolly, watchfully.

She lived in a separate building behind a two-story wooden house. The building, a garage at one time, had been converted at little expense into an apartment.

Inside it felt colder than out. Gray Eyes could not stop shivering. He laughed and tried to control the quaking, but it would not let up. Tracy turned on a large gas wall heater. The red spread of flame from the heater was the only light on the room. "I'll make some tea," she said.

She filled a pot of water and snapped on a two-burner hot plate. While she waited for the water to boil, she lit some candles. The room was decorated with beads, dried flowers, dolls. It heated up quickly. Gray Eye's shivering subsided. "Never had anything like that," he said.

She smiled. "Oh, really?"

Gray Eyes seated himself on the bed. It was a water bed and he swayed and the water sloshed around and he felt ill. "Say, are you a junky?" the girl said.

"No. I just need some rest."

"I can dig a junky. Or a narc. Something sexy about a cop. I went with a cop once. He wanted to marry me."

She turned on the television set. There was an electronic ping-pong game circuited through the set. "Cute, huh?"

"Nice."

She offered him some wine. He declined. She lit up a marijuana cigarette and passed it to him. He waved it away.

"You want to sleep? Is that it?" she said.

"I can't sleep."

"Bad dreams?"

"Oh, they're all right."

They played electronic ping-pong, which she was very good at. He couldn't win a game. "Let's play strip pong," she said after a while. "Like strip poker only it's strip pong."

They played and Gray Eyes lost consistently. When he took off his shirt she looked at the gash in his arm. "What's that?" she said.

"Cut myself shaving."

"A bullet done that," she said. "I know all about those things."

She noticed the tattoo on his chest. "Hey, we match," she said, taking off her jersey. Above her left breast she had a sloppy tattoo of a dagger with the word EVIL through it; above her right breast, a dollar sign.

She turned Gray Eyes toward the mirror and admired the artwork on their bodies. "What does a person do with this little booger?" she asked, tracing her fingers over Gray Eyes's stick figure tattoo.

"You touch him anyplace and see where it leads you."

"You a meth freak?" she said, touching the word.

"No."

"Who is the little booger?"

"He's my carbon copy. You know we all have a carbon copy somewhere. It exists in another world."

"I heard that somewhere."

"It's like if you kill a person in this world, in another world you missed him."

"Yeah, I heard that. I shot someone once," she said. "A nigger. The dude tried to turn me out. If I'm going to be a whore, I don't need a nigger mack."

"Did you kill him?"

"No."

"Well, in another world you did kill him."

"I hope so. He messed up my whole life. That was back home. I had this really neat apartment and all and I had to split town. Every pimp in the city was after me. Hey, I'll tell you one thing: if I turned out, I could be one definitely fine whore. You know what I'd do? I'd put my hair in pigtails and shave my beaver and pass myself off as a little girl. There's a lot of perverted old guys who go for little girls like that. Heads of big corporations. They love a scalped beaver." She kissed his tattoo. "Where will this little booger lead me?" she said.

"Where you from?"

"Davenport. Iowa."

"He'll take you to Davenport."

She grew thoughtful. "I have a kid back there somewheres," she said. "I got involved with this nigger dude there and he gave me a kid. And that's the for sure truth."

"I know it."

"And I had to give the kid up. You know, this nigger dude he'd get an attitude and beat the shit out of me. He wanted to turn me out. I took his gun and shot the dude. The cops traded me off—tit for tat. And that's the definite truth." She displayed a large brown birthmark on her upper back. "My mother used to tell me my father was Harry Belafonte," she said, indicating the birthmark. "I never knew my real father and that's the truth."

Gray Eyes did not say anything. "You don't believe me. That's the truth," Tracy said.

They played a few more games of pong. Gray Eyes was naked. Tracy took off her remaining clothes and began to suck on him. She stared at him all the while.

"What are you looking at?" he said.

"I like to watch you watching me." She got up and took a pair of handcuffs out of the nightstand drawer. "They're real," she said. "I had this narc boyfriend. Can I put them on you?" Tracy said.

He smiled slowly and shook his head, no, thinking how the world was taunting him: guns, handcuffs, Strahan. His arm ached where the bullet had sliced it.

"Put them on me," she said, her eyes bright with interest for the first time that night.

He cuffed her hands behind her and locked them together.

"Now fuck me," she said. They made love and it was indifferent to Gray Eyes.

"I'm tired," he said after a while.

"That's all right, babe," she said. She lost circulation in her arms and they had to stop and unlock the cuffs.

She started to doze off. Gray Eyes studied himself in the mirror. The small man on his chest seemed to be laughing. He slapped his hand over his heart. The laughing stopped.

"What?" Tracy said, through half-closed eyes.

"Do you have a car?"

"No."

"I need to take a trip," he said.

"You're a junky and you need to score."

"See any tracks on me?"

"Maybe you take it under the tongue. Let me look at your tongue." He stuck out his tongue and she examined it. "Maybe in your dick," she said.

He dozed off for a short while. His mother was alive, kissing him. They kissed passionately, then he realized he was kissing a man: Cervino.

He jolted awake. He got up and by the light of the glowing heater began to dress. He realized Tracy was not asleep. She was watching him. "I got to get to New York," he said.

"What's in New York?"

"Some good friends. I have to pay them a visit, then I'm heading for the Coast."

"Take me with you," she said.

"What for?"

"I touched that little booger you got on your chest. I want to see where he'll lead me."

She told him of a car they could boost and he took a hanger from the closet. Downstairs he slipped the hanger between the rubber and glass, hooked the lock button, and opened the door. The car was an old Caddy and he had no trouble getting behind the ignition and jumping the wires.

As they drove across the bridge heading away from Duquesne, she displayed a small revolver. "Cute, huh? Smith and Wesson Centennial."

"What do you got that for?"

She shrugged. "It belonged to my boyfriend. Undercovers use them." She held it up for him to see better. "Enclosed hammer. They can shoot right through their pockets and the lining won't catch on the hammer."

The sight of the gun sickened him. "Put it away," he said.

She looked hurt. "We could blow away some fucks with this," she said. "Don't you like to have a good time?"

They drove onto the parkway leading out of the city. "This is going to be some fun, babe! Shake and bake," she said, bouncing in the seat. "Which way?"

"Get off the next exit and we'll take Route Thirty."

"You're running, aren't you, Jim?"

"My name's not Jim."

"No?"

"I'm Buddy Gray Eyes."

"Gray Eyes? That's cute," she said. "Well, you're out of time, for sure, Buddy Gray Eyes."

"What's that supposed to mean?"

She laughed, still bouncing. "You know the song?" She sang in a flat voice: "*Yes, you are; yes, you are / You're so out of it you're on a star. / Baby, baby, baby, you're out of time.*"

"Hey."

"Really."

The road ahead was empty, icy, cold white under the gooseneck parkway lamps. Gusts of snow buffeted the car.

"All I'm going to miss is my pong game and my water bed," Tracy said. "All the rest is no big deal." She sang in empty exultation: "*You're out of touch my baby / my poor discarded baby, / I say baby, baby, baby, you're out of time.*"

# PART 2

# 12

AKIBA MOLDAVAN couldn't remember when he had seen as much snow. It blew in against the bus window in thick waves. The Greyhound moved at a crawl, overtaking trailer trucks, campers, cars stranded by the side of the road. Huge bulldozers appeared from time to time out of the snow, lurching, grinding, bucking in furious mechanical attempts to clear the turnpike.

It was an impossible task. The snow was a deluge making gray ghosts of everything.

"Look at that," the man next to him said. "Damn." He was a thin black, immaculate in freshly pressed suit, starched white shirt, burgundy tie. He was drinking Wild Turkey from a pint bottle. "I got to be in Yonkers, New York, by one P.M. Funeral."

"You might make it," Akiba said. It was not yet dawn.

"I might make it," the black man agreed. "Then again I might not." He offered Akiba a sip from his bottle. Akiba hesitated, then accepted.

The bus was packed full. The airport had been closed and people with pressing affairs in New York, though desirous of wings, had been forced to settle for wheels.

It was a curious crowd: a few obvious businessmen, but many strange-looking types, vague deep night hustlers who seemed desperate for flight. Burned-out hookers? Dope dealers? Was it a plague of crazies or just average folk expressing their creativity?

Since leaving Pittsburgh Akiba Moldavan's anxiety had increased. Thoughts of Kabbalah held him thrall. Everywhere he saw images of the *Sephirot:* in forms of skeletal trees along the road, ice patterns on the window.

Into what was he entering, what zone of hopelessness?

Julie Tripp had told him all she knew of the two people Buddy Hall would seek out. Akiba had formed an idea of them: vicious types without conscience, nihilistic, dangerous.

Adele Morath, an ex-model, had introduced Buddy Hall to heroin and pseudorevolutionary madness; Earl had been an ex-con, dope dealer, part of Alex Zayas's California group. They had returned to the East Coast together. Julie Tripp had no idea where they could be found.

And so Akiba Moldavan had flung himself out into the brutal *tohu* night to search for them, and through them, to find Buddy Gray Eyes.

The black man next to Akiba drained the bottle of Wild Turkey and reached into a paper sack under his seat for another. He offered the first swallow to Akiba. "Just look on me as a Saint Bernard dog leading us through the North Pole," he said.

Akiba, whose drinking was confined to an occasional nip with the old-timers at the synagogue after Sabbath services, was feeling the effects of the liquor.

"I hope I'm not imposing," the black man said, "but is there a particular reason you're wearing that hat?"

"It's not a hat, it's a beret," Akiba said. "And I'm wearing it because I'm Jewish."

The black grinned. "All right," he said. "*Mazel tov. Good yuntiff. Chob nischt can kahach.*" He waved his Wild Turkey in the air. "I speak the *mama-loshen,* you see. Thirty years I worked for Mrs. Saperstein up on Murdock Street. You know Mrs. Saperstein?"

Akiba had to admit he didn't. "Fine woman. We was

like *mishpachah*. When she died it was like one of my own." The black man sighed. "I'm goin' to bury my son. Spic stuck a knife in his heart."

"I'm sorry."

The black man stared at his bottle. "*Meshugga*. I tol' that boy that New York was no place for him, that them spics there would just bring him grief and sadness. They get you all full of dope, you know, and they just bring sadness to a person. He wouldn't listen." The black man sighed. "*Chob nischt can kahach*," he said. *I don't have any strength*. He brushed a tear from his eye, blew his nose in a large white handkerchief. "Whew!" he said after a long swallow of Wild Turkey. "*Shicker as a goy!*" He laughed loud and long, then grew serious again. "What can you say about a son who gets himself stabbed to death, Rabbi? I mean, what did God have in his mind?"

"He works on a level we cannot comprehend," Akiba said, knowing his answer was woefully inadequate.

"But is there a reason?"

"There is a design. We must try to discover that design, try to come close to God, imitate his actions in the world."

"You mean kill for no reason? Is that what you mean by imitate his actions?"

Akiba's head was foggy from the alcohol. "This is all a test. We are given a choice. And when we do the godly thing, we affect God. We reach Him. That's what this all is—reaching toward God."

"But what for? I don't mean to be disrespectful, *Rebbe*, but what the *fuck* for?"

"There is a reason for your son's death. God wants something from him and He wants something from you—even as He wants something from me. And—and—"

"I hope there was a reason, 'cause if there weren't, this whole thing is a raw deal, that's for shit sure, excuse the expression."

"We are in prison," Akiba said. He realized he was drunk. "Yet there is a glorious, unbearably beautiful light shining toward us from a magnificent palace. We see a faint glimmer from that light. We see, then we don't. And if we break out of the prison—the light might disappear for us altogether. But it is there! And—and—the light shining from that palace—is—the weakest, most ordinary light in the palace. And yet if we could see it—!"

He was talking to himself. The black man had fallen asleep.

Of course, Akiba thought. Raving again. Still, he knew he was near the heart of a great mystery, though he could not communicate what the mystery was. And he felt, yes, it would always be like this: the closer one came to the heart of that awesome, divine enigma, the more difficult it would be to communicate it. He would appear foolish and more foolish, the closer to God he came, until at last, when he was like Izzie, the moron, he would be truly with God.

The bus ground its way through the churning snow. People grew quiet. The black man next to Akiba Moldavan snored softly, his mouth open.

Akiba watched the snow, thinking: Out there is a vortex, and within the vortex is imprisoned a great secret. The snow danced and whirled beyond the window and Akiba tried to project his mind into the snow. If he could just concentrate sufficiently, he would plunge to the heart of the night and snow and all would be revealed.

It was nearly two in the afternoon when the bus pulled into the terminal on the West Side of Manhattan. New York was at a crawl, everything subdued, buried in snow.

The snow was still falling.

There was no possibility of getting a taxicab. He walked up Eighth Avenue toward where the old Madison Square Garden had once been. It was gone, of course, as well as the cafeteria that had occupied the corner opposite the Garden. He crossed over to Broadway.

The snow had soaked through his shoes. Before leaving he had returned home only to pick up his *tallith*, *tefillin*, an electric razor, and a few items of clothing. He had neglected to take galoshes and his feet were wet and numb with cold. He had no gloves either and he kept his hands jammed down into his overcoat pockets.

He realized now he had thrust himself into this enterprise with no plan, no preparation. He would come to New York. He would allow the whirlwind of the *tohu* to sweep him to Buddy Gray Eyes.

Where should he start?

He turned east on Fifty-fifth. The wind sliced at him. Tears came to his eyes. His nose began to run. He had no handkerchief. He hunched down in his overcoat and hurried along Fifty-fifth Street.

When he and Buddy Gray Eyes had been sixteen years old, they had hitchhiked to New York; they had stayed at a hotel opposite the City Center. The idea came to him that this is where he should begin. The hotel would provide a link, albeit foolish, tenuous, to his old friend. By contacting an element of the past he would create a bridge to the future.

The hotel, the Griswald, had changed drastically. Akiba sensed it the moment he entered the narrow lobby. Once it had catered to a music crowd, symphony and ballet lovers who would come to the city for a few days, take their meals at the Russian Tea Room or the Automat on Fifty-seventh Street, and spend their time at Carnegie Hall and the City Center. In those days the Griswald was ripe with serious purpose, culture.

Akiba and Buddy had stayed there because it was possible to hustle chess games. They had remained a month in New York, the summer of their sixteenth year, hustling chess and pool.

At the end of July they moved their operation to Atlantic City where they were able to stay at the Traymore on the boardwalk and spend their days on the beach, their nights playing Ski-Ball in penny arcades, or wandering the Steel and Hammond piers.

The first sign to Akiba of change at the Griswald was the desk clerk. In the old days the clerks were mostly failed musicians, frazzled, slightly dotty. Now he was faced with a sullen thug, a swarthy, pockmarked Mediterranean—a Moroccan or Algerian, Akiba speculated.

He looked for the chess lounge to his right. It had been replaced by a dimly lit bar. Two hefty women, one white with a black wig, one black with a blond wig, sat in the lobby in hot pants and platform shoes, eyeing Akiba. As he moved to the elevator, the white girl made a soft kissing sound with her lips.

The room was pleasant enough, but he was distressed to discover that the television worked badly and the steam heat gave off a constant oppressive hiss. The bedspread, also, displayed more stains than good hygienic practice would seem to dictate.

He phoned Ruth. Her voice sounded tired and edged with tension. "Emmanuel Rose called this morning. He said you had a run-in with Frankenthal yesterday. Frankenthal is withdrawing his support from the institute unless Rose is put in charge. He called you, and I quote, 'a pompous madman.'"

"We all know that. Right?"

"Your father was very upset when he got off the phone."

The split in Akiba's life was clear; on one hand, the very real problem of his father and his institute; on the other, magic, metaphysics . . . madness.

What could he say to his father? That I am dedicating my existence to the redemption of a murderer? I am crawling toward the roots of Kabbalah and between Kabbalah and *teshubah* for Gray Eyes I will think about Rabbi Emmanuel Rose and the institute?

He told himself he should be occupied with what is concrete and real, yet his soul cried out for something more, a sacred purpose. "Put him on the phone," he said.

"I gave him a pill. He's sleeping. Then Hannah began to babble and I had to sedate her, too. All I do around here is give people pills." She said this without rancor, in a soft, weary voice.

"Do you think I'm a pompous madman?"

"What other reason was there to marry you? Handsome and rich you're not."

He wanted to tell her he loved her; he couldn't do it. It had always been that way with him: he just could not pronounce the words. "Ruthie," he said, "don't worry about me—"

"I am worried," she said.

"I know, but everything is all right. I'm fine."

"Just be careful."

"Yes."

"Are you wearing your galoshes?"

"No. I forgot them."

"Oh, Akiba. Please, please take care of yourself."

After he replaced the phone on its cradle he sat there for a moment feeling selfish and small, guilty.

He stretched out on the bed, stared at the ceiling. A network of cracks spread from the lighting fixture; they merged with smaller cracks, then the very texture of the paint.

"I must do this," he told himself.

He felt lost, foolish, uncomfortable in his own skin. Is there anyone in this world as ridiculous as I am? he asked himself.

"*I must do this*," he said aloud.

He unpacked his overnight bag, then performed the *minhah*, the afternoon prayers. During the nineteen benedictions, the *amidah*, he poured out his heart, particularly in the benedictions for repentance, for forgiveness, for redemption, for healing of the sick. He prayed for his father and sister. And he prayed for Buddy Gray Eyes.

Afterward he removed his damp clothes and draped

them over the back of a chair in front of the hissing radiator. He turned on the television and slid under the bedspread. The set was a jumble of lines, but the sound came in clear. A game show was in progress. He looked at the window. The snow was still coming down, a shifting, diagonal flow, the movement magical, hypnotic.

He slept and dreamed of the old days. He and Buddy were in Atlantic City walking down the boardwalk. A pretty girl in a diaphanous dress strolled by them and winked at Akiba. The breeze off the ocean was cool, salt-sharp, the sound of the ocean a soothing whisper. He loved his friend. In the dream it began to snow and everything looked inexpressibly lovely and he found himself thinking how extraordinary it was for there to be snow in the middle of August.

He awoke with a start. It was dark outside. In a panic he rushed to perform the *maarib*, the evening prayers, which must be done at sundown.

He glanced at his watch. It was only a few minutes past four. The surrounding buildings had thrown his room into shadow. He still had time till the *maarib*.

He called his brother. Yakov's voice came on the line thin and breathy, distant. In the background he could hear loud, dissonant, electronic music. "I have to see you," Akiba said.

"Where are you?"

"The Griswald."

His brother laughed, a laugh without feeling, soft, mirthless. "The Griswald is a whorehouse," his brother said.

"Well. Perhaps I can bring a spark of the sacred into the profane. Can I see you now?"

"I'm having some people over this evening."

"It's important. I only need a few minutes."

There was an uncomfortable pause. "All right," his brother said very softly. He hung up without another word.

Akiba watched the afternoon dark glide into the blackness of night. He sat staring at the wall and his heart ached for the gulf between him and his brother. And even as he thought of his brother, he saw Buddy in his mind's eye and the pain he felt inside was immense. Why, why, did he have this constant ache for everyone? Everyone was lost, he felt, and somehow the fault was his. Why? Why should he feel responsible?

He performed the *maarib*, "Blessed be He who brings the evening twilight," and within it, the *hashkivenu*, the prayer for protection and peace during the night.

There was a foot of snow on the streets when he emerged from the hotel. It was still coming down. A heavy silence seemed to envelop everything, broken only by the intermittent whine of a trapped car.

He made his way to Park Avenue and up Park to Seventy-second Street, plodding through billowing curtains of white, as huddled, arctic people, hair and brows frosted, hurried by him.

His brother owned a brownstone at Seventy-second and Second Avenue. The lower portion was his studio. Yakov lived on the top two floors.

Akiba stood in a cozy reception area and waited.

The receptionist, a striking girl in her mid-twenties, was on the phone. "He can shove it, then," she was saying in a quiet, incongruously demure voice. "The work was done and if he wants to be an asshole about it, that's his problem. But I assure you, Yakov has every intention of getting what's coming to him."

She nodded to Akiba while she listened to the person at the other end of the line.

Akiba studied the reception area. The walls were lined with magazine covers his brother had photographed: *Harper's Bazaar, Vogue, Mademoiselle*. From where he stood Akiba could look up three stories to the ceiling of the building. It must have been a theater at one time. There were leaded glass windows facing the street, and a balcony directly above the reception area. On the balcony railing a number of black pinpoint spotlights had been mounted. Akiba tried to make out the pattern on the leaded windows; from his angle it was not possible.

"Yes, yes," the receptionist cooed. "I understand that." She paused. "Melvin, darling," she said with great patience, "tell that cheap, lying cocksucker to go fuck himself."

She hung up and waved Akiba through a door into the main section of the studio.

There was a scattering of people in the place, tall, bearded men, leggy, angular women. There was a bar and a red-jacketed man offering hors d'oeuvres from a platter.

His brother, barefoot, clad in a silk Oriental robe, was seated on a low-slung leather couch. He rose when he spotted Akiba and moved across the room to him. He was in his forties, running to flab, bald on top with a fringe of long red-blond hair and tired, sad eyes. He sported a reddish beard flecked with gray.

They shook hands and Yakov's grip was without energy. His hand seemed devoid of muscle and bone. "Well," his brother said, "shall we talk about the weather?"

Akiba smiled. "We should be able to do better than that."

"Don't expect *profound* conversation from me, brother. I long ago gave up that sort of thing. There is nothing so boring to me, at this stage, as *interesting* conversation. As you can see, I surround myself with people who have absolutely *nothing* to say." He leaned close to Akiba and spoke in a confidential tone without looking at him. "I even fall asleep during sex. The other night while we were having *at it*, that little girl over there said to me"—here he waved in the direction of a pudgy girl in a silk pajama outfit—"'No wonder people get paid for this.' She looks like a girl who should be working in Woolworth's, right? Well, as a matter of fact that's exactly where I found her. What can I do for you? Glass of Manischewitz?"

"Some other time."

"What are you doing here?"

Akiba was suddenly aware of how shabby he must look in his ragged overcoat, cheap beret. He felt desperately foolish and embarrassed. What was he doing here?

The gulf between him and his brother had never felt greater. Who were these people? Models, ad agency men, glamorous appendages of smart-set hustle, purveyors of modernity's sheen? And his brother, integral accomplice, polishing the outer shell of the world: Yakov Moldavan, the prodigy who had known by heart at the age of fourteen two tractates of the *Talmud* with commentary . . .

"Can we speak privately for a minute?"

"A minute," Yakov said.

Akiba followed him up a stairway to the balcony, which overlooked the main room. For a flabby man his step was light and graceful. When he was young, he had been a terrific tennis player, and Akiba wondered if he still kept at it.

They entered the bedroom area. It was surprisingly monastic: a low bed, a bedstand, books, a radio. No rug on the floor, nothing on the walls. There were open sections overlooking the studio on one side, the reception area on the other.

Akiba could now see the leaded windows clearly. They depicted biblical scenes. "Abraham and Isaac, Cain and Abel," Yakov said. "This place used to be a *shul*. I rented it, not because I like living in an old *shul*—as a matter of fact, I loathe it—but because I *need it*." He paused for a second and made a small motion as though grinding a knife into his heart. "An irritant, a reminder," he said quietly. "But, please, let's not get into all of *that*."

"I don't intend to."

"What do you want?"

"I'm searching for a woman. She used to be a model. Her name is Adele Morath."

"Yes, I knew her," Yakov said. "She's a whore, a junky, a police informer. Other than that she's a terrific lady. What do you want from her? Syphilis? Cancer?"

"Where is she?"

"Brother, she's not what you would call a very *nice* or *desirable* person. I think you should tell me why you want to find one of the, if you'll excuse the expression, *scumbags* of the earth?"

"Do you remember Buddy Hall?"

Yakov smoothed his beard with his forefinger. "The fellow you went to school with. His father was a racketeer."

"Yes."

"I remember him."

"He murdered a man."

Yakov looked directly at Akiba. His look was dead, sad, unnerving—a man stripped of belief in anything. "Who?" he asked.

"Old man Cervino."

"The candy store?" Akiba nodded. "Why?"

"I'm trying to find that out."

His brother picked up a small box of transparent slides and studied them against a Tensor lamp next to the bed. He looked hunched, tired, old, and Akiba was reminded of a man who had come to visit him years before when he had his first synagogue in a small town in Ohio. The man was of European background, prominent in the community. He was very active in the Catholic Church. When Akiba had closed the door to his study, the man said to him in a dull voice: "I was raised an Orthodox Jew. My whole family was wiped out in the camps. I am a Jew no more." Akiba had asked him why he had come to see him.

"I don't know," the man had said. "Please don't mention it to anyone." He had left after a few uncomfortable minutes. He never returned.

He had gazed at Akiba with the same sad, dead look he had just seen in his brother's eyes.

"What does this have to do with Adele Morath?" Yakov said, setting down the box of slides.

"I think Buddy Hall might be here in New York. Adele Morath was a girl friend of his at one time."

"You've come here looking for this murderer?"

"Yes."

"What are you going to do when you find him? Ask him to give himself up for old times' sake? Have you had anything to do with him over the years?"

"No."

"Then what are you doing, Akiba?"

Akiba was thinking, Is there anyone in this world more ill at ease, more stupid, than I am? "I'm going to find him and bring him *teshubah*," he said.

Yakov turned from him abruptly and walked to the far end of the room. "I can't get involved in this," he said. "This is madness. Do you understand?"

"No. I'm doing this with a design. I am following Kabbalah."

"Kabbalah? Black and white magic? Tear out the heart of a hen and place it under your tongue, wring the neck of a mole, make a candle from the finger of a dead man?"

"No," Akiba said patiently. "The Sephirot. The Thirty-two Paths—"

"Akiba, Akiba. This is insane."

Akiba suddenly flared up: "You say it's insane because you'd rather believe that God is a cover on some glamour magazine, *Cosmo* or *Vogue!*" He was shouting. "Something is out there, powerful, mysterious, *sacred*. And He touches you, even as you touch Him. I believe. I believe that whether you call it quantum physics, splintering light, subatomic particles—He is there. He is real. This world, *this*, is the illusion, the garment, the skin." Akiba was breathless, profoundly ashamed at his outburst. "I believe this," he said. "I believe."

"'From the side of the mighty evil serpent a spirit is stirred up which roams about the world—'" Yakov said.

"The *Zohar*. You remember?"

"I can't get it out of my head. Perhaps a prefrontal lobotomy—" He scratched slowly at his beard and for an instant Akiba saw in him the rabbi he might have become. "This friend is on the other side?"

"He is. He is in *tohu, sitra ahra*."

"Oh, Akiba, Akiba." Yakov Moldavan's voice was filled with pain.

"I believe it," Akiba said.

"Yes, yes—"

"And you believe it, too, somewhere."

"To try to come this close to God is to reach out toward madness," Yakov said. "You saw what happened to our sister—"

"Coming close to God had nothing to do with that."

"Oh, yes. It was Our Father in Heaven and our father on earth. Blessed Rabbi Isaac."

"You're wrong in this bitterness and hatred for him," Akiba said. "He is a pillar of righteousness and he has been stripped of everything he loved—his learning, his children—"

"He never loved his children. He loved God. That was enough for him."

"They're trying to take away his institute, Yakov," Akiba said. "I didn't come here to plead for understanding—"

"Don't, then!"

"He has nothing now. Nothing."

"I'm dead, remember," Yakov said. "He sat *shibah* for me."

"Yakov—"

"I hope your belief is strong, brother, the paths of the Sephirot tied into your heart like veins and arteries. Because if there is a gap, the slightest doubt, you will be left empty and alone. This world is all pimps and whores." He said this without emotion, his face a mask. And Akiba knew he was talking of himself.

Yakov sighed and lifted the phone. "See the girl at the desk downstairs," he said. "She'll tell you where to find Adele Morath. Be careful, though. Adele Morath is a sick, dangerous woman."

"The dark Sephirot, the dark Shekinah," Akiba said.

Yakov shook his head in disgust. "Don't come back

here," he said. "I want nothing more to do with such foolishness."

As he reached the stairway, Akiba looked back at his brother. He was turned away from him. He was staring out at the leaded glass windows.

Adele Morath's apartment was located in a luxury building at Seventy-sixth Street and First Avenue. It was one of those buildings that cater to singles—three secretaries to an apartment, roommate computer programmers, young lawyers, discreet call girls.

The lobby was a monument to outrageous taste: nearly the size of a football field with grass-green rug and lemon-yellow furniture. It sported a fountain—a cupid with water pouring from his mouth—and an enormous mural of Indians meeting with woodsmen while bayou birds with ridiculous stork legs pranced about. The name of the building was the Flamingo.

The name of the doorman, proclaimed on a tag above his heart, was Sal. He refused to ring Adele Morath on the house phone. "It's important I see her," Akiba said.

"How important?"

Akiba pulled out his wallet and showed him a card identifying him as a chaplain in the Pennsylvania penal system. "There are a few buildings in this city that have a no tipping policy," Sal said, breathing clam sauce on Akiba. "John-fucking-law or no, this isn't one of them."

Akiba slipped a dollar out of the wallet. The doorman palmed it without looking at it and ushered him into the lobby. "I hope you send that cunt up for life," Sal said, fawning after Akiba as he steered him toward an elevator in the far wing of the building. "She's doing hundreds a day in Johns alone, and who knows what else. Talk to the IRS, too. I'm sure they're interested. I'm warning you, though: mention my name, I'll deny everything."

Adele Morath answered the door wearing a low-cut flapper dress with a lot of fringe at the hem; it had nearly as many stains as Akiba's bedspread at the Griswald Hotel.

She was quite beautiful, though wasted. She had long black hair. There was a general air of dirtiness about her. She might have been thirty, but looked older. When Akiba told her he was a friend of Buddy Gray Eyes, she hesitated for a moment, then admitted him into the apartment.

She offered him a glass of red wine, which he declined. She poured one for herself, then seated herself on the raggedy couch. She was tired. She kept yawning.

The apartment was a studio badly in need of cleaning. There were dirty dishes scattered all over the place and the ashtray overflowed with cigarette butts. The drapes were closed. The room was dim and gloomy.

The only elements of cheer were two life-sized color photographs of Adele Morath when she was younger.

"What do you want from Buddy? I haven't seen him in five years, you know."

"I heard he was coming here."

"What for?"

A fat dachshund waddled in from the kitchen, heaved itself up onto the couch, and threw itself against Adele. "This is Miss Amaranth," she said, introducing the dog to Akiba. "Her name in Greek means 'a flower that never fades.' Classic. I always liked the classics. When I was a model, they said I had a classical look. My nose held me back. See the curve of my nose? I had a nose job and the jerk left me with this curve. Asshole." She massaged the bridge of her nose and did not speak for a while. "Buddy in trouble again?" She picked at a scab in the crook of her arm.

"Yes."

"Bad?"

"Yes."

"Well, that's the kind of weird unit he is. Don't you just love it? He always zigs when he should zag. You a good friend of his?"

"At one time we were, yes."

"I can't picture that," she said.

"Why not?"

"He would be such good friends with a Jew."

"He's Jewish himself."

"Not really," she said. "Oh, I know, supposedly he was born a Jew, but I know better. I would never take him for a Jew anywhere. I can always tell a Jew. First time I laid eyes on you, I knew you were a Jew." She laughed. It was a harsh, unpleasant laugh. "How come you're not wearing a little thin gold wristwatch and a medallion around your neck? All you Jews wear them."

"I wasn't aware of that."

"All the Jews I know. So what's the deal?"

"What do you mean?"

"You're after Buddy and there's a deal involved. You're either working with the law or against them."

"No."

"You tell me you're a good friend of his. He has no friends."

"I thought you were his friend. You and Earl."

"We were tight like a fist. Then he burned me, that Jew bastard," she said. "You got to admit it—there's no rat like a Jew rat. Does that get you mad?"

Akiba did not answer.

"Get mad. I don't care. You see, there was me, Buddy, Alex Zayas, and Earl. We were doing good works in the world, liberating oppressed peoples and shit like that. So we met this very holy Harvey Krishman Zen Buddha asshole, another weird unit, white robes, shaved head, and very into turning people onto scag. He claimed he did it with holy intentions—and the money wasn't bad either. At any rate there was a mixup and Harvey Krishman ended up being beat for eighteen thousand dollars." She yawned, scratched at her face. "Am I talking too much? I take these vitamin shots, Ritalin mixed with B-fifty-two. My doctor says I'm too introverted. He says get out of yourself, talk, you have all these things inside, express them. What was I saying?"

"Something about this Zen Buddhist—"

"Some people burned him. I'm not mentioning names. He took it all very well, wrote me a note: 'You have a bird's karma. Fly with the wind, motherfucker. How could I have done such an honored thing?' Poetic. Don't you just love it?"

"What about Buddy?"

"What about him?"

"You said—"

"That was the last I saw of him. Alex Zayas began to act like a commissar, you know, put us up against the wall, so Earl and I departed the set." She shook her head slowly, smiled, settled some old score in her mind, then stared hard at Akiba. "It's a dog-eat-dog world. If you're not biting it, you're not making it." She grew pensive. "I like Buddy. I like Buddy very much. I'm sorry he's in trouble." She was staring at herself in the mirror, adjusting her dress, pursing her lips. "Well, nothing moving but the clock," she said.

"Buddy's going to come here—"

"No, I don't think so—"

"Why not?"

"Ask him when you see him."

"Where's Earl?"

"That's a deep question."

"Will you give me the answer?"

"I doubt it."

"I have to find him. I have to get to Buddy. It's desperately important."

"Don't tell me sad stories. I've heard them all. You've done everything once, I've done it twice." She stared at Akiba. "You remind me of an uncle of mine. He's a dentist. The same angry eyes. A lot of Jews have those angry eyes.

Look," she said, matter-of-factly, "let me have a hundred dollars."

"What for?"

"A party."

Akiba shifted uncomfortably. "No."

"I'm not pretty enough for you?"

"How do I find Earl?"

"You give me a hundred bucks."

Akiba swallowed. His throat felt very tight. He felt stupid and exposed, completely incompetent. "I'd have to write you a check. I don't have that much cash."

"How much do you have?"

"Just enough to get around on."

She stared at herself in the mirror, as though to ask her reflection what she should do. "Okay, give me a check," she said.

Akiba took out his checkbook and began writing. "Make it out to cash," she said.

He handed her the check. She lifted her dress over her head. She was standing there in a pair of bikini panties. She wore no bra.

Her body was thin, but well formed. Akiba looked at her and a great sadness filled him. Her long black hair covered her breasts. She pushed it back. There was an ugly scar between her breasts, a pentagram. "Alex Zayas carved that," she said, her voice suddenly filled with shame. "He wanted to cut out my heart. That's as far as he got. I'll have it removed one of these days." She stood in front of him and there was a dark anticipation in her eyes, not passion, but a certain animal eagerness. She smiled and it was awkward and pathetic; Akiba noticed one of her teeth was broken. "Well?" she said.

"No. No, thank you."

"What do you Jews want?" she said. He did not answer. "My uncle risked his life in the war for the Jews. He killed people for the Jews. I'm sick of hearing about the poor

Jews. What about all the Germans who were killed in the war? I was in an elevator in Bloomingdale's last week and this fat Jew woman with thin bird legs tried to walk right over me. 'I vant to get out here,' she said with a thick Jew accent. If I would have had a gun I would have blown her head off."

"Where can I find Earl?"

"He has a coffee shop on Thompson Street in the Village. It's called Earl's. Why don't you want me, you Jew bastard?"

Akiba moved toward the door. He was trembling with shame. "Go on. Take a walk," she said evenly. "You and your gold watch and medallion. Take a walk."

Akiba turned at the door to face her. He could feel his lips trembling. He could weep with shame. She cupped her hand under one breast and shook it at him. "What are you staring at me with those angry eyes? Take a walk, creep."

Akiba took a walk.

# 13

"You'll like Earl. He's good people. He's like the older kid on the street who everybody looks up to. The best ball player, knows all the right moves—"

"Uh-huh."

"There were a lot of people looked up to me at one time, but then again, before that, I looked up to a lot of people, and that's the way it would go."

Buddy Gray Eyes and Tracy drove slowly through narrow Greenwich Village streets in the stolen Cadillac. He had been on a talking jag, just rambling on for hours.

Earlier his arm had been bothering him and they had stopped at a shopping center in Rahway, New Jersey, and picked up some cotton pads and bandages and they had patched up the wound.

There was no bleeding and very little pain, only a dull ache.

He had dozed most of the way across Pennsylvania. Tracy had stayed off the turnpike and when he awoke, she was lost in a jumble of New Jersey back roads.

He had been thinking, half dreaming, about his mother. It was strange how close her presence had come to him since she had died. For some years he had had little to do with her, then she died, and afterward he could not seem to get her out of his mind.

She was with him every night in his dreams, whispering

to him, smiling at him. And he was always always trying to reach her, trying to apologize to her.

There was the ancient man with eyes of no color and his mother. And he dreamed of them every night.

On the road he had dreamed of an accident. An ambulance was on the edge of the highway and two attendants were lifting someone into it. He rushed to the ambulance and saw it was a young woman, very beautiful; she was bleeding, dying, and he saw it was his mother. She was young, not yet twenty; she was smiling. He hugged her to him and begged her not to leave.

Her face was up very close to his and her look was peaceful. "I have to go," she said and her voice was like music, quiet, quiet, gentle. And there was no regret in her voice.

He had awakened then, and while Tracy took the car up one back road and down the next, he continued to think about his mother. He was very small and she had bought a plastic toy viewer for him. He would hold it up to the light and turn a knob, and film panels would move through it. He couldn't remember what was on the film, but he remembered his mother cuddling him on her lap and smiling and whispering to him. He remembered the smell of her, delicate, the fragrance of flowers.

He remembered the chicks they would buy at Easter time; and the rain that fell over the park beyond their house. And Cervino's store.

As Tracy searched for the road to New York, he had begun to talk. He went on about school yard fights, neighborhood heroes, football games. He replayed old football games as though they had occurred yesterday.

Tracy had said very little and it really didn't matter. He was in high school, playing ball. He could feel the spongy turf beneath him, the brittle cold of autumn days, smell the grass.

Certain plays unfolded in minute detail. He was crouched behind the center, the linebacker opposite had a scar above his lip, the guard was wearing a rubber pad over his left elbow; he took the ball, felt its pimpled surface, turned it in his hands until he had the sharp edge of the strings; he saw his set-back coming forward, and he faked the ball to him and started around the end. His heart was pounding. He saw faces in the stands and recognized his mother and father.

And he could see with perfect clarity his receivers spreading out across the field and everything was right. His place was right, his world was right. He threw the ball and it was perfect; the trajectory arched as though he himself had limned it in the sky.

Nothing in his life would ever be that right.

"Uh-huh," Tracy said. "I see what you mean, for sure."

And now, moving along Bleecker Street, he had come all the way down to Earl. "I'm sorry for going on like this," he said. "It's just that there are so many people that mean so much to you and you mean so much to them and you want to give them their due if only with a few words."

"Hey, babe, for sure. It's neat communicating with you like this. It's not often people get a chance to communicate," she said, her voice as dead as her eyes.

"So anyway, Earl was like an older brother to me. I'd do anything for him and he'd do anything for me."

He had a twinge of doubt: there had been a rupture. He wasn't sure what it had been about. Funny, how the distant past was so near, while the close past hardly seemed to have existed.

They parked the Caddy on Thompson Street at the corner of Bleecker. It was early evening now.

Before Gray Eyes left California, someone had told him Earl was out of prison and running his own luncheonette on Thompson.

They found it on a block that contained a pizza parlor and a hero sandwich stand. A sign said: "Earl's Coffee Shop—All Night Breakfast."

Inside, a bald-headed man was frying up a batch of

hash-brown potatoes on the griddle. There were three Spanish-looking men and an Anglo girl seated in a dark corner of the place. A jukebox played a jazz pachanga, a weird, syncopated sound of the late fifties.

Gray Eyes and Tracy seated themselves at the counter. Gray Eyes suddenly felt ill at ease, lost. What if Earl didn't embrace him, didn't take him in, didn't set things right? How would he get back to Alex Zayas and the Coast if Earl couldn't come through?

The man frying the potatoes ignored Tracy and Gray Eyes. Gray Eyes picked up a pair of spoons from the counter and began to click them together in time to the music. He whistled out of the side of his mouth, a rapid, trilling sound, and the spoons and whistles worked in perfect accompaniment to the jukebox sound.

"Hey, babe, that's so good," Tracy said. She bobbed her head about and slapped at the counter.

The bald-headed man turned from the griddle. He had a large, knobby head and a thin, hunched body; he wore tinted prescription glasses. "Tell Earl a friend of his is here," Tracy said.

"What friend?" the man said without emotion. He had a slurred, nasal voice. He glared at Gray Eyes.

"Hey, Earl," Bud said. "Earl. Say hello to Tracy."

The bald-headed man did not say hello.

Buddy rubbed the spoons together in his hands and looked confused. "Hey, Earl," he said, "aren't you happy to see me? Don't you want to know how things are out on the Coast, how everybody's doing?" Earl did not answer. "Things are really percolating out on the Coast, I mean Alex Z. has it all tight, baby, and it's fine. Fascinating people in his camp now, beautiful people seeing the light of his vision, you know. Celebrities. They call 'em celebs. Earl."

Earl just stared at Gray Eyes. Gray Eyes pushed the spoons away and shook his head as though to clear away some disturbing image. "What is it, Earl?"

"You tell me," Earl said.

Gray Eyes leaned close to Tracy. "I don't understand," he said and there was fear in his voice.

"This is the dude, huh?"

"This is him. We were tight like brothers—" In his mind he saw the glorious sands of the California coast; people playing volleyball on the beach; the surf, an undulating sweep of spume, racing from pier to pier along the clean, crescent bay. They're waiting for him. All his friends.

"He doesn't seem to know you," Tracy said.

"I know him," Earl said. "Sleazoid scumbag. You cost me a three-year bit, you motherfucker, you and your celebs on the Coast."

"I cost you?" Gray Eyes said. The pain and confusion on his face were immense.

"He snitched me off," Earl said to Tracy. "I made him for a snitch, I never made him for a snitch on me."

"Earl, you're wrong—" Gray Eyes said.

"Tell me about it."

"If someone snitched you off, I'm sorry. You served a bit. I didn't know—"

"You didn't know—"

"A lot of things went down in that set. There were a lot of accusations. It's vague in my mind. I'm out of all that now, doing fine—"

"You don't look so fine."

"Gimme some coffee, man, you'll see me perk right up. How's your coffee here? You got good java? Hey, Earl, I'm going back out to the Coast. I'm going to straighten everything out with everybody. There are a lot of misconceptions about me."

"Yeah."

"Remember when Waxy went out behind an overdose and a dope fiend friend of all of us saved him? Injected him with saline, poured ice over his balls? And Waxy gave the guy up when tit came to tat. And you said to him, he was a *friend*, how could you snitch him off like that? And he told you, friendship is one thing, but business is *business*. Remember?"

"Yeah, I remember."

"Well, I was never *low* like that."

Earl picked up a large bread knife and balanced it in his hands. "Tell me all about it. Tell me about the Coast while you're at it, the celebs, the sun."

"What do you want to know?"

"Isn't it true the sun hits the freeway there and it bakes the automobile exhaust and that lead when it bakes it eats away the brain so you find a lot of very crazy and contemptible people? Isn't that the way it is on the Coast?"

Gray Eyes looked genuinely hurt. "No, that's not the way it is at all."

Earl put the tip of the bread knife against Gray Eyes's chest. The Spanish-looking men and the girl at the table had turned their attention to the counter and were watching with blank-faced impassivity. "Tell me about Alex Zayas," Earl said, pressing with the point of the knife.

"Alex is beautiful."

Earl pressed harder on the knife. It dug through Gray Eyes's shirt and brought up a pinpoint of blood. Gray Eyes did not flinch. "Why do you think he's beautiful?" Earl said.

"He has compassion, he's very spiritual."

Earl laughed, keeping the knife point against Gray Eyes.

"What do you want here?" Earl said. He continued to press the knife to his chest, just below the heart. A small stain of blood had formed on Gray Eyes's T-shirt.

"I missed you, Earl," Gray Eyes said with deep feeling. "You know, you reach a place in your life where you realize you're losing things. People who were dear to you—"

"You got fucking gall, man, heaping this shit on me," Earl said.

Gray Eyes was becoming increasingly agitated. He gazed about the luncheonette as though he were trapped in a nightmare. What was going on? Earl had been like his own heart. Why was he treating him like this? Yes, there had been some hassle, a mixup between them on the Coast, but—

He noticed the three men and the girl staring at him and a great fear spread over him.

"Look, Earl, I don't know why you're doing this. I'm in a tight spot and I *need* you. And I hate to bring it up like this, but I think you owe me—"

Earl's eyes flashed for the first time. "Do you want this in your fucking heart?" he yelled. "I owe you?"

Gray Eyes brushed his hand past his eyes as though to dispel some terrifying apparition.

One of the Spanish-looking men at the table in the corner got up. He had a snub-nosed .32 Harrington & Richardson Sidekick in his hand. "What is it?" he asked, poised behind Gray Eyes and Tracy. He looked as though he should speak with an accent, but he didn't.

Gray Eyes turned. "What do you want? What are you, the *man*? The *heat*?"

"Fuck no," the Spanish-looking man said.

"What do you want then, maricón?" Gray Eyes screamed.

"Hey, keep it down," Earl said. He waved at the man, who replaced the gun in his waistband and sat down. "Don't go round calling people maricón," the man muttered. "There are women in the room."

"Maricón," Gray Eyes yelled, out of control.

"Easy, babe," Tracy said.

"Okay, okay," Earl said, smiling thinly.

"Look what you did, Earl. This is my best shirt and you ruined it. Is that the way to treat a man who's like your brother? Why are you coming on with me so hard, man?"

Earl shook his head and laughed. "Crazy fuck," he said, his tone softer now. "What can I do with you?"

Gray Eyes smiled and Earl laughed louder. He laughed until tears came into his eyes. "Your best shirt," he said.

The three men and the girl at the table looked uncomfortable, as though the joke was on them. "I swore if I ever saw him again I'd kill him," Earl said to Tracy. "But what are you going to do with him? He's like a little kid or a puppy dog."

"Bow wow," Gray Eyes said, smiling.

Earl poured out two cups of coffee and set them down in front of Gray Eyes and Tracy. "You want eggs," he said.

"I'll take some," Tracy said.

"Sure, anyone wears a rag says 'greed' will take anything," Earl said.

He scrambled them up eggs and bacon and poured himself a cup of coffee and the three of them sat at a table. No one spoke for a while. Earl stared out the window. "This snow is messing my business all up," he said.

"Which business is that?" Gray Eyes said.

"Any one you want."

Gray Eyes leaned across the table and took Earl's hand. Earl looked at him, bemused. "*Amigo*, believe me—"

"Anytime anyone says 'believe me' I know they're lying," Earl said.

"That thing you mentioned, I don't remember the details—"

"I remember them perfectly," Earl said.

"As I recall, someone took off this Hare Krishna freak—"

"Jerry O."

"Jerry O.? Was that his name? I thought it was Babba Das Rum Dum or something."

"Jerry Ohrenstein."

"I didn't know that. Right. At any rate, someone took him off. And in spite he set up a whole pile of people, including me, you, Adele. I slipped away and was trying to get the whole thing straightened out, I was *mobilizing*, you know, when Adele misread the whole thing and began spinning tales on everybody—"

"Adele did that?"

"That's the way I heard it. That's the way I remember it. My memory's not too good, but—"

"How about this memory? You made off with eighteen thousand dollars. And you arranged it so *adroitly* that a whole shitload of people took a fall. It was just like dominoes, man. And you did that."

"I did that?" Gray Eyes said.

"Oh, yes."

"If I did I'm sorry," he said very simply, like a small kid.

"Gray Eyes," Earl said, grinning a thin, skull-like grin. "Doesn't he have pretty gray eyes? You should have seen him when he was young. Prettier than Tony Curtis. What do you want from me, Buddy?"

"I want to get back to the Coast."

"What's the trouble?"

Gray Eyes did not speak for a long moment. "They're trying to say I dusted a guy."

"They're trying to say that, huh?"

"Yes."

"Did you dust a guy?"

"Not in my heart."

"I'll tell you something. If you gave me your brown to punk, her snatch, and a key of the best Corine, I wouldn't help you. If you told me you were dying and wanted to call an ambulance, I wouldn't give you a dime."

"You wouldn't?"

"That's right. You were a good kid at one time, Gray Eyes, I really liked you—"

"It was Adele's fault—"

"It was her fault," Earl said to Tracy. "She took the needle and put it in his arm."

"More or less."

"Which led to rank behavior and scumbaggery, with take-offs and setups and all sorts of treachery. Hey, I played the game a long time, Bud, and I'll be playing it until I'm dead and that's what tells me to tell you, *adiós*. You're fucking limitless bad news."

Gray Eyes, looking desperately depressed, remained quiet. Earl got up from the table and went behind the counter. He stirred the potatoes on the griddle. Tracy watched him. She did not take her eyes off him; but there was nothing in the look: just dead eyes. "That man wrote you off, babe," she said to Gray Eyes.

Gray Eyes stood up, confused, hurt. "What do we owe you for the eggs and bacon?" he said.

"Four and a quarter."

"Give him a discount," Tracy said, "for friendship's sake."

"Like the man said before, friendship is one thing, but business is business," Earl said.

Gray Eyes moved to the counter and laid a five-dollar bill on it. "I'm sorry, Earl," he said. "If I did something not right I wish I could make amends."

"Go see Adele," Earl said. "Explain everything to her, how you were mobilizing. Tell her how much you want to get back to the Coast, to the sun and celebs."

"My friends are all out there."

"Sure they are. They're waiting for you. They miss your smile and wit."

"Where can I find Adele?"

"Remember the Flamingo?"

"Swimming pool on the roof, hookers stretched out on the astroturf, soot coming down from the big Con Ed chimney?"

"That's the place. That's where she is."

"I thought you two'd be together."

"Naw, I gave up on that. I couldn't never sleep, you know, for fear she'd cut off my balls and trade 'em for weight."

"She's good people, Adele."

A quiet smile passed over Earl's face. "That's your problem. You always only see the best in people."

"Hey, Earl, what a nice thing to say!" Buddy grabbed Earl's hand and licked it and laughed foolishly. He barked like a dog and whistled and continued to laugh.

As he and Tracy reached the door, the Spanish-looking man intercepted him. "Take back what you said before," he whispered in Gray Eyes's ear.

"Hey, did I offend you? I'm sorry. Whatever it was, I take it back," Gray Eyes said, and he and Tracy moved out into the snowy night.

Shaken after his encounter with Adele Morath, Akiba Moldavan had returned to his hotel. He watched the news on television, then tried to sleep. He lay there, cold with anxiety; he felt cut adrift, foundering. He thought back on Adele Morath mocking him, mocking the Jews.

All his life he had encountered that sort of hate and he had never grown a thick skin toward it. What was it that they wanted from the Jews? he asked. Christian, Muslim—what was it they wanted?

Were they resentful because the Jews had been the first chosen to bear God's witness? Were they hateful because they weren't in on the ground floor? Were the Jews despised, as Hitler once said, because they had given the world a conscience?

The room was freezing. Chattering with cold and anxiety, he got out of bed and checked the radiator. It was not working. He toyed with the valves. Nothing happened.

He called the desk. "Room eight oh six. The radiator's not working."

"So?" the clerk said.

"How about giving me another room?"

"They're all the same."

"The whole hotel is without heat?" The clerk did not answer. "What are you doing about it?"

"Doing? I'm not doing anything." The clerk's voice was muffled, toneless.

"But that's stupid!" Akiba yelled. He waited for the

clerk to say something. He waited a long time. The line was dead. The clerk had hung up.

Outside in the street giant snow-removal machines groaned in the night. The snow had abated but was still coming down. The wind buffeted the loose-fitting window sash; freezing air poured into the room.

Akiba piled the bed high with whatever he could find: his overcoat, towels, even the plastic shower curtain. He still could not sleep.

He sat up in the bed, snapped on the gooseneck lamp, and dialed the operator. She put him through to Pittsburgh.

Ruth had just been thinking about him, was about to phone. "I was afraid you'd be asleep," she said.

"Consider the odds," Akiba said. "The very moment I decided to call you, you were thinking the same thing. It's a miracle! Or how about this? As far as anyone knows, we people on earth are the only living things. Statistically, we don't even exist."

"What are we making such a big *megillah* about, then?" Ruth said.

"And with all the statistical nonentities on earth, what are the odds that you and I would meet and get married?"

"Astronomical."

"And be happy and you be so terrific—"

"Mind-boggling."

They both laughed and Akiba felt better now. "How are things?" he said.

"A detective visited the house. Strahan. He was looking for you. I gave him Yakov's address."

"Ah, Ruthie—"

"The police should be searching for Buddy, not you." She paused. "I don't know what's going on in your head," she said.

"You think I'm becoming *meshugga*?"

"No."

"This afternoon I saw Yakov. He doesn't believe in anything. He's lost. I look about me. Everyone is lost."

"You were never lost like that," she said. "You always had your belief."

"I had considered certain possibilities. A possibility is not a belief."

"And now?"

"I am following the paths of Kabbalah."

"And these paths? Where are they leading you?"

"I don't know."

"Are you sure they even exist?"

"Maybe they don't exist. Maybe I'm chasing shadows. But that is what I have to do—"

"Why?"

"To know God. Once and for all, to know Him."

"But He is unknowable. You've always said that. How will you be certain that you've found Him?"

"I'll know!" Akiba suddenly shrilled, and as he did so, he felt shame and his fear returning.

There was a quiet hum over the line, a twanging sound like a faraway harp and it seemed to Akiba that he could actually hear the vast distance between him and his wife, an echo over that distance, a low moan of wind traveling across snow and mountains and superhighways, shopping centers, factories, rivers, bridges, bringing with it a feeling of infinite smallness and loneliness. Small and alone again.

"Do you understand?" he said.

"Do what you have to do."

"Please. Do you understand?"

"What room is this?" A voice had cut into the line, a husky, arid voice: the desk clerk.

"Will you get off the line!" Akiba yelled.

"I thought it was someone else. This isn't Booker?"

"No. I'm talking long distance. Get off!"

"Oh," the desk clerk said, and clicked off.

"What was that?" Ruth said.

"This hotel—it's just impossible."

"Relax now, Akiba."

"Do you understand what I was talking about?"

"Yes, I understand," Ruth said, and Akiba realized that she did not understand—how could she?—and this realization was devastating to him. If she couldn't understand, who could?

After hanging up he tossed in bed for what seemed hours. When he fell asleep, it was to dream about Adele Morath and his brother. Yakov was taking pictures of her, Akiba watching. She removed her dress and stood before him, fingering the pentagram carved between her breasts, while his brother moved around her squeezing off pictures. He noticed his brother had a tattoo on his arm, a stick figure golem.

"I'll break your motherfucking head," someone was yelling. "You hear? I'll break your motherfucking head." A woman screamed. There was a sound of a lamp crashing to the floor. Muffled voices. Laughter. A door slamming. Latin music. Akiba was awake. In the room next to him people were carrying on, pimps and whores, he was certain.

Should he call the desk? Oh, no. If they couldn't handle radiators that didn't work, what would they do about violence, degradation? For all he knew the desk clerk was there in the middle of it, urging them on.

He fought to concentrate on the Tree of Sephirot. He could only see the stick-figure form of the golem. I am entering a nightmare, he told himself. And it was true.

All the planes had been grounded at Greater Pittsburgh Airport so John Strahan just waited. He sat on a plastic chair in an observation area overlooking the field and watched the snow fall.

He opened his little spiral notebook and studied it. The list of tasks to accomplish seemed meaningless. He tried to concentrate. Had he forgotten anything? Yes. Car chains. They were still in the garage. He had meant to put them on before he left town. He printed neatly: CAR CHAINS. He would be sure to take care of that when he returned home.

He toyed with the chess problem, white to mate in three; relinquished it unsolved after a while.

At dawn the snow began to ease up. He had a breakfast of sausage and eggs. The breakfast didn't rest well in his stomach. His stomach began to pain him, a vague burning sensation.

He moved back to the observation area, watched the ground crew clearing the field for take-off, and thought about Gray Eyes.

An image kept turning in his mind, roiling there: Gray Eyes and Kitty Lou in a torrid embrace. He saw them as he remembered them in high school, both young, beautiful; their bodies churned together.

How could something that had happened so many years ago still torment him? he thought.

He crossed to the stainless steel water fountain and drank deep. "Put out the fire," he said to himself. The pain in his stomach eased.

He entered the men's room, moved to the urinal. The enamel edge was sprinkled with wiry pubic hairs, and Strahan pissed with a sense of revulsion. His whole world was infested with cock hairs. Cockroaches. Cock hairs. A wave of nausea came over him, but passed. He washed his hands thoroughly then splashed water on his face.

Plane service had started up again. By ten o'clock he was on his way to New York.

Akiba's wife had furnished him with Yakov Moldavan's address; Strahan went there as soon as he arrived in Manhattan.

He was surprised by the cool gloss of the operation. What had this to do with Akiba Moldavan? The receptionist forced him to wait a half hour. When he was finally shown into the studio, he found himself treated with brusque indifference.

He had no idea who Akiba's brother was; no one in the room resembled him.

The receptionist, passing through the room, pointed

toward a pudgy man with long reddish blond hair and a beard. Strahan caught the pudgy man at the door.

Yakov Moldavan, barely glancing at the credentials Strahan offered, kept a rapid tap-tap going with his sandaled foot while occasionally giving out an order to an assistant in a soft, sibilant voice. He did not apologize for the interruptions, nor did he look directly at Strahan.

The receptionist had reappeared and was hovering near the shoulder of Yakov Moldavan. "Sissy, talk to this man," Yakov said.

"I want to talk to you. Where can I find Akiba?"

"He's staying at the Griswald. Now please!"

"Don't be a hard-on," Sissy said pleasantly.

Yakov Moldavan started back into the center of the studio. "Hey," Strahan called out. "Don't turn your back on me like that." Yakov Moldavan turned. His face was a flat, Buddha mask. "I'm here all the way from Pittsburgh on my own time and I won't be treated this way," Strahan said. He had been thrown off balance at first, unwittingly forced to assume a position of deference. He had never conceived of Akiba Moldavan's brother in this way, a modern American success, slick, rude, condescending. Now he had recovered. He would be satisfied. "Don't shrug off murder, my friend. A man has been killed. We'll do what we have to do to bring the killer to justice. You may think that photographing a lot of skinny women holding boxes of soap is important, but I'm here to tell you the death of a man is more important."

"What do you want from me?" Yakov Moldavan said in a quiet voice.

"Let's start by being civil, sir."

"Give him the name of the girl," Yakov Moldavan said to the receptionist.

"What girl?" Strahan said.

"Your killer's ex-girl friend. I'm sorry if I seemed rude. I have a lot on my mind."

He moved quickly to the far end of the studio, trailed

by assistants. The receptionist handed John Strahan a slip of paper with the name and address of Adele Morath. "Okay, you've made your point," she said, "now get the fuck out."

The doorman at the Flamingo told Strahan he had just missed Adele Morath. He leaned close to Strahan, buddy-buddy. "If I were you," he said, sliding the bill Strahan had passed to him into his pocket, "I'd check out the Ravished Duck." He nodded toward the corner where a peppermint-striped canopy proclaimed: RAVISHED DUCK RESTAURANT. "She's there for lunch almost every day. She and the bartender got a little business going, but don't quote me. He's a fucking Turk, for chrissake."

Adele Morath was sitting at a corner table by herself. She was wearing butterfly sunglasses and drinking white wine. The Turk behind the bar pointed her out.

"Eyeballs pinned?" Strahan said, slipping into a chair next to her.

"What's that supposed to mean?"

"Anybody who wears sunglasses in a dark restaurant I figure's been banging dope."

"I have a serious condition of the retina," she said. "That's why I wear these."

"Really?"

"My eyes are very sensitive to *lame assholes*. Now, if you want to raise shit around here, that's your prerogative, but—"

Strahan looked over at the bar. The Turk had moved opposite the table and was watching the two of them. Strahan displayed his badge. The Turk moved away. Adele Morath, staring straight ahead, made no sign she even saw it. "Where's Buddy?" Strahan said after a while.

"You'll have to get in line."

"The other guy reached you?"

"Kike," she said under her breath.

"I can make things tough for you," Strahan said softly.

"What makes you think they're not?"

"Your friend whacked a guy out. I'll talk to some people and they'll lock you away until your nose is running like a faucet."

"I don't know what you mean. I'm not a *dope fiend*, if that's what you're hinting at," she said defensively. She removed her sunglasses. Her eyeballs were pinned. "This is harassment. Now get out of here—I don't talk to dirt, I walk on it. Ferzi!" she called to the bartender. "Tell El Creepo here to take a stroll."

"Keep polishing those glasses, Ferzi," Strahan said. Ferzi kept polishing.

Strahan leaned across the table. "What you don't seem to understand is you're a *cockroach* to me. Your life, what you really are inside, your sensitivities, mean *nothing* to me. Cockroach, you hear?"

"This is nothing but pure harassment," she said. Her eyes darted rapidly about the room as though searching for someone to rescue her. The Turk was slicing oranges into neat wedges.

"You don't know what harassment is, cockroach," Strahan said.

She covered her face with her hand and fought not to weep and Strahan was satisfied: he had cut her. She knew she was a cockroach. She kept her face averted as though hiding from the world. "I don't know anything about Buddy," she said. "I haven't seen him in years. I saw that Jew friend of his yesterday. Try Earl. He has a place on Thompson Street in the Village, a coffee shop." She was at the point of weeping, but she didn't. "You had no right saying those things to me. I'm a person, a human person."

"Is that right?" Strahan said, rising. "I didn't know that. You look, act, and smell like a bug."

He walked quickly out of the place. The Turk did not look up from his orange wedges. Adele Morath lit a cigarette. She stared at herself in one of the mirrored columns. She winked at herself. Her reflection, an aging, pale, skull-face, nodded and smiled and winked back.

Tracy and Gray Eyes stood on the east side of First Avenue on the corner of Seventy-sixth, opposite the Ravished Duck. They stood in the entranceway to a discount shoe store. Gray Eyes had had another attack of the chills.

He stood leaning against the glass, his hands jammed deep into his pockets, his body hunched over while he trembled.

The man who owned the store, an older man in a gray sweater, was watching the two of them through the glass door.

"C'mon, babe," Tracy said with no hint of compassion. "You're calling attention to yourself. I mean you look like a real down junky."

"I can't help it," he moaned, his teeth chattering violently.

"You got some kind of condition there for sure," Tracy said. "You ought to do something about it. That man is definitely watching us."

Gray Eyes glanced over at the man. He reminded him of Cervino, the candy store owner. Thick wool sweater, same gentle stoop to his body. "Let's go," Gray Eyes said. He started out of the entranceway. "We'll go back to the pizza place," he said.

"They were definitely looking at us funny there. This is a bad scene, babe."

"Did I ever promise you different?" Gray Eyes said, and Tracy had no answer.

The night before, after leaving Earl, they had driven up to Adele Morath's building. They had sat in the car outside the place for several hours while Gray Eyes tried to decide what to do next. Tracy had grown bored and sullen. She had the radio tuned to a hard-rock station and she bounced and twisted on the seat in time to the music. "This is no fun at all. I want to *boogie*," she said more than once.

Gray Eyes was reluctant to go into the building. He had become infected with rat paranoia. Everyone hated him; they were all out to do him in. Earl would have dropped a dime on him—to the police or to Adele. Either way the cops would be waiting for him. Everyone had a deal to cut. Earl would cut his, Adele would cut hers. And it would all come down on Gray Eyes.

He and Tracy sat in the car opposite the building until after two A.M. and he saw no sign of the police and still he could not bring himself to go in.

And it was not only rat fear that held him back. Suppose everything was all right. How would Adele react to him? Their relationship had been freighted with so many complications, weird complexities. She had helped turn him into what he now was. She was the first great love of his life. And he had ratted her out.

Julie Tripp had meant much to him, had been in all ways a better person to him. But Adele Morath had been the first. Gray Eyes had been Adele's Julie Tripp, the dope virgin initiated into that scary sodality, hundred-dollar-a-day habit, rank junkydom.

Should she reject him now, refuse to help, turn him in, the betrayal would be shattering. Somewhere deep, deep inside he had always believed that when everything went against him, he could go back to Adele. She would forgive and take him in, protect him, no matter how desperate the circumstances.

He had felt Earl would look out for him, too, yet Earl had turned against him, branded him as an informer. It cut him deeply that he had been misunderstood. His behavior had been so much more intricate, cunning, than mere informing, but how to explain it? It had involved Alex Zayas, various loyalties, trading people off, an elaborate construction that through no fault of Gray Eyes collapsed like a house of cards. Someone had informed—that was true—but in his heart of hearts Gray Eyes did not believe it had been him. Still, everyone had been buried; Gray Eyes had been cursed as a rat. And now he was certain that what had been interpreted as a rat action in the past would engender a rat action in the present—at the very least a total rejection of him by Adele.

"What do you want from this girl?" Tracy had asked in the car.

"She'll hide us for a while, get us some money."

"So we can get to the Coast? The celebs? Sun? Like the man said, getting your brains baked on the freeway? I'd say that sucks, babe."

"No, there's the ocean there and it's something special. There's no ocean like the Pacific Ocean—"

"It's just water like any other ocean, that's definitely for sure. I've seen water and I'm not impressed. Hey, this is no fun at all. I want to do some *boogieing.*"

He stared at her for a long time, trying to read her impassivity, trying to get beyond the flatness in her eyes. She would flash life and warmth, then turn it off like an electric light bulb. "What are you hanging with me for?"

"Beats me. Just looking for a little fun, babe. Shake and bake."

They checked into a small hotel on Eighty-sixth Street, the National. It was filled with hookers. The room cost them an outrageous twenty dollars. They were down to their last fifty.

Tracy had miraculously scored some Dolophine; how or when Gray Eyes had no idea.

He declined to join her in fixing up. "I've bested all that," he said.

"Best the best? No way," she said.

He watched while she broke open the capsules and emptied the powder into a bottle cap. She dissolved the Dolophine in some water, cooked it, and prepared to shoot it up. A globe of fluid glistened at the end of the needle, and Gray Eyes felt an excitement spread out from his heart: the tattoo man on his chest was doing a dance.

Tracy watched him watch her and she smiled a quiet, private smile. "Take some, babe," she said. "I'm not a pig."

"For my bad arm," he said. "It's killing me."

"Sure. For your bad arm."

He shot some of the Dolophine and could hear the little man on his chest clapping his hands.

They made love. While he moved inside her, Tracy kept her eyes open, studying him. He couldn't read her and was not sure she had enjoyed herself.

She sensed his concern and said, "You're a fabulous dude. You junky dudes are all so *good*—when you can get it up."

"I'm not a junky," he told her. "A junky is an addict and that's not me. I never use this garbage. My arm—"

"Definitely. For sure," she said. She mimed laughing up her sleeve. "Really." She lay close to him for a while. "Did you dust a man like you told that Earl dude?" she said.

He stared at the ceiling, but did not speak. "Hey, you don't have to justify anything to me," Tracy said. "You dusted the man because of your own personal reasons and I respect that. There are worse things in this world, babe, than dusting a man."

Gray Eyes smiled. The tattoo man on his chest was leaping and twirling, performing riotous somersaults—extraordinary acrobat! "I'm The Destroyer," he said simply.

"For sure, babe," Tracy said. While she drifted off to sleep, Gray Eyes lay awake staring at the ceiling.

His arm was throbbing now under the bandages. It felt hot and swollen. He couldn't sleep. He shifted on the bed. Outside the window a blue electric sign, NATIONAL HOTEL, burned around the edge of the shade. He got up to adjust it.

Tracy sat up with a jolt. She stared at Bud. Her eyes were wide and clear, totally awake, just staring at him as though she hadn't been asleep at all, as though she had been watching him through closed lids the whole time. "What?" she said.

"Nothing. What's the matter?"

She didn't say anything. She lay back on the bed, staring up at the ceiling. She closed her eyes and was immediately asleep.

Gray Eyes, suffering deep night paranoia, did not trust her. Who is she? Why has she come along with me? he thought. What does she want? The whole thing could be an elaborate setup, a *trap*. His mind was speeding, electric sparks spitting across the brain cell terminals, cutting red traces in his head. He knew what was happening. He had read about it in the newspaper, about experiments done on rat brains. He had a rat brain, didn't he? Ask Earl, Adele. Ask the legion of junkies, scrammers, dealers, all those who perpetuated the myth of him as informer. Informer! He had tried to protect them and they branded him as rat. . . .

The article had said: rat brain cell receptors fit lock-and-key with opiate molecules, morphine. Lock and key. His brain. Rat brain. Rat karma brain. Perfect fit. Those receptors were there to take up a natural opiate produced in the body. Beta-endorphin. He had written it down somewhere. That was his problem. Rat brain beta-endorphin. A lack of synthetic opiate would draw an overload of beta-endorphin on the system, inducing rat brain, rat karma paranoia. Speeding. Spit, *zap*, red traces in his head.

The little man on his chest was doing cartwheels, spinning with laughter. Pointing at him, accusing him.

He returned to the bed and closed his eyes. Molecule fitted to molecule, electric sparks coalesced and now the room had become a school yard. Small kids gathered about him. He began to whistle. The tattoo man on his chest howled with joy. The kids formed a circle. "Ring around the rosy, pocket full of posies, ashes, ashes, all fall down. Ring around the rosy, ring around the rosy . . ." A woman was calling to him off in the distance—his mother—"Buddy, Buddy," as Gray Eyes whistled and danced and led the kids to Mr. Cervino's store for penny candy. "Bud-dy!"

The next day Gray Eyes and Tracy had been back at their post, parked up the block from the Flamingo Apartments. They had walked to the corner to get a better view, had had a pizza breakfast at the stand across the way, then moved to the shoe store where he had been attacked by chills. They moved back to the pizza stand and drank coffee from Styrofoam cups and his shivering subsided.

He had still not decided what they would do. He had lost confidence in the idea of going to Adele. He told Tracy they would follow the little man on his chest. "He'll give us a sign. He always does," Gray Eyes said.

Horribly bored, she felt the idea had little to commend itself.

She brightened a bit when Adele came out of the Flamingo and entered the Ravished Duck. "She's a skank, man," Tracy said.

There was some truth in the comment: time had not treated her well. But, then, it had been less than kind to Gray Eyes, too. "Ten years ago," he said, "she was the most beautiful girl in the world. She had personality problems, though."

"What does the little booger say?"

"We go with her."

"All right," Tracy said.

Tracy and Gray Eyes were at the counter in the pizza stand when Strahan arrived at the Flamingo.

Gray Eyes moved to the window and leaned against the glass. "What's the matter, babe?" Tracy said.

Gray Eyes thought he might be hallucinating. "How did he get here?"

"What's that, babe?"

"That man—"

"What about him? He's just a man, babe. You all right?"

Gray Eyes did not answer. "Hey," Tracy called to the thin Italian behind the counter. The man wore a paper cap with "Hires Root Beer" on it, had greasy black curls down his neck. "You don't have a pyramid here, do you?"

"What?"

"Pyramid, like they have in Egypt."

The man laughed. His curls danced. "No," he said, pounding out a flat circle of dough. "No pyramids here."

"Not a brick mother," Tracy said. "Just a little thing."

"No, nothing like that."

"My friend here is sick. We put him under a pyramid, that fixes him right up."

Tracy rubbed the back of Gray Eyes's neck with her hands. "Feeling better?"

"Oh, yeah. I'm fine."

When Strahan came out of the apartment building and headed for the Ravished Duck, Gray Eyes was certain he was not hallucinating. It was Strahan all right, that tense, rolling gait of his, the affectation of a boxer's glide, a tough guy who never really had it. Gray Eyes knew John Strahan very well, knew his heart and guts, and knew both were rotted with fear.

A little while later Strahan came out of the restaurant. It took him some time to get a cab on the snow-clogged street. He glanced over at the pizza stand and Gray Eyes began to shiver again.

They had not been spotted though, and Strahan departed, leaving Gray Eyes devastated, rat brain receptors charged once more, fighting that terrible feeling that a conspiracy of extraordinary proportions was afoot. Egypt. Pyramids. John Strahan.

How had Strahan made it here? Who had tipped him to Adele?

Gray Eyes was trembling. He was soaked with perspiration. "You've got a jones," Tracy said.

"No. No."

A well-dressed man in his early forties arrived at the Ravished Duck. A chauffeur-driven Mercury Grand Marquis waited while the man entered the restaurant. A few minutes later Adele came out with the man and the two of them entered the Mercury. They sat talking in the backseat while the chauffeur lit up a cigarette.

"Let's go," Gray Eyes said. They left the pizza stand and hurried up the block to their car, the stolen Caddy. The Mercury pulled off, heading uptown on First Avenue.

With Gray Eyes at the wheel he and Tracy sped around the corner after them, just catching the flash end of yellow at the traffic light.

The Mercury went east at Seventy-ninth Street, then north on York. At Eighty-sixth Street it went east again. Adele and the man got out in front of a red brick house on East End Avenue. The chauffeur pulled off in the Marquis. They entered the house. The house, incongruous for Manhattan, was small, neat, with gables, and resembled something to be found in Connecticut or upstate New York.

Gray Eyes brought the car to a halt on the Carl Schurz Park side of the street.

An hour later Adele came out of the house. "Now watch this," Gray Eyes said, as Adele entered a waiting cab.

"What?"

"She just made her hundred. Now she'll skip uptown to cop."

Just as Gray Eyes had called it, the cab with Adele turned uptown on Third Avenue. Gray Eyes and Tracy followed in their car.

At One Hundred Tenth Street she got out and entered a store, San Juan Lunch. She sat in a red leatherette booth.

Gray Eyes entered the luncheonette after her.

She didn't seem at all surprised to see him. Her expression softened when he slid into the booth next to her. "Oh, Buddy," she said softly. She leaned her head on his shoulder and laughed quietly.

"How's everything?" he said.

"Fine."

A diminutive Puerto Rican brought coffee. The two cups steamed on the gold-speckled plastic tabletop. The place smelled of bug spray. "What was happening on the Coast?" she asked.

"Oh, you know, the Coast is the Coast, all kinds of things happening there. What's been happening here?"

"I got a dog."

"Hey!"

"Cute little thing. She's like my baby."

"Who's your connection these days?"

"No one special."

"Uh-huh." Gray Eyes watched a cockroach staggering along the chipped green wall paint. "What did the cop, Strahan, want?"

"Oh, him? Yeah. Well. He wanted you."

"Sure."

"And there was another guy came by. An old friend of yours from high school. A Jew. Akiba. He didn't tell me his last name."

Gray Eyes grew quiet. Akiba! What was he doing here? How, Akiba? Akiba Moldavan!

Julie must have contacted him and he must have searched Adele out. But why? What did he want? He was thinking: My whole past is chasing after me, the universe is closing down on me. My past will hound me until it drives me to the far stars.

It did not trouble him. He did not fear it now. It was not paranoia, but a tangible fact.

He rubbed his arm. It ached terribly.

"What's wrong?" Adele said.

"A little hole there. Thirty-eight police special."

"Someone shot you? Why?"

He smiled. "Why not?"

Adele ran her hand over his face. Her hand was very soft. She always came through when you were sick and hurting, Gray Eyes was thinking, on the rims. Get on your feet, though, and she'd chop you off at the knees. "What did you do?" she said.

"The cop told you, didn't he?"

"You killed someone."

"I guess so."

"Jesus. Why?"

"I had my reasons." He pointed a finger at the center of his forehead. "They only make sense here." He sipped at his coffee. The cockroach had fallen off the wall and was on his back on the next table, legs in the air, struggling. "When I was all jammed up, I thought of you, you know?"

"Yes?"

"I figured I could come to you." The cockroach's legs were churning, like a bicyclist going uphill. They began to move slower and slower, then suddenly snapped in. The cockroach curled into a tight, rigid ball. "I have to get back to the Coast, to Alex," Gray Eyes said.

"Whatever for?"

"Alex will make everything right."

"I can't put you up, you know," she said. "They watch me. They'd force me to trade you. I don't want to do that."

"Just help me get to the Coast."

"I can't do anything for you. Really. You know that." She smoothed his hair back with her hand. "You don't look good, Bud. You look tired and down." She laughed nervously. "How do I look?"

"Fine."

"You can tell me the truth. I look like a strung-out, wasted, junky whore. Don't I?" He did not answer. "The joint would have been good for me. I could have got my shit together," she said. "What about you? Riding the habit, or is it riding you?"

"It's dead," he said. "I rode it into the ground, broke its back."

"Ah, that's so good, Bud."

"You know me—I never really had an addictive personality."

"You're one special, weird unit, Bud."

"Oh, yeah."

"Why'd you kill the man?"

Gray Eyes sat there staring down at his coffee cup. "Let's just say I felt like it." He saw in his mind's eye his mother when she was young. She was on a ferris wheel, laughing and screaming and holding Buddy to her. Then he saw her dying, saw her wasted body, her face without flesh, the horrible rot of her leg, and he was suddenly filled with a sense of death everywhere, the bug-spray smell of death, cockroach curled in a death ball. "Can you help me in any way?" he said. "Give me some money. Anything. I thought I could depend on Earl, but it didn't work out. Now the police are here. I had this girl in Pittsburgh. She must have cut a deal."

"You don't have much luck with women."

"That's the game," Gray Eyes said. "If I can just get back to California—"

"What about all those people you burned, all those politicals?"

"Politicals, my ass. They were nothing but dope fiends."

"If that's what you believe—"

"Everybody's making me out to be a rat. You, Earl—"

"Rat karma," she said.

"That was you, not me—"

"Never! A rat is the lowest. A rat is disgusting," she said.

"Oh, yes. You were a rat. Big one, with a long tail."

"I was forced into it," she said.

"Right. Okay." They sat in silence. Adele lit up a cigarette. She had begun to get twitchy. Her concern for Gray Eyes had melted away. She had been offended to have been saddled with the obloquy of ratdom.

"Can you do *anything* for me?" Gray Eyes said.

"I don't think so."

"Please."

"You had no right calling me that."

A young black man wearing an ankle-length tan leather overcoat appeared in the doorway leading from the back of the store. The skin on his face, neck, the backs of his hands was piebald, great colorless patches edged with black. He stood in the doorway, staring down the aisle. "You have to go," Adele said.

"Your connection?"

"Yes."

"He's pretty."

"Just go." She reached into her pocket and slid a piece of paper onto the table. It was the check Akiba had given her. "That's the best I can do," she said.

Gray Eyes stared at the check and smiled. He studied Akiba's signature. He had changed over the years, but it somehow still retained a schoolboy's scrawling innocence. He kissed the signature, then stood up. The man in the doorway continued to stare. He had a yellowish tinge to his eyes. "Hey, maybe we'll see each other sometime," Gray Eyes said.

Adele spoke in a tiny voice, a choked voice. "Why did you do what you did to me? Why did you burn me like that? Why did you abandon me like that?" She was fighting tears. "You always told me you would take care of me."

"Rat karma."

"You just threw me away. You gave me up to all that scum."

The man in the rear doorway had his head cocked to listen. He was frowning.

"I never wanted to."

"Oh, yes."

"I could blame you, too, you know."

"For what?" she said, tears in her eyes.

"Forget it."

"My mother always told me, don't get involved with a Jew."

Gray Eyes said nothing. He pocketed Akiba's check and left through the front door.

The man with the piebald skin came close to Adele. "What was that?"

"Some creep hassling me."

"Is that so?" the man said. "Hassles are a drag, man. Hassles are bad. I don't like no hassles with no one."

"Yes," Adele said. "What do you have?"

"I have bags and balloons. I have loads. I have decks. I have all that good shit."

"That's so great. It really is," she said, and followed the piebald man out through the rear door.

# 14

It was dawn when Akiba Moldavan climbed out of bed. He had not slept at all. The night had been filled with screams and laughter, doors slamming, the sound of footsteps pounding up and down the hall.

His nerves were electric under his skin. He ached with fatigue. He looked at himself in the bathroom mirror and was shocked at how pale and drawn he appeared.

Back in the main room he took his *tallith*, prayer shawl, out of its bag. He examined the *zizith*, fringes, and recited in Hebrew, "Bless the Lord, O my soul; O Lord, my God. You are very great; You are clothed in glory and majesty, wrapped in a robe of light; You spread the heavens like a tent cloth."

He thought of Buddy Gray Eyes and tried desperately to find a bridge to God, to approach the luminous center of His Being. The effort was brutal, exhausting.

He concentrated with all his strength on a Kabbalistic meditation, struggled to awaken his spirit: *"For the purpose of unifying the Holy One, blessed be He and His presence, I wrap myself in this prayer shawl with fringes. So should my soul and my 248 limbs and 365 veins be wrapped in the light of the fringes, which is 613. And just as I am covered by a prayer shawl in this world, so should I be worthy of a dignified cloak and beautiful prayer shawl in the world to come—in the Garden of Eden. And* through the fulfillment of this command may my soul, spirit, holy spark, and prayer be saved from obstructions. May the prayer shawl spread its wings over them and save them 'As an eagle that stirs its nestlings, fluttering over its chicks.' And the doing of this mitzvah should be considered by the Holy One, blessed be He, to be as important as fulfilling in all particulars, details, and intentions, the 613 mitzvot that depend on it. Amen, Selah."

He spread out the shawl before him and spoke a *berakah*, prayer: "Blessed are You, Lord our God, King of the Universe, who has sanctified us with His commandments, and commanded us to enwrap ourselves in a *tallith* with zizith." He summoned up all the belief within him, opened the cage of his heart, felt his spirit, an ailing bird, wings beating against the weight of the wind, strain to rise, move now into terror-filled skies—a wasteland without limit—wheel, scream, cry out to God to reveal His face, buffet across the indesinent void toward the *Ein Soph*, the Unknowable, the endless soul of God. Akiba prayed and prayed for the bird of his spirit to come to rest there, if only for an instant!

The gulf was so vast, the desert between Man and the Master of the Universe . . .

He covered his head with the prayer shawl, and before letting it rest on his shoulders he said in Hebrew: "*How precious is Your kindness, God. Man can take refuge in the shadow of Your wings. He is sated with the fat of Your house and from the stream of Your delight he drinks. Because with You is the fountain of life and in Your light do we see light. Send Your kindness to those who try to know You, and Your righteousness to the good-hearted.*"

He then took his *tefillin*, phylacteries, out of their sack. He put on the *shel yad*, wrapped the leather thong around his left arm and hand, placed the leather box over the muscle on the left arm; then the *shel rosh*. As he wound its thong around his head, centering the box just above the hairline, he prayed in Hebrew: "Blessed are You, Lord our God, King of the Universe, who has sanctified us with

His commandments and commanded us to wear *tefillin*." He finished the donning of the phylacteries with these words from Hosea: "And I will betroth thee unto Me in righteousness and in justice, and in loving kindness and compassion. And I will betroth thee unto Me in faithfulness; and thou shalt know the Lord." The Hebrew word for "to know" employed in the verse was *daat*, the same word used for sexual congress, and Akiba spoke the words with passion, trying to embrace God, to know God in love as one knows a woman, to pour his whole being into God.

He spent the morning in his hotel room, wasted by a sense of hopelessness; the paths of the Sephirot were a maze, all was lost. Gray Eyes had by his actions proclaimed there is no God, there is no Universe, there is no World to Come. Nothing he had seen had countervailed this.

Gray Eyes had usurped the Sephirot, transformed light to dark, spread black tendrils to snare Akiba, drag him through blind passageways, destroy him even as he had destroyed the old man.

He paced the room, paused to stare out the window. The snow had almost stopped, a few vagrant flakes gusting about from time to time. The day was gray. Traffic crawled on slowly, but moved. Horns honked, a weird clarion dissonance, rising, diminshing, bleating again.

If he could have discovered a *reason* for Gray Eyes's action, the faintest outline of a human *why*, he could go on. But there was none. No trace, no spark, no reason.

He closed his eyes and fought within himself to bring up a spark, to ignite his soul. Our actions affect God. I am doing this for God, he told himself.

Four entered the garden. One died, one went mad, one became an apostate . . .

He had done this, he had come this far. He would not turn back.

And then the fiery tree began to blaze. Limbs of Sephirot, limbs of Holiness burned bright behind his eyes.

"I will do this," he yelled to the empty room. "I will do this, I will do this. Yes, I will do this."

Outside the sky was leaden, the day bitter cold. The falling snow had turned granular, covering the recently cleared sidewalks with a thin, ricelike layer. Beneath the grains of snow were patches of ice. The slush at curbside had formed a blackened, frozen crust.

He hurried through the streets oblivious to the cold, to the ice and slush. The Sephirot blazed in his skull.

On the subway ride to the Village he awoke as though from a dream. He hadn't remembered leaving the hotel, hadn't remembered boarding the train.

He found Earl's coffee shop without difficulty, a snake of neon spitting across a dark tenement facade. Inside, a large black man in a dashiki played chess with a bony-headed bald man—Earl. There was no one else in the place.

Akiba moved to their table, studied the board. Neither of the men acknowledged his presence. He stood there.

The black man had a mate in two and Akiba wondered if he saw it. Yes: he executed it perfectly.

The bald-headed man gazed up at Akiba through tinted glasses. "What the fuck do you want? I hate a fucking kibitzer." He shoved the chess board away and moved behind the counter.

"I'm looking for Earl," Akiba said. Earl did not answer, but set to work scraping down his griddle.

The large black man got up. He moved to the counter and leaned across it. "Give me my four dollars," he said.

Earl banged open the cash register and removed four one-dollar bills. The black man grabbed the bills, returned to the table, and packed up his chess set.

"He learned his chess in the joint," the black man said, "and he gets mad when someone lays a little *finesse* on him, some Nimzovich, some Capablanca. It's all *position* and his position was hopeless, you know that."

"It was hopeless," Akiba said.

Earl looked up from the griddle and glared at Akiba. The black man departed. "You said my position was hopeless. What did you mean by that?" Earl removed his tinted glasses. His pupils were unnaturally large—black, buglike dots. His speech had a slow, deep, ragged quality, like a phonograph playing off-speed. "Hopeless, motherfucker? Hopeless?" His head dipped down in slow nods toward the counter. "Had the game won till you walked through the door." He jerked his head up and looked with blank eyes at Akiba.

"Are you Earl?"

Earl moved back to the griddle. He began to slam utensils around. "Get out of here, I'm closing up," he said.

"I'm trying to find Buddy Gray Eyes."

"If you're the fucking heat, you're ridiculous."

"I'm not the heat. I'm a friend of his."

Earl scratched his bony head vigorously. His face looked like yellow parchment; it sagged with folds of skin. He had thick eyelids and thick bags of skin below the eyes. The skin of his face seemed to be pulling away from the bone of his face, all of it drooping down, a thick, slow run, like ice cream off the side of a cone.

"I know where he is," Earl said. "Outer-fucking-space. You'll find him, all right. Dead." Earl stared at Akiba with his huge, black-dot, pinned pupils. "He sold out anyone who ever loved him, that traitorous fuck."

"I need to get to him."

"Why?"

Akiba stared into the man's eyes, into the depths of the dope eeriness there. "I just need to," he said.

Earl took a pack of cigarettes out of his shirt pocket, removed one, and lit up. He thought for a while, forgetting the match. It burned down to his fingers; he jerked his hand and flicked it away. "He was a good kid once. Then he chucked it all into the cooker. Dope fiends are garbage. You hear me? Saw myself in him, saw him crawl to the cooker, saw him weasel and rat, and it's fucking painful.

It's painful. When he walked through that door yesterday—"

"You saw him yesterday?"

Earl looked up. "He's trying to get to California," he said. "If he means anything to you, don't let him go back there."

"Why?"

"Don't you see? Everybody's been using this fucking kid. They pushed him into junk, they pushed him into that political stuff, they pushed him into being a ratfink, they pushed him probably into even murder. Don't you see? Don't you see?"

"No."

"Ah, get out of here. Leave me alone. The whole thing sickens me."

"Help me find him."

"How? Walk up and down the streets of New York calling out his name? Scour the highways, train tracks, jet streams, between here and California? How?" He drew a cup of coffee from the urn, sipped at it.

Akiba got up from the counter. The gray day was turning dark. The inside of the coffee shop was dim now.

"I know why he killed," Earl said very simply.

"Why?" Akiba said.

"There was nothing else in this world for him to do." He began to laugh quietly. He leaned against the griddle and laughed and laughed. He began to hum to himself, laughed softly and hummed as though party to an extraordinary secret.

Unnoticed, a man had entered the coffee shop. There was a soft click as the door eased shut, and Akiba turned.

It was impossible to make out who it was. He was silhouetted against the afternoon light beyond the door.

"Move, skinhead, and you'll be picking pieces of skull out of that french fryer," the man said. He was holding a gun in his hand.

"Just call me Mr. Freeze," Earl said.

The man edged forward into the light. John Strahan. The light caught glints of his steel spectacle rims; his eyes appeared unnaturally bright.

Strahan smiled tightly at Akiba, then moved to Earl. He stared into his eyes. "You're out there, aren't you?" he said.

"I'm cooking at my own speed."

"Where is he?" Strahan said.

"You tell me."

"Cockroach!" Strahan said.

"I trusted you, dude," Earl said heatedly to Akiba. "Can't trust no one in this fucking life." He threw his coffee cup against the stainless steel backing behind the griddle. The plastic cup bounced harmlessly off. Earl looked as though he would weep with anger.

"Simmer down," Strahan said.

"Go fuck yourself."

Strahan cracked Earl along the side of his head with the revolver; Earl dropped to one knee. A crease of blood appeared on the bare skull above his ear; a thin trickle ran down the fleshy flap of his ear. "Damn," Earl said, shaking his head to clear it. He started to get up and Strahan kicked his leg out from under him. "Where's Gray Eyes?" he said.

"Who is this crazy fuck?" Earl said to Akiba. He began to crawl alongside the counter, heading for the back of the coffee shop.

"Stay where you are, cockroach," Strahan said. He came up close to Earl, who was cowering against the base of the counter.

"I got bad migraine," Earl said. "Don't hit me again, please."

"You want a cure for your migraine?" Strahan said. He placed the barrel of the gun against Earl's head, the tip in his ear. Blood from the gash on his head accumulated on the tip. He cocked the hammer back on the gun. Earl began to weep. "Oh, shit, man, why are you doing this? He's going to kill me. Oh, shit."

Akiba felt himself flooded with weakness. "John, let the man alone," he said.

Strahan pushed with the tip of the gun barrel, and Earl's head was squeezed in tight against the counter base. "Was he here?"

Earl was sobbing quietly. "You're fucking crazy, man. You're crazy."

"Was he here?"

"Yes. Yes."

"Where is he now?"

"I don't know."

Strahan smacked his head again with the revolver. Earl, in desperation, lunged forward and attempted to grab Strahan around the ankles. Strahan kicked out. His shoe caught Earl in the mouth. Earl brought his hands to his mouth and spit his dentures into his cupped palms. Blood flowed from his mouth. "My false teeth, man. You fucking broke my false teeth," he whined pathetically.

"Where is he now?"

Earl was weeping, spilling tears and blood onto the floor. "Goddamn Gray Eyes, turned and burned me so many times, caused me nothing but heartache in this life. What do you want from me? I don't know nothing. I swear to almighty God." He buried his head in his arms and wept.

Strahan drew back, eased the hammer shut on the revolver, returned it to its holster. He sat on one of the counter stools. "When I get him, I'm going to remove him from my life," he said to Akiba. "Don't try to stop me."

"Why do you hate him so?" Akiba said. Strahan did not speak. "Why?"

Strahan's eyes behind his spectacles began to blink rapidly; in the center of his gaze Akiba could see pinpoints of fear and this amazed him. He's afraid! Akiba thought. He hates and he will kill and he's afraid.

"The three of us grew up together," Akiba said, "shared the same childhood. Why do you have this hate?"

"I'm doing what I have to do," Strahan said.

"I won't let you kill him," Akiba said.

Strahan moved to the counter without taking his eyes off Akiba. Flashes of panic gleamed behind his spectacles. "I'm married to that cocksucker," he said. "I'll follow him wherever he goes."

"I won't let you kill him!" Akiba shouted.

Strahan looked small, sad. "The chosen people," he said. "You always take care of each other, don't you?" He appeared as though he wanted to say something more, but instead pushed past Akiba. He moved out of the coffee shop into the dark afternoon, hesitated just beyond the window, then was gone.

Ancient Jewish law, Akiba said to himself: a person pursuing another with the purpose of taking his life—*rodeph*. You must stop him. It is an obligation. You must stop him even if it means killing the pursuer. *Rodeph. Kabbalah. Rodeph. Rodeph.*

Earl was washing his false teeth in the sink behind the counter. "I'm sorry," Akiba said to him.

"Fuck him and the horse he rode up on," Earl said without looking at Akiba. He tried to cover his shame with bravado. "I was just conning him. I knew he wouldn't shoot."

"Your teeth—"

"They weren't mine, nohow. I won 'em from some spic playing chess. Now get out of here. You ruined my fucking afternoon, asshole."

# 15

GRAY EYES slept while Tracy drove. The roads were slick with ice, almost impossible, but they managed to keep going. The storm had kicked up again and appeared to be without end. They drove west into the heart of the storm.

He awoke to darkness. He was running a fever. He peeled back the bandage of his arm. The wound was festering.

"I think you should get to a doctor, babe," Tracy said to him. "You don't look too good."

"I don't want to go to a doctor."

He told himself that he was afraid of the police; a doctor seeing a gun wound would call them. It was something deeper, though: in his mind's eye he saw his mother dying. The chemicals used to fight her cancer had brought on an infection. Her leg had begun to rot. There had been no way to stop it, no doctor to cure it.

Tracy and Gray Eyes had planned to turn south halfway across Pennsylvania: that way they could escape the snow. Tracy, however, had come up with another idea. They would drive on to Davenport, Iowa, her hometown. She had friends there. They could hide out there and see that Buddy's arm was cared for. "What about the dude you tried to kill?"

"I beat the rap. Self-defense."

He was too sick to press her on it. The ache in his arm had spread out, seemed now to encompass his whole being.

Tracy drove the distance. They had a supply of MDA, methamphetamine, jolly beans Tracy called them, and Dolophine, and he would doze on the dollies while she kept popping speed.

At midafternoon they approached Chicago, skirted it, and followed I-80 across Illinois. They had been on the road almost twenty-four hours. The land, ominously flat, was a great white sea of snow all about them. The chains on their tires ground on through thick snow. The roads were passable, but barely so.

Tracy was talking about a man she had married when she was fifteen. Gray Eyes awoke, burning with fever, in the middle of the story. He had no idea how long she had been churning her words out. "That dude was like, unreal, you know. Dirty old man. He was like fifty years old, you know."

"What's that?" Gray Eyes said, bewildered. He thought he might still be dreaming.

"I know. You can't understand me. That's 'cause I talk into myself. Definitely. I was a breach baby and they pulled me out by my throat." She laughed.

On the radio Wilson Pickett sang, a moaning wail: "*If you need me, call me. If you need me, call me. Ah, but don't wait too long.*"

Tracy spoke through clenched teeth, her jaw muscles snapping with the amphetamine. "He had the best disappearing act I'd ever seen. He told me, you don't want to see me, I'll just disappear. And that's what he did. I just turned around one day, and, man, he was gone. Disappeared. I don't know how he did it. Weird."

"*If you want me, yeah, send for me. Honey, if you want me, Lord have mercy, send for me. Ah, but don't wait too long . . .*" The song was a mournful shriek, vibrating with the rev and strain of the car's engine. Buddy, his eyes closed, was slumped forward, his head resting on his hands. "Who?" he said.

"My husband. You'd never think he was fifty years old. He was a muscle freak and definitely very insecure. He would bad-mouth himself for sure and I don't know why. He was an *incredible*-looking guy and that had to work for him. At least for twenty-four hours. And yet he'd get insecure. And it would just make me sick to my stomach, make me want to throw up. I mean I just *hate* a person *that* insecure and I'd have to tell him, you're making me very sick to the stomach. And then he'd accuse me of being promiscuous. Is that what I am, promiscuous, I'd ask? He'd say, for lack of a better word. Promiscuous. I was only fifteen, what did I know? After he dematerialized I took up with an Indian, American Indian. A very together guy, *superficially*. But filled with all sorts of redskin hang-ups. You see, I've always been able to compartmentalize my life, fit in with all colors. Red, black, what-have-you. Definitely." She laughed, ground her teeth. "How you feeling, babe?"

"Not too well."

"We're going to get you to Davenport and get you all patched up. That Indian I was telling you about, he couldn't stand the idea that I was like communing on a meaningful level with other guys. It got him definitely very uptight and he took it as an attack on his masculinity and his Indian heritage. I respected his masculinity, for sure, but I didn't give a flying fuck for his Indian heritage."

Gray Eyes groaned softly. "Hey, babe, we're getting there. Then you're going to bag it until you're healthy. I'm going to take care of you. I have this very maternal streak, you know. I have three brothers and I used to take care of them." She laughed, tight-jawed. "The Indian accused me of sleeping with a state trooper. It was the truth. The trooper caught me with all sorts of chemicals for sure, dragging Main about a hundred and five. I balled him first time just off the side of the road, to beat that rap. Afterward we'd just meet any old time—out in the woods, down country roads. Anywhere. It turned me on doing him in a police car. The Indian made a big, heavy scene out of it. How could I make it, you know, with a pig? I said, look, I'll make it with a hunchback Chinese midget at high noon in the middle of Main Street if I feel like it. He raised all kinds of shit, broke my face, sent me to the hospital. That really grossed me out so I told him to suck off and I stayed away from him after that and the dude began to definitely harass me—you know, come out to the house and shoot out windows with a twenty-two and like that. I had this old VW and he tossed a Molotov cocktail through the window for sure and *destroyed the car*. That dude was a big politico at the university, you know? He didn't go to the school, he would just hang out and toss bombs and yell Red Power and that lame shit. After he wasted my VW I told the trooper about the dude and the trooper said I'll teach that redskin a lesson. For sure. Definitely. They picked him up and really beat the shit out of him, so he got really *rude*, you know, and laid some heavy motherfucks on them and like that, so the trooper shot him. Shot that redskin dude, *dead*." She laughed, her jaw twitching. "*D-E-A-D*. Custer's last stand in reverse." She continued to laugh. "I love a lot of blood and guts. I guess that's why you turn me on. Definitely."

It was just getting dark when they approached Davenport. They drove through Moline and Rock Island and crossed over the Centennial toll bridge into Davenport. "Hey, babe, look, the Mississippi. 'The Mississippi's wide and muddy, your momma's big and bloody.' That's what the jigs used to say. I'm going to get you all fixed up, babe."

Gray Eyes, his head lolling against the car window, watched the murky water rush by beneath the bridge, a viscous ooze that seemed both muddy and bloody to him. Blood was swimming in his eyes, the taste of it was in his mouth. He felt godawful, nauseated, feverish.

They checked into the All American Hotel on Main Street, between the Trailways and Greyhound bus stations. The hotel was old and run-down, but clean. No one in the narrow lobby appeared to be younger than seventy. The desk man looked at them with some suspicion, Gray Eyes felt, but Tracy said it was fever paranoia eating him up.

The elevator creaked its slow way upward, seeming to take forever. "Where we going, the planet Pluto?" Gray Eyes said.

"Fifth floor, babe."

He pressed against the vibrating walls, swayed, perspired. "Yeah," he said.

The room was large and pleasant, a suite actually, consisting of a sleeping area with a large, old-fashioned iron double bed, and a living room. The living room had a worn couch, an easy chair, and a blond wood coffee table scarred with cigarette burns. There were two bathrooms, one with stall shower, the other with a claw-legged bathtub. "Neat," Tracy said, inspecting the bathrooms.

Gray Eyes, shivering violently now, crawled into the bed with his clothes on. He curled into a tight, quaking ball beneath the heavy bedspread and blanket. "I have to get you a doctor, babe. Someone to look after that *arm*," Tracy said.

"No doctor."

"I'm going to get you some abortion hack who wouldn't dare go to the police. I have connections in this town. Some of those dudes really know their medicine, don't you worry about it." She sat on the edge of the bed. "C'mon, babe." She poured out some dollies in her hand and forced him to swallow them. Then she left.

Gray Eyes, in a deep, drugged sleep, was aware someone had entered the room, an older man, a doctor in a white medical coat. The doctor approached the bed, his expression serious, concerned. "Someone wants to see you," he said.

"Who?"

"Come with me."

"Where?"

"Not far."

"What about the girl?"

"This has nothing to do with her."

Gray Eyes felt apprehensive, yet sad, as though he would cry. The doctor reminded him of something sad and painful. What? He got out of bed. "What do I need?" Gray Eyes said.

"Nothing."

He followed the doctor out of the room into the hallway. Someone was moaning in a room at the far end. The moan was very loud and clear. The doctor opened the door to the stairway and they moved quickly down and through another door into an alley.

It was still dark outside. The alley was cold, littered with garbage. As he hurried after the doctor, something stirred in a darkened doorway and Gray Eyes looked over: crouched in shadow was a small child dressed in a snowsuit. He waved at Buddy.

At the end of the alley they came to a white brick building and Gray Eyes immediately knew somehow it was a nursing home. Strange, he thought, a nursing home fronting on this place. He followed the doctor inside.

The halls were white and empty, immaculate. The doctor opened a door and then they were standing in a hospital room. There was a woman lying in the bed, her body withered, doll-like. She had almost no hair on her head. Her face looked like a skull. It was his mother as he had seen her just before she died. Gray Eyes bent over her bed and looked at her leg; the flesh was suppurating. There was a heavy odor of seeping pus and death in the room. "How is this possible?" Gray Eyes said.

"We were able to keep her alive," the doctor said, and now Gray Eyes realized who he was: one of the doctors who had been treating his mother in her last days. "We've kept her alive all this time," the doctor said. Oh, God, Gray Eyes thought, all this time she's been suffering alone in this terrible room! No one knew . . .

He went to his mother and embraced her. She was trembling. She turned her face to him. Her eyes were wide and frightened and he began to weep. She was whispering something. He strained to hear, but couldn't make it out. "What? What?" he cried. He couldn't make it out.

He awoke, sobbing. There was a draft coming in through the partially opened transom; the room was freezing. He got up, closed the transom, then looked out the window. The streets were silent, dark, blanketed in snow. The snow was coming down easily, gently, and he stood watching it for a long while.

He moved back to the bed and turned on the lamp and peeled back the bandage on his arm. The arm was red and inflamed, the wound crusted with dried blood and stale pus. There was a sweetish odor coming from the wound and he realized it was the same odor his mother's wound had given off; it was the odor in his dream.

He called down to the desk for the time. It was five A.M. He sat on the edge of the bed, feeling desperately lost and alone. Where was Tracy? She should have been back by this time. He didn't trust her. She was a snake; he felt sure of it. She would sell him out. This very minute she was probably cutting a deal, bailing out of her own problems, trading him off.

He thought of Julie Tripp now. Of the women he had been involved with she had been the best; and he had blown it. Adele Morath, Tracy—they were both dope-fiend disasters, physical and emotional killers. They would cash you in at every turn.

Not so with Julie. He had been drawn to her because of an aura of wholesomeness, goodness, and he had not been wrong. He had needed health in those days as a suffocating man needs air. It had been absolutely imperative then that he turn his life around, salvage it. And for a while with Julie he had succeeded.

Then his death soul had taken over.

Where had it come from, Death Soul? He had first become aware of it as a small child; had come into his cellar and found his pet chick, mouth gaping as it fought for breath, dying. He had cradled it in his arms and cried. And his mother had comforted him.

Years later he had been at her bedside and in an eerie paradigm of present to past saw her mouth working in the same desperate way, trying to drink in life while death sucked it away.

Death Soul, a great black wing, had entered him then. He had become The Destroyer. Death Soul's emblem was tattooed above his heart.

As a child he had heard stories of the Kabbalah from Akiba. He had invented his own Kabbalah. Death Soul Kabbalah. He danced with the little man on his chest.

He knew, though, that Julie Tripp possessed another force. She was anti–Death Soul and she might have exorcised the blackness within him. Certainly she tried. The power of Death Soul, however, was too great. *Yetzer ha-ra.* The Destroyer.

Suddenly he longed for Julie. He saw her in his mind and her face was sweet beyond sweetness and a spark within him cried out for her.

He put through a long-distance call to Pittsburgh. "Little Julie," he said. "Ah, little Julie! I had a dream before. I dreamed about my mother. Julie, it was so real."

"Buddy, where are you?"

"On my way to see Alex. He's going to make it all right."

"Buddy, Buddy—"

He laughed and whistled. "I miss you," he said.

She did not talk for a long time. "What do you want me to do?"

"Come to me. Meet me at Lake Chandler. We'll go up in the mountains. No one can find us in the mountains."

"Where are you now?"

"All American Hotel, Davenport, Iowa. It's the perfect place for me, the all-American boy." He laughed again, whistled a trilling riff, laughed again.

"Wait for me. I'll come there."

"I feel like I'm dying," he said.

"I'll take a plane out. Wait for me."

"Julie, what I did seems crazy, but I had a specific reason for it, and I want to tell you about it."

"All right, Bud."

"When I see you."

"All right."

He hung up and stared at the ceiling. Was he awake now or dreaming? Had he just talked to Julie? Was his mother still alive, hidden away in a remote room, crying out for him? Had he actually *killed* a man?

The gray light of dawn appeared on the wall opposite the bed. He watched it climb upward and spread across the ceiling. He drifted off to sleep again.

He awoke to the sound of two men talking. He lay there, eyes closed, awash in a sea of incomprehensible talk. "The engines nowadays are made with these here smoggy device things in 'em," one of the men was saying. "An' the smoggy devices are also incorporated into the cams, unlike what everybody thinks."

"Oh, well," the second voice said, "you change your headers and your manifold and carburetor and, ah, maybe your ignition—"

"Uh-huh, that ain't the way to fly. What you got to do is change that bump stick, 'cause when you change that bump stick you can get rid of the smog device *completely,* an' that thing runs like *it's supposed to,* instead of like what the government says it's supposed to run like."

"For sure." A girl's voice, Tracy.

"I picked up a little 'sixty-five CJ-five Jeep thing there

and it had a little four-banger three-speed," the first voice said. It was low and drawly, not unpleasant, Gray Eyes thought; like warm water. "An' I got me a nice little 'seventy-two three fifty with low compression and all that garbage, slipped the old bump stick out, changed the intake manifold for one of them good aluminum jobs, and, ah, put a Holly carbureting on 'im and some headers."

"That moved 'im, huh?" Tracy said.

"Moved 'im? That nice little four-hundred-horsepower three fifty flat does third-gear burnouts," the second man said. His voice was higher pitched than the first's, irritating.

"And I'll bet that mother'll climb," Tracy said.

"It's got the torque. It'll idle up the side of a hill a motorcycle can't make," the second man said.

"There was this dude had a 'seventy-four CJ-five Jeep and he got him a four oh one full race Matador motor and put it in there. We were doing about four ten rear-end ratio with a four-hundred-horse three fifty Chevy against a four oh one Matador and flat blew his doors clean off the Interstate, made him eat his shorts. You couldn't believe it for sure."

"That was one scream-ass Jeep," the second man said. "For sure."

Gray Eyes, wide awake now, looked into the living room area. Tracy was there with two young guys, long hairs, one with a Jesse James moustache, the other bearded. The three of them were seated on the floor drinking beer from cans. He swung his legs over the side of the bed and sat up.

He could tell immediately by the tense twitchiness, the shining eyes, that they were all crazed and speeding, and his skin crawled and he was afraid. *She's going to do me in*, he thought in a panic.

Tracy noticed him. "Babe, this here is Apache," she said, indicating the one with the beard. "And this here, Corry."

"Is Apache your Indian?" Gray Eyes asked, dazed and

feverish and wondering what kind of nightmare *this* was. Apache and Corry laughed, simpering, and Gray Eyes felt goose bumps rising all over him.

"Hell, I'm no Indian," Apache said. He had the low, drawly voice.

"He's not the Indian, babe," Tracy said. "I told you, the Indian's dead. These are both friends of my brother Kevin."

"Which one is the abortionist?" Gray Eyes asked, and everyone laughed again and he felt very lost and alone.

Apache sat next to Gray Eyes on the bed. He smelled of motor oil. "Let me look at that arm," Apache said.

Gray Eyes held it up to him. "That's a mother," he said. He turned the arm around so Corry could see it.

"For sure that's a mother," agreed Corry.

"Definitely, for sure," said Tracy.

"Are you a doctor?" Gray Eyes asked of Apache.

"I'm not a doctor. Honest to God."

"Then what the hell are you doing with my arm?"

"Apache's very spiritual, babe. He'll be good for your arm."

"Right on, Willie," Corry said.

"Who's Willie?"

"Willie Coatimundi. That's her."

"She told me she was Tracy."

"Tracy Budwise, Willie Coatimundi, Tammy Wammy—she got all kind of names. Who knows who she is?"

"For sure, babe," Tracy said.

Corry gingerly lit a joint and passed it around. He lowered his head to Gray Eyes. There was a scab on top of it. "Apache healed my head," Corry said. "Had a hole right down practically to the brain. He healed it."

"He has heavy spiritual qualities, babe," Tracy said, taking a toke off the joint.

"Some gross pig put that hole in my head, night before last. 'Pache 'n' me we was gritting down in this here diner an' there was some *hassles*, you know, an' then all kind of shit come down from the black sky. There's this old boy, Rooter. You know Rooter?"

Gray Eyes shook his head. "He doesn't know Rooter," Tracy said, laughing silently, staring at the floor with her shiny, dead eyes.

"That's okay," Corry said, and continued. "Well, Rooter, he's kind of an asshole who works with the county police and he comes into the diner and starts to lay a whole load of bogus shit on us—"

"Bogus shit, man," Apache agreed. "For sure."

"Well, it just turned my teeth sour, you know. He snitched me off one time and seems like I've got a pig cloud over my head ever since."

"That's for shit sure," Apache said, not really listening. He was up and pacing the room, looking into drawers, checking out the closets. *He's looking to take us off,* Gray Eyes thought, and was relieved to know that he and Tracy were the poorest couple imaginable for a take-off.

"Old Rooter, he's for sure hassling," Corry went on, "so I take a butter knife and jab it in his gut. It was only a butter knife, couldn't do no harm—"

"He wasn't out to do no harm, babe," Tracy said. She joined Apache at the bathroom and showed him the tub. Apache turned the water on, let it run for a moment. *They're going to drown me,* Gray Eyes thought.

"Next thing I know there's a whole shitload of county pigs in the place and they're all climbing upside my face and this one takes him a little ball-ping hammer and *bip* gives it to me right on the top of the head, right in through the skull!" Corry began to laugh, a high, hysterical laugh, and Apache and Tracy joined in. They fell to the floor, laughing, pummeled each other.

"I woke up in there with my shirt all bloody and wrapped around my head. I said I'm going to bleed to death and you know what 'Pache said? Tell him what you said, 'Pache."

Apache looked up from the floor. "I told him, no he wasn't."

"For sure, that's what he said," Corry confirmed. "He waved his 'Pache hands over my skull, shazam-whizam!, and my head stopped bleeding and stopped aching and I was good old Corry again, definitely. Then he waved his hands again, at that cell door, and *five minutes* later they let us out of there."

Tracy got up and approached Gray Eyes on the bed. "He's going to fix you up, babe," Tracy said.

Apache suddenly leaped to his feet and began dancing around the room in a herky-jerky, idiot dance, snapping his fingers and jerking his head from side to side. "Go, 'Pache," Corry said. He went on like that for about five minutes, then he moved directly up to Gray Eyes, placed both hands over the wound, and said: "Heal thyself, motherfucker! Heal thyself!" He squeezed both hands over the wound. His hands were black with automobile grease. The pain was like an electric charge ripping through Buddy's flesh, excruciating; Gray Eyes thought he would pass out from the pain.

"Now up! Up!" Apache said to Gray Eyes. Corry pulled him to his feet. "March," Apache said.

Apache, Corry, and Tracy took Gray Eyes out into the hall, into the elevator, and down to the lobby. The night clerk, an older woman with a wattled neck and swollen sacs beneath her eyes, watched with indifference.

They dragged Gray Eyes outside. He felt as though he was floating. The day outside was fiercely cold, with a knife-wind slicing in from the Mississippi. "You're trying to kill me," Gray Eyes moaned to Tracy.

"Don't worry about it, babe, Apache is magic. I know he is."

"For sure he's magic," Corry said, holding Gray Eyes under the arms.

People hurrying to work through the frigid morning had begun to appear on the street. Corry propped Gray Eyes up against a parked automobile and Apache started doing his spastic dance around him. Tracy weaved from side to side snapping her fingers while Apache jolted and lurched around, grinning idiotically. Corry held Gray Eyes against the car, steadying him. The wind was ice blowing off the river; the metal of the car was ice under his back.

Suddenly, in the middle of a leap, Apache spotted someone down the block. "Pig!" he shouted, and without a break in motion bounded off in the direction of the river. Corry darted after him, running at his heels. They rounded a corner of a warehouse building and disappeared.

"Get me back inside," Gray Eyes said, trembling violently.

Tracy continued to stare off in the direction of the mud-colored river. She looked as though she might cry. "I scored some great meth and they split with it," she said sadly. "How you doing, babe?" Gray Eyes shook his head. He felt enclosed in an ice-block nightmare. Tracy led him, shivering and perspiring, back into the All American Hotel. "You can't trust no one, babe," she said. Though the words were directed at Gray Eyes, she was talking to herself.

# 16

AFTER the phone call from Buddy, Julie Tripp contacted Akiba Moldavan in New York. She knew she would go to Davenport to Buddy; she hadn't the strength to go alone.

He flew in from New York and they met at the Greater Pittsburgh Airport. They took the morning flight to Chicago. From there they would rent a car and drive the 150 miles or so to Davenport. Because of the snow the Quad City Airport outside Davenport was closed.

"He was obsessed by three things. His mother, his childhood, and this thing he called the Kabbalah," Julie Tripp said as they circled O'Hare field, preparing to land. "Some nights I would fall asleep to his voice going on and on as though I weren't there. He would go through things that happened to him as a kid in incredible detail. It was as though they had just taken place."

"But why Cervino? Why kill him?" Akiba said. "I'm sorry I keep pounding away at this thing, but it eludes me. Everything lately seems to elude me."

She liked him very, very much. There was a shyness and awkwardness about Akiba, a genuine goodness, that Julie Tripp admired and felt comfortable with. He reminded her in certain ways of Buddy. Small mannerisms: his smile, a way of cocking his head to one side when he listened, his self-deprecating manner. They were an interlocking of opposites: where Buddy was bold, he was hesitant; where Buddy was graceful, he was clumsy. And yet they could have been brothers.

It was his passion to go to Buddy, though, that caused her to feel something like love for Akiba Moldavan. "Why are you doing this?" she said now.

"I owe it to him for what he was to me at one time," Akiba said, struggling with the words. "But it's more than that. I can't explain it. And you? Why are you doing this?"

"He's part of me," she said, embarrassed as she spoke the words. Buddy stayed with her; she could feel him wherever she went, smell the odor of him, hear the tone of his voice.

And now suddenly she felt lost, lost, her life reduced to the thinnest margin of possibility. She was nothing without Buddy Gray Eyes.

White clouds scudded by outside the window and she thought, My life is a cloud; there is no center to it, no weight.

The plane had begun to descend, moving down in gradual, measured dips. It banked sharply out of the clouds and O'Hare field suddenly snapped into view beneath them with startling clarity.

On the ground they moved quickly through the terminal and outside picked up their rental car, a yellow Pinto.

The day was cold, gray. The sky was like slate. They took the Tri-state Tollway south out of O'Hare to Route 55 and got onto I-80 just west of Joliet. The roads were clear of snow, but treacherous, with intermittent patches of ice. The broad plains west of Chicago were carpeted with snow, but no snow fell.

Julie was at the wheel. A child of California, she had been raised with hot rods and she handled the little Pinto expertly, keeping just within the speed limit, shifting lanes with perfect ease, overtaking car after car. They moved relentlessly west and by midafternoon they were nearing Davenport.

Akiba watched the barren landscape, his mind turning over doubts, testing his actions. Today was Saturday and he had broken the Sabbath, first by answering the call from Julie Tripp, then by traveling. He had justified his actions: Under the doctrine *pikuah nephesh* a Jew has a sacred duty to do anything to save a human life—on the Sabbath, even on the Day of Atonement.

He was on a sacred mission of redemption; he was racing with *rodeph*, the murderous pursuer. He was following the paths of Sephirot, moving within its holy maze.

They drove through Moline and Rock Island, crossed the Mississippi into Davenport.

In the lobby of the All American Hotel several old people dozed on vinyl-covered chairs. The desk clerk watched a soap opera on a small, black-and-white portable television.

She didn't bother to consult her cards when Akiba asked about Buddy. "He's with this ratty-looking girl," she said.

Julie Tripp stood next to the desk feeling suddenly foolish and isolated. Buddy had a girl with him! Who? What did she mean to him? And what would Buddy and the girl say when Julie appeared at their door? He had called for her, though, hadn't he? He had said he missed her, that he felt like he was dying. Who was the girl then?

The clerk continued, "But they checked out this morning. The girl left a note for a Mister Patch. Your name Patch?"

"Patch? Yes," Akiba said.

The woman stared at Akiba, trying to determine whether or not he looked like a Mr. Patch. She handed Akiba the note.

In a childish scrawl it said: "Off to Calif. Tell my Ma we'll be droppin by to see Harry in Rock Spring, Wyomin. Thanx alot for takin off my jolly beans, you prick. Your former frien, Just Me."

# 17

"AND I want to pray specially for a bunch of sick people, that I want you to lay your head on the radio. Now put that empty purse on the radio, lay them tithes on the radio, put that dollar, three, five, seven, and above. You don't begin to get your money back and more till you give your ten percent out of every dollar. I don't care if you work on a job, somebody got an inheritance, old age pension, any money that comes in, ten percent belongs to God—"

"Hear that, babe? Lean your head against the radio."

Gray Eyes and Tracy sped through the freezing night picking up radio stations from Salt Lake City, Oklahoma, California.

During the day they had crossed the flatlands of Iowa and Nebraska, in below-zero temperature. They were now in Wyoming, heading toward Rock Springs in the western part of the state.

Tracy's stepfather, a man named Harry Garth, she said, had taken a job there as an equipment oiler. "He's making boss money there, babe, five sixty an hour, and he'll put us up for a while. Hell, he's been screwing me since I was ten years old so why wouldn't he put us up? And it's on our way to California."

Gray Eyes was too sick to argue. While Tracy handled the driving, he drifted in and out of nightmares. Ferocious prairie winds buffeted the car. The radio crackled out hillbilly songs, farm equipment auctioneers, rural home advertising programs—"washing machine, needs repair, seven dollars; newborn kittens, free to good home"—and ubiquitous pitches, some shrill, some mellow, for God, Jesus, salvation, and money.

"God blesses the giver, curses them that don't, curses breed hell, death breeds hell, raise that checkbook now, write to me now, let the Lord speak to you. I know God is speaking to thirty million people to send me a hundred dollars tonight and three people to send me a thousand dollars—"

"Send him a thousand," Gray Eyes said.

"For sure," Tracy said.

"He's speaking to me."

"Definitely. Come on, babe. Lay your head on the radio."

Gray Eyes leaned his head against the dashboard.

Curses breed hell, death breeds hell, and that's where he was, Gray Eyes thought. Definitely. For sure.

"Father, I come to you humbly tonight to fulfill the need of ten thousand people who need a miracle cure, give 'em that miracle cure in Jesus' name. That one that's sick, I command that arthritis, rheumatism, trichinosis, diabetes, blindness, deafness, hemorrhoids, heart troubles, stomach cancer, every disease to come out of the body, in Jesus' name."

"He didn't mention gunshot wound," Gray Eyes said.

"He means it, babe. Don't worry. Just put your arm against the radio there."

"Bless your homes, your business, your farms, your cattle, bless your neighbors, loved ones, they know that they're going to go to heaven, they want that they got a heaven to go to, they want to be saved, get that letter in the mail to me *today*, tomorrow never comes. We have a Holy Ghost tape for anyone sends ten dollars or more, we'll send it back return mail, and for everyone sends five dollars or more we will send a bonus gift, a red string prayer cloth, that red string is death on witchcraft—"

The signal began to break up and a shrill howl whistled through the preacher's voice as he continued to hammer home his box number and zip code. Send today, tomorrow never comes . . .

"Send him a thousand dollars," Gray Eyes said.

"We'll do it, babe, soon as we get it."

They were almost broke. They had in fact run out of money earlier that day between Omaha and North Platte. While Gray Eyes slept in the car, Tracy had entered a gas station in Kearney, Nebraska. They had been running on empty for miles; it was absolutely essential they get gas. She displayed the Smith & Wesson Centennial and forced the kid who ran the station to fill up the Caddy. Then she relieved him of nearly sixty dollars.

When Gray Eyes discovered what she had done, he exploded: "He'll have our license number. Every cop in the state will be looking for us!"

"He's not that smart, babe, believe me. He didn't even look at the license plate." To be on the safe side, though, they left the Interstate and followed back roads into Wyoming.

The cold and wind were brutal, sending long shrouds of drifting snow across the frozen blacktop.

In Cheyenne, well after midnight, they wandered deserted downtown streets, looking for a place to get a bite to eat, finally finding Reno's Bar and Grill, a place of wood and linoleum that smelled like a latrine. It was just opposite the Union Pacific Railroad yard. The bar section was closed, but a counter served food and they both had chicken-fried steak. Gray Eyes ate very little. Tracy kept imploring him to "chow down so's you keep your strength, for sure," but he smiled and whistled and just toyed with the food.

There were perhaps a half dozen men in the place. They

wore heavy wool or canvas jackets, cowboy hats and boots.

Above the counter were mounted several animal heads—a mule deer, a wildcat, a buck elk. One creature, weird mutant of the blasted plains, had a devilish head growing out of what appeared to be its hindquarters. "He's cute," Tracy said to the waitress. "What is he?"

"A yahoo."

"What's a yahoo?"

"South side of a moose goin' north," the woman said, and this brought grins to the men seated at the counter.

Tracy paid for the meal and she and Gray Eyes went back out to the car. Tracy was brooding. "I don't like the way that old bitch made fun of me," she told Gray Eyes. "You wait here."

Five minutes later she came running back to the car, jumped in, and burned rubber squealing away from the curb. In one hand she carried the Smith & Wesson, in the other a fistful of bills. "Count it up, babe," she said, handing Gray Eyes the money. "See if we got a thousand."

Tracy raced the car up and down back streets, took corners at insane speed, laughed, and banged the wheel.

They had made it to the highway out of town and once again they were forced to travel the back roads.

Gray Eyes had tried, but couldn't count up the money. Tracy took it from him and as she moved the car seventy miles an hour across ice- and snow-streaked highway counted it up. "Damn," she said, "nothing but fifty and eight dollars. Now we'll never get that red string prayer cloth that's death on witchcraft."

At daylight they entered Rock Springs. The town sat on a high desert plateau swept by snow and dust. They drove along through crumbling buildings, deserted gas stations, ticky-tacky mini-shopping centers.

They passed a closed-down movie theater, the Starlight—on its marquee was *The Sound of Music*; the Oasis Bowl Coffee Shop; Silver Spur Dining and Bowling. Everything was shut down and boarded up. The Jack-of-Diamonds Tavern, the Wel-Com-Inn, the Bon Aire Motel. All boarded up.

The wind was a howl now, lashing the surrounding desert, the boarded-up buildings, the icy highway.

They were in the middle of a windstorm, and snow and sand whipped across the empty landscape, eerie in the gray, dust-thick morning.

Gigantic eighteen-wheel trailer trucks moved along the highway, their tailgates edged with rectangles of red lights, resembling great square packages decorated for Christmas.

"This town shows me nothing. For sure, babe," Tracy said.

They spent the morning searching for Harry Garth. Tracy ran the car all over the desolate town; she would spot some decaying concrete building almost lost in blowing sand, come to a skidding halt, and leave Gray Eyes in the car with motor idling, while she inquired about her stepfather.

Gray Eyes sat hunched over in the seat, lulled by the hum of the heater, while country music interspersed with rural chatter about skip loaders, harvesters, feed prices, secondhand cars, emanated from the radio.

He thought he was a kid again, traveling out to California with his parents. His mother was holding him on her lap; he could smell the extraordinary fragrance of her.

He thought it was spring and everything smelled of flowers.

He awoke to a blast of cold air as Tracy jumped back into the car. "I found him!" she shouted. "I found him!"

Gray Eyes had never seen her so animated about anything. Eyes wild with excitement, she hurtled the car through the sand and snow haze.

"He's working about thirty miles the other side of town, the new Jim Bridger Power Plant they're building out there."

Although it was midday, the town was dark with blowing sand. They moved to the outskirts past acres of mobile homes barely visible in the snow and sand. "Temperature's ten degrees below zero, man told me back there, babe. Sure is a cold mother. How you feeling, babe?"

"All right," he said. He felt no pain, just a quiet, warm throb that enveloped his whole body.

They continued on through miles and miles of desert, through horrible areas of mangled land where soda ash, trona, and coal had been dug out of the ground in fierce, sweeping gashes. The land itself was so barren, so forbidding, that the intrusions on its surface appeared benevolent: to think there were people who cared enough for this vast, godforsaken desolation to expend the effort to violate it!

Eventually they reached mobile homes again, a whole city of them, thrown up with no particular pattern or evidence of amenities, just huge wooden crates thrown every which way in the desert.

Interspersed with the mobile homes were large canvas tents. "Imagine, babe, living in a *tent* in this weather! I sure hope ol' Harry's doing better than that," Tracy said.

They arrived at the power plant. Tents and mobile homes had been erected up to its fence, and the plant loomed out of the haze like some great cement monster, breathing thick black smoke from rows of enormous concrete stacks.

Once again Tracy left Gray Eyes in the car while she went inquiring after Harry Garth. On the radio a preacher with a honey voice crooned out his pitch: "I mail 'em back the same day I get 'em, it costs me a nickel a letter. If I save them letters up, somebody writes me dying with cancer, they may be dead and buried by the time I answered them. Listen, people, this is not a play thing with me. I believe this is God's business and it's serious business, just as if we had a store down here, if we had a market, or if we was selling insurance."

Tracy was back in the car now. "He's just along the

road, in one of those mobile homes. I knew he'd never be living in one of those tents."

They bounced up and down unpaved roads through the desert, Tracy maneuvering between mobile homes, trailers, tents, portable latrines, concrete shower facilities.

At times the dust and snow were so thick it was impossible to make out where road ended and desert began—not that it much mattered. "Look for Skylark Lane. He lives on Skylark Lane."

They passed Deertrail and Buttonwillow and Jacaranda, signs sloppily painted on standing posts, signifying dreary, haphazard ruts through the brutally corrugated desert terrain.

At last she located Skylark. She slowed the car to a crawl, straining to see her stepfather's mobile home.

It was a gray rectangle, twenty feet by eight. The name "Garth" was painted on the front door. Tracy hesitated before getting out of the car. "Hon," she said to Gray Eyes, "would you come in with me? If we're going to stay with Harry a bit, he should meet you like you were my fiancé. He's old-fashioned that way."

A dark woman in her late thirties answered the door. She was unnaturally thin, with leathery skin and patches of missing hair.

The inside of the mobile home was as colorless as the outside. There were a vinyl-covered day bed, a vinyl chair, and a plastic table. The television set was on, but not much of an image was getting through, just ghosts of soap opera faces. "Oh, Harry isn't around no more," the woman said, shocked that someone should be asking for him. "He hasn't been around for months."

"Where is he?" Tracy said.

"Harry's dead. He put a thirty-thirty in his mouth and blew his head off."

"You're shitting me," Tracy said, angry.

"Honest to heaven. There's not much to do up here, you know, an' I think he just got to gettin' bored. He was having a lot of problems with his teeth, too, you know, and then, he was a terrible drinker, rotten disposition and like that. I'm sorry. I hope he didn't mean nothing to you."

"No," Tracy said. "Not much."

In the car back to Rock Springs she drove without speaking for miles. "That asshole," she said at last with grim ferocity. "I wanted to surprise him, for sure. That asshole. That asshole."

By nightfall, after they had had dinner and filled up the car with gasoline, they realized they were almost broke again.

Tracy, who had discovered the red-light district in their whizzing around town, knew just what to do. She returned to the district, proclaimed on a billboard as "Fun City."

It was a sprawling, squalid area of mobile homes, campers, and trailers, spreading from the edge of town well out into the desert.

Construction workers, cowboys, miners, all made their way through the fiercely blowing storm along barely distinguishable dirt streets. Four-wheel drives, pickup trucks, cut-down hot rods, dune buggies were parked between the buildings among the frozen sagebrush, junked cars, and abandoned hunks of machinery.

The whores, mostly American Indians or Mexicans, sat behind the windows of their mobile homes and waved at the men, blew kisses, occasionally bared a breast.

"Don't worry, babe," Tracy said. "We're going to get you to California for sure." She took Gray Eyes into a place called the Way Out Inn.

It was one long room, a concrete floor, a bar, jukebox, and Formica tables.

Gray Eyes sat at the bar. Tracy ordered a brandy for him, but he did not drink it.

A song came from the jukebox, Merle Haggard singing: "When my blue moon turns to gold again / And the rainbow turns the clouds away / When my blue moon turns to gold again / You'll be back within my heart to stay."

Gray Eyes noticed that Tracy had left his side and was talking to an older man wearing a sheepskin jacket and cowboy hat.

The man paid the bartender and followed Tracy out into the night.

A few minutes later she reappeared at Gray Eyes's side. "Let's go, babe. Time to make tracks to California." She flashed some bills and they moved together out to the car.

As Gray Eyes fought the wind to get to the far side of the car, he stumbled over something. It was the man in the sheepskin coat. He lay on the ground between the car and a sagebrush-covered hillock. A stream of blood flowed from the top of his head across his face. His trousers were down around his knees. His sheepskin coat and hat were missing.

They were in the backseat of the car, along with a pair of heavy boots. "I figured him for about two bills, but we'll be lucky if there's a hundred here," Tracy said.

"He'll freeze out there," Gray Eyes said.

"He got enough antifreeze in him to keep him warm at the North Pole. An' I just give him a little love tap." She smiled. "When the lights went out for him, he was grinning with delight, up in that warm puss, having the best time of his life ever."

Akiba Moldavan and Julie Tripp arrived in Rock Springs in the middle of the windstorm. They drove aimlessly through wide stretches of empty desert, past abandoned mobile homes, caved-in concrete buildings.

The task before them seemed impossible. Where should they start? Where should they look?

They drove round and round; the town spread for miles about them, a wind-blasted catastrophe.

They searched all day, through motel lobbies, coffee shops, trailer camps, mining yards.

They could not find Gray Eyes.

At dusk they found themselves on a dirt road that seemed to lead nowhere. They were in an oil field. All about them unmanned rigs, like huge praying mantises, chugged and whumped without stop.

The car stalled out. It would not start. Julie fought not to weep. "Hey," Akiba said. He put his hand on her shoulder. He could feel her body trembling beneath it.

"It's just hopeless," she said. "Even if we were to find him, what would we do? He's lost, no matter what."

"I'm going to save him," Akiba said. "That's a promise."

She looked at him and smiled through her tears. "We can't even get this car started."

"If I do, will you believe in me?"

"Yes."

He took the key from the ignition and held it in his hand. "Aba cadaba, aba cadaba," he said. He blew on the key as though it was a pair of dice and inserted it again into the ignition. Julie turned the key. The car started right up.

They continued their search in town. At midnight, exhausted, they decided to give up. They would get some rest, then start out for Lake Chandler in the morning.

As they looked around for a motel, they passed a crowd at the side of the road. A man dressed only in trousers and a T-shirt was being helped into a sheriff's car. His face was streaked with blood.

They drove on by the neon front of the bar on the corner: Way Out Inn.

# 18

JOHN STRAHAN had lost him, lost Gray Eyes, traced him to New York and lost him. The slender leads he possessed had come to nothing: dead end.

He had returned to Adele Morath, tried to put pressure on her. She told him Gray Eyes had left town. She had no idea where he was going.

He had searched out Akiba Moldavan at the Griswald. He had left town, too.

He returned to Pittsburgh. "I followed him to New York," he reported to Busik. "By the time I picked up the trail it was cold."

Strahan had slept little the past four days; tired as he was, he could not slow down.

After leaving Busik he did not go straight home, but to the West Penn Recreation Center on Brereton, where he tried to get out his anger on the racquetball court.

It had not worked.

He arrived at the house after dark to find Kitty Lou in a brooding mood. She fixed him a TV dinner and made him feel lucky to get that.

Dressed in yellow pedal pushers, her hair done up in a beehive, she moved about the kitchen slamming drawers, banging pots and pans. "I made plans to go out ice-skating with Frank and Sue Ellen. Who knew when you'd be back?" Frank and Sue Ellen were neighbors over on

Phelan, one block away. Frank was a city fireman, a good-natured fellow whom Strahan found unbearable.

"Where are the kids?"

"At my mother's."

At seven Frank and Sue Ellen arrived. "You coming with us, Johnny?" Sue Ellen said. She had a Kewpie-doll face on a two-hundred-pound linebacker's body.

"I think I will."

"Why don't you sleep?" Kitty Lou said. "You look godawful."

"The exercise'll do him good," Frank said. "He's suffering job tension. I can see that."

At the rink Kitty Lou skated off on her own. Strahan sat in the observation area watching while she performed a whole series of skater's polkas and waltzes with a high school kid. The kid was blond and good-looking and Kitty Lou, skimming the ice with him, looked suddenly young and radiant and Strahan felt stripped of time, stripped of accomplishment. He was back in high school and Kitty Lou was skating with Buddy Gray Eyes.

The pain in his stomach was agony. He bent forward, pressing his gut with his clenched fist. "Put out the fire," he said to himself.

Frank and Sue Ellen were waving him down to the ice. A Latin tune had started up and Frank was trying to get everybody into a conga line.

Gray Eyes looked for Kitty Lou and the high school kid, but could not see them.

He moved around to the rear of the rink and drank deeply at the water fountain. The pain in his stomach eased a bit. Kitty Lou came out of the ladies' room. The high school kid was waiting for her. Strahan moved to her and pulled her by the elbow. "Let's get out of here," he said.

Frank and Sue Ellen joined them. "I thought you wanted exercise," Sue Ellen said. "You haven't even been on the ice."

They changed out of their skates, then crossed the parking lot to Pine Valley, an adjoining roadhouse. It was a green-gabled building with a neon pine tree sign; inside were plastic tables and a rainbow-lit jukebox.

Kitty Lou began ordering whiskey sours, drinking them down as fast as the waitress could bring them. She turned mean. "These kids suck," she said drunkenly, waving at the mostly young people on the dance floor. "I hate their guts. I could show them tricks they wouldn't believe." She glowered at Strahan. "What are you giving me the evil eye for?" she demanded.

"I'm not giving you anything."

"That's for shit sure!" She motioned to the waitress for another round of drinks. Strahan tried to wave the waitress off. "Over your dead body, mister," Kitty Lou said. "You don't run my life."

When the drinks arrived, Strahan tried to take hers away. She grabbed it back, took a long swallow, and spit the drink in his face. Then she threw the rest of the whiskey sour at him. He sat there, the drink dripping down his face and his shirt front. "Look at him, the lowest kind of person on earth," she screamed. "All he knows in this life is kick ass or kiss ass."

Strahan grabbed his wife by the wrist and yanked her from the table. He dragged her outside. Frank and Sue Ellen followed after.

In the parking lot Kitty Lou began to bawl. She leaned up against the car and wept bitterly. "I could have had a terrific life. I could have been living north of Forbes," she said over and over.

"Sweetheart, you just think you'd like that," Sue Ellen said. "But that wouldn't be a bed of roses."

Great tears streaked Kitty Lou's makeup, ran in rivulets down her puffy face. "I never wanted this," she sobbed. "I never wanted a life like this."

"What's that, sweetheart?" Sue Ellen said.

"I had the best tits and ass in the world and look at the miserable son-of-a-bitch I ended up with."

Strahan looked away. Everything is blurred now, he was thinking: ugly. When I find Gray Eyes, it will all be clear and simple.

Sue Ellen put Kitty Lou to bed while Frank and Strahan had a beer in the kitchen. "High-strung," Frank said. "That time of the month for her?"

"Yes." Strahan had a headache and he was desperately tired, but he knew he could not sleep. He took his notebook out and began to study it. "Do me a favor," he said. "Help me put on my chains."

"I don't think you'll need them," Frank said.

"You never can tell."

They went outside and put on the tire chains. Sue Ellen joined them on the street and Strahan walked them to their house on Phelan. Frank showed Strahan the paint job he had performed on the window frames. Sue Ellen pointed out a patch of frozen ground next to the door where she planned to grow flowers in the spring. "That should be nice," Strahan said.

"Oh sure. Flowers are always nice," Sue Ellen said. "Can I give you some advice? Give flowers to your wife. It never hurts to show a woman you care."

"Shut up," said Frank.

"It's none of my business," she said.

"That's right," Frank said.

She pressed her hand over her mouth and mimed turning a key in a lock.

Strahan left them and walked back up the hill to where his car was parked.

He drove over to Saint Stan's Church. The light in the parish house behind the church was on. Father Nagorski, who had been watching a rock show on television, came to the door in a pair of trousers and sleeveless undershirt. The

259

priest grinned sheepishly. "It helps me unwind," he said, indicating the set.

"Feel like going for a walk?" Strahan said.

"Sure."

The priest pulled on a thick turtleneck, then donned an old army field jacket. They walked north of Fifth Avenue, toward the Bluff. "Everything's changing and not for the best," Father Nagorski said. "I took the car into Andy Pavelko's for a tune-up and he presents me with a bill for nearly two hundred dollars. I need shocks, transmission work, brake job. I told him, 'You're givin' me a job all right, but it sure isn't a brake job.' It's all greed nowadays. Not brains or talent or hard work. Just greed."

They climbed the City Steps, a series of rickety wooden stairs built against a high hill that looked out over the downtown area.

The lights of the city spread like jewels below them. Fire from the mills along the rivers jetted in plumes of raw incandescence.

"I love this city, John," Father Nagorski said, moved. "Oh, how I love it. It's a tough city and sometimes it seems ugly, but I love it."

"I don't love anything," Strahan said. "All I know is hate. All I see are hustlers and thieves and murderers and I loathe them so badly sometimes it's like knives inside me, the hate I feel toward them, the animals and cockroaches in this world. Yet I know in some way I'm even worse than they are. And I can't help myself." He paused, twisting his hands together, groping. "I can't stop this terrific hate inside me. And the Jews—"

Strahan's breathing was coming fast now; he pressed his hand into his stomach. It seemed to Father Nagorski as though he was about to break down, that only a tremendous effort of will prevented this. "When I was a kid we lived in an old shack in Greenfield, while the Jews had mansions north of Forbes. An old Jew hired me once. I would travel out to his house on Friday night to turn on the lights for him, light the oven. He would give me a few pennies. The house had an old smell to it. I hated that smell, hated the people. I know it's crazy, but it's inside me. It's tearing at my life." His face was contorted now; he was on the verge of weeping, but he did not.

"Why don't you come back to the church, John?"

"I can't. I've gone too long with liars and murderers and thieves and I've become just like one of them."

Father Nagorski placed his hand on Strahan's shoulder. The muscles were tight, like metal bands. "I remember you as a kid, Johnny. You were a feisty devil, cute as the dickens. And now to see you like this . . ."

"He killed that poor, kind old man. He killed him."

"Johnny, please—"

"Walt, what am I going to do? I can't stop this hate." Father Nagorski attempted to hug Strahan to him and it was as though an electric current had passed through the detective. He pulled back sharply. "What am I going to do?" he said. "What am I going to do?"

"Johnny, let's just you and me work on this thing. Let's get down together on our knees and pray."

"I can't," Strahan said.

He turned away and started at a run down the stairs. Father Nagorski watched him as he moved rapidly, landing after landing in a zigzag pattern, down the steep hillside.

At riverside the mill fires burned with terrifying intensity. The sky was hot white, red, gold with their flame.

Father Nagorski wanted to call out to Strahan, to call out over the city and the fire, to shout the proper word, that specific word of love and redemption that would ease the pain consuming John Strahan.

But he couldn't reach him. No, he was moving across the avenue below now, moving into the jumbled streets and rotting tenements of the Hill District.

Father Walter Nagorski would have difficulty sleeping that night. A sense of loss, of misgiving grave and terrible, had assaulted his world. In the future he would mark it: he had walked the City Steps with John Strahan on a winter's night and Strahan had desperately needed help and he had been unable to give it.

The word had not come.

The night after, and the night after that: all the nights for the remainder of his life sleep would not come easy for Father Walter Nagorski. He would lie in bed and remember times on the ball field at Saint Philomena's, above the old coal mine, when a child would tug at his cassock, a small, thin, nearsighted kid, begging for attention, crying out to learn his secret: Father Walt, Father Walt, how do you do it? How do you hit the ball so far?

It had been John Strahan.

It was almost dawn. Strahan sat in the White Tower sipping coffee. Late-night junkies and pimps and whores drifted in and out of the place. The Man was there and deals were aborted. Pale, frail ghosts of the night shifted and snuffled, scratched and yawned.

Jo-Jo was there and Turtle and Mother and they watched what was happening with vague amusement. "You know your problem, John?" Jo-Jo said. "You take your job too seriously. Why don't you transfer to gambling and stash away a good bundle? Retire down to Miami Beach. By forty you could be a millionaire."

Turtle laughed soundlessly. Mother Shadman stirred his rice pudding. "Anybody seen Gray Eyes?" Jo-Jo said. "I was under the impression people were looking for him. They say Mother dropped a dime on him. Is that right, Johnny?"

"Mother would never drop a dime," Turtle said. "He'd call collect."

Mother Shadman looked uncomfortable. "Don't joke. Not about that," he said. His fingers were trembling.

No one spoke for a while. The short-order cook turned a knob, releasing steam from the coffee urn.

Three men entered. One of them was Sidney Hall.

He stood swaying just inside the doorway, his face

flushed with alcohol. He lurched along the counter and almost fell before seating himself.

The men ordered coffee. Sidney Hall turned toward Strahan.

"Cocksucker," he said. "Fucking low-life cocksucker."

"Malty," Turtle said to one of the men, "get him out of here."

The man called Malty and the other man pulled Sidney Hall to his feet. "He's a low-life, spreading those stories about my boy," he cried out, swinging his arms about him, slapping at the men ineffectually. "Low-life cocksucker."

At the door he attempted to grab the jamb. He writhed and wailed as the two men dragged him outside.

Strahan could see the three men wrestling on the sidewalk outside. Sidney Hall's mouth was open wide in a scream that could not be heard inside the White Tower.

At last the men succeeded in getting Sidney Hall into a cab.

"It's a father's love, John. Don't take it serious," Mother Shadman said. "He expected a lot from the kid."

"Everybody expected a lot from Buddy Gray Eyes," Turtle said. "Who can figure this life!"

No one spoke for a while. Jo-Jo took elegant drags on his cigarette, blew smoke circles. "Long night," he said.

The black dishwasher brought out a tray of cups. He nodded at Strahan. Strahan ignored him. "They're all long," he said.

"What's that, John?" Turtle boomed. "You got to speak up."

"He said all nights are long," Jo-Jo said.

"Only if you don't sleep," Mother Shadman said.

Strahan had just arrived home when the phone rang. It was Busik. "How about this, John? Girl and a guy held up a gas station, some hick Nebraska town. Car had Pennsy plates. Then they pull another holdup down the road in Cheyenne, Wyoming. Same car, same plates. Then they beat up on a deputy sheriff in another hick town. And the description, John. It sounds like our boy. And more—"

"What?"

"The car turns up in California. Small town in the mountains. I think you ought to get out there and see what's going on."

# 19

THE land they traveled through was like the far side of the moon: scalloped, frozen escarpments, dark volcanic buttes. There were no buildings, no people, no cars.

Akiba Moldavan and Julie Tripp had driven I-80 past the Great Salt Lake and Salt Lake City, into Nevada, through Elko, Winnemucca, Lovelock. At Reno they took 395 south. They sped through groves of piñon, juniper, and ironwood. They entered a stretch of desert, 8,000 feet high, and all vegetation ceased. Jagged peaks of the Sierras and the Wassucks etched a sky of gray vastness; the windswept plain between was immense, chilling.

Unsettling markers appeared: every few miles along the side of the road strips of bedsheet formed diagonal crosses held in place by stones. Each cross was the size of a man. They fluttered eerily at the edges. Who put them there? For what arcane purpose? Skydivers, road workers, some bizarre religious sect? They were present alongside the road for thirty or forty miles; then, abruptly, they stopped.

After a while the land grew more hospitable. Snow-dusted mountains bristling with pine and fir came into view, rusted water towers, stacks of hay, dark cattle grazing beneath the black hills. The basalt land was still bleak and empty of people, but it looked inhabitable.

They turned off the main road and began to climb up into the eastern Sierras.

It was night when they reached Lake Chandler. The daytime temperature had been in the fifties. With darkness the thermometer plunged. It began to snow.

They took adjoining rooms in a ramshackle wooden motel on the edge of the dark lake. After washing up they decided to go for a walk.

The town consisted of three or four wooden buildings and a one-pump gas station. They stopped at the gas station, the only place that seemed open.

Inside, a man in heavy mountain boots, twill trousers, and wool jacket sat, feet up on a scarred desk, staring at the snow.

Julie inquired about her family and friends. The man, who had only recently moved to Lake Chandler from Topaz, knew no one. He thought he had heard about her father and brothers, though. They had moved across the mountains to Merced—or was it Visalia?—he wasn't sure. Maybe the name wasn't Tripp. Maybe it was someone else.

They started back to the motel. It was dark now and they could see nothing of the lake. They stood on the road and looked out at a great expanse where earlier the lake had been. To Akiba it seemed as though the earth ended here. He felt a chill fear. They had come this far; there was nothing else. They were at the edge of God's earth.

Back at the motel they decided to get some rest; in the morning they would set out for the cabin where Julie and Buddy had once lived. It was in a remote area above the timberline; during the summer it housed trail crews and backpackers. Julie was convinced Buddy would be hiding out there.

Akiba could not sleep. He felt headachey from the altitude. He could not get warm.

Outside the wind moaned and the image of the emptiness where the lake had been returned to him, haunted him now with a sense of isolation, enormous, without end.

Where, where in the maze of *Sephirot* was he?

He thought back on the time when as a young man he had been forced to stay in the tuberculosis sanitarium in New Jersey. It had been winter and from his window he could see only snowy fields, whiteness stretching to the horizon. He had felt abandoned, deserted even by God, and the wind howling across the field seemed to be sweeping all hope away. In the night he would lie awake, damp with tubercular sweats, listening to the wind as a condemned man listens to the rustle and footfall of his approaching executioner. He felt he would never escape the place, daylight would never come, health would never return.

And then one night he had been touched by what he had believed to be God. He lost his terror of the wind. And he slept.

Had God come to him then? He was not sure. For if He had, where was He now? Why had He deserted Akiba?

In the next room Julie Tripp also could not sleep. She thought of her childhood, of Buddy, of the twisted life that had followed their meeting. And now she was here, cut adrift, lost.

What she had believed to have been love had taken her to this naked point of estrangement, estrangement from everything, her family, this home of her youth, herself as she once had been.

What did the future hold? If she should find Buddy, if they should come together on this day or the day after, what would she have?

The commitment of this strange, shy, awkward man, Akiba Moldavan, his passion to save his friend, seemed to her now the only element of solace, of surety in this life.

And where did that leave her?

She struggled to fight off the terrors of the night, forced herself to think of more pleasant times, of days with her father and brothers when they would ski the snow-heaped slopes together, glide down in graceful, exhilarating runs, glory in the brilliance of sun and snow, rejoice in the love they felt for each other. Had it ever really been like that? She wasn't certain, but she grew warm inside at the thought. All was safe, all was right. She slept.

Akiba, too, slept at last. He was in Atlantic City, gazing out at the beach. Pretty girls moved by in dresses delicate as the summer's breeze; the air was dizzying with a taste of salt, of taffy, of roasted peanuts. A cold wind began to blow in from the ocean. The sky darkened: a tidal wave approaching. He looked toward the horizon and saw gathering there huge, oblique shards of ice, great knives of silver and gray piercing the heavens.

He was aware of someone standing above him. Faint dawn light had filtered into the room. Two figures were at the foot of the bed. He realized they were holding pistols.

"Keep your hands where we can see them," a man said in a quiet voice.

Akiba sat up. "Slow, slow," said the other man. He snapped on the overhead light. The front door was open and Akiba could see the manager of the motel hovering outside in the cold.

The men holding guns on him wore gray quilted jackets over olive drab shirts. They wore olive trousers, dirty Stetsons, and western boots.

There was a sound in the other room and the taller of the two men pushed open the connecting door.

Julie Tripp, in a terry-cloth robe, was standing in the center of the second room. "I know you," the man said. The other man moved to where he could see Julie. "You know her, don't you?" the taller of the men said. "Jake Tripp's daughter."

"That's right," the second man said. "Come on in here." He motioned with the pistol. Julie entered the room.

The motel manager was now standing in the doorway leading outside. "This isn't them," the shorter of the two men said to the manager.

"I don't know anything about it," the manager said.

"The man had blond hair and blue eyes is what they said," the taller man said.

"Don't know anything about it."

The taller of the men put his gun away. "Sorry, Julie," he said. "Get dressed and we'll buy you breakfast."

They sat in the Hi Sierra Café, a drafty building made of thick, rude pine boards. Julie was having pancakes. The men, who were from the Mono County sheriff's office, had piles of food in front of them: pancakes, eggs, bacon, ham, and squaw bread, a sweet, pulpy local specialty. Akiba had declined the café food.

"We got us a ticklish situation here," the short man said between mouthfuls. "Man and a girl come into town yesterday—blond-haired fellow and a short, dark girl. Hippie types, look like something a wolf swallowed and shit over a cliff. I haven't seen them for myself, I'm just goin' on the reports. Last night sometime they broke into the Ski Doo Sports Shop and stole a couple of pairs of skis, boots, and some firearms. They was spotted leaving the scene."

The tall man checked a notebook. "Remington seven-millimeter magnum with Redfield four-X scope, a Winchester two seventy with scope, and a used Winchester, model number ninety-four thirty-thirty. Also a couple of handguns, twenty-two pea shooters."

The short man continued: "Fellow with the Forest Service, name of Osgood, discovered a car abandoned up the hill a ways, an old Caddy with Pennsy plates. We did a routine check on it, and, lordy, seems it was stolen in Pittsburgh PA. Cops back there are interested in that particular vehicle because they had some big murder thing back there. They said pick 'em up if we could and they'd send out someone to take a peek at 'em."

"I don't like getting involved in no back-east murder case," the taller one said

"We had orders to bring this here hippie couple in for

questioning. The Ski Doo robbery, this murder thing. Spoke to the ol' boy down at the gas station and he says he thought you people might be the ones we was looking for. Any fool can see you're not hippies and this guy here got him dark hair."

"We got some men coming up from Bishop. I believe we'll wait," the taller man said. "I ain't getting up into no trees after no back-east hippies. Not with them carrying a Remington and two Winchesters with scopes. No, sir, my mother didn't have no idiot children, least of all me."

Julie and Akiba walked back to the motel, picked up the car, and drove along the narrow road that circled high above the lake. The road had recently been cleared, but had been snowed in again. It was fairly passable for the first mile or so, but the higher they climbed, the more difficult the going became.

The sun was up now and the day was brilliant. The sunshine reflecting off the snow pained their eyes with its brightness. The lake below was a wide, white disk of snow and ice.

At last they could go no farther on the road. They sat in the car with the motor running and the heat going. "The cabin's up there," Julie said. "It's a hike, though."

They left the car and began to push on through the woods. Akiba gasped for breath in the thin air.

An extraordinary sense of exhilaration had come over him. I have come this far, he was thinking. I have done this. Soon I will be face to face with Buddy Gray Eyes. I will discover the reason for his act. I will learn the dark side of God's mystery, black Kabbalah. I will learn what value my life has.

They climbed for nearly an hour. They were nearing the timberline when Julie stopped. Ahead they could see ski tracks cutting through the snow, barely visible under a recent downfall.

They examined the tracks: two sets of skis, moving to

the right, curving down a hill. "It must be them," Julie said. "The cabin's down there."

They pressed on through the trees. The tracks plunged a serpentine path deep into the woods. The forest was dark, the sunlight retarded by thick, snow-heaped boughs. They moved on a couple of miles. Everything was silent, shadowed, cold. They did not speak.

At last they came to a clearing. Up a steep rise was a wooden cabin almost buried in snow. The ski tracks led to the cabin.

It had begun to snow again.

There was no sign of movement in the cabin, no smoke coming from it.

They started to work their way up the hill. Akiba thought of the stolen rifles, the scopes. If Gray Eyes was up there, he would have them in a scope at this moment. He would hold Akiba's life in his hands: one rifle shot and it would be over. Would Akiba even hear it?

He looked over at Julie. Her face, flushed with cold, was impassive. Is she concerned with the possibility of her own death? Is she afraid?

They neared the cabin, their breath fogging up in the brutal cold, the falling snow.

"Buddy!" Akiba called out. The snow was falling very fast now, almost obliterating the cabin. "Bud!"

There was no answer. No sign of anyone within. "Buddy! It's me. Akiba!"

They were at the door of the cabin now. Akiba waited for the rifle shot, took a breath, expecting it to be his last. He felt no fear, and he was surprised at this.

The only sound was the fierce moan of the wind.

Akiba pushed at the door. It swung open. He and Julie entered.

The inside of the cabin was dark except for a slab of light from the open door, which illuminated a patch of the room.

There was a sharp, metallic sound of a rifle being cocked. Someone stirred in the shadows. "Hello, Akiba," a familiar voice said quietly.

John Strahan stepped into the square of light.

# 20

THE Mono County sheriff's men had three snowmobiles with them, two 298-cc Polaris TXs and a 528-cc Evinrude & Johnson J Phantom. They carried several 5.56 Stoner carbines, an Armalite 7.62 AR-16, and a 7.26 M21 with Leatherwood variable power scope.

The sheriff's men had arrived with Strahan at the cabin over a fire road across the back of the mountain. After turning Akiba and Julie over to two of the deputies, Strahan, spectacles fogging in the cold, dressed in wool watch cap, quilted jacket, quilted trousers, joined a discussion on how the search should proceed.

The sheriff's men believed Gray Eyes and the girl were not far off. They had found an abandoned fire, bandages, and fresh ski tracks. The tracks led away from the rear of the cabin.

A helicopter attempt to follow the tracks was considered too risky; a squall of snow was blowing.

It was decided that two men familiar with the mountain area would start out in the Polaris TX snowmobiles; they would maintain radio contact with the rest of the group, track the fugitives, and when the weather eased up, the helicopters could be brought in.

Strahan insisted on accompanying the men on one of the snowmobiles. He was a fair skier and had had some experience with snowcats. "I know the Evinrude and

Johnson," he said. "I used to drive an OMC two forty-four-Q."

"Well, these here got the float-type carburetion," one of the sheriff's men said.

"Bendix?"

"No. OMC."

"No problem."

"Hell, it's all right with me," the man who seemed to be in charge said. "You know this fella. You can talk to him. Take the J Phantom."

A monumental rage, born of impotence, had been building in Akiba Moldavan. "Don't let him go with you. Please!" he shouted as the men prepared to leave.

"Look, mister," one of the sheriff's men said, "I don't know your business here, but I suggest you mind it and not matters of the law."

"He wants to kill him. Don't you see that? He wants to kill him."

"Maybe he deserves killing," the sheriff's man said.

The other men smiled.

The snow had let up briefly. The rear windows of the cabin presented a sweeping view of mountain expanse. A steep slope fell away from the cabin down to a broad, treeless area that seemed to stretch for miles. Two sets of ski tracks cut the snow, intertwined ribbons raveling toward the horizon.

One of the sheriff's men was studying the terrain through a pair of binoculars. "There they are," he said.

Far across the tundra two antlike figures could be seen moving across the limitless white. Akiba started for the window, but was stopped by one of the men. "Just sit back down there like a good boy," he said.

Buddy is in the void, Akiba was thinking. He is lost in snow. He is lost.

He has committed a certain act. Why? And I have come after him. Why?

Strahan, the pursuer, in an instant will be out there chasing him down. With high-powered rifle and telescopic sight he will pick him off as though he were a clay bird in the shooting gallery at Kennywood Park. Buddy Gray Eyes will never be redeemed.

Why?

The track of the Sephirot will be destroyed forever. I will be destroyed with it. Why?

And suddenly Akiba Moldavan was rushing forward, past Strahan, past the sheriff's men, hurtling toward the door. He was through it, outside now and running, stumbling along the ski tracks.

He flailed at the snow, struggled down the hill, screaming: "Buddy! Buddy!"

His chest felt as though it would burst from the effort; his vision was blinded by the blood pounding behind his eyes. "Buddy! Buddy! Buddy!"

He realized he was howling, screaming down the hillside.

And now he was aware of someone pushing along behind him, thrashing through the snow. It was Strahan. Akiba could sense the thrust of his body against the snow, hear strained gasps of breath; then he felt his grip on his shoulders. He twisted to get away, but Strahan had his arms around him now and was pressing him down into the snow, and for an instant they were both sixteen years old on the ball field in Greenfield and John Strahan was punching and kicking at him.

They fought in the snow, rolled through it, slid down the hillside.

Strahan's hands were around Akiba's neck. Akiba tried to get away, but Strahan was on top of him now. Akiba looked into his face. His spectacles were askew and the eyes behind them were bright with passion.

He forced Akiba back into the snow, shoved his head under.

Akiba fought for air, but it did not come. Strahan's

fingers were like steel on his neck. Snow heaped in on him and the world was silent and everything was closing down, becoming black.

He heaved and bucked, trying to break Strahan's grip, to rise up above the snow. He could not.

The tidal wave of my dreams, he was thinking. It is sweeping me under.

And then he felt himself being lifted up. The brilliant white of snow and sky stabbed at his eyes and it was painful, but he was free. He could breathe.

One of the sheriff's men on skis was holding him. Strahan, a few yards away, struggled for breath. He had his spectacles off and was trying to clean the snow from them. His naked gaze seemed curiously empty, the eyes small and ineffectual, the look of a lost animal, a mole suddenly bared to light.

"We don't want no trouble now," the sheriff's man was saying, as he helped Akiba up the hill.

Strahan moved up the slope behind him. At the cabin he started for the group of men at the snowmobiles.

"He'll kill him," Akiba said, his voice hoarse, torn, barely audible.

No one seemed to care.

Speeding over the snow, John Strahan experienced a sudden euphoria: they had the quarry on the run. They would pursue him until he could not go on. He would cut Gray Eyes down on this blanket of white as though he were an animal.

It was like hunting in the Alleghenies. Every winter he and Jack Palmer would take off a week and track bobcat, deer, hare, and fox. In the old days they would go out on snowshoes or cross-country skis; the last three or four years they had used snowmobiles.

Strahan felt regret: Jack was not here. He would revel in the thrill of the chase, the triumph of the kill. His regret was quickly supplanted by exhilaration. What a hunt this was! What sublime prey awaited his bullet's trajection!

The snowmobile purred easily over the thick, woolpack snow, a seemingly endless blanket. There was an occasional loud crack as the machine's runners snapped a dead branch. They came to a stand of pines and sped on through lanes of white between the tall trees, following the ski tracks, which grew ever fainter under a gentle fall of snow.

Strahan's whole body tingled with excitement. *I'll have him. Soon. Soon.*

*All pain for me will end. I will be free. I will have him!*

As they moved once more out onto the tundra, the lead deputy brought his snowmobile to a halt. He studied the landscape through binoculars. "If they continue off in that direction, they'll be heading toward wilderness. If they veer left, they'll be heading back toward civilization, Chandler Valley or Mono Lake."

"If they keep on into the wilderness, I say let them go," the second deputy said. "This weather they won't get far, I guaran-damn-tee you." He radioed back to the men on the fire road that the hardtop between Chandler and Mono Lake should be patrolled. "They might be looking to fake us out and cut back onto the road. I'll say one thing: where they're pointing now is a losin' proposition."

For the next hour Strahan and the two deputies followed the ski tracks. The snow was falling heavily and the going was slow. They moved at little better than a crawl, the snowmobiles bucking and whining through intermittent drifts; they would hit a mogul and take it at a good run, then bog down again.

Gray Eyes and the girl appeared to be following a corridor running south between a populated area to the east and rugged desolation to the west. "They might be heading for Chandler Valley," one of the deputies called out. "That's resort area and that could be trouble for us."

They were moving lower now, into brush and trees, the

altitude dropping from about 12,000 feet to near 9,000. The terrain was generally downhill and the feeling was that Gray Eyes had been successful in lengthening his lead. They were coming into a thickly wooded area. At times the brush and trees were so tightly woven that the men on the snowmobiles had to circle off in a wide arc to avoid the tangle. Two people on skis going downhill had the advantage, maneuvering through narrow gaps in the wood where the snowmobiles could not possibly follow.

They came to a clear run. The lead deputy called out over the whine of his engine: "We got to pick up the pace. We're losing them."

Strahan had noticed: in the open areas the ski tracks were less and less visible under the heavy snowfall.

Panic, which forced out all sense of cold and discomfort, seized Strahan. Gray Eyes would escape. If he made it into the heart of the wild, there to die, it would give Strahan little comfort. Strahan needed Gray Eyes's blood. He must have him framed against white. He must scope him, then cut him down. That would be his only satisfaction.

The tracks, dying, faint, gray bands, spun through a scrim of white flakes into a tangle of trees and bush. The lead deputy veered off to the right in order to avoid the dense wood. The second deputy followed.

Strahan powered forward. He hit into the wood at full speed, the snowmobile slamming through branches and brush, thin limbs whipping at him as the machine bumped and roared forward. He cut the motorized sled left and right, avoiding the trees, slicing through thickets of shrub and baby pine. A low branch whacked against his shoulder, snapped loose. He broke through at last into open land, gusts of snow squalling off the plain. He had managed to follow the ski ruts through the wood, but now as he careered over a small rise, the ruts disappeared, inundated by the surging, heavy fall of white.

Strahan brought his machine to a halt, stumbled into the snow, and fought to discern a lead. The two deputies appeared now, circling around the wood on their machines. The three men gathered on the rise and surveyed the wilderness in front of them.

It was a wide, sloping plain. The surface was empty, white, virginal under thick billows of snow. "Damn snow just outraced us," the leader of the deputies said.

Strahan flung himself forward against the slope and, on his knees, began sweeping at the snow with his gloved hand. He could find no trace of tracks.

The snow swirled and buffeted down on them. Twisting flutes of snow sped across the plain below. "Let's push on a bit," the lead deputy said. "Maybe we'll pick the trail up."

They moved back to their snowmobiles and eased down the long slope. There was no sign of the tracks. The snow had effectively obliterated the marked surface of the plain.

The slope curved to the left and they followed it down, across open, clean land heaped by surges of snow. Trees rose high above them on the right and the snow appeared to be pouring down out of the trees. They continued on.

They came to a small, iced-in lake and crossed it, driving in blind snow. They had nothing to follow. At the far end of the lake the two deputies wanted to turn back. "It's going to be dark in another hour or so. We'll never pick 'em up," the lead deputy said.

Strahan insisted they go on. "They're not about to climb back up into the trees," he reasoned to the deputies. "If they're running, they're going to keep going downhill."

They started forward again, but Strahan had a problem: his machine began to handle erratically; he could not maintain normal speed. "The track," he called out to the deputies. "It's binding on me. I must have knocked it out of adjustment going through the wood."

He drove the front of the machine over a frozen mound;

the snowmobile tilted forward on its runners, elevating the track. "Let's hope it's not torn or the idler pivot's damaged," one of the deputies said.

"It could be the sprockets or sprocket clip, or the axle bearings," said the second deputy.

"Goddamn," said Strahan. "She bogie wheel or slide rail?"

"Bogie wheel," the lead deputy said.

They checked the springs that pressed the bogie wheels against the track. They adjusted the rear idler gears. "Start 'er up," the lead deputy said. Strahan started the engine. "Now, just give it enough throttle to a point where the clutch and drive train are set in motion."

"I know." The track revolved a half dozen times and Strahan turned the engine off.

"No problem," said the second deputy. "She's just not centering herself." He made a few more adjustments. "Now if we got free play and self-centering, we're in business. If not, we got a bent arm or the suspension's shot."

They tried it again and this time the track operated correctly, with sufficient play on either side as well as proper spacing.

The three men were numb with cold. The sky was beginning to darken. "We can't go no farther, now," the lead deputy said.

At that moment luck turned for them. The snow stopped. A fierce wind howled across the desert of white in front of them, sweeping the plain, whipping up dancing crests of snow. "Let's take a look-see," Strahan pleaded. They moved forward across the snow plain.

They had gone two hundred yards when suddenly the lead deputy called out: "Over there!"

To their right the wind had exposed the immediate surface of the plain; thin, ghostly bands appeared, were blown over with white, then appeared again: ski tracks.

With a whoop the three men revved the snowmobiles up and sped forward. They dashed to the base of a hill where the tracks were fresh and clean and they followed them to the top.

They gazed down across another expanse of white. A ridge of trees rose up beyond the plain. Two figures on skis were plodding toward the trees.

Strahan raised the 7.26 M21; peered through the Leatherwood power scope. The back of a man on skis heaved into his sight: Gray Eyes bent forward, bucking against the wind, poling toward the trees. The figure bobbed in and out of the scope. Strahan couldn't freeze it. "You'll never make that shot," the lead deputy said, and Strahan knew it was so.

"We'll catch them now," the second deputy said. Strahan lowered the rifle and they started on down the slope, heading across the plain and into the trees.

Halfway down they split up, one deputy going left, the other right, and Strahan speeding straight down the middle.

Strahan realized he was trembling. It was not from the cold.

To Gray Eyes it was all a white dream, a dream of purity. He was not conscious of pain or fever or cold. He was sailing a white sea, a white cloud. The feeling was exquisite. He was flying, outracing the vacuity of his being.

Occasionally a stab of freezing air would shock him into self-awareness. Then he would feel the burning in his lungs, the tearing pain radiating through his limbs as his tortured muscles fought for oxygen. And he would see the girl beside him, Tracy, her eyes fanatical, her whole being driven by intorted demons, a tiny bundle of madness fighting the wind. He would laugh. "You can do some skiing there, little one."

"What did you think, babe? Think you were with a lemon?"

Then he would be caught up once again in the wide sigh of the breathing mountain, in the powdery tuft and cloud, floating, floating, floating . . .

They were in trees. Tracy had stopped. She was gasping for air. "I got a cramp," she said, doubling over and massaging her calf. "How far, babe?" Her face was constricted with pain.

"What?" Gray Eyes was suddenly aware of the ground, the trees, his fleeing mortality. He was pouring perspiration. His arm throbbed, a boundless agony: his whole body pulsated with it.

"Where are we going?" Tracy gasped.

Gray Eyes shook his head and laughed. He had long lost their bearing, had no idea where they were. They could keep on in the same direction and be swallowed up by the mountains; it might be spring before they'd be found; summer; perhaps years; centuries! It would be a fraud on the future, everyone convinced he had escaped, and he and Tracy, frozen like prehistoric mammoths in glacial ice, are discovered and dug up a thousand years hence. They would be a sensational find, put on display: twentieth-century man and wife caught on walk. The puzzling needle marks in the flesh? Vitamin shots . . .

They were being pursued; of that he was aware. Occasionally, over the past hour, he had heard the piercing whine of snowmobile motors sounding above the moan of the wind. The sound had grown louder. They could hear it now very close.

"Let's go," he said to Tracy. He drove his poles into the snow and kicked off down a small slope; he leaned low and thrilled to the feel of speed as he accelerated into a stand of pines. He felt as though he was being carried along by the wind. It was so easy! This was it, what he had always desired in life: momentum without effort.

At the bottom of the slope he turned and looked back at Tracy. She has not moved. "Come on," he called to her, his voice barely carrying above the roar and sputter of the approaching snowmobiles.

"I can't, babe," Tracy said.

"We're almost there," he said, although he had no idea where there was.

"Fuck you, man," Tracy yelled, her expression fierce. She poled down the slope angrily, moving on past Gray Eyes with a look on her face, driven, implacable, beyond desperation: a tiny Eumenide flying across the snow.

He followed after her downhill through the trees, poling easily, gliding, and as the angle of the slope steepened, just bending low and hurtling down the curving drop.

The sound of the snowmobiles enveloped them now, cracked and sputtered and whined, increased to a deafening roar.

And then they were really plunging down. They had hit a rutted path and the hill dived deeper and they flew with it, leaning against the wind. "Whoopee," Tracy called out, bending low and thrusting forward with the hill's angle.

Gray Eyes had lost a sense of where he was: it was summertime and he was sixteen at the Kennywood Park swimming pool with Kitty Lou Ozimek, taking the long, fluming metal slide into the water; he could hear the sounds of the kids all about him; somewhere music played. He would evade John Strahan, her boyfriend, and take her into the tunnel of love . . .

They came hurtling over a mogul and continued to career down and now he was back on the mountain. Sounds carried up to them on the wind, sounds that mingled with, then superseded the snowmobiles: shrieks and laughter and shouts. He *had* heard them!

Their path was a tributary flowing into a wide run: skiers, hundreds of them, gliding, leaping, sliding, flopping, moved at them, past them, from all directions!

They were coming down a giant slope. The area below was thick with skiers. There was a yellow brick lodge; a huge parking lot filled with cars, vans, motor homes. Ski lifts glided gracefully the length of the hill.

On the main run Gray Eyes and Tracy zigzagged between young kids and older folk, people in fancy nylon outfits, colorful sweaters, scarves, capes, hoods, masks. An icy funnel, curved toward the run's end, sent them joggling down to the slope's base near the brick lodge.

There was music, laughter, screams. The sound of the snowmobiles could no longer be heard.

At the bottom they swerved to a stop, sending up a spume-spray of snow. They kicked off their skis next to the brick lodge.

They walked through the lodge, past lift lines and ski lockers, cafeteria steam tables and vending machines. A sign informed them: Chandler Valley Ski Area.

"Hey," Tracy said. "Fantastic!"

"I ever lead you wrong?" Gray Eyes said, musing still on Kennywood Park, the swimming pool slide, Kitty Lou Ozimek.

"You're something else, babe."

In the parking lot a family was loading a station wagon. The motor was warming up; no one was behind the wheel. "There we are," Gray Eyes said. He diverted the owner's attention while Tracy slid in behind the wheel. "Is that Chandler Valley?" Gray Eyes said, pointing back at the lodge.

"Yes," the man who owned the station wagon said.

"I don't know. You're sure?"

"That's Chandler Valley. Right."

Tracy had the door open opposite the driver's side. Gray Eyes backed up to it, still pointing off in the opposite direction. The man's family looked on, bewildered, as Gray Eyes entered the car. "Well, I thank you very much, sir," Gray Eyes said.

Tracy squealed like a little kid as they sped south. "Oh, babe, that was beautiful, for sure. You knew where you were headed and we did it."

Gray Eyes, pale and ill, feverish, hallucinating, juggled in his mind the two realities, the mountain and the amusement park, and found it all wondrous: to be skiing in winter one second and in a flash sliding into a summertime swimming pool! "Everything's fine," he said, smiling. "We're home free now."

For he knew somewhere at the end of the road was Alex Zayas.

Strahan sat with Akiba Moldavan and Julie Tripp in the office of the sheriff of Mono County. Strahan had been trying without success to have them held as accessories to criminal flight.

Now he was experiencing some backlash. The sheriff's people, humiliated at having expended so much effort on a chase that had brought them nothing, turned surly. The fugitives were headed south in a stolen car and the south was Inyo County. Let Strahan go down there and play Big Chief City Detective.

"Can we leave?" Akiba asked.

"I don't see why not," the sheriff said.

Strahan stared out the window without speaking. As Akiba started for the door, he suddenly wheeled around and punched him. The blow caught Akiba at the side of the head. He grabbed the desk and hung on. A deputy, stepping between them, pushed Strahan away.

"Go back to Pittsburgh!" Strahan shouted.

"It's not that easy, John."

"Go back," Strahan said. "Go back."

Later, after Strahan had left and one of the detectives was delivering their rented car, Akiba and Julie were informed that the Los Angeles police had been called in on the case. The stolen station wagon had been found in Santa Monica, parked near the beach in a shut-down lot.

"That Pittsburgh cop," the deputy said, "is he playing with a full deck? When I told him the news, he didn't know whether to laugh, cry, shit, or go blind. Just another day's work, I told him. But he whooped and hollered, used his damn tail for a whip, larruped himself out of here. It ain't like a cop to get that emotional, you know?"

# PART 3

# 21

The day was cold sunlight, the ocean roiling. Though not entirely deserted, the cement walk along the beachfront was quiet. An old couple huddled under a blanket on a bench. A group of men played chess on concrete tables.

Several young winos congregated on the sea wall, sharing a poorboy of muscatel. A blond man with grotesque cantaloupe muscles, in polo shirt and jeans, exercised on a set of parallel bars in the sand, oblivious to the sharp, cold morning wind gusting off the ocean.

Gray Eyes, desperately ill, probably dying, turned to look back at the bluff above the Santa Monica beachfront. "My mother was staying there when they took her to the hospital."

"Where?" Tracy said without looking back.

"That hotel there. The Sovereign."

She knew he was in end-of-the-road shape, but there was no way for her to cope with it, so she kept dropping pills, Ritalin and Quāaludes, alternating her ups and downs, trying to secure some magic equilibrium. The wound in his arm gaped now, seeped pus.

He would not go to a doctor or a hospital. He raved on about his mother. Tracy and Gray Eyes continued along the walk, moving the distance between Santa Monica and Venice. ."The last words she said to me were about my shirt. It was a pink shirt. 'Buddy, that's such a beautiful shirt,' she said. I sat there for two days holding her hand and talking to her. I told her all the things I never told her when she was conscious. She kept moving her lips but no sound came out. Just whispers. W*h*ispers, w*h*ispers, w*h*ispers." He shuffled along, rambling, talking to the wind. "And her eyes were rolled up and you could see the whites and she was so thin. And she would breathe in and then the sound would come out, a panting moan. Hour after hour while I sat there telling her how much I loved her. And when she died—when she died—the moaning sound stopped first. Then she just breathed out a small, soft sigh and I noticed the pulse in her neck just quit. Just like a clock that has run down. It just quit."

"Where are we going, hon?"

"What?"

"You said we had to get to this guy, Alex. You said you knew where to find him."

"Right," he breathed. "The canal."

"Where's the canal?"

Gray Eyes made a vague motion with his hand. They continued on. The buildings grew shabbier, run-down. Old Jews with gray faces moved slowly by, dragging swollen and arthritic legs. They passed nodding junkies, crippled juice heads. A leather-jacketed low-rider argued with his toothless woman; a skin-head black, dressed in shorts and tank top shirt, oblivious to the cold, bopped along, feeling no pain. An ancient man harangued a bearded homosexual dressed in knitted frock, earrings, panty hose, and pumps. "You're lousing up the neighborhood," the old man yelled. "I have to sit in my room all day, staring at the wall. I'm afraid. This place used to have some great delicatessens. Now I have to walk five miles to Zucky's in Santa Monica for a corned beef. You faggot creeps have made my life a hell."

"I'm sorry you feel that way," the homosexual said in

an elegant voice, smiling with infinite patience. "Still, I thank you for having given me a glimpse into your world." He pursed his lips, made a kissing sound, and sauntered away.

Tracy and Gray Eyes came to a picnic area situated between the beach and the walk. Two winos, one black, the other white, played chess on the brick parapet. A black woman was yelling and waving a wine bottle at the black playing chess. "Nigger, you better be able to run," she yelled.

"I can run," he said, not looking up from the chess board.

She approached him and shook the wine bottle at him. "You better be sure you can run."

"I'm sure," he said.

The woman, confused, retreated to the walk, muttering. On the parapet next to the chess players a dumpy blind girl, bundled in a heavy sweater, sat, her swollen, distorted face turned to catch the rays of the cold sun.

Long hairs, chicanos with cotton bands around their heads to keep their black locks out of their eyes, tossed a Frisbee around on the grass. A thin junky played a guitar while a girl in peasant dress and no shoes, shaggy hair under her arms, blue eyeshade, a crazed look on her face, danced around. "Do it, babe," Tracy called out. "Do it." Tracy executed a few slinky, hip-wagging steps on by.

"All right," the girl said, clapping her hands.

"Alex was always special," Gray Eyes said. "He had learned from life and he never did anything wrong."

"I get the picture."

"He had learned love and compassion. It didn't matter who you were, what you had done."

"A special dude."

"Oh, yeah."

They passed a small brick building, "The Way, the Truth, the Life Church" painted next to the door; then the

Continental Hotel, a fleabag. In the lobby of the Continental old Jews and wine-heads shared the broken furniture, stared out over the gray sea.

A mist was rolling in across the water, a thin, puffed-cotton shroud. "Look at that, babe," said Tracy, indicating the mist. Gray Eyes just stumbled on ahead, yellowish drainage seeping from under his jacket sleeve.

Farther on they passed a small blue and white stucco building, a synagogue. Someone had painted a black swastika near the door and it had been imperfectly whitewashed out.

Gray Eyes smiled. "My mother, she just—my mother," he said. "She just—" He hummed softly.

"Where's this place?" Tracy said. "What does it look like?"

"Hmm?"

"This house we're looking for."

"It's very pretty. Yellow. Like a flower."

They turned off Ocean Walk and moved along Washington Street, past low-rider bars and boarded-up hot dog stands, cafés, and fish houses. They found the lane leading to the canal. "Maybe you ought to go alone," Tracy said. She felt canceled out by all she had gone through, all she had done with a man she didn't even know. She felt a peculiar, rare loyalty to him now—was it because she suspected he was dying?—yet she also felt she should save herself: save herself for what, she wasn't quite sure, nor was she even sure she wanted to be saved.

The houses along the Venice canal were run-down, wooden, with sagging porches on the water's edge, gray picket fences, peeling enamel, broken windows. The water that stagnated in the canal was an oily green like dumped paint. Ducks somehow existed on the water and Tracy paused on the concrete bridge over the canal to watch them. Three young kids, two blacks and a white, tiny ragamuffins, were following along the canal after the ducks with a potato sack. "Duck dinner," Tracy said, laughing.

Gray Eyes laughed back, but he wasn't aware of the ducks or the canals. He was aware only that his body was enveloped in pain so pervasive it formed a floating cloud for him to walk on. He strolled on pain, cavalier as any down street dude, smiling and humming and sashaying along.

On the other side of the bridge Tracy spotted the yellow house. It was clean and well kept with a prissy neatness that immediately distinguished it from the other houses on the canal.

They moved off the bridge, down to the water's edge, through the yard of the first house, and then onto the porch of the yellow house. Gray Eyes leaned against the porch railing, his arm dangling at his side, fluid gathering at the edge of his jacket cuff, dripping from his hand. His eyes were closed now and his breathing was shallow. Tracy shook him. "Babe? Babe? Are you all right? We're here, babe?" He did not answer her, but just stood there with his eyes closed. The door to the house was open. They entered.

The inside was a chaotic contrast to the exterior: no furniture, stripped walls, floor strewn with broken glass, old newspapers, rags.

An elderly man was seated on a torn sofa cushion in one corner of the room. He was surrounded by empty wine bottles.

"Alex?" Tracy said.

The man laughed. "That'll be the day," he said. "Buddy Gray Eyes?"

"Yes."

"What's wrong with him?"

"The thing is he's sick," Tracy said, "but there are reasons why he definitely can't go to a doctor."

"Oh, I can understand that," the man said.

"I think he's really bad off, for sure," Tracy said.

"Oh, take him to Alex. Alex will know what to do with him. Oh, Alex wants to see him so bad."

Gray Eyes laughed and hummed. "I told you, didn't I?" he said.

"The place above the merry-go-round. He remembers."

"Oh, yeah."

"The merry-go-round," the old man said.

"Yes," Gray Eyes said.

He and Tracy left the canal area and started back toward Santa Monica. They moved along Main Street, past pawn shops, army and navy emporiums, cheap furniture stores.

"We're going to see Alex," Gray Eyes rhapsodized. Despite the pain, the sickness, he was ecstatic. Alex Zayas was purity, health. Alex Zayas worked miracles.

He had loved few people in this life and Alex Zayas was one of them. Alex had done terrible things and terrible things had been done to him, yet he had learned how to care for people, how to be merciful and just to them, how to elevate them.

When all the world had marked Gray Eyes down as an informer, Alex had believed in him and stood by him, defended him.

Alex would save him once more.

They were at Ocean Avenue now, moving past beach high-rises, oceanfront bicycle paths, a pitch-and-putt course where old folk trundled golf carts along, playing out their last days at sea's edge.

Gray Eyes paused to watch them, even as he had paused not long ago to watch the kids at play in the Colfax School yard. And he realized how far he had come, past bitterness and despair, to this realization: all those that live are beautiful. I am coming to Alex, he thought.

They reached a short hill overlooking the Santa Monica pier, watched gulls dive and wheel above the ocean. The water was blue-green, ridged with foam, eddied with swirling shades of black, constantly shifting, yet from their vantage point, having an appearance of weight, of grave, marblelike opacity: it was an ocean in which nothing could sink, from which nothing could be reclaimed. "We're here," Gray Eyes said, and he suddenly felt as though he might not make it.

The ground was swaying gently like the roll of the ocean, the movement of the palm trees on the palisade above the ocean.

He stood at the top of the hill and took in deep drinks of air and he was a child again in Atlantic City, standing on the boardwalk with his mother. "Smell that salt air!" his mother would say, always. "You'll feel like a new person. Oh, that salt air!"

And yet years later she had lain just blocks from here, awash in salt air, dying.

They moved down the hill toward the rust- and duncolored wooden building that housed the merry-go-round. A few teen-age couples strolled in an arcade along one wall of the building. There was a shielded oval balcony above the merry-go-round. A set of wooden stairs led to the apartment above.

The merry-go-round started up, moving in a slow, gliding circle, calliope music pumping out, squealing and whistling, the carousel picking up speed, spinning now, and Gray Eyes did not think he could get to the top of the stairs.

"Babe, you're almost there," Tracy said. And he forced himself to go on, to reach Alex.

Around the balcony above the carousel they came to a steel-plated door. Tracy pushed a buzzer, but the sound of the calliope drowned out any noise it might have made. She pounded on the door.

It opened and a man, moving with feline grace, ushered them into the apartment.

The man was very tall and had long, flowing, shoulder-length gunmetal-black hair. He was wearing a tank top shirt and canvas ducks. He wore no shoes. In the waistband of his trousers was a 9-mm Parabellum Walther Automatic.

His face was scarred and punched in like a prizefighter's.

His age was hard to determine. He might have been thirty; he might have been fifty. He wore a tiny gold crucifix in one earlobe.

Despite the ruggedness of his features there was something sad and kind in his look. He pulled Gray Eyes to him and hugged him for a very long time. "Oh, Buddy," he said. "What did they do to you?"

Gray Eyes looked up at the man without comprehension, a look pathetic, frightened, confused: the look one sees on the senile old, the long-abandoned insane. He had been in Atlantic City with his mother, the Steel Pier, and now—? "It's Alex," the man said quietly.

"Alex," Gray Eyes breathed. "Alex, Alex."

And Gray Eyes wept.

It was late night when Julie Tripp and Akiba Moldavan arrived in Santa Monica. Fog had come in from the ocean and the town was very still, very quiet. Headlights and street lights gleamed in ghostly aureoles and Akiba felt a terrible presence of time: even as this fog smothers everything, time is consuming us.

I am near the crown of the Sephirot and Buddy Gray Eyes is near it also, he was thinking. He is on the other side, in dark Sephirot and I must get him into the light.

Yet time is spinning away, time destroys, time obliterates.

They drove through the fogged-in streets, past gray, clapboard beachtown buildings, and the idea was a powerful corrosive in Akiba Moldavan's thought: I am losing out to time.

In the Lurianic Kabbalah they spoke of *tzimtzum*, a vacuum created when God withdrew from Himself into Himself; and *shevirat ha-kelim*, the breaking of the vessels: the primordial light of creation spills over, its sparks falling into demonic spheres of being.

There must be a restoration, *tikkun*, when all the fallen sparks, the lost souls are salvaged.

If a person could salvage one spark, that spark could light another and holy, holy, the light of the world could be saved.

And yet time is sweeping it all under, fog is smothering it. "Where is this man, Alex Zayas?" Akiba said.

"He's always on the move. They had a place out in Venice, on the canal," Julie said. "They also had an apartment above the merry-go-round on Santa Monica Pier."

Where is Buddy Gray Eyes? Where? With the limbs of dark Sephirot, the black paths of the other side, crown of night lights.

Akiba closed his eyes, thought of Atlantic City, the Steel Pier, Kennywood Park; he saw the Tree of Sephirot and spinning amusement park lights in his head. "He's at the pier," he said, and Julie steered the car in that direction.

Akiba felt an enormous tenderness for the girl with him. It surprised, moved him. She carries a spark of divinity within her, the spark that shall light the way, he thought. With the spark of this young woman I shall dispel darkness, effect redemption.

"In Kabbalah we talk of evil being a vacuum, a place from which God has removed himself. Yet even there a faint essence of God remains." He was thinking aloud; Julie Tripp watched him out of the side of her gaze and he realized how strange his words must sound. "They say God is in that vacuum as a fragrance is in the vial after it has been emptied of its perfume. You, too, are that fragrance."

She smiled and he felt foolish. "I'm crazy," he said.

"No, I understand," she said. "God is in everything, even the bad. The world would be just too lonely without God."

"You are a spark," Akiba said. "You glowed within Buddy, warmed the dark within him."

They turned down a short hill and parked the car in a lot opposite the Santa Monica Pier. Through the fog they could just make out the form of the merry-go-round building.

A few sad yellow lights still burned on the pier and Akiba and Julie moved from the car into the cold, damp air and walked toward the lights.

The merry-go-round building was shut down for the night. They tried the door and it was locked. Akiba shook the door and beat on it, but no one came.

He called out for Buddy. No one responded. The only sound was that of the breakers crashing against the pier supports.

They left the merry-go-round and walked along the pier. They passed a fortune teller's parlor, a seafood restaurant, a shooting gallery, all closed for the night.

At the end of the pier they found an open hot dog stand and they entered; they stood inside a glass enclosure while Julie had a corn dog and coffee.

The ancient pier beneath them groaned and creaked as waves slammed into its pilings.

"We're looking for a man called Alex Zayas," Akiba said to the griddle man. "He used to live above the merry-go-round. Do you know him?"

The griddle man raised his chin. There was a terrible scar running across his neck. "I know him," he said, his voice a rasp, barely audible. Akiba stared, appalled, at the scar's crusted redness. "The world needs revenge," the man said. "People wouldn't be in nuthouses if they could have revenge. I'll have it. I'll have revenge. Now get out of here, punk." He turned from them and occupied himself at the griddle. He would not speak to them again.

"Alex never needed a reason for his actions," Julie said as they walked back toward the parking lot. "I asked him once why he did what he did. He got down on his knees before me and swore none of it was true. It was true, though. Yes, it was true." She was quiet for a while. "You see—he raped me once." She said it simply and without emotion.

"Did Buddy know?"

"I could never tell him. He would have confronted Alex

and Alex would have killed him. And that's the way that world was."

As they neared the merry-go-round building, Julie hesitated. "What?" Akiba said.

"Alex's people," Julie said.

In front of the merry-go-round building two men stood as though waiting for someone: a man with braces on his teeth and a shaved head, and a man with a Fu Manchu moustache.

"Hello," the man with the braces said.

"Where's Alex?" Julie said.

"He's gone. A long time ago. Months ago." His voice was very quiet.

"Have you seen Buddy Gray Eyes?"

"I haven't seen him and I haven't seen Alex. Everybody's gone." Both men were looking off toward the beach walk beyond the pier.

"You're sure?"

"Oh, yes. Yes."

As Akiba and Julie continued on to the parking lot they saw the man with the moustache enter the merry-go-round building. Julie started up the car. The calliope began to sound from the building, a weird shrilling sound that grew in intensity, whirling out of the fog, the banshee cry of a spirit in agony.

Alex Zayas parted a curtain over the window and the room was suffused in light. On the back wall were two life-sized posters, one of Jesus, one of Lenin.

There were six people in the room—four men and two women.

Two of the men had dark, chicano looks: the man with the shaved head and braces on his teeth and the man with the Fu Manchu moustache.

The other two men were older and looked to be laborers. They wore workboots and overalls covered with white dust. One was balding. The second had his head shaved also.

The girls were very young and dark and had small, ratty faces with scarred complexions.

Alex led Gray Eyes to a mattress at the far end of the room and put him on it. He passed his hand over Gray Eyes's brow and looked into his face with infinite kindness. "Remember how we always speculated on the Crown? Where it was, how you reached it? After you left I went through a terrible time. I kicked the habit like we said we'd do and when I had finally purged my system of chemicals, it came to me in a very real and certain way: I am the Crown."

"Gnostical Leninism," the man with the braces said. "It's Kabbalah, but it's more—"

Buddy's eyes were glazed and for a moment he appeared dead. He was breathing though, and his fingers worked in a rubbing motion as if trying to feel something in the whorls at their tips. "He's on the last path," Alex said. "He's coming home."

Tracy noticed, in a corner, partially covered by a tarpaulin, a stack of weapons: carbines, automatics, shotguns.

Alex Zayas cradled Buddy in his arms and stroked his hair. Buddy's eyes were closed and he looked as though he was asleep.

"Let him rest," Alex said. "He's had a hard trip." He looked at Tracy and smiled a quiet, sad smile. "He's safe now."

Later, Alex disappeared into a back room. One of the girls removed a deck of Tarot cards from her jacket pocket. She spread them out on the floor. "Take one," she said.

Tracy chose a card, turned it face up. It was a Five of Pentacles. "We see here a man and a woman without money, very poor," the girl said in a voice barely above a whisper. "They pass a window with a candle in it. There is snow on the ground. They are living in misery, on the run, outcasts. They are in vast, vast darkness. They have not yet realized the supernal light. It means this: poverty, loss of home, desperate loneliness. Lovers unable to get together, unable to rest, unable to find a bed together. There is a bond between them, mutual unhappiness. Dark night of the soul."

Tracy did not speak for a very long time. "Yes," she said at last. "Yes, yes."

Alex returned to the room. He spoke in quiet tones to the man with the braces and the man with the moustache. They left the apartment.

Alex took Buddy in his arms once more. Buddy's eyes opened and he stared at Alex with a very lucid and direct look. He smiled. "I was dreaming," he said. "Oh, it was beautiful."

"We must talk," Alex said. "I have a confession to make."

"No confessions. They're useless."

"Yes, yes—but—"

"No guilt, no confessions."

"You must hear this," Alex said fervently. "All you've suffered, all you've gone through—it was because of me."

"No confessions!"

"I was the informer. You took the blame. It was me. I didn't do it easily. Understand that. You see—everything we had worked for, *everything* was in jeopardy."

"You, Alex? You?"

"Yes."

"Oh, Alex—"

"I'm desperate, now. I need you. I need your help. We're so near to the light, yet a great black cloud threatens. It could come down on us, obliterate us, and the world would never even know we existed."

Alex's disciples stirred uncomfortably.

"You need my help?" Gray Eyes said.

"Once they hook onto you, they never let go. They want more and more. They want names, they want people set up. They treat you like a junky, a common dope fiend." Alex Zayas's voice was high and tense, his expression pained. "I am the Crown now, but what is my Kingdom?

These half-dozen assholes? Remember what we used to talk about? A group of comrades who were tied to each other like the arms and legs of a single body, the limbs of a tree? Well, I'm clean now. I'm the Crown. I could have it all. We—you and I—and yet—?"

"What Alex? What do you want?"

"I swore I would take care of you, Bud, and I will. I made a phone call before. They're putting it all together."

"Putting what together?"

"We are going to atone, you and I."

"You're turning me over to them," Gray Eyes said.

"God is justice and I am created in His image and I will mete out justice."

"You'll kill me and deliver my body—"

"Only a life can atone for a life," Alex said. He bared Gray Eyes's chest, revealed the tattoo man. He circled the head of the man with his forefinger; he smoothed it over the word METH. Then he leaned down and kissed the figure, there.

One of the workmen had moved to the weapons pile and picked up a Mossberg M500 shotgun. He cracked the breech and inserted two cartridges.

The two girls left the apartment. The workman with the shotgun stood between Gray Eyes and Tracy.

The music of the carousel down below suddenly started up, thudded and whined beneath the floor, growing in intensity as the merry-go-round speeded up.

"I tried to make the best deal for all of us," Alex said, "but my man is playing hard to get."

"You're going to kill us," Tracy said.

"He's suffering," Alex said. "You, too, are suffering. We shoot an animal to put it out of its misery. Why treat a human being any worse? The Crown will be absolved. I'm saving you, Gray Eyes. I'm saving us all."

He made a small nodding motion to the man with the shotgun, then backed away.

The music below thundered, screamed, deafening, cacophonous.

"You're my heart and soul, Buddy," Alex said. "I love you."

The man with the shotgun leveled it on Gray Eyes but Gray Eyes did not remain still: he moved forward off the mattress with incredible quickness, drove his head into the groin of the man with the shotgun.

The gun went off, but Gray Eyes had grabbed the stock of the gun, swinging it to one side. Two shots shattered the window.

Alex screamed, but his scream was drowned out by the sound of the calliope.

Gray Eyes ripped the shotgun from the grip of the man in work clothes and, wielding it as a club, fought his way to the door.

Alex Zayas struggled to extricate the Walther Automatic from his waistband. Gray Eyes hit him with the stock of the gun, caught him on the shoulder, and drove him against the wall. The automatic flew from Alex Zayas's hand and slid across the room.

Tracy had rushed the door. The second workman leaped forward to grab her, but Buddy Gray Eyes was on top of him, smashing at him with the shotgun stock.

Tracy forced the door open and she and Gray Eyes made it out to the wooden oval above the carousel. The man with the braces, the man with the moustache, and the two girls were riding the merry-go-round, waving their arms and laughing.

Alex Zayas was out of the apartment now, moving in extraordinary bounds along the balcony. He leaped forward, grabbed Gray Eyes around the neck, and drove him onto the wooden floor. He held him by the hair and slammed his face against the floor.

Gray Eyes forced himself forward, thrashing to get out of Alex Zayas's grasp.

Through a gap in the balcony wall overlooking the carousel he could see the man with the braces on his teeth, the man with the moustache, and the two girls, rising and falling astride the spinning wooden horses, while the discordant calliope shrilled and shrieked and whistled.

Alex was whispering now, his voice filled with pain and fervor: "Buddy, oh, Buddy, this is for all of us—"

The workmen were moving around the balcony, one with a carbine, the other an automatic. Tracy clawed at Alex, trying to free Buddy Gray Eyes. She was screaming and her voice was trapped in the dissonance of the calliope, was buried in its harsh wail.

Alex had Gray Eyes's neck in a viselike grip between forearm and bicep. His arms, like stone, recalled to Buddy the arms of Cervino, the same adamantine hardness. Alex's arms crushed in on Gray Eyes and he knew Alex was trying to squeeze out what remained of his life.

A dark curtain seemed to be closing down on everything. The music had become muffled. Everything was spinning now, not only the carousel, but the building, the pier, the whole world.

"For you, Buddy, for all of us," Alex Zayas said. Gray Eyes could see the two men in work clothes move forward, trying to sight their weapons. Alex's body blocked their angle; they could not get off a shot.

Tracy's face was close to Gray Eyes's now. Her mouth was open wide; he could see the fillings in her teeth, dirty gray, the sharp animal edges of the teeth. He could see the bone and sinew of Alex Zayas's wrist; a bold blue vein pulsed swollen where the wrist joined the hand. And now Tracy's teeth came down hard on the wrist and he could see in stupendous, anaglyphic clarity the bite of the teeth as they cut into the wrist.

He knew Alex was howling now, but it had become part of the muffled roar into which he was sinking and he was indifferent to it.

Alex thrashed backward, flailed at Tracy. She leaped past

him, and Gray Eyes realized she had gone over the edge of the balcony, down onto the plaster canopy of the carousel.

Gray Eyes followed her, rolled free of the balcony, felt himself falling. He hit the canopy and slid to the floor.

The men in work clothes opened fire. The scream of the calliope was augmented now by a deafening fusillade. Chunks of plaster exploded off the carousel top; the floor was raked with splintering wood. The man with the braces, the man with the moustache, and the two girls flung themselves from the spinning merry-go-round and scurried for the door. A piercing cry of sirens now sounded very loud, very close.

At the rear of the building Tracy had found a fire exit and was fighting to unlock it. Gray Eyes threw himself against the door. It swung open and the two of them pushed forward. They were outdoors now, on the ocean side of the pier. They hurried to the pier's edge over thick, slippery beams.

There was a ladder leading to the beach and they went down it, and then they were on the wet sand with ocean water swirling about their feet.

They moved along under the pier, stumbling through seaweed-twined pilings. When they emerged, they were at the beach walk.

Everything felt pure, light, easy to Gray Eyes. He felt no pain, no fatigue.

He had found Alex. He had learned the truth about him. Alex had been the one. Alex had ratted him out. Now he could rest.

They put up at the Continental Hotel, facing the water on Ocean Walk, fifty feet from the beach. The room was a dirty yellow and smelled of bug spray and disinfectant.

While Gray Eyes drifted in and out of consciousness, Tracy tried to figure out what to do. From time to time he would awaken and stare at himself in the mirror. "I look like my mother did when she was dying," he said.

"You're not dying."

"Why are you here?" he said. "Why do you stay with me?"

She could not explain it, but his dying was for her an objectification of her living: she could see in him the decay of herself. By caring for him she was caring for herself. She was mourning herself. She must save herself.

At last he slept and she was afraid he was dead. She lay next to him on the bed and held his wrist in her hand. She lay awake like that through the night, feeling the shallow beat of a dying man's pulse.

# 22

The concrete walk was deserted. A light rain was falling. The sky above was heavy with clouds, the ocean dark, angry.

Off the walk, squatting under a brick overhang, three kids in rubber wet suits lipped cigarettes. They were no more than ten years old and had stringy blond hair down to the middle of their backs. It was impossible to tell whether they were boys or girls. With pinched faces and feral eyes, they watched the rain as though it were a personal affront, a conspiracy against their lives.

John Strahan sat in the Sea 'N' Surf Restaurant in Venice, facing the strand and the sea and the kids in wet suits.

He sensed he was near some sort of collapse. He had not bathed, shaved, slept in he could not remember how long. The pain in his stomach was constant now. What is happening to me? he thought.

I am becoming absorbed into Buddy Gray Eyes. The two of us are becoming one.

Nothing matters though, he told himself; only that I finally get him. Then I will be clean again; then I will sleep; then the pain in my stomach will stop.

He had been in the Santa Monica–Venice area two days. The only lead had blown up that morning, a gang of crazies who had offered to trade in Gray Eyes, then got into a shoot-out with one another on the Santa Monica Pier.

The local police doubted that Gray Eyes had ever been involved. The leader of the gang had been taken in on a whole load of charges. Strahan had rushed to the jail, but had been too late.

The man had killed himself.

Strahan had seen the cell. The man had cut a wrist and scrawled on the wall in blood: "Not the crown, but Judas." Then he had wrapped his shirt around his neck, tied it to the bars, and jumped from the upper bunk.

Where did that leave Strahan? I am at the ocean, alone, he told himself. Yet he felt with a desperate certitude that Gray Eyes was near.

Two other people were in the Sea 'N' Surf, a cramped beach hangout with six tables, concrete floor, wicker walls: an elderly black with an enormous gray Afro and a man with a long beard, a single gold earring, plum-colored woman's dress, and nylon stockings over hairy legs.

They were arguing quantum physics and the zodiac.

Strahan dunked a sourdough roll into his coffee and tried to figure out what next to do.

He opened his small spiral notebook. He came across a note: Edmund Husserl, Phenomenology, consciousness in relationship to objects. What was that all about? Oh, yes, a book Mother Shadman had been reading.

He thought about childhood, Cervino's store, his first meeting with Akiba Moldavan and Buddy Gray Eyes. The paths they had traveled since then!

What had happened on that day? What relationship did it have to the murder of the old man?

What jagged shard of time did Gray Eyes carry from that day to this?

He pondered a chess problem he had written down months ago. White to mate in three. It was futile: he could see only Gray Eyes, Akiba Moldavan, Cervino.

He thought of the chess master Capablanca. Someone

had once asked him how many moves he thought ahead. One, he answered. Only one? Yes, but always the *right* one.

Where was the right move now? Why hadn't it presented itself to him? White to mate in three. Buddy Gray Eyes, Akiba Moldavan, Cervino.

He was at rock bottom now, desperate. The middle game had been played out; the end game was racing ahead out of control, pawns hurtling toward the queening rank.

Diagonals, horizontals, verticals, knight moves: herky-jerky skips and jumps, one, two, and over, one and over two.

Where would Gray Eyes turn up next?

He had prowled the ocean walk from Santa Monica to Venice. He had been in every low-rider bar, down-dope hangout. He had scoured the piers, the beaches, the canals, the side streets.

The pain in his stomach would never leave him, he could not rest, until he had found Buddy Gray Eyes, found and killed him.

It would never be different. It was end game in his life.

A young girl soaked with rain, strung out, entered the Sea 'N' Surf. She's a dope fiend, Strahan thought. She's on the rims.

The girl glanced at him and he sensed a dart of fear in her look, a recognition.

She seated herself toward the sea, facing away from Strahan, and ordered coffee.

She drank the coffee in a rush, glanced back at Strahan once, then hurried from the store.

Strahan moved after her out onto the strand. She was going at a half run along the rainswept walk. Strahan began to jog after her.

She reached the Venice Pavillion and disappeared down a ramp. Strahan followed her. The rain was coming down heavier now, stinging his face.

The girl had fled into a circular, open air, seaside arena, a cul-de-sac used for picnics and rock concerts in season. A concrete wall curved around the arena, enclosing it. There were concrete tables and wooden benches and a canvas-covered stage area. It was raining very hard now and for an instant Strahan thought he had lost the girl. Where had she disappeared?

Then he saw her behind the platform stage, circling the edge of the arena, trapped by the concrete wall.

Strahan caught up with her. Through an aperture in the wall the ocean could be seen lashing the rocks on which the pavillion was constructed.

"Hey," Strahan said. "Don't I know you? Aren't you from Denver?" She huddled against the wall, shook her head. "What's your name?"

"Mary," the girl said. She was wet and shivering.

"You're not from Denver?"

"No." She would not look him in the face. "You from Denver?"

"That's right."

"You don't look like anyone from Denver."

"Is that so?" Strahan said.

"You ever been in New York?" the girl said.

"Naw. You?"

"Naw."

"Why'd you ask?"

"You look like a back-east type, is all."

"Not me. What did you say your name was?"

"Mary. Slocam. They call me Sloke."

"Where you from, Sloke?"

"Frisco."

"What do you say we get in out of the rain? You live around here?"

"No."

"Where do you live?"

"A long way from here."

"All right. What do you say we go back to that place and have some coffee?"

"What do you say we don't?"

"It's crazy standing in the rain."

"It's all right."

"You know, you're a very attractive girl. You have a great look to you. The first moment I saw you I was attracted to you."

"Really?"

"That's right."

She stared at him for a long moment. Ah, yes, Strahan thought, she knows me. She's scared. This is it: I have her.

"Okay," she said. "Why not? Let's go back to that place. I feel like I could use a hot chocolate."

Hooked, Strahan thought. Cockroach caught. She knows me. She must be the one. Yes, I'm in the end game now.

"Weather for cockroaches," he said as they walked along the strand.

"That's funny. Weather for cockroaches."

"I hate cockroaches," he said.

"Everyone does. Definitely," she said. "For sure."

They sat in the Sea 'N' Surf sipping something called Hot Cinnamon Delight, made, according to the menu, from coffee, chocolate, whipped cream, and cinnamon. "Mmm, that's good," Strahan said.

"It's all right." The girl looked bedraggled and hopelessly lost. Her eyes were anxious with dope deprivation.

"You have a boyfriend?" Strahan said.

"Sort of."

"What does he do?"

She hesitated. "He's a cop."

"A cop?"

"Yeah."

"You like cops?" He grinned.

"Sort of."

"That's real interesting. Because, you know, well, you know—this is going to make you laugh—I used to be cop."

She did not react. She stared dully at him. Strahan pressed it. "Yeah, I been a cop in a lot of places."

She didn't speak for a long time. "Where have you been a cop?" she said at last.

"Oh, you name it."

"Pittsburgh?"

He smiled slowly. "Oh, sure."

She took in a deep breath. "What's the matter?" he said.

"Don't hurt me," she said.

"What makes you think I want to hurt you?"

"Cops always hurt people."

"Not necessarily. People sometimes get involved in things that are way over their heads. And then a cop can pull them out of a jam." Strahan continued to force a smile, to talk reasonably. Inside, the tension was extraordinary. His stomach, his arms ached with it. It's her. The girl with Gray Eyes. The girl on skis. I have her.

"You guys play people like yo-yos."

"Some people are yo-yos." He stirred his Cinnamon Delight. This is the moment, he thought. Easy. "Where is he?" he said quietly.

"Who?"

"Gray Eyes."

She sat motionless for a very long time. "How did you know?"

"I recognized you recognized me."

"That could be a nice title for a song," she said. She looked sad, infinitely sad, lonely, lost.

"He's dying," she said.

"Take me to him." He held his breath, waiting for the answer.

"Please, don't make me. I don't want to do that."

"Come on—what did you say your name was?"

"What difference does it make?"

"Look, I like you. I think you're a good kid."

She studied his face. "Do you really like me?"

"I like you a lot."

312

"Really?"

"Yes."

She toyed with a paper napkin on the table, slowly shredding it. She gazed out at the rain.

"Please," he said. "No one cares about him, except maybe you and me. It's a shame what they're doing to him. He'll die like a dog and those sons-of-bitches will be happy. They'll leave you with nothing but a hunk of cold flesh. Please." He could hardly breathe, the words were coming so fast. "We've known each other since we were eight years old. We hung out at the candy store together, had the same girl friend, played football on the same team. He was my best friend."

"He's good people, isn't he?" she said. "I don't know why he did what he did."

"He had his reasons. Don't you worry though, he's going to beat this thing because I'm going to help him. He'll never find a friend as loyal as me."

"Would you get him to a doctor?"

"I'll see he gets the best."

"And you won't tell him I snitched?"

"Oh, no."

"Because I think he has respect for me and I wouldn't want him to lose it."

"No. Let me call the hospital. Where is he now?"

"The Continental Hotel, just down the walk. Room five. Don't tell him I snitched. And please, take care of him." Strahan leaned close to her and kissed her on the cheek. She grabbed his arm and held on. She was trembling. "Do you really like me?" she said.

"Of course."

She was fighting tears. "I always had a thing for cops," she said. "And they always fucked me over."

"I wouldn't do that," he said, pulling away from her.

"Will you come back to me?" she said.

"That might be a little tough."

"What am I going to do?" she said. "I hurt inside."

He peeled off a twenty-dollar bill and passed it to her. "Get high," he said.

"For sure."

The rain had stopped by the time Strahan reached the Continental Hotel. There was one old woman sitting in the lobby, knitting a cap. She was smiling and talking to herself. Strahan went to the desk. There was no one behind it. "He's shooting up," the old woman said. "Spic junky."

Strahan went behind the counter and found a key in the slot for room number five.

He climbed a wooden stairway that smelled of must. There were no lights on in the hallway at the top. He removed his .38 from under his jacket and the backup .32 from the holster on his hip.

There was a fine, sensual pleasure in holding the gun. He thought of that day, oh, so many years ago, when he and Gray Eyes had met for the first time, that day in front of Cervino's, when they had fought and he had been beaten. Some humiliations you never forget. The ones when you are a child are the worst.

They stay with you, they reside forever in your gut. And they fester and grow. Things are heaped on them.

And he despoiled my wife when she was pure. And he ridiculed me on the football field. And he slaughtered an innocent old man.

And he is a Jew.

And now: I will blow him away. And all the pain inside me will cease forever.

He thought of Walt Nagorksi and a sudden uneasiness came over him. The priest certainly would not approve.

But, then, Father Nagorski was at ease in the world, lived his life without effort, had his belief and was secure in it.

He remembered as a kid being tortured by an awareness

of that ease, that sense of rightness: "But how do you do it, Father Walt, how do you hit a ball so far?" There were things in this world which were overwhelmingly mysterious, yet held the key to everything. Some people did them so simply. How do you hit a ball so far?

He could never learn that and he could never learn to live with what Buddy Gray Eyes had become in his life.

Father Nagorski cared for people, knew love, forgiveness. These were things beyond Strahan's ken, although he yearned for them, admired their purity, wished, oh, how he wished, he could have exhibited them.

And yet there were things that John Strahan could accomplish that were beyond Walt Nagorski's achievement. On the chess board, for instance, the priest lacked an instinct for finality; he could not clinch it. That's why Strahan always won over him. He knew how to bide his time, accumulate advantage, shut down avenues of escape, crush his opponent. Years ago he had collared a professional hit man. The killer had told him: My world is like chess and when you off a dude it's checkmate.

Strahan would checkmate Buddy Gray Eyes.

Walt Nagorski didn't understand the pain in Strahan's stomach. He must have satisfaction, he must have release. There were wrongs in his world and they had coalesced in the existence of Buddy Gray Eyes, his *ontological* presence. Phenomenology, Mother Shadman had said: consciousness in relationship to objects. Strahan knew all about that. He knew that a bullet could do away with all the complexities, the ambiguities of philosophy: effect a change with extreme prejudice, cancel a dude's mail, as they say.

And now a realization came to him as he stood in the darkened hallway: the present had nothing to do with the past. The humiliation he had suffered, the hate he felt, his sense of right and wrong, his wife's deceptions, his inadequacies, bad eyes, pain in the stomach were irrelevant. When you canceled a dude's mail, it was as though he had never ever existed. One, then, could move into the future, demonstrate a particular consciousness in relation to objects *from this time forward*. Once he had rid his world of Gray Eyes, everything would change; he would enter a fresh dimension. He was not even certain he would return to his wife. Perhaps he would take up with the girl at the Sea 'N' Surf, Gray Eyes's girl. They would rent a room on the ocean. They would get down and bang dope. He would become a different person.

He probed the hallway for the first door, felt its raised number, moved on to the next, feeling the face of each door until he came to five. He located the keyhole and inserted the key. He turned it quickly and swung the door in. He crouched low and, keeping both guns at arm's length, entered the room.

It was empty.

He searched the closet, overturned the bed. The room was empty.

There was a pile of bandages on the floor. The room stank, an oppressive odor of putrefaction.

He sat on the bed and waited. Through the window he could see the angry, slate-colored ocean. The day grew dark as afternoon bled into night. No one came.

He sat in the dark, waiting. He sat motionless on the edge of the bed. His heart was empty of feeling. Gray Eyes: gone. Where? When? White to mate in three. He still had not solved it.

With the light of dawn he was still seated in the same spot.

# 23

WHAAAAAAAA, whaaaaaaaa, whaaaaaaaa, cars swooshed by in the night, tires churning rainwater, headlight beams slashing across the wall, dying out, returning with yet another diagonal slash of light.

It was deep night and Akiba Moldavan could not sleep.

The night before, after Akiba and Julie Tripp had encountered the two men from Alex Zayas's group, they had returned to Ocean Avenue and taken rooms in a small hotel there.

They had slept a couple of hours, then gone out again. They had returned to the merry-go-round. It was shut down.

It had begun to rain.

They spent the whole day in Venice and Santa Monica, visiting old hangouts of Buddy Gray Eyes and Alex Zayas.

It rained all day and though they were wet and tired, they continued on.

The Tree of Sephirot glowed within Akiba now; he could feel its powerful, radiating presence: it was inside and it was all around him.

I am approaching *Kether*, the Crown, he thought. I have struggled through the twenty-two paths, the ten limbs, and I am coming near the Crown.

"Everything's different," Julie said, "like a shattered mirror." They could not find Gray Eyes or Alex Zayas.

Places she had known were altered, people no longer there. All was familiar, all was changed. Alex had been seen, had not been seen. He was down the block, he was dead. Buddy Gray Eyes? Who? Snuffles, shifting looks, sighs. He's gone. Where? He's never been here.

"He is near," Akiba insisted to Julie. "He is near."

But where? How to find him?

They had come back to the hotel that night, exhausted.

Akiba had lain in the bed and people appeared to him out of an uneasy half sleep: the man with the braces on his teeth, the man with the moustache. They performed obscure gestures, exchanged elusive glances. They knew Gray Eyes was near. No one would tell where.

These are *kelippot,* Akiba told himself, demonic shards, shattered light.

He sat up, huddled at the edge of the bed. He prayed and his prayer was filled with confusion. To whom was he praying? For what?

At last he dozed off. The Tree of Sephirot spread just beyond his reach. It was immense, tangled. Julie Tripp sat at its gnarled roots, staring straight ahead with a look of such fragility and need that Akiba felt a sob rise up within him.

She was staring at him and she was blind.

He awakened to the sound of the cars passing in the rain outside, the shifting play of light and shadow on the wall; then he drifted off to sleep again; once more the Tree of Sephirot opened up before him, erupted in a slow, barely perceptible distention; Julie Tripp knelt on the ground before it.

She was moving her lips in a soundless entreaty. Akiba watched himself move toward her. The tree above them glowed with dark, mysterious calorescence, immense, inexorable.

He lay out beside Julie Tripp and pulled her to him. "I love you," he said.

He awoke with a start, flooded with weakness, heart racing.

"I love this girl," he said, and he trembled with the thought. I am madness. I am ego and desire.

Now he told himself: It's not her I love. It is the Shekinah. I love the Shekinah and out of that love I will redeem Buddy Gray Eyes. I will redeem myself.

I am in *tohu*, the dark other side where men thrash in confusion, lost. I am in *tohu*, I am in despair.

I must get to Buddy Gray Eyes. If I die in the process, I must get to him.

He dressed and walked out onto the balcony. The street was slick with rain although it was not raining now.

In Julie's room next to his he could see a light. Was she awake now? he wondered. Was she thinking of him? Had they shared the same dream?

Why had he been touched so deeply by this girl? Why?

It was her essential goodness, her dedication, he decided. She loved Gray Eyes even as Akiba had loved him. In her own way she had committed herself to his redemption.

And she was seeking her own redemption.

She had reached out to Akiba. They had held each other. They had embarked together on the madness and sanctity of a man's restoration, the *tikkun* of Gray Eyes. She had become the shadow of Akiba's heart even as dark Kabbalah was the shadow of the light. She had become for Akiba a glow of the Shekinah, a spark of the spark.

The light emanating from Ein Soph is blinding, he was thinking. We view it through many veils. We recognize its fire by the faint light of a dying ember.

And that is the love I feel for this girl, Akiba Moldavan thought.

He knocked softly at her door. "It's Akiba," he said.

Julie Tripp admitted him to her room.

She wore a terry-cloth robe over a thin gown. She was unimaginably beautiful.

They didn't talk for a long while. Akiba felt awkward, foolish. He had brought this girl to the far Pacific shore; they had arrived in fog, racing time. They had found only their own helplessness.

Why are we here? Whom do we question? Where do we go?

What could he offer her?

Gray Eyes is here, near, calling out to us, Akiba thought, yet how do we find him?

How? How?

Julie Tripp sat on the bed, stared at Akiba. He realized he, too, was staring and he was embarrassed, but he could not take his eyes from her.

No one in his life had appeared as beautiful as she in this moment.

"I was thinking about you," she said. "And I couldn't sleep." He did not speak. "Akiba, come here." He did not move.

She removed her robe; underneath, through the gown, he could see the pink of her flesh, the darker pink of her nipples, the wedge of her sex. "Come here," she said.

Sadness flooded his being. Regret. His life was regret. My belief is a fraud, he was thinking. I have deserted father, sister, wife, children. I have entered a fun house chase, a chase of bleak absurdity—leading where?

*Tohu* was not Gray Eyes's world, but his own. He had become Gray Eyes's mirror image.

His whole life had led to this—a motel room on the ocean's edge, a bed with a young girl, a gentile in whom he has invested qualities of the Holy Shekinah.

What a wasteland my life has become, he thought. I am worse than Yakov, my brother. I am *am haarez*, an ignoramus, and worse. I have sacrificed my life for this moment.

Regret, regret. The *tohu* was the crucible of regret.

What could his life have been if he had turned away

from the world of his father? He might have gone into law, business, medicine, owned a great house, worn fine clothing, traveled the world.

He might have belonged to country clubs, excelled at golf, played the stock market, had a wife of impressive style, entertained clients. He might have gloried in the world, been dazzled by it.

He might have slept with a woman as beautiful as Julie Tripp.

But he had dedicated his life to Kabbalah.

"Come over here, Akiba," Julie Tripp said quietly.

"You don't want me," Akiba said, and it took all his strength to utter the words. "By sleeping with me you think you'll have Buddy. It's not so."

She drew her legs up under her and wrapped her robe around her and her shame was enormous. She huddled like that on the bed and her body was wracked with sobs. She fought them and she did not utter a sound.

And the pain within Akiba was so great that he felt he would shatter with it. Oh, God, he said to himself, that You have made us so pathetic! Where is our glory, where is our magnitude, where is our belief?

He rushed from the room along the concrete balcony, down the iron steps. He moved at a run across Ocean Avenue, heading toward the beach walk.

He heard Julie call his name and he ran faster. At the walkway leading down to the beachfront he stopped and turned.

Julie Tripp, a coat over her robe, was rushing toward him. "I am crazy, but I have dedicated my life to Buddy's redemption!" he shouted at her and his voice sounded against the thunder of the ocean and was lost in it.

She came to him and leaned her head against him and trembled under his hands. "I love him," she said. She held tightly on to him. "I love him, I love him."

The night was cold, the air damp. The rain had stopped.

The sky was very low and black. Wind rustled the palm trees along Ocean Avenue as they walked toward the pier.

Shivering in the cold, they moved down the iron and concrete stairway to the walkway beyond the pier. The ocean pounded the beach and they stood leaning on a retaining wall and watched the great animal heave of its weight, its white froth fury muscling the shore. Gusts of sand rose and swirled along the beach, dwarf tornadoes dancing beside the ocean walk.

"We'll find him," Akiba said to her. "He's here. I know it!"

They moved away from the wall and continued along the walk toward Venice. There was something ominous in the damp dark of the ocean walk, something threatening. Dark Kabbalah, dark Sephirot.

He was pacing its paths.

They passed skeletal monkey-bars projecting from the sand, weird runic forms laced against the night sky; boarded-up hot dog stands; a darkened paddleball court.

They passed the Sea 'N' Surf, dark, boarded up; the Way, the Truth, the Life Church; the Continental Hotel; the Teferith Jacob Synagogue.

At the scarred *shul* Akiba paused and wondered: Does it still minister to souls, and if so, whose? So poor, so desolate, he thought, moved by the pitted blue and white plaster facade, the battered iron gates shielding the door, the obscene scrawls of graffiti, the ugly shadow of a painted-over swastika.

He thought, of course, of his own synagogue, of the poverty there, of the old Orthodox Jews trying to hang onto a way of life that was doomed by time, culture, prosperity, Jews of another world, Jews lost, Jews dying. He was carrying in his heart the glowing, delicate filament of a faith he knew was being consumed in the speed and flash of the modern world.

His heart ached for his father and for all the old Jews

who were being engulfed inexorably by modernity's holocaust, the roaring firestorm of great cars, television, electrical gadgets, neon. The flames of Hitler's ovens, he thought, could not consume the spirit with as much fury as the mushrooming inferno of the atom world.

He and Julie walked the three-mile distance from Santa Monica through Venice, to Washington Street on the edge of Marina Del Rey. Behind them now was despair, despair of sea walk rummies, dying junkies, beachfront hustlers, confused, lost, shuffling old-timers, oceanside losers. Ahead were the sleek high-rises of the Marina area, the woodsy town homes, the brilliant yachts, the plastic and concrete condominiums.

They turned on Washington Street. Just up the block was an all-night hero sandwich stand. They entered and ordered coffee and doughnuts at the counter.

In the rear of the place, at a Formica table, nodding out in junk-filled reverie, sat the man with the moustache, the man with the braces on his teeth, and Tracy.

They looked over at Akiba and Julie, and though the two men recognized them, it didn't much seem to matter.

"It's all Kabbalah," said the man with the braces on his teeth as Akiba approached. "The First Cause." He waved his hand ineffectually.

The man with the moustache was shaking his head. "He was the Crown, the Messiah, and he's dead." He stared up at Akiba with an expression of extraordinary pain and incomprehension. "He was unifying everything."

"He's with his Father now," the man with the braces said.

"Someone laid the goods on him," the man with the moustache said. "Set him up."

The man with the braces laughed. "You, man. Don't shit me. You set him up." He bobbed his head up and down for emphasis.

"That's a lie!"

"You, baby, you." He grinned broadly and the braces

were like barbed wire over his teeth. "You cut yourself a deal."

"What are we going to do?" the man with the moustache moaned, at the point of tears.

"Hey, baby," the man with the braces said, "he'll be back. He'll walk this earth again. And if he don't he was nothing but a motherfucking jivester."

"No!" the man with the moustache said.

"Baby, the First Cause is still the First Cause," the man with the braces said. "And Kabbalah is still Kabbalah."

The man with the moustache was inconsolable. He covered his face with his hand and wept quietly. The man with the braces dipped his head lower and lower in short, junky nods. Tracy remained impassive, staring at the window glass. "Where's Gray Eyes?" Akiba asked.

"Wow, Gray Eyes," the man with the braces said, his lids fluttering. He laughed to himself. The man with the moustache composed himself, lit up a cigarette, kept it to his mouth with two fingers, and permitted his thoughts to sink into quiet clouds of smoke.

Tracy was a hood-lidded statue, a frozen wax doll. "He got Gray Eyes for sure," she said after a while.

"Who's that?"

"That Pittsburgh cop."

"Where?"

"What difference does it make?"

"Tell me. Please."

"The Continental Hotel," she said, scratching the side of her face. "Definitely." Dead eyes, dead heart.

A man and a woman entered the place, two clean-cut young people on a date. The man with the moustache watched them as they put in their order at the counter. Suddenly he jumped up, almost knocking over the table, and ran toward them. He grabbed the young man by the shirt front and threw him against the wall. He slapped him several times hard across the face. The young man cringed, trying to protect himself. "What's my name?" the man with the moustache demanded.

"I don't know." The man with the moustache slapped him again. "They call you Baby Lobo or something like that."

The man with the moustache flung him to one side and returned to the table.

He seated himself and resumed puffing on the cigarette. "Did you know him?" Tracy said.

"I didn't know him. But he sure knew me." He smiled quietly, at peace with himself.

It was just getting light out when Julie and Akiba arrived at the Continental Hotel. The Spanish junky, a cadaverous man in a purple nylon net shirt, scarred face and arms, was wide awake behind the desk, listening to a transistor radio through an earplug. He steered them to room five on the second floor.

The door was ajar. Akiba and Julie entered. A man was seated, staring out the window.

"Buddy," Akiba said softly, approaching the man.

The man did not turn for a while. When he did, his face was devoid of expression. "He's gone," John Strahan said softly.

"Where?"

"I don't know," Strahan said, his voice empty, beyond defeat. He continued to stare out the window, talking to himself now: "That day at Cervino's when we were kids. He beat me up. Why? Later he took the woman I loved. Why? Why did he do those things to me?"

"Leave him be," Akiba said. "Go home."

"I can't," John Strahan said. He leaned his face against the window and moaned like an animal in pain.

Suddenly, he slammed his forehead against the glass. It cracked, but did not shatter.

One lens of his spectacle cracked also and the pattern of both was a central stem with spreading limbs.

"John," Akiba said, but Strahan did not respond to him; he continued to whimper, his eyes bright with agony, and Akiba knew that he had crossed some dark threshold in his soul.

Julie and Akiba returned to the ocean walk. The light, filtered through mist, was like gray stone; the air was damp and heavy.

An old man came to Akiba out of the Teferith Jacob Synagogue. "*Du bist a yid?*" he said. Are you a Jew?

"Yes."

"Come. Come. We need a *minyan*."

Akiba asked Julie to wait for him on one of the ocean walk benches; he went with the man.

Inside the synagogue the men of the congregation nodded in greeting. They were old, pathetically so, shabby, unshaven, dressed in frayed clothes, ill-fitting charity garments worn long beyond the time when the men possessed the flesh to fill them out.

There was fear in their eyes and a desperate need for belief and Akiba was profoundly moved: they were so near the presence of *Malakh ha-Mavet*, the Angel of Death, these survivors of faith. Poor, ill, dying, every morning they pursued a small, passionate mission, searched out a minyan, attempted in their own way a simple *tikkun*, the restoration of God's pure dominion.

The interior of the synagogue was painfully drab: wooden benches; a functional *bimah*, the platform on which the *Torah* was read; an unimpressive ark. It smelled of mildew, of the sea.

Someone handed Akiba a *tallith* and prayer book and the *shaharith*, the morning service, began.

They went through the benedictions, *yotzer*, light, and *ahavah*, love, then the *Shema*, "Hear O Israel, the Lord is our God, the Lord is One," followed by *geullah*, the benediction for redemption.

Akiba prayed fervently, prayed as he had never prayed in his life. Redemption was near, so near, if not for many, then for one: if one man can be redeemed, it is as the redemption of the world.

And Akiba felt the Tree of Sephirot within him and all about him.

Its pattern had been in the shattered window in Gray Eyes's room, the shattered lens in Strahan's spectacles. It was in the lines on the faces of the men of the congregation, in the cracked plaster of the synagogue walls. It was everywhere.

Through the *amidah*, the prayer done standing after the *geullah*, the prayers for repentance, forgiveness, healing of the sick, he felt Gray Eyes within him, his childhood friend was part of him and he prayed with a fervency that obliterated the world of *kelippot*, shells, demons, dark Kabbalah, that knew only the world of light.

His soul had merged with the soul of Gray Eyes, his twin, his shadow, and a *tikkun*, the restoration of the Divine Vessels, was a breath away. Near, so near. He could feel it, within him and without, he could almost touch it: *Parsufim*, a completion of the Supernal Configuration.

The *amidah* was followed by the prayers of supplication, the *tahanun*, and then there would be *keriat ha-torah*, the reading of the law.

The old man who had summoned Akiba to the *minyan* now moved to the ark containing the *Torah*, drew back the *parocheth*, the curtain separating the ark from the Sanctuary.

An audible sound, a moan, passed through the congregation. These men who had seen so much in their lives: dreams unfulfilled, aspirations delayed, suffering, horror, loved ones gassed and incinerated, children rejecting the most sacred beliefs of their fathers; these courageous bearers of the faith looked on in dismay.

Crammed into the ark, huddled against the *Torah*, was Buddy Gray Eyes.

The blue-gray irises of his eyes had rolled to white and his breath came in shallow, barely audible gasps. The rotating whites of his eyes presented a vision of emptiness, of blindness, the Shekinah in exile, the eyeless virgin.

No one moved. Then Akiba rushed forward. He pressed his body against his friend.

As though hoisting the *Torah*, he lifted him from the ark, staggered under his weight down from the *bimah* onto the main floor.

He set him down on a bench against the wall and passed his hand over his face.

Gray Eyes breathed deeply, and the irises of his eyes came into view, the extraordinary coloration, the blue-gray opalescence of Gray Eyes, seeing, cognizant.

"Akiba. Akiba, my old friend."

"Oh, Buddy."

"Remember—we talked of the golem and the Tree of Life and the Tree of Death?" Gray Eyes said, and his voice was small, childlike, and the two of them were kids again, resting under the buckeye trees of Frick Park.

"Yes."

"Akiba," he said very quietly.

"Why did you kill the old man?" Akiba said.

"Let it go, Akiba," Gray Eyes said.

"I can't."

Gray Eyes ran his tongue over his lips. "It's tied together like the heart, the veins, the arteries. It moves from then to now," he said.

"Yes?"

"He loved me."

"Cervino?"

"I had a pet chick and it died. I had never known death before that time. I wept and my mother comforted me. And later, many years later, she died and it was the same."

"But Cervino—?"

"I stole from him, that day I first met you and John Strahan. Strahan told the old man. The old man took me to his back room."

"What happened there?" Gray Eyes smiled, shook his head in remembrance. "What?" Akiba said.

"The old man forgave me," Gray Eyes said in wonderment. "He hugged me and his arms were like stone. He loved me and so years later I killed him."

Akiba waited for a reason. None came. "But *why?*" he said at last.

Gray Eyes stared at him with a look of absolute clarity. "Death is love," he said, as though this were the most obvious fact of all. "Death is mercy. Don't you see that? Why else take a helpless animal? Why else my mother? Don't you see, Akiba? I am The Destroyer who brings mercy to the innocent. Mercy to them, mercy to the innocent of the world."

And Akiba realized as he held Buddy Gray Eyes, he was with the Sephirot and its shadow, dark Kabbalah and light.

"Save me," Gray Eyes breathed.

"Yes."

"Save me."

"There are three things necessary for redemption—"

"I remember," Gray Eyes said.

Akiba wiped the perspiration from his friend's face. "Repeat after me—" Gray Eyes stared up at him. His look was bright and suddenly ferocious and he bared his chest and the stick figure golem, the Tree of Death, danced on his skin. Gray Eyes threw himself forward, flailing at Akiba. He struggled to his feet. Akiba attempted to restrain him, but he broke away, broke through the ring of old men surrounding him, moved at a run up the aisle and out of the synagogue.

It had begun to rain once more, a fine, mistlike spray. Buddy Gray Eyes stumbled into the rain and began to run along the ocean walk.

Seated at a window in the Continental Hotel, John Strahan saw the door to the synagogue swing open, saw a figure moving away along the ocean walk, and he knew it was Gray Eyes.

And he knew he would get him this time.

His revolver was out of its holster now, the cold heft of it in his hand sending a thrill through his whole being. Yes, he would have him at last.

And he was out of the room, leaping the wooden steps to the lobby in twos and threes, then out through the lobby and onto the walk. He raised the revolver. "*Buddy!*" he yelled.

And Buddy Gray Eyes turned to face him, his arms opened wide as though to embrace John Strahan.

And now Akiba Moldavan was there and he put himself between the two men.

And Akiba knew: if a man pursues another with the intention of taking his life, he is *rodeph* and it is justifiable for anyone to prevent this, even by taking the pursuer's life.

And more: Buddy Gray Eyes had himself taken human life and for *teshubah*, repentance, he must confess his sin to God, vow never to repeat it, and repay what he has taken. He must give up his life for the life he has taken.

And Julie Tripp was there now also, fighting with Akiba, trying to pull him out of the line of fire.

Akiba was not to be deterred. His existence had distilled itself to this essence: bring his friend *teshubah*.

It was a unification of the Sephirot, a supernal configuration, the victory of light over dark, the Tree of Life over the Tree of Death.

He yanked away from Julie and came straight toward Strahan. "Move! Get out of the way!" Strahan was screaming.

Yes, I will kill him if I must, Akiba thought.

Strahan ducked low, attempted to evade his advance. "Gray Eyes! Gray Eyes!" he screamed. "I want you, beautiful Gray Eyes!"

Akiba had him by the arm now and he fought him, fought with a desperate ferocity, sure of what he must do: *rodeph*, and he must prevent it and then there must be *teshubah* for Buddy Gray Eyes.

The two men went down on the rain-slick walk. Strahan thrashed and screamed, struggled to get free, but Akiba would not let go. He hung on with all the strength he had, all his purpose, all his belief.

He had hold of the barrel of the revolver now, bent Strahan's gun hand back, twisted hard, and the revolver came out of Strahan's grip and Akiba scrambled to his feet.

At the margin of his vision he could see Gray Eyes moving down the walk, stumbling; and Julie Tripp was rushing after him.

Strahan came up after Akiba and Akiba swung out with the gun. It caught Strahan on the side of the head and his body sagged and he fell. He tried to get up; he had his hands around Akiba's legs and his grip dug into the flesh of his thighs. Akiba put the gun to Strahan's temple and he wanted to pull the trigger, but he could not. He hit Strahan again and this time he rolled over, moaning on the walk.

Buddy Gray Eyes was running, running, running down the morning beach walk with its gathering lost crowd, past crumpled winos and nodding dawn junkies, surfers in black wet suits, guitar strummers, Frisbee-tossing kids, old chess players. At last I'm dead, he was thinking. It is merciful. At last.

The ocean roared in his head, the pitted and mutilated facades of oceanside buildings pulsated in his gaze. He could see beyond the pier, high above the ocean walk, way, way, far away, the Sovereign Hotel and his mother was dying, she was whispering to him. "You're a good son, Buddy. You're a good son," over and over again, and he has beaten it all, beaten life, beaten dope, beaten the loss of heroism, the waste of his being. The irises of his mother's eyes are rolled back, the whites rotating, her breath a loud moan, the pulse in her neck is running down, running down: stopping.

He felt the cool of the rain on the walkway as he slid facedown across it.

And Akiba Moldavan, old friend, dear old friend, is leaning over him. And Julie Tripp is there. And he looks for his father, but he cannot find him. He finds other men there, ancient men, impassive men. And tattooed beach people, and men in black motorcycle jackets. But his father is not there.

Akiba Moldavan is holding a revolver and that seems extraordinarily strange to Buddy Gray Eyes. He wants to tell him, no, you are not meant for guns, but he can get no words out.

*And a chick is dying and he is pressed close to his mother, and then the rain is falling.*

And Akiba is laying the revolver down on the walk and Gray Eyes sighs, knowing that is good, that is how it should be.

And Akiba is talking and Buddy Gray Eyes is repeating after him the *viddui*, the confession. First Akiba Moldavan has whispered, "Many have said the *viddui* and lived; many have said it and died. Repeat: May my death be an atonement for all the sins, iniquities, and transgressions of which I have been guilty against Thee . . ."

Gray Eyes wants to raise his head and kiss Akiba Moldavan but he cannot.

*He is in the rear of Cervino's candy store and the old man is holding him, hugging him to him, forgiving him.*

"Repeat: The Lord reigneth; the Lord hath reigned; the Lord shall reign for ever and ever."

"The Lord reigneth; the Lord hath reigned; the Lord shall reign for ever and ever. The Lord reigneth; the Lord hath reigned; the Lord shall reign for ever and ever."

He is saying the *viddui* and Akiba is saying it with him, holding his hand, comforting him. The feel of his presence spreads a bounteous warmth over him.

Cervino moves to a glass jar at one corner of the room, removes a piece of sugar crystal candy and hands it to him. It sparkles like a diamond, showering the room with blinding light.

"Blessed be His name, whose glorious kingdom is for ever and ever. Blessed be His name, whose glorious kingdom is for ever and ever. Blessed be His name, whose glorious kingdom is for ever and ever."

Gray Eyes wants to say more. He wants to say the sea is swallowing me up. Your tears are scalding me. My mother said I was a good son. You are my true friend. But instead he repeats after Akiba Moldavan: "The Lord He is God. The Lord He is God. The Lord He is God. The Lord He is God. The Lord He is God. The Lord He is God. The Lord He is God."

Then: "Hear, O Israel: the Lord our God, the Lord is One."

Good-bye, Akiba, he wants to say, but he is dead.

John Strahan lifted his revolver from the ground and walked back to the Continental Hotel. In room five Tracy was lying nude on the bed.

He closed the door and removed his clothes. He tried to enter her, but could do nothing. "What is it?" she said drowsily.

He did not speak. She smiled. "You did come back to me, Daddy," she said, and drifted off to sleep.

He put on his clothes and moved to the window. He stared down on the walk. An ambulance was there. They were removing Gray Eyes's body.

Strahan fingered the fracture in his spectacle lens.

Later Tracy awakened and went out. She returned with a glassine envelope of heroin. They shot up together.

With the drug's first rush Strahan realized this was what he had been seeking all his life. It was a revelation, yet he could not articulate what he saw: there was in the air, in symbols of the purest black and white, a chess problem and he could not solve it, but it did not matter. Afterward he realized the pain in his stomach had disappeared. It never returned.

# EPILOGUE

There are no miracles, Akiba Moldavan had decided. There is just life, which encompasses death, and it moves in a manner that is strange and ineluctable.

And yet: Rabbi Isaac's *Talmud* had come back to him. He could speak.

Yakov Moldavan visited Pittsburgh and there was a reconciliation. And money was made available by Yakov for the institute and it was saved. All these things happened.

Gray Eyes was buried, at Akiba's insistence, in the holiest section of the Orthodox cemetery. This did not please Emmanuel Rose, but he accepted it. After all, Rabbi Isaac was recovering. The Moldavans were on the ascendancy again.

Mother Shadman was at the funeral and he wept for Buddy Gray Eyes and he whispered to his coffin as it was lowered into the earth, "Nobody dies. There is no death."

Sidney Hall stared straight ahead and he did not weep for his son. Neither did Julie Tripp weep, nor John Strahan's wife, who was there also.

Hannah Moldavan was subdued throughout the ceremony. Julie Tripp held her by the hand. Julie Tripp had decided: she would become a nurse. She would become a companion for Hannah and Rabbi Isaac.

In the days that went after, a marked change came over Akiba Moldavan. He became content, even conventional, a man without serious passion or aggressive conviction. He performed his tasks at the institute and at his synagogue in the Hill District correctly, if unimaginatively. He dreamed of becoming a lawyer or a doctor, but he knew it would never be. He gained weight. He thought about taking up chess again.

He believed.

John Strahan had disappeared. There were rumors: someone had seen him in California. He had become addicted to heroin; he had been in prison. No one knew. No one tried to verify these things.

Jack Palmer chewed gum and shook his head and stared out the window of the Public Safety Building, wondering: Who will hunt with me in the deep of winter?

John Strahan was written off by all concerned: except Father Walter Nagorski, who thought of him when night came and he could not sleep.